# ROSEMEAR

## QUINN NOLL

*To the OG and my pride and joy*
*Dewey, Willie, Jeeves, Johnny Bananas, and Jo Bean*
*You are the best part of me and I'll love you forever.*

*And to my dear friend Cyndi*
*A woman who never met a person, alive or dead, she couldn't make laugh.*
*Thank you for supporting me and joining in my wacky, sometimes creepy, paranormal investigations.*

*But next time, don't forget to bring the sage.*

*When the sins of the dead collide with the secrets of the living, nightmares are born.*

# CHAPTER
# ONE
## *ABIGAIL*

*The Weeping Time*
*March 2–3, 1859*
*Ten Broeck Racetrack*

Abigail Charles shivered in a shadowed corner near the auction block, watching from beneath half-closed eyelids while waiting her turn. The Savannah winds howled, and the rain was merciless, a near-biblical deluge with a ferocity seventeen-year-old Abigail had never witnessed.

It was proving to be a record-setting day in more ways than one.

Hundreds of people stood around her, wide-eyed, unprotected from the elements, and trembling with fear. Some yearned for anonymity, while others, shoulders slumped, stared with vacant eyes at the platform before the horse stalls, resigned to their fate.

Resting an arm around Abigail's waist, securing her to his side, stood her true love and soulmate, Prophet Jones. He looked down at her and nodded imperceptibly before giving her a reassuring squeeze.

As if, by doing so, he could miraculously alter their circumstances and save them both.

But he understood he could not. His only hope was that they would be sold together.

Days ago, four hundred thirty-six people had been forced to travel by steamer or rail to a racetrack in Savannah, Georgia. There, in what would become the largest slave auction ever recorded, young and old stood solemnly together, heads bent in both prayer and sorrow, waiting to be sold to the highest bidder.

All at the behest of one man—Pierce Mease Butler.

Laden with gambling debts and heavy stock market losses, slaveholder Pierce Butler had decided the quickest way to solvency was to sell nearly half of the enslaved people he currently owned. His only stipulation was that, wherever possible, families that had spent a lifetime together on his plantation would not be separated.

As Pierce Mease Butler and his employees were renowned for brutality against their laborers, the stipulation was a glaring example of hypocrisy and willful ignorance.

Because, despite his request, families *were* torn apart in a matter of minutes. Hearts were broken and lives shattered as the forlorn took turns moving to the center of the arena, one by one, to learn their fate.

Clutching Prophet's hand at her waist, Abigail watched, wide-eyed, as a man with massive arms wearing a tattered shirt stood stoically at the center of the raised wooden platform. Tobias Baker, the first to ascend the auction block steps on this, the second day of the sale, was a twenty-two-year-old skilled carpenter with a gentle heart and warm smile. Eyes pinned on his twelve-year-old sister, Frances, Tobias followed the auctioneer's demands to open his mouth, lift his lips, raise his shirt.

Another man, the auctioneer's assistant, prodded, poked, and inspected Tobias—much to the crowd's delight—from every angle, in every humiliating way.

But Tobias did not object. He hoped his compliance would help him curry favor with the crowd. If it did, he might be able to persuade his new owner to purchase Frances as well.

The group had been at Ten Broeck Racetrack for two days, soaked to the skin amid a torrential downpour without reprieve, while hundreds of men gawked at them. Some spectators shouted instructions to the auctioneer; others took notes and asked about a bondservant's health.

*"Hey, Mr. Auctioneer! How old is that one in the back?"* or *"Make him smile! I want a worker with good teeth!"* or even, *"Does he come with kin? I'm needin' a soft woman to keep me warm at night, gents!"*

The men would hoot and holler, chuckling at the occasional derogatory comment or vulgarity, excusing each other's behavior as merely 'good ol' boy' humor.

It was a disgusting display that played out time and time again throughout the arena, epitomizing the self-absorbed, callous disregard these men possessed for the enslaved.

People, entire families, were being auctioned off like cattle with nary a thought.

Abigail wiped the rain from her face and swallowed hard, fearing she would soon vomit. A notorious slave trader and the man in charge of the auction, Joseph Bryan, stood on the middle step of the auction block, holding Tobias's arm and shouting out numbers.

In minutes, the gavel came down on the speaker's podium, and Tobias, having the coveted skill of carpentry, was sold to a man from Alabama who owned a construction company.

Although many had been sold before him during the two-day auction, he had fetched the highest price thus far.

As soon as Tobias left the auction block, a greasy-looking man with round glasses who snorted when he breathed walked into the crowd. He pointed at Prophet, and Abigail tensed.

Prophet, in overalls and a white shirt, his hands stained

from ironwork, merely pulled his shoulders back and stood tall, seemingly unconcerned. Giving Abigail a final squeeze, he strode to the front of the arena and ascended the platform. Once he was atop the auction block, his gaze met Abigail's before he dipped his head and turned away, unable to witness the pain in her eyes.

The two had met in Darien, Georgia, on Butler Island, a coastal rice plantation owned by Pierce Mease Butler. Prophet worked on the property as a blacksmith, while Abigail tended the Butler home and cared for the family's children.

The two had fallen instantly in love, dreaming of the day when they would be free to marry.

Dreaming of emancipation.

But until all talk of abolishing slavery was acted upon, until the civil war began, the young lovers were considered merely as human property owned by a wealthy White man.

Lost in the past, Abigail jumped when she heard a bang at the podium.

"Sold to the gentleman from South Carolina!" the auctioneer barked, pointing the end of the gavel at the back of the room.

She froze, her stomach lurching.

*Prophet's been sold! Prophet must move to South Carolina!*

And then, defeated… *Prophet is leaving me!*

Sobbing openly, Abigail watched as her love, tears staining his dark cheeks, was led away from the auction block.

If Abigail knew it would be the last time she'd ever see him, she might not have made it through the rest of the day.

But she didn't know.

Part of her had hoped the same man who purchased Prophet would take her too; another part recognized the futility of that wish. Prophet's new owner had spent an obscene amount of money to buy him.

There would be little left for a female laborer with very few skills.

When her turn came to ascend the auction block, she felt numb, indifferent to her fate. What did it matter, anyway? Her parents were dead, killed in a fire when she was only fourteen; a younger sister, Chloe, had succumbed to yellow fever a year later.

Abigail had no one…no one except Prophet.

And now, she didn't even have him.

She listened to the shouts of the men as they bid against each other, each vying to win the pretty little Abigail, with her smooth skin and quiet disposition, until her eye caught a distinguished, burly man in the back row.

He was studying her, mumbling to no one in particular while debating the merits of buying the woman on the platform.

Moments ticked by as Abigail, palms sweating, waited. Finally, the man pushed his hands off his thighs and stood.

Joseph Bryan stopped spewing numbers, eyes on the big man. "Don't I know you, sir?"

The man said nothing.

Seconds later, a smile of recognition spread across Joseph Bryan's face, and he snapped his fingers. "I know, I know! Hawthorne, right? From right here in Savannah? I'd no idea you were here." He looked around, assuring himself that Hawthorne was the wealthiest man in the room and could afford to pay a high price. Satisfied, Bryan asked, "Are you interested in this female, Mr. Hawthorne?"

William Hawthorne removed a pipe from his jacket pocket and lit it; the fragrant scent of tobacco filled the space. "Not interested, Bryan. Determined. So, whatever the last bid was on this young Negro woman, double it and let's get this over with."

And just like that, Abigail Charles would leave the only home she'd ever known and walk, blindfolded, into her new life.

And her worst nightmare.

# CHAPTER
# TWO

Isabella Boyd stood outside the massive building, studying the crumbling stone foundation, the broken windows, and the sagging roof. A nearly two-hundred-year-old wooden sign hung crookedly over the entrance, the letters now faded but still legible.

*Rosemear.*

Isabella assumed the home was named by a previous owner, a ritual common in the South.

Sighing softly, she turned and glanced at the man behind her. "Seriously, Spencer? You told me this was a unique 'fixer-upper.' All I see is a dilapidated and potentially dangerous house that needs to be razed."

Her husband of ten years raked a hand through his blond hair and gave her a boyish grin. "I know, I know," Spencer said. "But ignore the exterior for a minute and close your eyes as I walk you through the possibilities."

"Possibilities?" Isabella snorted. "You mean besides renting a bulldozer?"

The sounds of laughter halted their conversation. Turning, Isabella scanned the front yard for her children. "Samuel? Eleanor? You kids be careful, you hear? No telling what debris or animal dens are on this property."

"Yes, Momma," Samuel called from somewhere on the side of the house.

"We promise!" Eleanor's voice followed her brother's, the hint of a giggle unmistakable in her tone.

Isabella turned back toward the house. "Okay, Spence. Hit me with your 'vision' for this place. Because honestly, I see nothing but hard labor, tens of thousands of dollars, and heartbreak." Her tone was flat, bordering on boredom.

Because she'd been here before—inside Spencer's mind, privy to his grandiose plans.

It was exhausting.

"You may be right," Spencer said, brows raised. "Or," he said, drawing out the word, "maybe this place, Rosemear, becomes a dream come true." He took her in his arms. "Look, Izzie…"

Isabella raised an eyebrow. *Izzie.*

She hated that nickname. Whenever it left Spencer's lips, she immediately pictured an overweight, hairy man with slumped shoulders and thick glasses worn dangerously close to the end of his nose, tinkering with a cuckoo clock. And the alternate he sometimes used—*Belle*—was almost as bad, conjuring images of black-draped vampires or wolf-like beasts, their fangs dripping with blood, merrily chasing little girls in the forest.

If she had to have a nickname, she preferred Bella.

Although, to be fair, she had no issue with anyone else calling her Izzie, Belle, or Bella. Only when those names left his lips did she feel like falling onto her sword.

While aflame. Blindfolded and bound, hands tied behind her back.

Spencer shrugged sheepishly. "Sorry. Look, *Bella*," he corrected, "we've all had a rough couple of years. You, in particular, have been through the worst kind of hell. But this is our chance to hit the reset button." He brushed a wayward strand of hair from her face. "Instead of looking at this as an uphill climb, why not look at it as a new beginning? A fresh start, away from Tampa and all our awful memories there."

Isabella's heart, already broken in several places, seemed to fracture even more. "There is no fresh start or new beginning that will heal a wound that won't stop bleeding, Spencer," she said, annoyed that he seemed to be moving forward while she could still barely breathe. "Please don't assume relocating will erase the hole in my heart."

"No, of course not, love. Forgive me? I just want to build memories that bring us joy instead of pain. Nothing can do that better than starting in a new town. It's like beginning with a clean slate, a blank canvas. I think Savannah could offer us that." He took a step back from her, gesturing toward the house. "I think Rosemear could be our do-over."

A thin bead of sweat ran down her temple, and she wiped it away with the back of her hand. The sun's brilliance was near-blinding; the temperature a stifling ninety-two degrees.

Sighing, hands on her hips, she studied the house again, trying to see what he saw. "Okay, Spencer. I promise to keep an open mind if you promise to admit defeat when we walk inside and start to hyperventilate."

Chuckling, he glanced at his watch. "Deal. Say, we still have about twenty minutes until the realtor arrives. She's showing another property downtown and might be a little late." He grabbed her elbow and guided her toward the side of the house. "I heard there's a gazebo surrounded by a beautiful garden out back."

Isabella hesitated. "What about a pool?" she asked, voice strained. "Does it have a pool?"

Spencer put his arm around her shoulder. "No, love. No pool, no hot tub, not even a sprinkler system."

The tension coiled inside drained from her body. "Okay, then. Let's have a look."

"Momma! This yard is huge!" Ellie cried, her five-year-old legs pumping hard as she ran toward her parents. "And look! A tire swing!"

Isabella caught her daughter just as she jumped into her arms. "I see that," Isabella said, smiling, "but it looks a bit worn, Bug. I'm not sure it's safe."

Samuel, wielding a long stick like a Japanese sword and making 'whoosh' sounds as he moved, spun across the yard toward his family. "Don't worry, El," he said between thrusts of his stick, "I'll try the swing first, so you don't get hurt."

"Thanks, Sammy!" Ellie said, clapping her hands in excitement.

Isabella's heart swelled as she studied her son. Sam had Spencer's blond hair and goofy grin, but that was where the similarities ended. Both the Boyd children looked eerily like their mother—small noses, high cheekbones, the striking gray of their eyes. And, while Samuel's hair was wheat-colored, Ellie shared her mother's chestnut shade.

"Find any buried treasure, son?" Spencer asked.

Isabella cringed, and Sam rolled his eyes. "Ninjas don't look for buried treasure, Dad. They fight bad guys and do surveillance on their enemies and stuff."

Spencer nodded and ruffled the boy's hair. "Fair point, my nimble friend. So how goes the recon? See anything cool out here?"

Before Sam could answer, the sound of car tires crunching over stones caught their attention. Spencer clapped and began hurrying toward the circular driveway. "Come on, gang! That must be the realtor!" He turned to face them all and, jogging backward, said, "This is exciting, right, kids?"

Samuel smirked and started to run, positioning himself in front of the group.

"Hey," Spencer called out, laughing and chasing after his son. "Where's the fire?"

Giggling, Sam ran faster.

Isabella's stomach clenched. "Samuel Daniel Boyd! Slow down before you end up in an alternate universe!"

"Okay, Momma!"

Ellie, suddenly quiet, moved closer to her mother. She grabbed Isabella's hand, and, walking slowly, they rounded the front of the building and walked to the top of the driveway.

A moment later, Ellie shivered and stopped in her tracks as if hitting a wall. She looked back toward the house, her tight grip on Isabella's hand almost painful.

"What is it, El? What's wrong?"

Ellie turned fully toward the house, eyes pinned on a cracked second-story window.

Isabella faced the house as well, following her daughter's gaze. She saw nothing.

"Hey," Spencer called out, sensing the lack of movement behind him, "what's the hold-up? What's wrong, El?"

Ellie, face pale, remained silent.

"You boys go on ahead," Isabella said. "We'll be along in a moment."

With a shrug, Spencer put a hand on Sam's shoulder. "Come on, Sammy-me-boy. Race ya!"

Isabella watched them run for a moment before crouching in front of Ellie. "Okay, baby, tell me—what's up?"

Ellie was still staring at the second floor. Her damp hand squeezed Isabella's fingers even harder.

Confused, Isabella looked again toward the window that held her daughter's fascination. And still saw nothing.

"Come on, Bug," Isabella said finally. "There's nothing there."

Ellie popped her thumb into her mouth, a habit she'd broken two years earlier. "I don't… I don't like it here, Mommy. I'm scared."

"Of what, baby?"

Ellie dragged her gaze from the house and faced Isabella. Bottom lip trembling, the little girl whispered, "The people in the window. They don't want us here."

Isabella's pulse kicked up a notch. Frozen in place, she whispered back, "What people, Bug? Who doesn't want us here?"

Ellie turned back to the house. After a pause, she said, "The people who live here."

Isabella frowned. "Oh, honey, there is no one living here. Not anymore. The last owners moved out months ago."

Ellie shook her head. "I don't think so, Momma."

Isabella stood again and, feigning nonchalance, said, "It's fine, El. This place is for sale because the owners moved out. And, of course we're welcome! Who wouldn't want to hang out with a Boyd?"

But even as the words left her lips, Isabella shuddered. Her voice seemed an octave too high, the rhythm of her speech a little too quick. It was a tone she used to convey to her children that everything would be okay.

She wondered now if it was Ellie she was trying to convince. Or herself.

They hurried forward, trying to catch up with Spencer and Sam. Just as they neared the driveway, Isabella dared to throw one more glance over her shoulder. Her heart skipped a beat as, scanning the second-floor windows, she watched a panel of tattered lace curtains—curtains that had fascinated Ellie and had been completely still moments ago—move aside a few inches before quickly drop-ping back into place again.

As if someone were peeking through the window.

Isabella felt the hair on her neck stand on end as she digested what she'd just seen.

Or thought she'd seen.

Because although she wanted to believe she was cured of the demons that had once visited her mind, still, every so often that little finger of doubt would nag at her. Were the auditory and visual hallucinations, the missing snippets of time, and the over-whelming fatigue she'd suffered in the past truly gone? Was she delusional to believe that her mental state was now stronger than it had ever been?

That it was near 'normal,' whatever that might be.

But like an unwanted houseguest, familiar insecurities had re-surfaced of late. She feared that the echoes of voices and terrify-ing images that had occupied her mind, spawned from the tragic events of three years ago, were still there.

Lurking in the recesses of her brain, faded but present.

As a result, it was becoming increasingly difficult to decipher whether she'd fully recovered from her mental collapse or had just deluded herself into believing it so.

Staring at the house now, she couldn't shake the feeling that it had been neither a delusion nor a draft pulling that curtain back.

It felt more deliberate.

It felt as if someone were studying them, assessing them.

Watching them.

"Thank you for meeting with us," Spencer said, shaking hands with the realtor, Suzanne Johns. He put an arm around Sam's shoulder, pulling him close. "This is my boy, Samuel. We've been doing some 'recon,'" he winked at Sam, "and the grounds have a ton of potential. We're looking forward to seeing the inside."

Suzanne pasted on a smile, hiding how much she hated showing this house. "Of course," she lied. "Happy to help."

"Great! Now, if I could just find the rest of my family…" he said, words trailing off. Then, smiling at their approach, he addressed Suzanne again. "Ahh, here they are. Suzanne, meet my lovely wife, Isabella, and our precocious little five-year-old, Eleanor."

Still holding Isabella's hand, Ellie tilted her face to her mother. "Momma, what does percosis mean?"

Isabella smiled. "Precocious. And it means you're a very special little girl."

Ellie smiled, satisfied with the explanation.

"Thank you for coming out," Isabella said, shaking Suzanne's hand. "I know it's a bit off the beaten trail. What can you tell us about this place?"

Suzanne lifted a shoulder. "Plenty. There is a lot of history here, a lot of tragedy." She thumbed through her listing notes. Even though she'd shown this property dozens of times, she always needed to refer to her 'cheat sheet.'

It was as if her mind willfully, purposefully, made sure she would forget all she knew about this house and the darkness surrounding it until it was time to dig it up again with another potential buyer.

"Let's go inside, and I'll give you the highlights," Suzanne said.

They moved to the house's entrance, where a bifold-type shuttered door—originally red but worn with age and time—beckoned them inside. Isabella tipped her head back and studied the wooden plaque above the door she'd spotted earlier. The word 'Rosemear,' burned into the weathered oak, had a beautiful, yet somehow ominous, ring to it.

Suzanne stopped near the door. "The home's architectural style is called English Regency. A popular design from the early 1800s to about 1830, it's best known for using a stucco exterior and utilizing symmetry in all the workmanship. Every design or structural element in the house occurs in pairs—paired windows and doors, a double staircase, matching columns in the foyer. The builder was going for harmony and balance. He even went as far as to create several false doors to maintain the symmetrical look of the home."

Isabella nodded, then pointed at the sign above the door. "Rosemear? Was that the name of a previous owner or something?"

Suzanne shook her head. "As far as I know, no one with that name lived here. It could be just one of those things people used to do, you know? Give their homes a name?"

Spencer raised a brow. "Pretty specific name, though, wouldn't you say?"

Suzanne agreed. "I suppose it is." She lifted the lock box, entered the combination, and removed the key nestled inside. Unlocking the shuttered front door, she swept an arm out in invitation. "After you," she smiled.

Isabella hesitated. "Um, is it safe to enter? I'm no architect, but the foundation looks questionable, and the roof is in tatters."

Suzanne smiled, but it seemed a sad, 'You've no idea what you're getting into' kind of smile. "According to the listing agent," she began, "you could move in tomorrow. That is, if you don't mind sharing the space with some field mice and oceans of spider webs. Structurally, though, it's safe."

"Your lips to God's ears," Isabella muttered.

Suddenly buzzing with energy, Sam tossed his stick aside and blurted, "Are there ghosts here?"

Suzanne's initial shock at Sam's question quickly turned to discomfort. "Um, do you believe in such things, Samuel?"

Sam shrugged. "I dunno. Never seen one before, but it sounds pretty cool."

At a loss for how to respond, Suzanne merely nodded before

leading the group inside. They moved through the front doors of the house and into the foyer. Two white pillars, intricately carved and in remarkably good condition, stood ten feet apart in the center of the entryway, reaching beyond the first floor before terminating at the ceiling on the second level.

Impressed, Isabella had to admit the place must have been stunning back in the day. She looked overhead, noting an intricate chandelier hanging in the center of the foyer. Two metal hearts—one upright and the other inverted—were woven together above a gas-driven lantern.

"How lovely," Isabella said. "I'm surprised the owners left this. Do you know the story behind it?"

Suzanne nodded. "A little. The legend goes that, before emancipation, the enslaved would try to find unique ways to communicate with each other. This piece," she said, nodding toward the ceiling, "was created to let others know that they were here, that they existed."

"Like a thumb in the eye to the slaveholders?" Spencer asked.

"A bit. Back then, the enslaved were forbidden to learn to read and write. As such, they didn't have the skills to keep a journal or diary and let others know they were here. So, instead, they created art with hidden meanings. In this case, the entwined hearts and outer leaves are meant to convey a message."

"What kind of message?" Isabella asked.

"That everything is connected in some way. According to local historians, it refers to the saying, 'As above, so below.' Loosely translated, it means there are countless layers of the universe, each conceived in the mind of God. We are all connected in some way, all intertwined, and whatever you sow in the physical world, you reap in the spiritual one."

"Huh," Spencer said. Then, chuckling, he added, "So be good, for goodness' sake!"

Isabella swallowed her embarrassment. Spencer had an

uncanny knack for missing the point. Ignoring his ignorance, she said, "That's somehow both beautiful and incredibly sad."

"It is," Suzanne agreed.

"Whatev," Spencer said with a shrug. "Getting back to the real world, though—are you seeing these columns, babe? The marble tiles and the double staircase? I mean, who has that?"

Isabella did her best not to roll her eyes. She and her husband had very different opinions on what was important in life. He equated respect with status. In his mind, if you lived a glamorous life in a home worth lots of money, you inched up a notch in social standing.

Isabella thought that was a load of crap.

She'd grown up in a wealthy family. Her parents had started an investment firm and had done amazingly well. When they were killed in a home invasion several years ago, Isabella and her brother, Daniel, were left with a vast amount of money. Her parents had also set up a generous trust fund for their current and future grandchildren.

Daniel, ten years older than Isabella, had no children and, at forty-three and without prospects, it appeared he never would.

Indeed, Isabella had much experience with the pitfalls that came with great wealth. She knew what money could and could not do. Extraordinary wealth could not make someone a good person. Her parents had socialized with some very affluent people— successful entrepreneurs who lived luxuriously within the walls of their majestic manors.

Most in that circle had maids, butlers, and personal assistants who saw to their every whim and desire. In Isabella's experience, though, all the help in the world couldn't change a person's character.

Because, despite an easy life, many of her parents' friends remained spoiled, self-absorbed assholes.

Giving her husband a disapproving look, Isabella said, "You're right, Spence. I would guess that not many people have an entry like this. Still, a double staircase in an otherwise dilapidated home doesn't make me jump with joy."

Spencer's brows furrowed, and his neck veins pulsed. "Well," he said stiffly, "since we've just started this tour, how about we finish it before declaring the entire building 'dilapidated.'"

Uncomfortable, Suzanne cleared her throat. "Well, then, shall we check out the rest of the home?"

They nodded and continued the tour.

"The kitchen is this way," Suzanne said, veering to the right. "Mind the construction materials scattered about. The last owners…" She stopped, unsure how much to say.

"The last owners what?" Spencer asked.

Suzanne's face looked pained. "Uh, there's a complicated history there."

Confused, Spencer asked, "How complicated? Did something happen here we should know about?"

"Such as?" Suzanne said, stalling for time.

Spencer looked back at Sam and Ellie, currently playing 'red light, green light' while trying to catch up to the adults. He lowered his voice. "Such as a suspicious death or known homicide or some other horrendous crime that may someday affect the resale value of our investment?"

Suzanne cleared her throat again. "Well, um, the previous owners left in a hurry, you see," she answered.

Isabella chewed on a fingernail. "Why, though? Did you ever find out why?"

Suzanne said nothing, continuing toward the kitchen.

Isabella looked at Spencer, who merely shrugged. They followed Suzanne, keeping their eyes on the floor as they stepped around power tools and mounds of debris.

"Come on, guys," Isabella called out to the children. "Watch your step here."

When they arrived at the kitchen, Suzanne swept out an arm

before pointing to the farmhouse table in the center of the room. "I figured it would be easier to show you rather than attempt to explain," Suzanne said. "The last folks who occupied this property didn't even stop to clean up before they hightailed it out of here."

Isabella was stunned.

Dinner dishes, some with remnants of desiccated food on them, littered the kitchen table. It was as if a family had sat down to eat, received an urgent phone call, and left.

Never to return.

"Jesus," Spencer whispered. "Why wouldn't the sellers clean this mess up? How do they expect to get top dollar?"

Isabella inwardly sighed, struggling again not to roll her eyes. Spencer's fascination with the bottom line was growing tedious.

"I really don't know," Suzanne said sadly. "Truthfully, I get the impression they don't much care if they get top dollar." She looked at Spencer and added, "Which is why, per our conversation, it's being sold 'as is.' I think you could get an excellent deal on this house."

At the moment, Isabella didn't care much about the purchase price. She was trying to understand the reasons behind the previous owners' hasty departure.

"Suzanne," Isabella said, "I know that, according to many real estate laws, you are under no obligation to disclose the home's history. That is, *unless*," she said the last word forcefully, "we specifically ask. To be clear, the way these people left bothers me. So, I'm asking you point blank: did anything violent, illegal, or nasty occur in this house?"

Suzanne looked around the room, eyes dull, as if she'd been asked this question a million times and was weary of answering. "According to my broker, this home does have a history of misfortune."

"Such as?" Isabella asked, her heart quickening.

"Such as the Hawthorne murders," Suzanne said, defeated. She knew the sellers would rather keep that information to themselves, but questions were bound to arise when a homeowner vacated their property as they had.

In the dead of night and without explanation.

Still, Isabella was correct. Suzanne was under a legal obligation, not to mention a moral one, to disclose the home's history when asked.

"You're joking," Spencer said, incredulous.

She blew out a breath and leaned her hip against the kitchen sink. "I'm not. The murders occurred in 1859, nearly two hundred years ago. The home's original owners, William and Lillian Hawthorne, were killed. William was found on the floor in the parlor, while Lillian was discovered face down on the mattress in the main bedroom. There didn't appear to be any signs of a struggle, leading locals to believe the couple either knew their killer or were poisoned first, incapacitating them and allowing the killer to land the final blow."

Isabella gulped. "And that final blow was?"

"A very long, very sharp knife," Suzanne said. "They each had several penetrating wounds, some deeper than others. Lillian had over a dozen stab wounds, but William… um, William had at least forty-seven. I've heard that two of those forty-seven stab wounds were delivered to his eyes."

"Sweet Jesus," Isabella whispered.

Spencer clasped Isabella's shoulder. "Were the perpetrators ever brought to justice?"

"Maybe," Suzanne said carefully. "Locals claim that an enslaved young woman, sold by one man and brought to Rosemear by another, was responsible for the killings."

Isabella's hand flew to her throat. Toying with a cameo necklace that nestled just above her breasts, she asked, "What happened to her?"

Suzanne sighed. "No one knows for sure. Any records kept back then were destroyed in a fire. All we have to go on is hearsay and the stories passed down from generation to generation."

"So, nothing, then?" Spencer asked, his voice clipped. "You can tell us nothing else about her?"

Suzanne shrugged. "I can tell you what the rumors are about her, about this place. And I can tell you her name was Abigail. Abigail Charles."

# CHAPTER
# THREE

After Suzanne completed the tour of Rosemear, Isabella stood, arms folded, in the empty dining room, trying to envision how the room would look furnished with her family's belongings. Although she remained unconvinced that Rosemear would be their "forever home," as Spencer had promised, she did admit to feeling a particular pull toward the place.

Still, the information Suzanne had given them about the property's history was gnawing at her.

Never one for hysteria, not particularly convinced that inanimate objects, such as houses, held some residual essence of their previous owners, she nonetheless was rattled by the history Suzanne had shared with them.

"After the murders," Suzanne had explained as they stood in the kitchen, "I believe the Hawthorne children remained here until the last heir died in the early 1920s. Since then, four other families have called Rosemear home—three of them met with some kind of tragedy, and the last one stayed for only about two months." Looking around, she'd added, "And, it would seem, escaped with only the clothes on their backs."

Isabella frowned. "So, they, what? Just ran out of here?"

Suzanne stared blankly at a far wall, momentarily forgetting she was not alone. "Like a cat shot in the ass," she muttered finally.

Spencer frowned. "People don't just run from their homes mid-meal, never to return." He nodded at the table. "What happened here, Suzanne?"

"No idea. The only information my office received was that the owners, John and Macy Cates, had an emergency and needed to sell the house immediately. I do know they have a little boy who is desperately ill, so perhaps that was the issue."

Isabella stared at the dirty dishes. "You mentioned the young girl, Abigail Charles. What can you tell us about her and the Hawthorne murders?"

"Not much, I'm afraid. At least nothing verifiable. As I said before, the records kept at the time were destroyed by fire. Local legend has it that Abigail was in love with William Hawthorne. When that love was unrequited, she went mad with jealousy against both him and Lillian. Poisoned the couple first before slaughtering them."

Spencer's mouth twisted in disgust. "Talk about a coward's way of doing it. Weak with poison, the Hawthornes wouldn't have stood a chance."

"I don't know," Isabella said. "Maybe the Hawthornes were abusive, and Abigail was only saving herself."

"Or," Spencer countered, "maybe she was psycho."

Isabella bit her tongue.

"Anyway, where was I?" Suzanne said, more to herself than anyone else. "Oh, right. So, aside from knowing that the last surviving child remained here until he died in 1923, that's the extent of what I know. You may be able to gather more information from the town hall or local library." She paused. "Look, I know this history is a lot to process, but I still think this can be a fabulous home. And to be fair, the Hawthorne tragedy was more than a century ago. Different times."

"Yes, they were," Spencer offered. He took her hands in his. "Look, we can't objectively look at the past through the eyes of the present, right? Life was very different back then. Right, Suzanne?"

The realtor gave a half-smile before nodding.

Isabella said nothing, instead mulling over the one thing Suzanne had said about the sellers that turned her blood to ice.

*The last family escaped with only the clothes on their backs.*

Not left, not relocated, not moved out because of extenuating circumstances.

*They escaped.*

"Come on, Bella," Spencer had pleaded after following her to the dining room. "Can't you feel it? It's like, I don't know, a missing piece of the puzzle or something. Life would be so perfect here. *We* would be so perfect here."

Isabella chewed on her lip, indecisive. Spencer took it as an open invitation to push harder.

"It's the best of both worlds," Spencer said. "MacMillan's headquarters is right here in Savannah. They've already agreed to let me transfer, and I'll even get my own office! Let's face it—hospitals and medical facilities will always need a pharmaceutical rep, right? I can make a ton of contacts here, and on travel days, the airport is close by." He snapped his fingers as though his next point was merely an afterthought. "Oh, and Julia is planning on driving this way next week. Thank God she's willing to relocate."

Isabella nearly groaned aloud. *Julia.*

Clenching her teeth, she forced herself to bite back a caustic remark. Julia Cox, Spencer's assistant, was a twenty-eight-year-old blonde with a flawless face, perfect teeth, and a body most women would kill for.

She was also the principal reason Spencer and Isabella's marriage was in a freefall.

"Um… you promised me you were going to find another assistant, Spencer," Isabella said, hating the way her voice rose to a near-whine when she said his name. She didn't understand it. She'd long since come to grips with the realization that her marriage had been on life support for years, Julia or not.

Still, the sting of betrayal can sometimes take longer to mend than a broken heart.

Spencer stared at her momentarily, pity in his eyes. When he finally spoke, it was with a condescending tone generally reserved for a child. "Babe, I'm looking for someone else. Truly, I am. But times are tough, and no matter what we think of Jules as a person, she's damned good at her job. I wouldn't have achieved the success I've had on my own." He patted her back. "Right now, think of her as a temp, huh? Just until I find someone to take her place."

Isabella turned to a window, finally giving in to the temptation to roll her eyes. Leave it to Spencer to play the "I'm doing it for the family" card rather than admit to the legitimate reason Isabella wanted Julia out of their lives.

*Because she fucked you, Spence. Several times. And you fucked her back.*

He rested his hands on her shoulders and looked out the window. "The whole thing with Julia is… well, I'm trying to make it up to you. But if you keep throwing it in my face, we can never move on."

Isabella stiffened, her eyes darting around the grounds. Suzanne and the kids were somewhere on the other side of the house.

Isabella didn't want to do this now; she *shouldn't* do this now.

She did it anyway.

Laughing bitterly, she turned to face him. "Throwing it in your face? For real, Spence? And here I was, thinking we could have a normal conversation about how that woman makes my skin crawl. Every time I hear her damned name, all I can see is her beneath you, naked, in my bed."

Spencer had the decency to cringe. "I get that, Bella. I do. But to keep rehashing it—"

"Is throwing it in your face?" Isabella finished for him, cheeks flushed. "That's what I'm doing?"

"No, that was a poor choice of words on my part. But let's look to the future instead of dwelling on the past, okay?" He lifted her chin and said, "Just think of it, Bella. Picture us fixing the place up, returning it to its former glory, living here with Sam and Ellie. Savannah has a great school system, wonderful doctors nearby, and plenty of space for an art studio. And Luna—don't forget Luna is close by."

Isabella's best friend, Luna Lake, lived on the beach in a three-bedroom cottage in Hilton Head, about forty minutes from Savannah. An overachiever, she worked two jobs—one as a nurse practitioner for a neurology group in Savannah and the other in an art gallery closer to Hilton Head. She had never married, insisting she was "still waiting for my knight in shining armor to save my ass."

But she was never lonely. Her roommates, a cat named Little Ricky, and two cockatiels, Lucy and Ethel, saw to that.

Isabella sighed, knowing she would agree to the move before Spencer even started his 'upsell' of the place. Whether they would live here together as husband and wife remained to be seen.

"Okay, fine. We'll try it."

Spencer hooted and clapped his hands.

"But," Isabella said sternly, "I won't move the kids in until we fix the foundation and the roof. Also, we need to make sure the heat pump works. And what about cooling? We have to—"

He cut her off. "I'm on it. I took down the phone numbers of some companies Suzanne recommended for the exterior work. And I'll get some window units until we can get central air."

"And the heat pump?"

"Don't worry so much, Bella. I got this."

Isabella shuddered. The last time Spencer had said those words, her world collapsed, casting her into a void she feared she'd never escape.

*"Don't worry. I got this,"* he'd said all those years ago.

But in fact, he didn't.

He didn't have it at all.

After putting in an offer for Rosemear that was thirty thousand dollars below the asking price, Spencer and Isabella drove the five hours back to Tampa with the kids, each sharing the top three improvements that meant the most to them should the offer be accepted. For Sam and Ellie, the 'must haves' were cable television, the latest gaming system, and separate bedrooms.

All things Isabella and Spencer had already planned for.

Besides the essential building improvements—a new roof, replacement windows, a new furnace and water heater—Isabella's 'wants' included central air and vac, an outdoor kitchen for entertaining, and a security system with cameras.

"A security system?" Spencer asked, pulling into a gas station. "What do we need that for? Rosemear is in the middle of nowhere."

"Precisely why I'd like a security system, Spencer," Isabella said. "You're gone for days, sometimes weeks at a time. I would feel better if we had a camera system or something. Maybe if we'd had one before…." She stopped speaking, waiting for the crushing ache in her chest to subside.

Spencer picked up her hand and kissed her knuckles. "Don't

do that, okay? Don't torture yourself. It was an accident, plain and simple. A camera wouldn't have mattered." He unbuckled his seat belt. "We need gas, and I could use a big-ass coffee. Do you have any cash? I'm tapped out."

Isabella sighed, reached into her purse, and handed him a twenty.

"Sweet! You want something?"

"Can you grab me a water and some ibuprofen? I'm getting a serious headache."

"Sure. Be right back."

Watching him walk away, Isabella hit the lock mechanism and glanced at the back seat. Sam and Ellie were snoring softly, Ellie's hand linked with Sam's.

Isabella smiled.

Five minutes ago, they were arguing about who could burp the loudest; now, her youngest sought the familiarity and security of her older brother's touch. Despite their protests to the contrary, they actually liked each other.

Sighing, trying to ignore the drumbeat pounding in her brain, Isabella rested her head on the back of her seat, closed her eyes, and drifted off…

*She was in a sea of color, running through an open field of wildflowers and alfalfa, laughing as the bottom of her bright yellow dress twirled in the wind.*

*"Momma, wait up!" a tiny voice yelled.*

*Isabella stopped, tipped her head back, and smiled, the sun's brilliant rays warm on her face. She turned and crouched low, arms wide, and waited for the little girl with the rosy cheeks and blond curls to reach her.*

*"Got you, little one!" Isabella said, lifting the child easily.*

*The child giggled and squirmed before burying her face in her mother's shoulder.*

"I love you, Momma," the girl whispered.

"And I love you, baby. So very, very much."

Isabella hugged the child in her arms. She felt a tug of fear, of horror, even in this dream world, though she could not remember why.

Ignoring her unease, she smoothed a hand over the little girl's back. At the moment, all she wanted was to stay in that meadow that smelled of honeysuckle and lavender and sunshine and never let go.

She heard the muffled sounds of a man's voice in the background, lost among the bird songs and the brush of the wind. Turning her head slightly, she listened closely but could not hear what was being said.

Disregarding the voice for now, Isabella nuzzled, tickled, and bounced the little girl on her hip, swaying back and forth, soothing the child with a rhythm as old as time.

But something was wrong. The child was no longer giggling, no longer hugging back.

Instead, the little girl was limp and eerily still. Rivulets of water dripped from her hair onto Isabella's shoulder.

And again, the man's voice. This time, clear as day, Isabella heard what he said.

"Don't worry. I got this."

Frantic, Isabella looked around but saw no one.

Her stomach clenched. She knew if she moved—if she broke the spell of the dream and looked down at the child in her arms—the image would stay with her forever.

She could never unsee it.

She looked anyway.

Her vision homed in on two tiny, chubby arms, waxy pale beneath the blinding sun, hanging loosely at the child's side. She snapped her gaze away, fear pooling in the pit of her belly as a scream gathered in her throat.

The field of fragrant wildflowers had faded, morphing into a dark body of water.

A distant voice, carried on the wind, whispered, "Don't worry. I *got this."*

*Isabella blinked rapidly before shouting. "Help! Oh, God, please! Someone help us!"*

*Silence.*

*Suddenly, she was no longer among a pasture of beautiful flowers. Instead, she was standing on tippy-toes in the center of their pool in Tampa, heart pounding, the pungent scent of chlorine burning her nostrils.*

*Wide-eyed and limbs trembling, she forced herself to look, really look, at the lifeless form she cradled in her arms.*

*Disbelief, followed by horror, assaulted her mind. She was suffocating, melting into a puddle of nothingness. The moment she looked down, she'd ceased to be consequential and a part of the living.*

*Instead, she was content to wallow in this in-between world, this land where life and death intersected, where the only thing guaranteed was the raw, mind-numbing pain that had begun to devour her.*

*Because the cherubic child Isabella had held in that field, the giggling one with the beautiful blue eyes and long, black lashes, was staring back, eyes open but unseeing. Her head lolled to one side, and her swollen tongue peeked out from beneath parted lips.*

*As if cursing her fate; as if she wanted to say just one more thing.*

*"Spencer!" Isabella screamed. "Help me!"*

*But the only response, so faint she couldn't be sure it was real, was five words.*

*"Don't worry. I got this."*

*Isabella pulled the child closer to her chest and howled. It was a primal scream of unimaginable loss.*

*A cry with neither a beginning nor an end, born from a heartbreak only another mother could know.*

*It was the soul-crushing grief of losing her two-year-old daughter. Anna Rae Boyd.*

"Mom!" Sam yelled, shaking Isabella's shoulder. "Wake up!"

Isabella jumped, startled, and looked around. They were in the car, still in the gas station. She'd only dozed for a few minutes.

"Oh, sorry, Sammy. Did I wake you?"

"You were screaming, Momma," Ellie said softly. "Crying, too."

Self-conscious, Isabella touched her wet cheeks. She wiped her face with the back of her hand, then turned to face Sam and Ellie. "Sorry, guys. Must have been a nightmare. I'm fine now."

Sam squinted. "You don't look fine," he said doubtfully. "I think you look, like, sad." Then, in a near-whisper, he asked, "Was it about Anna?"

Isabella studied her son—furrowed brow, pinched face. Although Ellie was far too young to remember the tragic day she'd lost her twin sister, Samuel was six years old at the time and re-called it all.

The pain of loss, his parents' heartbreak, Isabella's subsequent hospitalization.

It was a burden much too heavy for a nine-year-old boy to carry.

"Nah, it wasn't about Anna," Isabella lied. "It was probably another football dream. You know the one—me trying out for Tampa Bay and them saying I was too slow. Personally, I think they are making a huge mistake!"

"Go Bucs!" Ellie shouted enthusiastically.

Sam frowned but said nothing.

Cupping a hand over her ear, Isabella picked up a pen from the console and pretended to speak into it.

"Ladies and gentlemen," she said, voice deep, "welcome to the walk-on tryouts for the Tampa Bay Buccaneers! This year, a particular hopeful, Isabella Boyd, has captured the eye of several coaches...."

"Mom!" Sam whined, rolling his eyes.

A knock on the car window caused them all to jump. Holding

a small bag between his teeth and carrying two large coffees, Spencer smiled through the glass. Isabella reached across and opened the driver's side door.

"I got you a latte along with the water. Maybe the caffeine will help your headache."

He handed her the coffee and the bag, which was heavier than she expected. She opened it to see a bottle of water, a small tin of Advil, and two juice boxes.

Isabella looked up at him, surprised. It had been years since Spencer had demonstrated such thoughtfulness.

It made her nervous.

He tapped the inside of the driver's door with a palm. "I'll just gas up the car, and we'll be on our way!"

Five minutes later, tank full, they got back on the highway.

"How much longer, Daddy?" Ellie asked, slurping up the last of her juice through the straw.

Spencer glanced in the rearview mirror. "About twenty minutes, little lady. Think you can last that long?"

Ellie nodded, then asked a seemingly random question. "Can we get a dog?"

Isabella chuckled. "A dog? Wherever did you get that idea, El?"

"I-I think a dog will keep us safe."

Spencer frowned. "We've never had a dog and have always been safe, Ellie. A dog is an enormous responsibility. They need to be fed, groomed, and walked." He lifted his eyes to the rearview mirror again. "And you gotta pick up their poops, ma'am! A whole lotta poops! As I said, dog ownership is a big deal. Maybe we can talk about it when you get older."

"But me and Sam could take care of it! Right, Sammy?"

Sam bobbed his head. "Yes! Dogs are cool! We promise to feed and walk it and clean up after it. We'll even give it a bath when it's stinky!"

Spencer shook his head. "Sorry, guys, but it's too big of a job at your age. And Mom and I don't have the time to devote to a dog right now, especially if we move."

Isabella turned and smiled at her children. "We're not saying never, kids. We're just saying not now. Besides, if we get the Rosemear house, we'll get a security system and cameras to keep us safe."

Ellie's eyes welled with tears. Turning her face to the window, she said under her breath, "If we move to Rosemear, that won't be enough. Nothing will be enough."

The only one who heard her was Sam.

It was shortly after four p.m. when they arrived home in Tampa. After unpacking the overnight bags they'd used for the hotel the night before, Isabella headed into the kitchen to start dinner. She found Sam and Ellie at the table, each with a sheet of blank paper. An old cookie tin served as the container for dozens of crayons.

"Hey, guys," Isabella said. "I'm going to start dinner. Any requests?"

Sam stopped coloring for a moment and looked up. "How about McDonald's?"

Isabella frowned. "Nah. We've been so busy looking at real estate that we've had McDonald's three times this week. How about chicken?" She started pulling pots and pans from the cupboard.

Ellie made a face. "I don't think I want to eat chicken anymore. Grace Rooney says they have to kill a chicken so we can eat it! They cut off its head!"

Sam nudged Ellie's shoulder. "Of course they kill them, dorkus. How else you gonna eat 'em?"

Ellie looked between Sam and Isabella, tears in her eyes. "Is that true, Mom? Do they cut off their heads?"

Sam laughed. "Oh my gosh, El. You're so dumb sometimes."

"Mom!" Ellie cried, kicking Sam in the shin. "He's calling me names!"

"Ow!" Sam said, rubbing his leg. "She kicked me!"

"Did not!"

"Did, too!"

Isabella banged a skillet on top of the stove. She was exhausted and stressed about the house offer, and the headache that had begun hours ago refused to let up. "Enough! Ellie, you keep your feet to yourself, you hear? And Samuel, stop calling your sister dumb."

"Yes, Momma," they said in unison.

"Hey," Spencer called from the front porch. "Where's my family? Ya'll come out here for a minute."

"Last one to the door is a butt munch!" Sam smirked, glancing at Ellie, the last few moments forgotten.

They jumped up from the table, squealing with delight, and ran toward the front of the house.

"Slow down, both of you!" Isabella called after them. "I have no intention of spending my evening in the emergency room!"

Isabella dried her hands on a dish towel and walked to the porch door. Sam and Ellie were already sitting on the steps, hands between their thighs, watching Spencer pace on the walkway.

"Okay, we're here, Spence. What's going on?"

Spencer held up his cell phone and grinned. "Guess who I just got off the phone with?"

Isabella stared blankly. She was too tired for guessing games.

"Aunt Luna?" Sam asked, hopeful. It had been nearly two months since they'd seen Luna Lake. Isabella and the children missed her terribly.

Spencer, however, did not. He and Luna were, most of the time, like oil and water.

"No, not Aunt Luna," Spencer said, wrinkling his nose as if he'd smelled something foul.

"Okay, we give up," Isabella said wearily. "Who was on the phone?"

Spencer grinned again. "Suzanne, that's who! She presented

our offer to the owners of Rosemear, and they accepted immediately! Crazy, right? It's only been a few hours! And because we won't need to apply for financing, we can move in immediately!"

Isabella bristled. Yes, she had money and could purchase five homes similar in price to Rosemear and never break a sweat. But knowing Spencer expected her to foot the bill while not risking a dime of his own money pissed her off.

While Isabella was busy seething, Sam was clapping his hands, jumping up and down. He was looking forward to Rosemear's bigger rooms, larger yard, and the well-built tree house out back he could explore.

Ellie, however, looked miserable. She dropped her head and crossed her arms over her belly.

Noticing the change in her daughter, Isabella came and sat next to her on the step. "What is it, peanut?"

Ellie laid her head on Isabella's shoulder. "My tummy feels funny."

"Are you hungry, El?" Spencer asked.

"N-no. My tummy just feels icky." She looked up at Isabella. "Can I go to my room to lie down, Mommy?"

"Of course, baby. How about I bring you some chicken noodle soup in a bit? Sam, can you get your sister settled inside?"

Sam nodded and followed Ellie into the house.

"Okay, Spence," Isabella said, standing again. "Assuming we do this, I still want all the things we talked about done before we move in. I'm talking about the roof, the foundation, the works. Agreed?"

Spencer pumped his fist in the air. "Yes, ma'am! You got it! I'm going to make some phone calls. We need to call a realtor and get this house on the market!"

He took the porch stairs two at a time, then stood beside her and kissed her cheek. "You'll see, Bella," he whispered in her ear. "This move is going to change everything. Finding this place was like, I don't know, fate? Like we are supposed to be there."

As he disappeared into the house, Isabella's thoughts were no longer occupied with upgrades or improvements or the décor scheme she would use in Rosemear.

Instead, like waves crashing to the shore, her mind was filled with the dire warning from her daughter's lips earlier that day.

*They don't want us here.*

# CHAPTER FOUR
## *ABIGAIL*

*Rosemear*
*May 21ˢᵗ, 1859*

Clyde Baldwin twisted his cap in his hand, a sweat-stained knit shirt snug against his generous belly. His heart kicked up a notch, and his gut soured at the thought of intervening, but he knew it had to be done.

"Um, boss?" Clyde began, his deep baritone bouncing off the barn rafters. "You maybe ought to stop, huh? Looks like the boy is close to meetin' Jesus hisself right about now."

Near breathless, William Hawthorne ran his tongue across his bottom lip, tasting blood. He'd probably bitten that lip a half-dozen times over the last five minutes, a habit he'd picked up as a boy.

Whether on a date with a pretty girl, performing a challenging task, or right before he took the kill shot while hunting, William's top teeth always found his bottom lip.

And it had happened just now as he rained justice down on his property.

Dragging a thumb over his still-bleeding lip, he nodded at his plantation overseer. "Might be right on that, Clyde. I think the boy has had enough."

Turning his attention to the back of his right hand, William examined the surface, palpating his bruised and bloodied knuckles. He flexed his swollen fingers several times, wondering if he'd broken a bone in his forty-nine-year-old hands while delivering his brand of punishment.

A moan from below dragged William away from his inspection and back to the present. He glanced down at the crumpled form at his feet and, using the tip of his boot, pushed hard at the man's shoulder.

"Hey," William said evenly. "You hear me, son?"

The man grunted and rolled heavily onto his back, kicking up a cloud of dust that lingered like smoke.

"Get up, Young Joseph," William ordered, spitting blood onto the barn floor. "You need to get yourself cleaned up and back to the fields."

But Joseph, a month shy of his eighteenth birthday, remained on the ground, whimpering.

William bent forward. "I said," he growled, "to get your ass up! I mean it, boy! I ain't playin' here!"

Joseph groaned once more before slowly returning to his side.

"That's it," William soothed. He stepped back a few feet and plopped down on a hay bale. "You know what your problem is, Joseph? It all comes down to respect and gratitude. You have no respect for my home, my things, and no gratitude for the blessings the good Lord has seen fit to give you." He rubbed the knuckles of his hand, the flesh there tight and tender. "Do you know how much I spend on seed, boy? How much of my hard-earned money I spend on my crops?"

Using one arm to support his ribs, Joseph sat up. His left eye was swollen shut, his jaw was aching, and his lip was split. He held back a sneeze as dirt from the barn floor tickled his nostrils.

A sneeze now, through ribs that were most likely broken, would be his undoing.

The room spun when he tilted his head back to face his attacker. There was a throbbing at the base of his skull that, combined with the relentless sensation of reeling, created waves of nausea. Using his good eye, he squinted at William and willed his body to stop shaking.

"No, I don't believe you understand," William continued, "because, if you did, you wouldn't be out there in the midst of a workday, sleeping in my fields, content as a baby sucking on his momma's teat."

Joseph wiped the sweat from his brow and tried to focus on moving, but getting back on two feet seemed insurmountable.

And it had little to do with the beating he'd just taken.

This morning in his quarters, Joseph had woken up feverish and damp with sweat, unable to stop shaking. The pounding in his head was surpassed only by the fire in his throat—a hot and relentless pain that burned brighter with each swallow.

Joseph had tried his best to ignore his symptoms.

But, as the day wore on and his temperature climbed, he'd found it nearly impossible to swallow or take a deep breath.

"He looks sickly, Father," a male voice said from the barn entrance. "Feverish and such."

William rose from the hay bale and faced his twenty-one-year-old son. "He's not sick, Edward. He's lazy."

Edward frowned and moved further into the barn. "But it's Young Joseph, Father. I don't expect we have a better worker out in those fields, except for maybe his father."

There was a soft shuffling from behind, and Edward turned. "Well, if it isn't Ms. Abigail Charles!" he said, smiling brightly. "How are you this fine day?"

A smile touched Abigail's lips, but she said nothing. Her eyes brushed over Edward and William before she spied the young man on the ground.

"Oh, mercy!" she gasped, gathering her skirts and rushing to Joseph.

Kneeling before him, she reached out, gently touching his swollen eye. Looking over her shoulder, she spoke. "I can take care of this, Mr. Hawthorne, sir. I can fix him up, right as rain, so's he can get back to work straight away."

William eyed Abigail. "That right, little one?" He rubbed his chin, the friction of fingers against his five-o'clock shadow like sandpaper. Lowering his gaze, he brazenly gawked at the mounds of flesh peeking over the neckline of her dress. Reluctantly, enjoying the view, he dragged his gaze from her breasts back to her face. "And how about the sickness? My boy thinks Young Joseph here looks sickly. What do you think?"

Abigail's heart fluttered beneath her worn dress. She was terrified of this man. "Um… I think Mr. Edward has a keen eye for such things. If he say Young Joseph is sickly, he sickly."

Edward smiled at her. "Thank you, Abigail."

She nodded, then turned back to Joseph and squeezed his hand.

"All right, enough of this nonsense," William said wearily. He looked at Edward. "So, what would you have me do? Give him the day off? A brief vacation? What message will that send to the other workers?"

Edward chose his words carefully. He and William disagreed on many things, but the most notable difference between the two was their opinions about slavery. William believed it was a White man's God-given right to hold another in bondage, while Edward believed no person had the right to own another human being. To that end, he swore that once his father was gone and the plantation left to him, he would make it his mission to free all those enslaved at Rosemear.

Even if it meant cutting back on his crops; even if the South hadn't yet accepted that emancipation was a genuine possibility.

"No, Father. I'm not asking you to give Young Joseph a vacation. But if there is even the slightest chance he's contracted diphtheria or scarlet fever, shouldn't we err on the side of caution? Diseases like those can spread like wildfire and cripple our operation."

William pursed his lips. "You may be right, son. While disciplining the boy, I could feel the heat just bubblin' off his skin."

Edward nodded and discreetly winked at Abigail. "Then, for sure, it's best to isolate him. Our family has seen firsthand how dastardly these illnesses can be."

William grunted. "Fine. I'll leave it to you and Abigail to deal with." He turned toward the barn door. "Come, Clyde," he said. "We have more fields to inspect."

Clyde nodded. "Be right with ya, boss."

After William walked outside, Clyde donned his cap, pulling the brim low. His gaze flicked from Edward to Abigail, and he frowned, unable to hide his disdain. On more than one occasion, he'd witnessed a familiarity between them, a mutual admiration that angered him. Finding Edward's eyes, he grunted, "You know, Mr. Hawthorne, there's a saying around my parts that might do you a bit of good."

"And what saying would that be?" Edward asked, unnerved by the venom in Baldwin's tone.

Clyde lazily picked at a tobacco-stained canine tooth. Glaring at Abigail, he said, "The saying goes that sometimes… well, sometimes a body don't find out a snake is venomous till they get themselves bit."

Edward smirked. "I'm not afraid of snakes, Mr. Baldwin. Or overseers, for that matter. But I do appreciate the warning."

After helping Abigail get Young Joseph back to the enslaved quarters and into bed, Edward stood awkwardly in the dusty driveway, waiting for Abigail to return outside.

Pacing a circle, hands in his pockets, he tried to ignore the small voice in his mind, urging him to leave, telling him that nothing good could come of this strange infatuation with Abigail.

A louder, more commanding voice in his mind reminded him that when Adam and Eve ate fruit from the forbidden tree, their betrayal became the genesis of all sin.

And that voice belonged to his father.

Shaking his head—as if the motion could wipe Abigail from his mind—Edward turned to leave. The creak of the cabin door stopped him, and he turned to find Abigail, hands clasped in front of her, standing on the porch.

The sun bathed her in brilliance, highlighting her cheekbones, full lips, and smooth and perfect skin. Edward hitched a breath but remained otherwise still. He feared any movement would ruin his vision and snatch this cherished memory from his mind forever.

"Did you hear me, Mr. Hawthorne, sir?" Abigail was saying. "I fear Young Joseph has the fever. He's burning something awful."

Edward cleared his throat. "Um, yes, you're probably right, Abigail. I suppose if he isn't better by tomorrow, I should fetch the doctor. It may be diphtheria or the yellow plague that ravished Savannah five years ago. Hell, maybe it's even scarlet fever. In any case, we don't want any of those diseases spreading on the plantation, do we?"

Abigail gave a subtle shake of her head.

"Perhaps while we wait to see if the doctor is needed, we could have some men move Joseph to the barn. I know it's not ideal, but several cots are already set up for the stable master and groomsmen. It's certainly cooler and more comfortable than the slave quarters, and separating him from the others will help contain the infection."

Abigail wiped her hands on her apron. "That'd be most kind of you, sir. I will have Virgil and Abraham set Joseph up in the barn."

When Edward didn't move, Abigail said, "Was there somethin' else you be needin', Mr. Hawthorne?"

Edward smiled. "Call me Edward, Abigail."

"Oh, no… no," she stuttered. "No, sir, I can't do that. I can't show such disrespect to you or the Hawthorne family."

He dug into his trousers, removing a pipe and a nearly empty tobacco satchel from a side pocket. Holding up the crumpled pouch, he shrugged. "Guess I'm out of tobacco." Then, winking, he added, "Good thing I know a place where they grow it."

Abigail smiled shyly.

Edward studied her for a moment. "You've been with us for a few months now, am I right?"

She nodded.

"And in that time, you've done everything my father and his wife have asked of you, haven't you? I mean, I've seen you jump from performing household tasks to helping in the fields when we are short-handed, to grooming horses and mending fences when need be."

"Yes, sir," she said quietly.

"Well, Miss Abigail, I believe such loyalty deserves a reward." He stuffed the pipe and tobacco bag back into his pocket. "So, tell me… If you could have anything right now, anything in the world, what would it be?"

Abigail pushed her shoulders back, somehow feeling her pride was in jeopardy. Or worse, feeling like the question might be a trap. Although Edward Hawthorne had been nothing but agreeable, she was unfamiliar with kindness for the sake of kindness.

Because, except for Prophet Jones, anyone who had ever shown her tenderness had an ulterior motive.

Head held high, she descended the steps and faced him. "I'm not needing anything, Mr. Hawthorne, sir. I have plenty to eat and all the fabric I need to make my clothes. It's so much fabric that I have enough to make new aprons for the cooks. And your daddy saw fit to give me my very own room, right there in the main house. I expect I have all that I need, Mr. Hawthorne. Not many nowadays can say the same."

Edward raised a brow. "So, there's nothing, then? Not more

firewood to keep you warm in winter? No sweet treats to eat or costly perfumes? How about fine silks or fancy shoes?"

She slowly shook her head.

Lowering his voice, he added, "What about your freedom, Abigail? I know of a system called 'The Underground Railroad.' It's composed of people who are secretly working to ensure every man, woman, and child lives free from the chains of slavery. I believe it is this group of fine individuals who will bring an end to the barbaric practice of enslaving others." He reached out to grab her hand, then thought better of it. "Honestly, these folks, these wonderful souls, can help transport you north, where slavery does not exist. You can be free."

Abigail, eyes downcast, shook her head. "Meaning no disrespect, Mr. Hawthorne, but free to do what? To go where? Freedom is just a word, sir. True freedom means nothing without a means to survive that life and a person to share that life with. I have no skills, no place to go, and nobody waitin' on me if I did. I have no one."

Her simple admission, as if she were resigned to spending a lifetime alone, tugged at Edward's heart. "That must be very hard for you. Is there nothing I can tempt you with?" The voices in his head, cautioning him about the dangerous territory he was entering, returned.

He ignored them.

"Surely, there is something," he said. "Some gesture or gift to make you feel better? How about a decadent meal accompanied by the finest champagne? Or a sunset walk on the beach, where the scent of the ocean and the colors of the sky make you think you've surely died and gone to heaven."

Abigail tilted her head, trying to decide if his offer was genuine.

He winked at her. "Or both? Nothing says we can't do both dinner and a beach walk."

Abigail closed the distance between them. Heart pounding, she stopped mere inches away from him, far enough to be respectable but close enough to see the tiny lashes at the corners of his eyes and smell the scent he'd applied just that morning.

Searching his face, fearing a swift and angry response to what she was about to say, she hesitated.

"Abigail?" Edward croaked, devouring her scent. Her sweet breath, combined with the aroma of lavender soap, enveloped him. Edward fought the urge to close his eyes and steady himself. Being this close to her was thrilling.

Thrilling and dangerous and utterly terrifying.

It was as if she were his greatest strength and most supreme weakness, giving him life while simultaneously ripping the air from his lungs. Standing mere inches away, breathing her in, was a temptation he'd never before experienced. He fought the urge to wrap her in his embrace, to kiss her lips, to worship her in his arms.

Oblivious to Edward's desires, Abigail mulled over his offer, debating whether or not it was sincere. Eventually, the flames of apprehension were doused by the only thing that kept her going most days: hope. "Very well, then. In truth, Mr. Hawthorne, there is one thing I want. One thing I've dreamed about but knew would never come to be, could never come to be."

Time stopped. Edward held his breath, waiting, hoping she would say his name, tell him it was him she wanted, him she needed.

*The forbidden fruit.*

Instead, to his utter shock, Abigail whispered, "Teach me to read, Mr. Hawthorne, sir. I want to learn how to read."

Water sloshed over the sides of the weathered bucket in Abigail's hands as she made her way to the barn. Setting the pail on the ground near the barn entrance, she wiped a hand across her forehead and stretched her back.

"You all right, Ms. Abigail?" Virgil asked from behind her.

She turned and smiled at him. "Yes, Virgil, I'm fine, thank you. Just bringing in some clean water for Young Joseph."

He nodded. "He in a bad way, that boy. I pray the Lord don't see fit to take him."

Abigail dried her damp hands on her apron. "Although prayers are most welcome, Virgil, I believe Jesus means for us to help ourselves when we can."

"He surely do," he said with a nod. He took off his cap and twisted it in his hands. Abigail was a confident, smart, and pretty lady. Her presence made Virgil, usually a smooth conversationalist, positively tongue-tied.

Still, he tried.

"You, uh, you got a heart of gold and the touch of an angel, Miss Abigail. I-I don't rightly know what any of us would do without you here, taking care of us. Young Joseph is lucky to have you. We—well, we all are."

"Nonsense, Virgil. I just do what needs doin', same as you. And right now, I'm fixin' to help Young Joseph break that wicked fever."

With a grunt, she lifted the bucket again and hobbled into the barn, moving carefully to minimize water loss.

Virgil grinned at her retreating form. "Well, if'n anyone can do it, Miss, it'd surely be you."

Abigail rinsed a white cloth in the pail of cool water, wrung it out, and gently placed the rag on Joseph's head. He jumped at her touch, his hand grabbing her wrist.

"What happened? Where am I?"

Abigail shushed him. "Hush now, Young Joseph. You have the fever. Mr. Edward Hawthorne gave permission to house you in the barn while you ailing."

Joseph looked around. "The fever? You mean the yellow plague?"

Abigail shrugged. "Ain't no telling. Could be that, or it could be what took young Master Hawthorne last year."

Joseph swallowed hard. "The diphtheria?" His voice cracked with fear. "Tell me true, Miss Abigail… Am I gonna die?"

She submerged the rag in the bucket again, squeezed it, and placed it back on his forehead. "You stop with such foolishness now. Ain't nobody dyin' on my watch. I'm gonna see to it. And Mr. Edward said if you get much worse, he'll fetch the doctor."

Joseph eyed her suspiciously. "That what he say? You know, Miss Abigail," he swallowed with difficulty, "you need to use care with the company you been keepin'. Just as an eagle don't fly with a duck or a fox don't frolic in a hen house, we need to mind our place here at Rosemear."

She stood. "What are you going on about, Joseph?"

He lifted his body slightly and rested on his elbows. "It's just a warning, Miss. Mr. Edward, well, he not all he looks to be. I seen him drunk on many a night, ranting 'bout one thing or another. And he got an ugly temper, that for sure."

Abigail stiffened. "Mr. Edward been nothing but kind to me, Young Joseph. He even say he gonna teach me…."

She stopped herself from completing the thought. No one could know about Edward's offer to teach her to read. There was too much at stake for both of them.

"He gonna teach you what?" Joseph asked.

"Never you mind." Lowering her voice, she added, "Virgil Lewis, you best stop telling tales about Mr. Edward. Talk like that can land you in a heap of trouble." Sighing, she turned and headed for the door. "I'll bring you something to fill your belly shortly. Until then, I'll leave you to your rest."

Once outside, Abigail closed her eyes momentarily, trying to stop the hammering in her chest. She looked around, ensuring that she and Joseph had been alone.

Spies were everywhere on this property—she'd known that since the first day she arrived.

Whether paid workers looking to gain favor with the boss or enslaved laborers just hoping to survive, William Hawthorne had eyes and ears all over Rosemear.

She walked toward the main house, anxiety twisting her stomach into knots. Periodically glancing behind her, she shuddered, wondering what would happen if one of William's spies had overheard Joseph speaking poorly of Edward Hawthorne.

When she reached the mansion's back door, she looked around one last time before slipping quietly inside, satisfied she was alone.

And never noticed the dark figure on top of the barn roof, hands resting on his hips, watching her.

# CHAPTER FIVE

*Rosemear*
*July 16th*
*Present Day*

Isabella bent forward, repositioned her hands, and pulled hard, dragging the rolled carpet over the hardwood and setting it against the far wall of the dining room. Sweat glistened on her forehead as, panting with effort, she gave the cumbersome bundle one more tug, trying to straighten it out.

And felt the nail on her third finger break nearly to the quick.

"Shit, shit, shit!"

"Mommy!" Ellie yelled from the bottom step of the staircase. "You said a bad word!"

Isabella stood and cracked her back. "Good ears!" she yelled back. "You're so right, Ellie-bell. Forgive me?"

Ellie jumped off the last step, veered left, and raced into the dining room. Arms extended and head thrown back, she twirled in the center of the room and sang a nursery rhyme, giggling at the echo that greeted her.

"Careful, sweet pea," Isabella said. "You'll get dizzy and fall down, just like London Bridge."

Ellie stopped spinning and skipped toward her mother, sneakers squeaking against the hardwood floor. "Are we really sleeping here tonight, Mom?" she asked, plopping down on the carpet roll. "We have no furniture and no lights, and my room still smells bad."

Isabella frowned. "Does it? That's odd. I cleaned every inch of that room yesterday, even the walls. But this house has a bunch of nooks and crannies, so it's possible I missed something. We'll look as soon as we're done here, okay?" She tightened the elastic band holding her high ponytail. "As for the other stuff… yes, we don't have all our furniture yet. But the movers are coming tomorrow with our bedroom sets, and I've ordered a ton of other stuff to be delivered here—stuff that was popular when Rosemear was built, like wingback chairs, a mahogany dining set, and a few Victorian couches. Wait until you see! It's gonna be epic! And so much fun to decorate!"

"What are Victoreen couches?" Ellie asked.

Isabella finger-combed her daughter's hair, tamping down a cowlick with a mind of its own. "Victorian," she corrected. "It's a style of decorating from way back when."

"But what about the dark?" Ellie asked. "It's spooky here in the dark."

"Well, we have electricity, but since I'm not sure how safe the lamps are, we'll use the flashlights, candles, and kerosene lamps your dad brought us. It'll be fine, El."

Ellie sighed dramatically. "No lights means no fun."

Isabella kissed her forehead. "Tell you what. How about you and me go shopping for light fixtures this week? Until then, this will be a grand adventure! Like camping out, only without the bugs!"

Ellie's shoulders sagged, but she nodded in agreement.

"In the meantime, how about you give me a hand unrolling this beast? Dad and Sam went to the lumber store, so it's just us girls to get the job done. Up for the challenge?"

Ellie raised a fist and shouted, "Yes! Girl power! Right, Momma?"

Isabella smiled. "Right, baby. Come over here on this side of the carpet, and we'll each take an end. We push on three. Ready?"

Ellie grinned and began counting. "One… two…"

A loud bang from upstairs caused them both to jump.

"Momma?" Ellie whispered.

Isabella wiped her hands on her jeans. "It's nothing, baby. Probably the wind, blowing one of the bedroom doors shut."

Ellie, eyes wide, didn't move.

"Bug? Aw, sweetheart, there's nothing to be afraid of. Like I said, it's probably just the wind. There are three windows with cracked panes upstairs that we still need to get fixed and, like, I don't know, a gazillion fireplaces in this house? Plenty of things that can contribute to a draft."

Ellie looked unconvinced.

"Come on, I'll prove it to you! Let's have a look. While we're up there, I can also get a good sniff of that stinky bedroom." She turned toward the foyer and smirked. "First one to the top—"

"Is a rotten egg?" Ellie interrupted, clapping her hands.

"Hmm, isn't it usually the *last* one that's a rotten egg?" Isabella said with a grin. "Anyway, in this race, the first one to the top gets to pick the menu tonight!"

They skipped, hand in hand, to the bottom of the staircase on the left. "How about if I go on that side?" Isabella said, pointing to the stairs on the right. "That way, we aren't running over each other to get to the top."

She hustled to the opposite side, pretending to be out of breath when she got there. "Boy, am I out of shape! I think you may beat me today, girlfriend! Just make sure to hold on to the railing, okay? Ready? On your mark, get set…."

"Go!" they said in unison.

Giggling, they ran up the steps to the main landing, Isabella deliberately slowing halfway up. When they reached the top, she locked on Ellie's face, widened her eyes, and mimicked the witch in 'The Wizard of Oz.' "You got me, my pretty! But next time, I'll get you! And your little dog, too!"

Ellie frowned. "But you said we can't have a dog."

"I said not now, El. I never said never." Attempting to change the subject, Isabella exhaled theatrically, then wiped the sweat from her brow. "It's so hot up here! I know heat rises, but this is ridiculous!"

It was true: even with daylight waning and the A/C window units running, it was stifling inside the house. The French doors on the exterior back wall, centered between both staircases, were open, allowing a slight breeze to enter the space. Beyond the doors, a small balcony overlooked the rear gardens. The view was stunning.

"See that?" Isabella asked. "These open doors would explain where a breeze was coming from."

Ellie pressed her lips together. "I don't know, Momma. I don't think those doors were opened before."

"Maybe Dad opened them before he left for the lumber store. Or, it could be that a blast of air from the air conditioners or a broken window slammed the door."

Ellie nodded, then took her mother's hand.

"Geesh, kid," Isabella said. "Your hand is like ice."

Ellie shrugged. "I know. It happens when people get ascared sometimes."

Isabella crouched down. She took Ellie's other hand, then raised them both to her lips and blew, trying to warm them. "It's pronounced 'scared.' And who told you that?"

Ellie dropped her head, suddenly fascinated with the floor. "No one."

"Eleanor Boyd," Isabella said sternly, "what have I told you about not being truthful?"

"But I'm not supposed to tell anyone, Momma," she said, shaking her head. "I—I promised."

"Baby," Isabella said again, lifting Ellie's chin and forcing eye contact. "What do we say about secrets?"

Shoulders slumped, Ellie dug the toe of her sneaker into the scarred floor and spoke in a sing-song voice. "Secrets, secrets, they're no fun; secrets, secrets, hurt someone."

"That's right. So, do you have something to tell me?"

She shrugged. "I-I guess. It was just... it was my friend, Martin."

Isabella frowned, scouring her memory. They had met some people in the last few weeks while working on the house. Most of them had young children, like Anthony and Joyce Rizzo, owners of the General Store, and Mike and Teresa Logan, who operated a local running/hiking club that Isabella wanted to join. Just yesterday, Sid and Claire Gibbons, operators of a family-run home improvement store, had personally delivered a load of pavers, along with a 'Welcome to the neighborhood' cherry cheesecake.

But, as far as she recalled, none of these people had a child named Martin. The only Martin she'd ever known was her best friend's brother, who had died twenty years ago. At the time of his passing, Isabella and Luna were just ordinary fourteen-year-old girls trying to make sense of a tragedy that would never make sense.

Martin Lake had been sick for two years before eventually succumbing to cancer three days before his twelfth birthday.

*Leukemia. The taker of children, the destroyer of dreams.*

Focusing again, Isabella, still crouching, released Ellie's chin and frowned. "Martin? Sweetie, who is Martin? Where did you meet him?"

Ellie held both hands behind her back, and her eyes found the floor once again. Another slam, coming from a back bedroom, echoed throughout the house.

Ellie's head snapped up, and she sucked in a tiny breath, searching her mother's face for an answer.

"You know, most times," Isabella said, standing again, "the

truth lies in the simplest explanation. My money's on the wind."

Ellie chewed her bottom lip.

"How about we discuss Martin later and play detective instead? I'm sure that, together, we can figure out the 'Mystery of the Banging Door'!"

As the words left her lips, the bulbs in the chandelier winked on and off.

Ellie tilted her head. "And the mystery of the blinking lights? Can we play detective on that case, too?"

Isabella held back a response, instead glancing down over the railing. The shadowy effect of the flickering lights on the ivy-covered wallpaper on the double staircase was chilling.

She hated that wallpaper.

The green of the ivy was much too vibrant for her liking, and the gold-rimmed leaves—meant to telegraph wealth—were far too showy for her taste. But now, the buttery tones of the foliage shimmered like a disco ball with each spasm of light, creating a creepy—rather than ugly—effect.

It was as if the vines had come to life, undulating and bending with each pulse of light.

Isabella felt a chill run down her spine. As crazy as it sounded, it felt like the ivy was snaking up the staircase walls, its sinewy tendrils reaching for them.

"Mommy?"

"It's okay, El," Isabella said, giving Ellie a wink as she snapped back to the present. "It's fine. We'll check all the doors until we find the guilty party."

Ellie tilted her head. "But what about the lights?"

"Not to worry. I'm sure the bulbs in the chandelier just need to be replaced." She held out her hand. "You know, Bug, moving into a new place always brings unfamiliar sounds. Part of the mystique and excitement of a brand-new home is learning all about its history and the quirks that go with the house. So think of the oddities as a gift—a kind of 'welcome mat' from the house to its new owners."

Ellie sighed. "I don't think you understand what Rosemear wants."

"What it wants? Oh, sweetie, Rosemear is a building, an object. It can't want anything from us because, well, it's not alive."

Ellie's lower lip began to tremble. "You're wrong, Momma," she whispered. "Rosemear *is* alive. And it's not happy."

Isabella stood in the west wing hallway, hands on her hips and eyes sweeping the doors on either side of the hall.

All of them appeared to be closed.

"Mom?" Ellie said, her tiny arm wrapped around one of Isabella's thighs.

"I'm not seeing anything. Heck, I'm not sure what half of these rooms are for." She patted Ellie's shoulder. "Come on, baby. Let's check each door on this side first; then we can hit the right wing."

They worked in tandem until they reached the end of the hallway. Isabella stood before the last door, the furthest one back, and twisted the doorknob.

It was locked.

She jiggled the handle several times. "What the heck?"

"Maybe Daddy has the key," Ellie said helpfully.

"Maybe. But why would he lock it? What could be in here that needs to be locked up?"

Standing on tippy-toes, Isabella stretched a hand overhead and swept her fingers along the top of the door frame.

No key.

"Okay, El," Isabella said, giving the doorknob one last twist. "I'll look for the key later. Let's head over to the east wing and check those doors."

Midway down the hall, Isabella stopped, sure she'd heard a child giggling.

But Ellie had run ahead and was nearly on the east side of the house.

And Samuel wasn't home.

Heart racing, Isabella followed her daughter down the hall, trying to look unaffected while rationalizing what she'd just experienced. The muffled giggles she'd heard seemed to originate from behind the door at the end of the hallway.

Inside the locked room.

But the mind has a remarkable way of explaining the unexplainable. By the time she'd reached the east wing, Isabella had already convinced herself the voices she'd heard were merely drafts, breaths of wind groaning within the eaves and floorboards of the house.

Because the alternate explanation was terrifying.

And led to a road she was unwilling, and unable, to travel alone.

In the east wing, Isabella stopped in front of the first bedroom down the hall and pointed at the hinge on the door. "Bingo! See this, El? See how the door is tilted crookedly in its frame?"

Ellie nodded. "Like the doors in a Dr. Seuss book."

"Exactly! The top part of the door is dipping to the right because the pin is rusted and partially broken. I expect that would make it rattle a bit in a strong breeze." She tapped the door. "It's heavy, too. The weight of the wood allows it to move side to side, instead of just forward and back."

"Like a regular door?"

"Yes, ma'am!" She leaned a hip against the jamb. "So there you have it, ladies and gents. Another mystery solved by Boyd

Investigations!"

Ellie frowned but said nothing.

"You know what?" Isabella said, brows raised. "We haven't checked out these rooms in detail yet. Let's look around, see what we can see. Then, we'll check out that smelly room of yours."

Noncommittal, Ellie peeked at her mother from beneath half-closed lids, her gray eyes fringed by long, thick lashes.

"Plus," Isabella said, rubbing her aching lower back, "by the time we're done, the boys should be back to help us lay the carpet. Sound like a plan?"

"Okay," Ellie said. "Can we look at that one?" She pointed to a blue door on the left. "I've never seen a blue door inside a house before."

Isabella shrugged. "Me either. But after seeing that ivy crawling up the walls, I don't know if we should be surprised."

Ellie reached the blue door first, grasped the knob with her palm, then pulled her hand away as if she'd been burned.

"Bug?" Isabella said, walking quickly to Ellie. "What happened? Did you get a splinter?"

Ellie massaged the hand that had touched the doorknob. "No, but it was hot, Mommy. Like on fire hot," she whispered, holding out her hand.

Isabella inspected Ellie's hand, front and back. "I don't see anything, baby," she said, placing a palm on the wooden door. "But the good news is the door is cool, so there's no fire inside. Let me try the knob."

Ignoring Ellie's "No!" Isabella grabbed the doorknob. "Downright chilly now, which is weird since it's like a furnace up here. Let's check inside."

Ellie shook her head and stepped away from her mother, moving to the middle of the hall.

Just as Isabella began to turn the knob, she felt her grip slip as a powerful tug wrenched the knob from her hand. The door flew open, slamming against the bedroom wall, the reverberation of wood against plaster shaking the oak beneath their feet.

Isabella slapped a hand over her heart. "Holy crap, that scared me to death! Must be drafty in here, too."

As she peered inside, still standing at the threshold, the first thing to hit Isabella was the stench. It was a combination of sweet perfume, frankincense, and some kind of chemical, like bleach or ammonia. Her stomach roiled, and she held the back of her hand to her nostrils.

"What the fu…." Isabella said, stopping before she finished the obscenity. "Um, I don't recall smelling anything during the walk-through, do you?" Mumbling, she added, "It's almost as if I've forgotten everything about the second floor. Did we even come into this room before?"

Ellie shrugged.

"Is this the smell you were talking about in your room, Bug?" Isabella asked. "I cleaned the walls, so maybe you smell bleach?"

Ellie shook her head. "No, that's not it. My room smells yuckier."

Isabella grinned. "Like Sammy's shoes?"

"Even stinkier." She paused, thinking. "Remember when that wild bunny got stuck inside the shed when we were at Disneyland? We came back, and Daddy was mad because the shed smelled really bad. And then he found the bunny." She widened her eyes and tilted her head, tongue lolling from her mouth, imitating the posture of a deceased animal. "Daddy said she got stuck inside the shed and didn't have any food or water."

"Yes, I remember. It was an unfortunate thing, wasn't it?"

"Yeah, well, that's sort of how my room smells. Like the shed with the brown bunny."

Isabella swallowed hard, replaying her daughter's words in her mind.

*That's how my room smells. Like the shed with the brown bunny.*

*The dead brown bunny.*

Backing up, Isabella ushered Ellie away from the blue door. "What do you say we head to your room now, kiddo? I can poke around in here later."

Ellie nodded and raced down the hall to her bedroom.

With one last glance inside the room, Isabella closed the blue door and followed her daughter down the hall, the nasty odor still clinging to her nostrils.

*Bleach. Perfume. Incense,* Isabella thought, disturbed. *What the devil happened in there?*

When Isabella walked into Ellie's room, she found her daughter sitting on the elaborate parquet floor, tracing an intricate pattern with a fingertip. The bedroom, located within the turret-style architecture on one corner of the house, was one of the prettiest rooms in the manor.

As soon as Isabella cleared the threshold, she wrinkled her nose. "Oh, boy, I see what you mean, Bug. This smell is different from the odor behind the blue door."

A series of taps from one of the three octagonal windows caught her attention. Walking across the room, she peered through the glass to find a large Southern oak, heavy with Spanish moss, looming to the left of the corner window.

"Ta-da!" Isabella said with a slight bow. "Another mystery solved by our investigative team! When the wind blows, I bet a limb knocks against the window pane, creating that banging sound we hear. Remind me to ask Dad to trim those branches back." She clapped her hands together. "Okay, let's see if we can figure out where that weird odor is coming from, shall we?"

Ellie sighed. "Okay, but I don't think you'll find anything. I think it's just the house telling us to get out."

"Get out? But we only just got here!" Isabella joked.

Ellie frowned. "It's not funny, Momma!" Then, under her breath, she added, "There are people here—people we can't see who died a long time ago—who want us to leave. Ghosts or something."

Isabella was caught off guard by the remark. "Ghosts? Oh, Bug. I think you've been watching too much *Scooby-Doo*. No one is here except us and the occasional spider looking for his supper. There are no dead people, no goblins, no boogeymen. Just us."

Ellie sighed and leaned backward until she was lying supine on the floor. Covering her eyes with the crook of her elbow, she remained silent.

"Ellie?" Isabella prodded.

Eleanor was quiet as her five-year-old brain searched for the right words. "But there are, Mom. There are ghosts. And they speak to me sometimes. Martin speaks to me. He says we're not safe here."

Isabella did her best not to react, her mind scrambling for a rational explanation. Had Ellie been sleeping okay? Was it possible the stress of the move, or even Anna's death all those years ago, had affected her more than she and Spencer realized?

Or could it be more than that? The thought slammed into her brain without warning, nearly bringing her to her knees.

*Oh, my God! Could Eleanor be experiencing the auditory hallucinations that accompany schizophrenia?*

Isabella's family had an extensive history of mental illness. Her great-great-uncle, Jonathan 'Jack' Duncan, had suffered from an unspecified form of psychosis that, according to her father, included both auditory and visual hallucinations. It began in his early teens, and back then, the treatment could be worse than the disease.

Jack went through life trying to convince his family that it hadn't been a troubled mind causing his delusions. Instead, he insisted they were a consequence of his psychic abilities, his sixth sense. He was certain his visions and the words he'd heard whispered in his ears were not hallucinations but a result of his ability to communicate with spirits. Until his dying day, he had claimed to 'know things.'

Things that were impossible to know.

Institutionalized at twenty and given electroconvulsive therapy six years later, Jack was never the same. He had died at age eighty-three, a shell of a human being, still claiming to have the "gift that only I can see."

In addition to her Uncle Jack, Isabella's maternal grandmother suffered from depression, and a second cousin—a man named Jeffrey—thought he was St. Sebastian, the patron saint of sports.

All because he fancied himself an athlete.

In truth, Jeffrey was neither a saint nor anything close to athletic. The man had the agility and coordination of a sloth and would be the last person God would choose to return to earth as St. Sebastian.

In addition, although not formally diagnosed with any psychological disorder, Isabella herself had been hospitalized for several weeks after Anna's death. The doctors called it a 'mental breakdown accompanied by emotional instability.'

Isabella called it hell.

So, yeah—the possibility that Eleanor had inherited the genetic blueprint of a troubled mind was not a stretch.

Willing her racing heart to slow down, Isabella sat beside Ellie on the floor. "He speaks to you, Bug? Martin does? What does he say, exactly? Who did he say we aren't safe from?"

Sniffling, voice muffled beneath the arm still covering her eyes, Ellie mumbled, "From the dead people, Momma. From the people in the wall."

# CHAPTER
# SIX

After Spencer and Sam had returned to the manor with a few pizzas, a bottle of soda, and a six-pack of beer, the family sat and ate, discussing their plans for the house.

Ellie, quietly nibbling her pizza, said little.

Once they'd finished, Spencer raised the lantern from the table and held it beneath his chin. In a chilling voice, the top half of his face bathed in shadow, he asked the children if they'd like to hear a ghost story involving a train conductor and his missing arm.

Horrified, Isabella stopped him immediately. "Bedtime!" she said, a bit too cheerily.

"Aww, Mom!" Sam whined. "I wanna hear a scary story! It's only nine o'clock."

"Yes, well, we have a big day tomorrow. Everyone is hitting the hay early tonight." She stood and pulled Sam to his feet. "Come on, Boyd children… Let's get your teeth brushed and faces washed for bed."

"Are we all sleeping together?" Ellie whispered.

"You betcha. I've set up our sleeping bags and pillows in a great big circle in the living room. Hopefully, the movers will be here tomorrow with our stuff, and we can finally sleep in our bedrooms."

"It's okay, Mommy," Ellie said with a shrug. "I don't mind when we all sleep in the same room. It's safer like that anyways."

"Safer?" Isabella asked. "What do you mean by…"

Sam, oblivious to his sister's fears, interrupted his mother. "But do we actually have to go to sleep, though? Can me and El talk for a little while?"

"Yeah," Ellie said with a yawn. "I'm not even tired."

Isabella raised a brow. "Not tired, huh? Okay, well maybe just pretend you're tired, then."

"Does that mean we can pretend to sleep, too?" Sam said with a grin.

Isabella rolled her eyes. "Your choice, but while you're pretending, I'll be dreaming of puppy dogs and ice cream."

Ellie grabbed her mother's hand. "I hope I dream that, too." Then, in a voice barely above a whisper, she added, "I don't want to have bad dreams anymore."

"Then don't, baby. If you tell your mind to have sweet dreams, it will listen. You know what my grandmother used to say?"

Ellie shook her head.

"She'd say, 'Dreams are the mind's way of sorting through the nonsense.' She meant that dreams help us figure out our fears and stuff. Does that make sense?"

Teary-eyed, Ellie nodded. "I guess so. But before we got this house, I used to have good dreams all the time. Now, I only dream about Martin and some sad lady in a long dress. Oh, and the people behind the wall. I dream about *them* a lot!"

After tucking in Sam and Ellie, Isabella headed back to the dining room, listening to the faint voices of her children as they discussed the pros and cons of being a superhero.

From the sound of it, there were very few cons.

*Just regular kids, having an innocent conversation while fighting bedtime. Thank you, Jesus, for this little bit of 'normal.'*

Because everything Ellie had just divulged about her dreams was miles away from ordinary.

It was terrifying.

Isabella entered the dining room and sat on the black and red oriental carpet, facing her husband. "Sorry about cutting you off before, Spence. I was worried that a scary story right now, given Eleanor's anxiety about Rosemear, might not be the best idea."

Spencer shrugged.

"Anyway, I'm not gonna lie about being concerned. Ellie thinks—scratch that—she's *convinced* that Rosemear is haunted."

Spencer took a sip of beer and stared at her. "Haunted," he said, a note of irritation in his tone. "Is that something our child told you, or is this an assumption?"

"An assumption? Christ, Spencer..." She blew out a breath. "No, I didn't 'assume' anything. Ellie has an imaginary friend, one she believes is a ghost."

Spencer took another pull on his beer.

"Did you hear me?" she asked, annoyed.

"Yeah, I heard."

"And?"

"And nothing."

Isabella frowned. "Excuse me?"

"Look," he said, sounding bored, "Ellie is a little kid. Kids are experts at spotting bad guys lurking beneath beds and boogeymen hiding in closets." He swept his hair away from his forehead. "Sometimes I feel like you look for trouble where it doesn't exist."

Isabella felt a rush of heat to her earlobes—a telltale sign she was close to exploding.

Very few things infuriated her, but being patronized by her husband was at the top of the list.

In the end, there were several reasons her marriage was failing—lack of intimacy, different ideas about child-rearing and finances, and his infidelity, for starters. But the arrogance of his tone, whether they were talking about the kids or money or the weather, always seemed the heaviest to overlook.

It was a constant occurrence, and she was sick to death of it.

Indeed, their union was living on borrowed time, and she couldn't even say she was sorry to see it go. Her feelings for the man she had once loved with every fiber of her being had changed.

Because he had changed.

Like layers of an onion, Spencer Boyd's true self had finally been revealed. He was a liar and a cheat—a thoughtless, egotistical man whose love of money and power was eclipsed only by his love of self.

Months before their daughter had drowned, Isabella discovered her husband's affair with Julia Cox and began divorce proceedings. If Anna Rae hadn't died, she and Spencer would be living separate lives by now.

But she did die, and that death had devastated her, both mind and body. She had neither the mental capacity nor the emotional reserves to pursue a divorce in those early months.

And now, nearly three years after Anna's death, it seemed a task too enormous for the moment.

She was still mourning, still gathering strength and searching for peace. The last thing she wanted to deal with was lawyers, courtrooms, and custody agreements.

"Anyway," Spencer continued, "while I applaud the whole

'mother bear protecting her cub' schtick, it seems you're turning this minor issue into a storm within a teacup."

Pushing back her shoulders, she pinned her gaze on Spencer. "Is that what you think, Spence? Because, just being honest here, my 'schtick,' as you so cleverly put it, is merely a mother expressing concern for her child's mental well-being. The last thing I would expect is for my worries to be ridiculed and ignored by the man who is supposed to protect her."

He frowned. "Now, hang on a minute, Bella. That's not what—"

Isabella cut him off. "I think," she said, standing, "that I'm going to look around upstairs again. You should get some rest. Big trip tomorrow, right?"

Sulking, Spencer nodded. "First trip of the month working in the Savannah office. I have a conference in Atlanta on marketing strategies in the early afternoon before I'm off to introduce MacMillan Pharmaceuticals to several hospital bigwigs in Charleston. If I can get my foot in the door in some of the larger medical centers—the ones with deep pockets and wealthy patients—I'll be set. I'll only be gone a few days."

Isabella nodded and bent down, picking up one of the two kerosene lanterns on the floor. "By the way, a door is locked upstairs on the west wing. I'm sure we checked all the rooms during our walkthrough with Suzanne. Do you know where the key might be?"

Spencer shook his head. "Locked, huh? Wasn't me. The kids, maybe? Anyway, Suzanne gave me a bunch of keys. I'll leave them on the kitchen counter tonight, and you can try them tomorrow. If we can't find the key, I'll have to take the door down."

"Right. Well then, goodnight. Don't forget Luna is coming tomorrow to help me with the movers."

A hint of something dark flashed over Spencer's face before he reined it in. "Yeah, sure. I remember," he said, voice bitter.

Isabella turned and headed toward the double staircase.

"Wait a sec," Spencer called to her retreating form. "How long is she staying here, anyway?"

Not missing a beat, continuing toward the stairs, Isabella tossed over her shoulder, "As long as she fucking wants, Spence. As long as she fucking wants."

When she reached the top of the staircase, Isabella held the lantern high, sweeping it back and forth over the darkened hallways. The night sky was inky black, the moon blanketed in a layer of clouds, affording not even the tiniest sliver of light through the French doors.

"Okay, so, yeah, it's a little creepy," she whispered. "Just keep moving."

She headed down the east wing hall, stepping lightly and holding her breath, an internal dialogue running through her mind.

*Why, out of all the doors in this house, is just one of them locked? Why is one door blue? What is that God-awful smell in Ellie's room? Why do I constantly ask myself questions I can't possibly answer?*

She continued down the hall and, passing the first two rooms on the left side of the hallway, walked directly to the blue door. Taking a deep breath, she haltingly reached for the doorknob.

It was cool to the touch.

Grasping the handle, she slowly rotated the knob before suddenly stopping, her hand frozen in place.

Something was moving inside the room.

Heart thundering, she pressed an ear against the wooden door. After a few seconds, she caught the unmistakable groan of the floorboards as someone, or something, paced inside. Her hand flew to her mouth as the thud of heavy boots marching across the old hardwood echoed through the door.

As quickly as it began, the pacing stopped, replaced by a scraping sound, like claws across a floor. Isabella recoiled, and she snatched her hand away from the knob.

*I swear to God…if I open this and find an animal, it's gonna be ugly.*

After several moments of trying to control her 'fight or flight' response, she wiped her damp palms on her jeans and, once again, put an ear to the door.

Silence.

Hand trembling slightly, she reached out and palmed the doorknob.

It wouldn't turn.

*What the hell?*

Confused, she rattled the knob back and forth, occasionally nudging the door with her shoulder. Less than thirty seconds ago, the knob had moved freely beneath her hand. "Okay," she said, frowning, "it's an old building, complete with the original hardware."

She tried jiggling the handle once more without success. Then, attempting to explain the unexplainable, she muttered, "Locks stick, wood swells. It's an ancient house, one with quirks and character."

Giving up for now, she whispered, "Okay, you win. But I'll be back." Rapping her knuckles lightly against the wooden door, she moved further down the hall to Ellie's room.

The creak of a hinge from behind caused her to turn.

Eyes widening in disbelief, she watched the blue door—unyielding only moments earlier—slowly swing open.

As if she'd passed some unseen test and been invited to enter.

It took two full minutes before Isabella's heart settled into a regular rhythm and she could think again.

*It's nothing—just the wind. See for yourself, scaredy cat!*

Holding the lantern at arm's length, she tiptoed back down the hall toward the blue room. Flickering shadows danced against the walls from the lantern light, creating menacing shapes and slithering contours that reached for her as she walked.

Threatening to grab her and suck her into the walls, into the very bones that shaped Rosemear.

Her heartbeat quickened once again, and she gave herself a mental slap. *Oh, for fuck's sake! It's just shadows!*

Inching closer to the threshold of the blue room, she peered inside, waiting for her eyes to adjust to the darkness. Her nose wrinkled reflexively as the same odor, the combination of incense and disinfectant that she'd smelled earlier, reached her nostrils.

Feet planted firmly in the hallway, she leaned her upper torso forward and swept the lantern's light from side to side, trying to assign an explanation to each murky shape.

*Come on, sugar britches, get a grip! This is your house!*

Commanding her feet to move forward, reminding herself to breathe through her nose, she stepped over the threshold.

The room was ice cold.

Isabella placed the lantern in the center of the floor and rubbed the chill from her arms. Swallowing back an irrational fear that she was in danger, that she was being watched, she slowly took in her surroundings.

The bedroom, one of two masters in the home, was immense. The wall to her right held a wood-burning fireplace with a thick marble mantel and an ornate mirror over the top. The glass, desilvered and speckled with black, gave the room an ominous feel.

Isabella shivered, trying to ignore the irrational thought that the mirror was waiting for her to peer into its marred surface.

Waiting for her to discover the mysteries of yore and unlock Rosemear's terrible secrets.

Rattled, she averted her gaze, instead inspecting the matching floor-to-ceiling bookcases on either side of the fireplace. Several hardcover classics, left behind by a previous owner, were scattered among the otherwise empty shelves.

She pressed two fingers against her temple, trying to massage away an impending headache. Her brain worked feverishly, sorting through the muddled memories of when she'd first toured Rosemear.

Suzanne Johns must have taken them through the blue room at some point. She must have pointed out the features, the size, and the beautiful oak flooring when they explored the house.

Yet Isabella remembered none of it.

She turned a slow circle in the center of the room, squinting to absorb its layout, straining to see beyond its shadowed corners. On the wall in front of her were two three-sided bay windows—each with a gabled roof—that overlooked the grounds behind the house.

At the far end of that same wall was an old-fashioned wardrobe at least seven feet tall, partly obscuring the double doors of what she assumed was a closet.

She picked up the lantern and headed toward the cabinet, wondering why someone would use a free-standing armoire rather than the built-in closet behind it. Goosebumps peppered her skin as her breath, now visible as a cloudy, mist-like vapor, came in rapid huffs. The room's temperature, already icy, must have dropped another ten degrees since she'd entered it.

*How is it so damned cold in here?*

Nearing the large armoire, Isabella raised the lamp overhead. Her eyes roamed over the two-door cupboard and lower chest of drawers before landing on the wooden pole that lay flat on the side of the dresser. Isabella had seen photos of armoires like this and knew the exterior bar could be lifted and locked, giving its owner additional space to hang a man's suit or a woman's gown.

She leaned forward, looking behind the dresser to see if there was enough room between it and the wall to open the closet door just a crack. She wanted a quick peek to see if the closet could be used for storage.

A skittering sound came from behind her. Yelping, Isabella spun and raised the lantern higher, expecting to see a drooling, taloned nightmare—a ghoulish, hideous creature fresh off the pages of a Dean Koontz novel.

Or a sharp-toothed, one-eyed beast who brought grown men to their knees, ravaged women, ate little children.

But nothing was there.

Annoyed, desperate to get off that frightening train of thought, she tipped her head toward the ceiling.

A gasp escaped her lips.

Every square inch above her, including the decorative molding surrounding the broken chandelier, was painted a robin's egg blue. The color was identical to the paint on the bedroom door.

Isabella's brows dipped into a vee as she inspected the ceiling from several angles.

"Yeah," she mumbled, voice dripping with sarcasm, "that's not weird. Who does this, anyway?"

Once the words left her lips, an icy hand squeezed her shoulder, its bony fingers digging into her flesh.

Simultaneously, a puff of warm breath whispered in her ear. *"Leave this place!"*

Isabella jumped, head whipping around the room. "Jesus Christ! What the..."

*"Get. Out!"* the same voice boomed.

No longer a whisper or a warning, the voice echoed off the walls and ricocheted off the tinted ceiling, leaving no doubt as to its intent.

Terrified, legs like jelly, Isabella bolted for the bedroom door, the kerosene lantern nearly slipping from her grasp.

"Oh, God, oh God!" she cried, breath ragged. "Shit, shit, shit! Spencer!"

Arms pumping, she sprinted down the hall to the staircase. Heart thumping wildly against her chest wall, she reached the landing without looking back.

If she had looked—if she'd been brave enough to turn around—she would have spotted the phantom-like hand, cast in shadows, as it wrapped its long, tapered fingers around the edge of the blue door.

Just before slamming it shut.

"Spencer!" Isabella yelled from the bottom of the staircase. "Jesus, Spence, you aren't going to believe this!"

She reached the dining room, trembling and breathless. Leaning forward, she put her hands on her knees and concentrated on her breathing. She was dangerously close to hyperventilating.

On the verge of tears, Isabella told him everything that had happened in the blue room.

"Wait, wait. Slow down, Iz," Spencer croaked, groggy with slumber. He'd fallen asleep on the dining room carpet. "You aren't making any sense."

Isabella's eyes widened as they darted around the room. Crouching closer to him, her voice barely above a whisper, she enunciated each word: "I'm telling you that the blue door was locked. When I turned the knob, it was locked. I swear it. But then it just… just opened on its own. And when I—I went inside, something touched me! And I heard a voice, a growl in my ear, telling me to get out!" Near hysterics, she continued scanning the room. "I'm not kidding. It was freaky as fuck!" She thumped her hand on her chest. "Christ, my heart is racing."

Spencer sat up slightly, body weight resting on his elbows. "You need to calm down before you have a heart attack. I'm sure there is a logical explanation for the door being stuck. You pushed on it, right? Jiggled the handle?"

Isabella frowned. "I-I guess?"

"Sure you did, as would anyone, right?" Spencer said, his smile condescending. "You just loosened it, love. It's an old house, and wood expands. It was stuck, that's all."

Isabella shook her head. "No, it wasn't stuck; it was locked.

I swear on my children's eyes, Spencer, it was locked and sud-denly opened." Then, more to herself than her husband, she mumbled, "Maybe Ellie was right; maybe there *is* something otherworldly here."

Spencer raked a hand through his hair. "Okay, so how the door opened will remain a mystery for now. What else happened up there?"

Isabella scrubbed her hands over her face. "I could hear move-ment inside, like someone was pacing. After a minute of trying to open the door, I gave up and walked away. Halfway down the hallway, it swung open."

"By itself?" he asked dubiously.

"Yes! On. Its. Own! When I entered, there were strange sounds, like a scuttling or scraping noise, but I couldn't pinpoint an exact location. It was like surround sound or something—everywhere but nowhere."

"O-kay," Spencer said, frowning. "What else?"

"As if that wasn't enough?" she shot back. "Jesus, are you even listening to me? There were shuffling sounds, followed by the scrape of nails or claws moving quickly across the floor. It was all around me."

"Ah, I see." Spencer's tone was, once again, patronizing. "Rodents, my love. I've seen plenty of evidence of them in the kitchen. The house is in the middle of a field, after all. We may as well have a sign that reads, 'Welcome to the Mouse House!' Why don't you call an exterminator in the morning, huh? Get it taken care of."

Isabella clenched her jaw. "It wasn't a mouse, Spencer. I'm not an idiot. I can tell the difference between a mouse and…some-thing else." She leaned closer to him. "Besides, that wouldn't ex-plain the voice. Or being touched."

A beam from the lantern caught his raised brow. "Right, right. You mentioned being touched as well, didn't you? Touched by whom?"

He was looking at her with pity, and she hated it.

She took a step back. "Well, Christ on a cracker! If I thought it was a 'whom,' I'd be calling the cops right about now, wouldn't I? It wasn't a person. It was something else."

Spencer sat up fully. "So, this 'something else' that supposedly touched you… It spoke to you as well? Do you know how crazy that sounds?"

Isabella's eyes widened. "That was low, Spence," she said softly. "Even for you."

He groaned. "Jesus, look, I'm sorry, okay? That came out all wrong. It's just a lot to absorb, especially with your history of…" He stopped himself from completing the sentence. "Look, Bella, all I'm saying is that if the roles were reversed, wouldn't you think it sounded a little out there?"

Isabella's face burned bright red. "If the roles were reversed, Spencer, I'd see you as frightened and upset. I'd listen to what you had to say and try to devise a course of action. What I wouldn't do is patronize you or insinuate that you're a headcase, you know? Yeah, that's something I would *never* do."

"Oh, come on, that's not fair, babe. All I'm saying is that doors opening or closing themselves and ghostly whispers in the ear sound a little bizarre."

"Well, frankly, I don't give a shit how it sounds. I felt a hand on my shoulder—felt every finger of that hand—and heard a male voice angrily telling me to get out. I'm not hallucinating, delusional, or bat-shit crazy!"

"No, no, of course, you aren't." Spencer studied his fingernails, then sighed dramatically. "Um, unless—well, unless you're…."

"Unless I'm what?" Isabella spat out, knowing what he was about to say.

Because, secretly, she was thinking the same thing.

*Oh, please, God! Not again!*

Instead of verbalizing that thought, she waited for him to speak, trying to convince herself that he was wrong.

"Unless you're relapsing," he said finally. "I hate to say it, but it *is* the elephant in the room, isn't it? Could you be experiencing a recurrence of your prior problem, babe? You know, after Anna?"

She stared at him, throat dry. It was one thing to deal with your own mind-numbing insecurities regarding your sanity; it was quite another animal altogether to have someone else validate your thoughts. "You think I'm having another breakdown?"

He wrapped his arms around his bent knees, eyes glued to hers but saying nothing.

She rubbed her brow. "Think what you want, Spence. We both know you will anyway. Whatever." She gripped the lantern tighter. "I'm going to bed. Tomorrow, I'll speak with Luna about it and see what she thinks."

He snorted. "Speak with Luna? That woman is a freak show, what with her moonstones, salt lamps, and essential oils bullshit. If you ask me, Luna Lake is the last person on earth you should seek advice from."

Isabella chuckled mirthlessly. "Then it's a damned good thing I didn't ask you, isn't it?"

She walked away, head held high, unable to see the anger behind his eyes nor hear the oaths he muttered beneath his breath.

And, by the time she entered the living room where the children slept, Isabella was too far away to catch the rhythmic *thump-thump-thump* of Spencer's clenched fists as they pounded against the dining room carpet.

# CHAPTER
# SEVEN

*ABIGAIL*
*Rosemear*
*June 21ˢᵗ, 1859*

"**I** am impressed by how quickly you are learning, Ms. Charles," Edward murmured over Abigail's shoulder. The sweet scent of bourbon tickled her nose, and she stiffened, Joseph's warning slamming into her brain.

*"I've seen him drunk on many a night, ranting 'bout one thing or another. He got an ugly temper, that for sure…."*

Abigail shook off the words before the rumor could germinate and jade her opinion of Edward Hawthorne. He'd been nothing but attentive, kind, and gentlemanly toward her. Never once had he so much as raised his voice in her presence.

*No,* she thought. *Mr. Edward is no threat to me.*

Sitting before a rolltop desk in Edward's bedroom, Abigail smiled and slid her chair to the right.

"Thank you," he said, pulling a wooden stool beside her. He

glanced at her work again. "Your letters are coming along quite nicely, Abigail."

"Thank you, sir," she said, her voice barely above a whisper. The cost if she were discovered unchaperoned in Edward's bedroom would be immeasurable. "I'm trying my best, even been formin' letters on the kitchen counter using a bowl of rice." She giggled softly. "That way, if a body comes near, I just erase the rice into a heap on the counter."

Edward chuckled. "Clever. Did you know that the best way to learn is by doing? That's why I created that alphabet workbook for you." He gestured toward the pages before her, filled with letters to trace and short sentences to copy. "The more you practice, the easier all this will seem. I can already see a vast improvement in your sentence structure and vocabulary."

For the last month, Edward had been sneaking Abigail into his room for reading lessons nearly every evening. So far, no one seemed the wiser, but the consequences of being caught necessitated extreme caution on both their parts.

Abby clutched the pencil tighter and returned to work, dutifully forming her letters while occasionally glancing at Edward. Each time she did, she found him smiling at her, engrossed in whatever she was practicing.

And each time her eyes met his, heat swept across her cheeks, and her belly did a little flip.

Clearing his throat, desperate to engage her in conversation, Edward said, "Have you met my sister? She's the eldest child in the family and quite a character." He shook his head, smiling. "What is it they call her? A free spirit?" He chuckled. "Would you believe Margaret wears trousers, rides horses bareback, and downs whiskey as easily as any man I know?" He shrugged. "And although Maggie can be a bit trying, I appreciate her company. I've no other living siblings, so it's nice to have someone who shares my interests."

"You had another brother or sister, then?" Abigail asked, eyes still on her work.

"I did. Elizabeth, my sister, was a few years older than me, and Martin, my little brother, was just four years old. They both succumbed to diphtheria." He shook his head sadly. "Yet another sister, an infant, died at birth."

Stunned, Abigail took a moment to respond. "Oh, mercy! I'm very sorry to hear about your troubles, sir."

Edward nodded. "Thank you." He stared out a window. "Did you know they call diphtheria the 'strangler of children'? The toxins produced by the disease close off the throat with a false membrane, making it impossible to take a breath. Elizabeth was just twenty-one when she passed in the winter of 'fifty-seven. Six months later, it took little Martin. Poor souls. What a horrid way to die."

"Surely is, Mr. Edward." Abigail brushed a hand over her skirt, smoothing the fabric. "I don't believe I've made Margaret's acquaintance, but I did meet your momma, Ms. Lillian, a few times. Handsome woman."

Edward raised a brow. "But not a pleasant one, right?" He sighed heavily. "Thankfully, Lillian is not my mother. She's our former governess who married my father a year after we placed my mother, Sarah, into the ground."

Abigail, unsure how to respond to that, instead asked another question. "How did your momma pass, if you don't mind my askin'?"

"I don't mind," Edward said. "Fact is, we aren't all that certain what took her. The best guess from the doctor was yellow fever, although she had no fever to speak of. Instead, she developed other symptoms that left her bedridden for weeks—nausea and vomiting, unbearable abdominal pain, and fatigue so extreme she could barely lift her head." He frowned. "What else? Oh, her hair changed. Once thick and long, it became brittle and sparse. I found clumps of it in her bedding one day." He shrugged. "I was only thirteen then, and changing her linens seemed all I could do for her."

"Oh, my," Abigail whispered.

"Yes, everything happened in the blink of an eye. Soon after the belly pains, my mother developed other symptoms—skin lesions on her hands and the soles of her feet, a burning sensation that blanketed her throat and mouth. It must have been torture for her."

"I can't even think of what to say, Mr. Edward."

He shrugged. "God's plan, I suppose. I'm thankful she is no longer in pain. As I've said, I was just a boy at the time, but I do remember how she suffered. I've no desire to watch anyone else I love experience such anguish."

"Surely is tragic, sir." She tilted her head in thought. "You say she have sores but no fever?"

Edward nodded. "Right. Strange, isn't it? Although she did have a yellowish tint to her skin, which is why Doc Coolidge decided on the diagnosis."

Abigail rolled the pencil between her palms. "Forgive me for sayin', but are you certain that what killed her? Seems her poor health maybe was from something else."

"Such as?"

Abigail adjusted the kerchief on her head. "My momma told me a story once about a rich White man, a fella name of Wendell Danvers. Seems Wendell, at aged seventy-two, got hisself a young bride of fifteen. There was talk of Wendell's cruelty to the girl, whippings and such. I believe her name was Leah."

"What happened?" Edward asked. "Did he beat her to death?"

"Never had the chance. Shortly after the marriage, Wendell got real sick. Same ailments that your momma had."

Edward nodded. "So he died of yellow fever as well."

Abigail shook her head. "Oh, he died all right, but it weren't from the fever. Old Wendell was poisoned—arsenic, most likely. It were his young bride who done it."

"Arsenic? How on earth?" Edward gaped at her. "Are you saying you think my mother was poisoned? Murdered with arsenic?"

Abigail noted something flash in his eyes, something she'd never seen in Edward.

Anger.

Not willing to risk his wrath, she put a hand up and stuttered, "Mercy, Mr. Hawthorne, sir, don't pay me no never-mind. Some days, I go on and on with my foolishness. Please don't be cross with me."

Edward frowned. "I'm not angry with you, Abigail. I just don't see how my mother could have been killed that way. Or why. Sarah Hawthorne was a caring and loving woman. I don't think she had an enemy in the…."

He stopped, suddenly remembering something.

Something huge.

An idea, an accusation, popped into Edward's head, and he ignored it. Standing, he walked to the nightstand, retrieved a vase containing a single rose, and brought it back to the desk. "Do you know how Rosemear got its name?"

Abigail shook her head.

"We never had a name for the place, other than the 'Hawthorne Plantation,' until a year after Lillian married my father," Edward said, taking a seat. "She found herself with child shortly after the nuptials and, in 1853, gave birth to my sister, Rosemary. As the youngest in the family, I was thrilled to become a big brother."

Abigail sensed another tragedy coming. "What happened?" she whispered. "What happened to baby Rosemary?"

"She came several months too early, you see. Rose was so small—small enough to fit in the palm of a grown man's hand. Poor thing never even took a breath."

Abigail gasped. "Oh, my! That's somethin' awful, Mr. Hawthorne."

He pursed his lips. "Edward. Please, call me Edward."

Abigail blushed. "Apologies, sir…er, Edward."

He rubbed his thumb and forefinger together, a habit he'd developed in childhood. The repetitive motion helped soothe him when he was distressed. "But yes, you're quite right. Rose's death was awful. After she died, Lillian named the plantation after her."

"Rosemear?" she asked.

"Yes. So 'Rose,' of course, was from my sister, and the word 'mere'—meaning small or slight—was sometimes spelled 'mear' in days of yore. I suppose my stepmother believed the latter spelling to be more feminine."

Abigail's eyes welled. "That surely is sad, Mr. Edward. But somehow beautiful, too."

"Yes, yes, it is. But enough about me. Tell me about yourself, Abigail. Do you have family?"

Abby put the pencil down, wanting to give him her full attention. "No, sir, not anymore. My parents was—I mean were—good Christian folk who never hurt no one. We lived on the Butler plantation, doing odd jobs, tendin' the young'uns and such. One day, a lantern tipped in the barn, kicking up a fierce fire. Mama and Pa died while they was tryin' to save the livestock." She clucked her tongue. "Fire killed a foreman named Skinny and five fine horses, too."

Edward patted her shoulder. "Tragic. I'm sorry to hear that. Do you have anyone else? A brother or sister, perhaps?"

Abby shook her head. "My baby sister, Chloe, left this earth a year after my parents. It was the fever that got her." Her gaze left him, and she stared, unseeing, at the corner of the room. "Fever took near fifty of us that year. Tried to take me, too, but I guess I's too stubborn to die." Her face fell for a moment, and she turned back to Edward. "Did I say that right? Don't sound right to me.

"Mostly right. If you substitute 'I'm' for 'I's,' it would be a perfect sentence," Edward said with a wink.

"Thank you, kindly," Abigail said. "Truth is, I've no family left. All I got is Prophet, and you know about him."

Edward nodded. "I do. Terrible thing to separate you two." He lightly cupped her chin and turned her face to his. "You know, Abigail, I could try to find out who purchased Prophet. Maybe I could even buy him from them."

Abigail gasped, uncertain she'd heard him correctly. "Oh, sweet Jesus! Could you really do that, Mr. Edward? Could you get my Prophet back to me?"

"I could try," Edward said, eyes twinkling. "But selfishly, I don't want to."

"Sir?"

Edward released her chin and rested his forearms on his thighs. "If I bring Prophet back, Abigail, I could forever lose my opportunity."

She picked up the pencil again and tapped it against the desk, trying to understand the meaning of his cryptic message. "I'm sorry, sir, but sometimes I ain't got—I mean *'I don't have'*—the sense the good Lord gave a goose. Opportunity for what?"

He pried the pencil from her fingers, laid it on the desk, and took her hands in his. With a wry smile, he said, "Nonsense, Abigail. You're smarter than you give yourself credit for." He waggled his brows. "You're so bright, in fact, that I'm surprised you haven't noticed my behavior. Given how I stumble over my own two feet and stutter in your presence, I expected how I felt about you to be embarrassingly obvious."

"Sir?" she said, still confused.

He brought her hand to his lips. "I've fallen in love with you, Abigail Charles. Hopelessly, madly in love with you."

She stared at him, wide-eyed.

Edward smiled and continued. "Yes, it's true. You're my first thought as I greet the rising sun and my final thought as I close my eyes to sleep. Having you near me is as vital to my life as the blood in my veins, the air in my lungs, the beating of my heart." He kissed the knuckles of her hand, one by one. "So, you see my dilemma. If I were to bring Prophet here, I'd lose any chance of making you mine."

Abigail tried to speak, but it was as if her vocal cords had become paralyzed.

"I know, I know—it's a lot to take in," Edward said. "I guess I'd hoped that if I shared my feelings, you would also share yours. About me, I mean."

She dropped her head and inspected the knuckles he'd just kissed. Clearing her throat, she finally found her voice. "Um, I don't... I don't know what to say, Mr. Edward. I appreciate all you've done for me. Truly, I do. And they ain't no doubt you a handsome man."

Edward smiled kindly. "*There isn't any doubt*," he corrected. "Remember, to be literate means to shy away from words like 'ain't.'"

Abby nodded. "Isn't any doubt you are handsome. But truth be told, I ain't never..." She stopped, correcting herself. "I have never thought of you in that way. To do so could see me on the wrong end of a hangman's noose."

Edward stroked his brow. "Please believe me, Abigail, that as long as there is breath in my body, no harm will come to you. You have my word."

Abby searched his face, looking for the truth. Edward Hawthorne was a rich and powerful man. Would he risk losing that position, that power, to protect her?

She wasn't sure that he would.

"Anyway," Edward said, rising, "I'm not expecting an answer right away." Then, with a sly grin, he added, "Unless you cannot help but declare your devotion to me by telling me you are madly in love as well."

Abby giggled.

"I'll take that as a maybe?" He bent down, kissed the crown of her head, and whispered, "We'll work this out, love. And, while we can't speak to others about our feelings, Judgment Day is coming. A revolution is nigh! My abolitionist friends talk of emancipation and the brave soldiers willing to fight for the rights of all the enslaved. When that day comes, when every man, woman, and child is free, there will be no need to hide our love in the shadows. Trust me?"

Abigail stood, her relatively short stature overshadowed by Edward's towering height of six feet four inches. Tipping her head back, she studied his face, still uncertain. On the one hand, she missed her love, Prophet Jones.

They'd planned a future together, one that included building a cabin, birthing strong babies, and being blessed with sweet freedom. When those plans were made, Abigail and Prophet were young, naïve, and pinning their hopes on a brighter future.

But Abigail was no longer that innocent girl. She'd seen how random life was, how unfair and utterly cruel it could be.

And she understood that she and Prophet would never be together without the dark cloak of slavery around their shoulders, weighing them down, imprisoning them.

Suffocating them.

But, with Edward as a lover, she would be looked after and cared for. She could enjoy more luxuries, more freedoms than she'd ever thought possible.

Decision made, she took one of his hands in hers. If she could not be with Prophet, she would salvage what was left of her life with a man who seemed to truly care for her. "As it happens, I do trust you, Mr. Hawthorne. With my life, if need be."

He bent down, lips close to hers. "Edward?" he breathed.

Leaning into his kiss, she sighed. "Yes. Edward."

Lost in their embrace, neither noticed the man standing in the rose garden, a scowl on his face, eyes pinned on Edward's bedroom window.

The following day, shovels rising and falling in sync, Abigail and

Virgil quietly cleaned the barn stalls. After several minutes of silence, Virgil was the first to speak.

"Miss Abigail? Why you doing a chore supposed to belong to Young Joseph? Just curious, mind you. I ain't complaining for the help."

Abigail leaned her shovel against one of the stall walls and massaged her back. "You know, Virgil," she said, parroting Edward, "to be literate means to shy away from words like 'ain't.'"

Virgil lifted a brow. "What's that you say?"

"Oh, never mind," Abigail said with a sigh. She grabbed the shovel once again. "I'm helping you because Young Joseph is still burning with the fever. He needs his rest to get well. Besides," she said with a lopsided grin, "everyone knows you muck like a one-armed mariner tryin' to row hisself from a storm."

"Yeah, yeah," Virgil said, laughing. "Maybe that my plan, huh? If'n folk don't think I can do the job, then…."

"Hey!" Clyde's voice boomed from the open barn door. "How 'bout more muckin' and less jawin'? Those stalls ain't gonna clean themselves!"

Virgil grinned, leaned closer to Abigail, and whispered, "To be literate means to shy away from words like 'ain't.'"

She covered her mouth with both hands, trying to quell her laughter.

An hour later, Abigail left the remaining stalls in Virgil's hands and headed back to the kitchen in the main house. She'd promised the cook, Cora, that she would teach her how to make sweet potato pie, just like her great-grandma used to make.

Halfway to the mansion, a large man wearing sweat-stained overalls and reeking of manure closed in on her.

Clyde Baldwin.

"Not so fast, Missy," he said, stepping in front of her and raising a hand to her chest, blocking her path.

Nervous, Abigail held perfectly still, trying to calm her racing heart. The overseer's hand was positioned between her breasts, palm flat against her skin. She knew that if she moved, his hand would follow until he eventually found one of her breasts.

It had happened before—on many, many occasions.

It was no secret around Rosemear that Clyde Baldwin was a pervert and a bully. If she lived to be a hundred, Abigail would never forget how Clyde treated her, how he made her feel. In his presence, her mind went blank, and her body froze.

Afraid to stay still, yet too terrified to move.

He was a vile man who'd stopped Abigail countless times over the last few months under the guise of giving her yet another chore to do. He'd get close, touch the center of her chest, and lick his lips suggestively.

Moments later, he'd feign losing his balance before groping her breasts with his hairy, paw-like hands, pretending the contact was incidental.

It always began the same—a hand to her chest, a fake stumble, fingers wrapping around one breast. He'd give a hard squeeze, smiling through rotting teeth while ignoring Abigail's racing heart.

Then, with a hearty laugh, he'd drop his hand and saunter away, his pungent odor and fetid breath lingering in her nostrils long after he'd gone.

It was a recurring violation, seemingly without end, that never ceased to terrify her.

Now, sounding much braver than she felt, Abigail threw her shoulders back and stared at his imposing frame. "What can I do for you, Mr. Clyde?"

He leered at her, eyes roaming up and down her body. "Oh, I can think of plenty you can do, Missy. But first, let me ask your opinion on something. Last night, as I was tending to the garden weeds, I couldn't help but notice Mr. Edward had a lady friend in his bedroom." He pointed toward the house. "Could hardly miss 'em, really. They was both at the window, close up together, seeming real familiar like. Most curious, don't you think?" He inched his hand to the right until he felt Abigail's nipple poking between his fingers. "You, uh, you wouldn't happen to know any-thing about that, would ya?"

Abigail's stomach lurched. "I can't say that I do, Mr. Clyde."

His hand grew bolder, moving from breast to breast and back again, occasionally pinching a nipple painfully between his thumb and index finger. "That right? Strange, on account of this particular lady friend looked awful familiar to me. You sure you didn't see nothin'?"

Her throat bone dry, Abigail moved her tongue around the inside of her mouth, hoping to discover a hidden pocket of saliva to help her swallow. "No, sir, Mr. Baldwin. I surely don't know nothin' about any of that."

Clyde snickered, squeezing each breast one last time before dropping his hand to his side. Watching her through hooded eyes, he spat a cheek full of tobacco juice near her feet and moved closer. "Listen up, girly," he rasped, his voice suddenly low and chilling, "I see you for what you are. And I know what you're up to. Things ain't gonna end well for you unless you remember your place on this plantation." He moved his mouth to her neck and dragged his tongue up its length until he reached her chin. Voice dropping an octave, he said, "You taste good, little girl. Like sweet tea with lemon and honey."

A single tear rolled down Abigail's face, and she clenched her teeth to keep them from chattering.

"Now," he continued, indifferent to her terror, "I may be wrong, but I expect you are gonna do something extra special for me, ain't ya?" He ran a finger slowly up and down her bicep. "Yessir, sure as

I'm standin' here, you got secrets. And if'n you want me to keep 'em, you best be really, really nice to ol' Clyde."

Abigail's eyes darted wildly around the property, searching for someone, anyone, to help her.

There was no one.

Stomach cramping in fear, heart galloping at the possibility she and Edward had been seen together, she searched for the right words to convince the overseer that he was mistaken. She must deter him from this path he was on.

Because if the truth were revealed about her and Edward, the ramifications for her would be severe.

Maybe even deadly.

But before she could assemble her thoughts and fight back, Clyde slapped her on the ass and, whistling a lively tune, headed back to the barn.

Leaving Abigail standing alone, knees shaking, wondering how in the world she would save herself.

# CHAPTER EIGHT

"Come on, Mom!" Sam yelled from the foyer. "You said we could explore outside before Luna gets here!"

Isabella stood at the kitchen counter, washing dishes and trying to ignore the unrelenting pain behind her eyes. Her ongoing battle with headaches had begun in elementary school, growing progressively worse as she aged. Now, in the third decade of her life, and after much nagging by her favorite nurse, Luna, she was finally considering seeing a doctor.

"I'll be there in a minute, Sammy," she said, wiping her hands on a dish towel. "Is Ellie with you?"

"Yeah! Come on, Ma! Maybe we can find something cool to show Dad when he gets back!"

The slam of the front door reverberated through the house, igniting another pulse of pain behind her eyes.

She rubbed her temples, trying to push aside the rush of irritation at the mention of Spencer. His reaction last night as she described her experiences in the blue room still annoyed her. Although her husband was a master manipulator and narcissist, his ability to minimize her fears and concerns continued to shock her.

In truth, the only person in the world who could make her feel like a simple-minded idiot was the man who'd vowed to love her forever.

That, combined with his condescending tone whenever she showed vulnerability, only reminded her of why she had been planning to leave him before Anna's accident.

And his affair with Julia Cox was only part of it.

She could finally see it, see past the grief of losing her daughter. The once beautiful tapestry that symbolized their union was now frayed, the fabric stained with greed, betrayal, and deception. Their marriage had been in serious trouble long before Anna's accident shattered their lives.

Indeed, the coffin had been assembled years ago. Spencer's affair with Julia merely supplied the nails to seal it shut.

She sighed heavily and walked toward the front door. When she reached the foyer, she tilted her head back and studied the double staircase.

All was quiet.

In the light of day, everything felt different. The shadows disappeared, and the creaks and groans quieted. The atmosphere, the very essence of the house, felt lighter, untroubled, when the sun was out.

For a moment, Isabella wondered if ghosts slept.

Or if she believed enough in the supernatural to accept the possibility they were real.

And if she didn't?

If she didn't, it meant her experiences upstairs had been created within her own mind, a punishment for a past transgression.

A transgression so vile, so revolting, it required a special kind of penance.

*Is Spencer right?* she thought. *Is what I'm seeing and hearing the result of a guilty mind—my mind—conjuring up boogeymen as a form of self-punishment or atonement?*

Mood darker now, she stepped outside, squinting in the sun's brilliance and making a mental note to search for her sunglasses. Those glasses, a handful of charcoal pencils, and a pair of emerald earrings had been missing for weeks.

"Hey, guys?" she called from the front steps. "Front or back?"

"Back!" Sam yelled from behind the house.

Shading her eyes with a hand, Isabella walked to the rear of the house but didn't immediately see her children. "Boyd offspring, call out!" she said, mimicking a phrase from one of their favorite television shows.

"We're here, Momma!" Ellie yelled. "We found graves!"

Isabella frowned. *Graves?*

Following the excited voices of her children, she walked to a clearing among some trees several yards behind the house. Sam and Ellie stood side by side, heads down, their backs to her.

"Whatcha got?" Isabella asked, peering over Sam's shoulder.

Sam grinned. "Ta-da!" he said theatrically, pointing to several headstones before him. "Dead people! I wonder who they are?"

Isabella moved past him and studied the small cemetery. There were six headstones, all of them small, each of them blank. A piece of what could have been a seventh stone lay beneath an ancient tree. "I'm not sure, Sammy. There isn't any writing on them." She scanned the ground several yards ahead and saw only a pile of stacked firewood and an old shed.

Since she and Spencer had yet to walk the acres of land that came with Rosemear, she had no clue what lay in their backyard.

"Maybe the names got washed away or something," Ellie said

helpfully.

Sam scoffed. "Words don't wash away from headstones, dorko. That's why they call it engraving. 'Cause it's engraved on a grave. Right, Mom?"

"Is that true, Momma?" Ellie asked.

"Yeah, it's true," Sam said with a smirk. "You *are* a dorko."

"Mom!" Ellie cried.

Short on patience, the pounding in her head growing louder, Isabella turned from the stones and faced her children. "Enough! Samuel, there's no reason to be unkind to your sister. And Ellie, I won't always be there to protect you. You need to stand up for yourself sometimes."

Ellie's beautiful gray eyes filled with tears.

*Well played, jackass!* Isabella scolded herself.

She bent down until she was eye to eye with her daughter. "I'm sorry I snapped, Bug. Momma has an awful headache and isn't thinking clearly. Forgive me?"

Ellie beamed, vigorously nodding her head. "It's okay, Mommy."

"No, it isn't," she said, kissing Ellie's forehead, "but I appreciate your saying so, honey. As far as engraving, when someone puts a name or date into concrete, it's most often permanent."

"Oh," Ellie said quietly.

"However," Isabella continued, squinting at her son, "old age or the elements can wear away the engraving. It's called erosion. So, it seems you're both right."

Self-satisfied, Ellie stuck her tongue out at Sam. He rolled his eyes.

Isabella turned back to the small cemetery and brushed away dirt from the closest headstone. "Nope, nothing here. Maybe this is some sort of pet cemetery?"

Before anyone could answer, they heard a series of barks

somewhere out front.

"I hear a dog!" Ellie screeched.

Isabella nodded. "Me, too. I'll be right back, nuggets. Do not go anywhere until I return, capeesh?"

"Yes, Mom," they said in unison.

Once Isabella was out of earshot, Ellie said softly, "I don't think it's a pet cemetery, Sammy. I think it's... I think Martin is here somewhere."

Busy hurdling over the back three stones, legs flying, Sam finally stopped and turned to his sister. "Martin? Who the H-E-double-hockey-sticks is that?"

"Sammy! Only Mom and Dad are allowed to say that! You're not supposed to swear!"

Sam rolled his eyes again. "Fine, baby pants. So, who the *heck* is Martin?"

"He's ... he's my friend."

Sam tilted his head and stared at her. "Your friend? We just moved here, dum-dum. You have no friends."

Ellie stamped her foot. "I do, too, Samuel Boyd! His, his name is Martin! He has black curly hair and blue eyes and likes to play hide and seek, and he might be buried right here on this property!"

"Oh, brother. You're crazy, El," Sam said, shaking his head. "You understand that if Martin *is* buried here, he can't be your friend 'cause he's dead, right? And imaginary friends don't count as actual friends."

Ellie's eyes filled with tears for the second time that morning.

"Okay, okay. Jeez," Sam said, contrite. "Don't cry, okay? I'm sorry." He walked back to her and placed a hand on her shoulder. "Come on, squirt. I'll help you look at the other headstones. Maybe we can find this Martin kid."

Ellie smiled, and, hand in hand, the two strolled the tiny cemetery, studying the chipped and decaying stones crawling with moss and ivy.

Several minutes later, they still had not located a 'Martin' among the ruins.

Isabella rounded the front of the house and came face to face with a massive, drooling, hairy monster.

She screamed and stopped short, losing her balance. Arms waving, hands grasping the air like a cartoon character, she fell backward and, with an 'oomph,' landed flat on her ass.

"Oh, shit!" a deep voice shouted. "Midge, no!"

"Come here, Midgey!" called a second, decidedly younger male.

Isabella covered her face as the slobbering beast licked her cheeks. "Oh, my gosh!" she said, laughing. "Wait! Just wait!"

"Midget, come!" the man said sternly.

The black behemoth whined briefly before trotting away from Isabella and returning to the man who'd commanded it.

"I'm so sorry about that," he said, jogging to her and extending a hand. "Midge is usually stand-offish with strangers, but it looks like she likes you."

"Lucky me," Isabella said, accepting the offered hand. "What the hell kind of beast is that anyway?" she asked, grunting as the stranger pulled her to her feet.

"She isn't a beast!" the boy said, offended. He was a stocky kid about Sam's age, with a mop of unruly red hair and black-framed glasses. "She's a beauty!"

"Matty," the man scolded gently, "remember your manners."

Chastened, the child dropped his head. "Sorry, Uncle Nate."

Nate smirked, then stuck out his hand in greeting. "Please accept my apologies. I'm Nathan. Nathan Decker." He turned to the boy and ruffled his hair. "And this overprotective kid is my nephew, Matthew."

Isabella shook hands with them both. "He isn't overprotective;

he's a good friend. I'm Isabella Boyd." She glanced around Nate's back. "And your black, furry horse over there is named Midge?"

Nate laughed. "Technically, her name is Midget. Not a horse exactly, but a Newfoundland."

"Same difference," Isabella said. Quirking a brow, the hint of a smile behind her eyes, she added, "Midget? Seriously? That's the best you could come up with for your two-hundred-pound dog?"

"One hundred forty-five, actually. She's on a diet now since she's put on a little weight hanging with Matty at my sister's house." Smiling, he cocked his head at his nephew. "Matty here swears he isn't giving her too many treats, but…."

"I'm not, Uncle Nathan! Honest!" Matty protested.

"Anyway," Nate continued with a shrug, "naming her Midget was my poor attempt at being clever. 'Course, I may or may not have been a little drunk when I did it." He smiled wider and winked.

Isabella's heart stuttered a moment, and her cheeks reddened. For the first time in a long time, she found her body responding physically to someone other than her husband. Confused, she averted her gaze.

"You sure you're okay?" Nate asked, concerned. "Seemed like you checked out there for a moment. Did you hit your head?"

*No, I checked out because you are stupid handsome with no ring on your fourth finger—a fact I shouldn't have noticed as a married woman.*

Isabella shook her head. "No, honestly, I'm fine." Tucking a wayward curl behind her ear, she asked, "Do you live around here? I don't think I've seen you before, and I definitely would have remembered Midget."

The dog moved to Isabella's side as if on cue and nuzzled her hand.

"Yeah, Midge is pretty unforgettable. As for me, I am currently crashing at my sister Marnie's house with her and this nutty ten-year-old." He bumped Matty with a hip.

Isabella felt an unexpected sadness wash over her. "Oh, so you don't live in Savannah, then."

"No, not yet. I am looking for a place, though. Hopefully, I can find something in the Garden District area. I transferred from a small PD just north of Atlanta to the Savannah police department a few weeks ago."

"I see. So, you're a police officer, then? Tough career choice."

"It has its moments, I'll give you that," Nate said. "But all in all, I love the job. I just wanted to do it closer to my family and the area I grew up in."

"Makes sense. Is your sister close by, then? I haven't had a chance to do much exploring yet, so I'm not familiar with many of my neighbors. You said her name is Marnie?"

"Yes, ma'am," Nate said with a nod. "Marnie Benson. She lives about two miles away, off that dirt road that looks like it goes nowhere. Do you know the one?"

Isabella absently stroked Midge's ears. "I think so. Is that the one with the ginormous oak tree at the road's edge? The Spanish moss hanging from its limbs is so eerie. It's like the tree stands sentry, loath to let anyone pass."

"You have a good memory," Nate said. "And a good eye. It does feel like that tree is guarding something, doesn't it? Something of great importance or value." He smiled crookedly. "Weird, but I've often felt like I had to, I don't know, flash my badge or show my passport to proceed."

"Yes, exactly right!"

"And once you pass through and can see that oak from every angle?" He stuffed his hands in his pockets and grinned. "Man, do you feel small."

Isabella smiled back. "Very true. I try to capture the raw beauty in nature, but I'm not convinced I can do that majestic oak justice. It must be hundreds of years old." A soft, almost whimsical smile touched Isabella's lips. "Oh, the stories it could tell...."

She waited for him to say something back, ask her a question, but he just stared for a moment.

Uncomfortable, she rushed on. "Because I'm an artist. That's-that's what I meant about capturing nature's beauty."

He gazed at her for another moment before finally speaking. "An artist, huh? What kind of art?"

"Watercolor paintings and charcoal sketches, mostly. I like to do outdoor stuff, like beaches, parks, etc. I've been, uh, sort of out of the painting scene for a hot minute and need to jump back in. I mean, the subject matter here in Savannah is endless! Just looking around this little corner of the planet, it's easy to see how Mother Nature..."

Isabella stopped at her mention of Mother Nature, suddenly remembering her children were out back and unsupervised. "Um... sorry, but I should go now. My kids are out back, hungry and alone. That sometimes proves to be a deadly combination."

Nate chuckled. "I understand. Well, we'll be off, then." He slapped a hand to his side, and Midget obediently came to him.

With a wave, the trio turned to walk away.

"Wait!" Isabella said, surprising both herself and Nathan. "My kids would love to meet Midge." Turning to the boy, she added, "And my son Sam is about your age, Matty. Maybe you could give him the inside scoop on Savannah's school system. After all, summer will be over before you know it."

Matty groaned. "Yuck—school."

Nate laughed. "Just wait until you have to work for a living, brother. School is gonna seem like a cakewalk."

Matty groaned again before running ahead to the backyard.

"He seems like a good kid," Isabella said. "I'm glad there is someone close to Sam's age nearby. I worry about him sometimes."

Nathan nodded. "Yeah, Matty is the best. His dad died recently, and he's been a lost soul ever since. Marnie is doing an amazing job raising him alone, but a boy needs a role model, you know? So

I stepped in and took up one of the reins to help."

"That's so sad," Isabella said, genuinely heartbroken for Matthew.

"It is. Thomas, Matty's father, was a great guy who was dealt a crappy hand in life. At the age of three, he lost an eye to retinoblastoma. Then, his parents died in a car wreck when he was only fourteen. After their deaths, Thomas turned to substance abuse to handle the loss. It took him four years of treatment and pain to escape that addiction."

Isabella listened, silently counting her blessings.

"Anyway, eventually, Thomas met Marnie, and all was right with the world. They lived a fairytale life until yet another cancer diagnosis shattered their peace. This time, it was in his brain and very aggressive. He died six months ago, less than a year after being diagnosed."

"Oh, how tragic." Isabella spread an arm in invitation, and they started toward the backyard, walking as they continued to talk.

"It was. So, when the opportunity came up to change departments, I took it. It felt like the least I could do for my sister. Besides, Matty is, literally, my favorite person to hang with. And, much to my surprise, he seems to enjoy my company as well."

Isabella smiled warmly.

"Anyway," he continued, "it's good to be home. And I'm glad my nephew is meeting your son. I don't think Matthew has many friends. He's an overweight kid who happens to be uber-smart and wears glasses, so…."

Isabella stopped and looked at him. "So, talk about having a target on your back?"

Nate nodded.

"Yeah, I get it," Isabella said, walking again. "Kids can be so cruel sometimes."

"You're not wrong, Mrs. Boyd."

"Isabella, please. And thankfully," she said, beaming, "Samuel isn't like that. He's almost too nice sometimes." With a smirk, she added, "Unless he's messing with his sister, Ellie. Then all bets are off."

Nathan laughed, a deep, masculine sound that made Isabella's knees quiver like Jello.

"I could tell you stories about me, Marnie, and my brother Ryan that are downright cringeworthy. Hard to believe we were so ugly to each other, yet we all survived to joke about it."

"Hah! I'd wager that my brother, Daniel, and I would give you a run for your money!"

They reached the back of the house and looked around the yard. Sam and Matty stood in the clearing near the unmarked headstones, while a giggling Ellie was draped across Midge's back, rubbing the dog's flank.

Nate smiled. "It appears as though your daughter has, wisely, joined 'Team Midge.' But those two boys, whispering and with their heads together like that? That can't be good."

Isabella jerked her chin toward the clearing. "Sam and Ellie found a couple of old headstones earlier. Bet you twenty bucks that Samuel is telling a ghost story about the dead people buried here and showing off in front of Matty while, at the same time, successfully scaring the bejesus out of his little sister. Win-win, right?"

Nate chuckled. "Sounds like. So, who do you think those stones belong to?"

"No idea. My first thought was some sort of pet graveyard, but now, I'm not so sure. It seems kind of a lot, doesn't it? If we are to believe that these markers represent pets, we can assume they are all from the same household since the stones appear identical. But six, possibly seven, pets buried here seems like overkill to me." She smirked. "No pun intended."

Nathan agreed. "Yeah, it does seem weird." He paused a moment, then pointed to the right. "Have you seen how far your property goes back? My friends and I used to hang out back there.

Rosemear always seemed to be either vacant or on the market." He gave her a boyish grin. "So, of course, we happily took advantage of that fact. We didn't just meet here, tell a spooky story, and leave. Oh, hell, no. We ran around the grounds, jumping out at each other from the shadows and whispering in the dark, trying to see who would scream first. Of course, all this was being done while drinking ourselves silly."

"Lovely," Isabella said dryly.

"It is, isn't it?" Nate joked. "It was an unspoken rite of passage around here once you became sixteen—sneaking onto Rosemear's property, drinking, staying out past midnight. Good times."

She smirked. "Sure, sure. Trespassing, underage drinking, breaking curfew. All good, clean fun for the youth of America."

Nathan laughed. "You got it. Anyway, I've roamed this land front and back. There's a small cemetery back there, probably the final resting place of Rosemear's original owners."

Isabella tilted her head. "Another cemetery? The realtor never mentioned that, but we've been shackled to the inside renovations for weeks. We haven't had much time to look around."

He nodded. "Right. I imagine you've had little time to dally."

Isabella chewed on a thumbnail. "What do *you* think, Nate? Who do these stones represent if the Hawthornes are buried a half-mile away?"

He rubbed the back of his neck. "No idea. I'd suggest visiting the town hall or maybe the library for answers. Either way, getting a property's history is never a bad idea." He put his thumb and forefinger between his lips and whistled. "Hey, Matty, my brother! We have a ton of stuff to do today. Let's get moving, huh?"

All three kids ran toward Isabella and Nathan. Midge trailed behind, her steps more of a saunter than a trot.

"Hey, Mom!" Sam huffed, breathless. "Can Matty come over to play later?"

"Manners first, Samuel," Isabella said with a smile. "Sam, Ellie, this is Officer Decker, Matty's uncle."

"Hello," Sam said.

Ellie's eyes widened. "A real-life policeman?"

Nate grinned. "Yes, ma'am. Nice to meet you both."

Sam bounce in place. "So, can he, Ma? Can Matty come over later?"

Isabella nodded. "Well, we have the movers coming, and Aunt Luna is on her way, but maybe dinnertime?" She glanced at Nathan. "Interested in breaking bread with us tonight? I'm making spaghetti and meatballs. Spencer—my husband—doesn't care for it, so it's become a ritual for us when he's away. Of course, your sister is welcome to join us."

"Thanks, but Marnie's shift starts at six. After Thomas died, she switched to nights so she'd have more time for Matthew's school activities. But Matty and I would love to come if it's not too much trouble. A homemade meal sounds much better than the menu I'd planned for us this evening."

"Which was?" Isabella asked.

"Franks and beans."

"Oh, well, that doesn't sound too bad."

Nate smirked, and, as a group, they began walking to the front of the house.

"Yeah, you'd think so," he said. "Except hotdogs and canned beans are all I know how to cook. We've eaten it three times this week. Even the dog is refusing the leftovers."

Isabella laughed. "Poor Midge."

"Poor Matty," Nate countered.

She chuckled again, enjoying the banter. It seemed a thousand years since she'd smiled so much. "That, too. Okay, see you at six? Bring Midge, too. Luna loves dogs."

With a salute, Nathan said, "Yes, ma'am. Until then, I'll be home, puttering around in the yard if you need help moving stuff in. Do you have your cell phone on you?"

Wordlessly, Isabella reached into her back pocket, unlocked the phone, and handed it to him. He typed in his number and handed it back to her.

"There you go. Holler if you need me."

Isabella watched them leave, feeling lighter than she had in years. But she also feared that this blossoming friendship with Nathan, lovely as it was, could prove to be a double-edged sword.

On the one hand, she felt somewhat guilty for being attracted to her new neighbor. She was, after all, a married woman, albeit in name only. But she also understood the need to feel something—anything—besides pain, anger, and sorrow.

Nathan was, she suspected, everything Spencer would never be.

So she silenced the prickings of conscience that tugged at her and, content, headed back to the clearing and her children.

And never noticed the dark figure with the scorching gaze glaring at her through an upstairs window.

# CHAPTER NINE

Isabella looked down at her clipboard, waiting for the movers to exit their truck, which was idling in the driveway. The sky remained cloudless, the sun just as bright as when Nate was there earlier in the morning.

Sam and Ellie sped by her on the front lawn, racing to be the first to find a buttercup in the grass.

"Hey," Isabella called out, squinting beneath the sun's glare, "have either of you seen my sunglasses? They've been missing for days."

"Not me!" Sam yelled.

"Me either!" Ellie said, hot on Sam's heels.

"Okay, well, keep your eyeballs peeled." Isabella glanced down at her clipboard once again before snapping her head up. "Oh, and stay off the driveway. Aunt Luna should be pulling up any minute, and that tank she drives will squash you like a bug."

Ellie giggled. "Okay, Momma!"

"Hey, squirt!" Sam yelled, waving a yellow-petaled flower at Ellie. "I win! I found one, see?" He held the blossom under his chin. "Look! Do I like butter?"

Ellie squinted, checking for the telltale yellow reflection at the top of her brother's neck. According to the childhood game, if a buttercup left a golden shadow beneath your chin, you liked butter.

"I-I think so?" Ellie said with a pout. "I've never played this game."

Isabella shaded her eyes, watching the movers exit the truck before focusing on her son. "Oh, yeah, I can see it from here, Sammy-me-boy. You definitely like butter!"

While perfecting her craft as an artist, Isabella had spent a semester in college researching several varieties of plants and flowers. She hoped to capture their subtle lines and shadings to embody them realistically in her paintings. When the term ended, she'd learned that a buttercup's bright, lemony color, combined with a unique, flat layer of epidermis cells, ensured that anyone and everyone on the planet would come up as a 'butter lover' in this game.

Still, it was an activity that kept the kids occupied, allowing Isabella to concentrate on her list, so she played along.

"In fact," Isabella said solemnly, "I would say you like it 'butter' than anyone I know!"

Sam grinned, pumping a fist in the air.

Ellie whined and dug a toe into the dirt. "It's not fair! Sammy, will you help me find one, too?"

"Yeah, come on, squirt," Sam said, pointing to an area near the front steps. "Let's look over there."

"Be careful, guys," Isabella warned. "The movers have to go in and out through that door, so don't block them, okay?"

The rumble and screech of the van's door lifting, followed by a raspy cough, caused her to jump.

"Excuse me, ma'am—didn't mean to startle you, but we're ready to get started. Had a miscommunication with dispatch on another job, but it's cleared up now. I mean, how the hell are we supposed to be in two places at once, am I right?"

Isabella, unsure how to respond, gave a tiny shrug instead.

"Exactly my point," the man said, climbing into the back of the van. "Anyway, first in the chute—where's this table go?" He hoisted his blue jeans up over his hips and ass before jumping off the rear of the vehicle. Once on the ground, he reached into the cargo area and, grunting, lifted out the butler-style coffee table.

Isabella studied the man for a moment. He was at least seventy-five pounds overweight, with sweat-stained armpits and a perpetual wheeze. 'Dirk,' according to the name embroidered on his shirt, was also middle-aged and breathless, his face currently a dusky gray.

*Is he always this bluish-gray color? Like a Smurf caught in a thundercloud? What would his name be, then? Stormy Smurf?*

Forcing herself to focus, Isabella tried to mask her concern. It wouldn't surprise her if the man clutched his chest, keeled over, and died right there in her driveway.

And without Luna's help, if 'Dirk' went down in a heap, he'd be toast.

Isabella could barely apply a Band-Aid.

Unwilling to risk him collapsing from overexertion, she directed him to the foyer. "If you could bring that one into the main entrance, that'd be great. I'll decide where I'm putting it once the other things for the living room are in place."

Dirk nodded, ribbons of sweat trickling down his temples.

"Um, can I get you a water or something?" Isabella asked.

"No thanks," Dirk rasped, adjusting his grip on the table. "We're running behind here."

Isabella watched him take the table inside before she went back to checking her list. Aside from the family's bedroom sets, a few treasured lamps, and the butler table left to her by her grandparents, Isabella had ordered all new pieces to reflect the era of the home. The living room and dining room furniture, all period-specific, was due to be delivered later today, while the items she'd purchased for the extra bedrooms, home office, and art studio would come in a few days.

Her cell phone rang, and she dug it from her back pocket, checking the caller ID.

Spencer.

"I didn't expect to hear from you so soon, Spence. Trouble?"

"Now, why does a man have to have a reason to phone his drop-dead gorgeous wife?"

Isabella nearly groaned. Her husband was nothing if not transparent. "But seriously," she deadpanned, "what's up?"

"Fine, don't play with me," he said. It was meant to sound light-hearted. Instead, it came across as passive-aggressive, almost threatening.

Like the false pleasantries and teasing banter one might expect from Hannibal Lecter.

Right before he ate you.

"So?" Isabella said. "What's going on?"

Spencer sighed dramatically. "Thing is, babe, these people at MacMillan are brutal! They have given me about a month's worth of work and expect it to be done lightning-quick. I know I promised to be only a few days, but it's looking closer to five or six."

Isabella chewed her bottom lip. "I see. Are you still, um, alone?"

"Alone? Well, not quite. Julia is here in Atlanta, if that's what you're getting at." Sighing dramatically, his tone bored, he added, "Look, I told you, it takes time to find a good assistant. But it's strictly business, I swear. Hell, with all the reading I'm expected to do and the graphs I'm supposed to memorize, I can barely get out of my hotel room!"

Isabella fumed. *A hotel room is where most of our problems started, jackass!*

She cleared her throat. "Okay, well, text me when you're on the way home, then."

"Sure, sure," Spencer said. "Don't I always take care of you, babe? You'll be the first to know. I swear."

Isabella heard the shuffling of papers through the phone line, followed by a distant knocking and a female voice that said, "Coming!"

"Expecting someone?" Isabella asked.

"Oh, uh, just room service," he said quickly. "Listen, I gotta run, Iz. I'll give you a jingle later. By the way, is Luna there yet?"

Isabella couldn't fathom why Spencer seemed hyper-focused on Luna's visit. "No, not yet. Why do you ask?"

"Just wondered, is all. You said you would talk with her about the weird stuff you heard upstairs. I just wondered if you'd had a chance to do that."

"Nope, but I will. She should be here very soon."

"Swell," Spencer said beneath his breath, though Isabella heard. "Okay, talk soon. Love you, babe."

"See ya," Isabella said. She clicked 'end call' on her cell and tipped her head back. She and Spencer had been together for a decade, and she knew him like no other—knew when he was hiding something, knew when he was lying.

Several thoughts bombarded her, each more disturbing than the next. But there were just two notions that she held onto, two thoughts bouncing around her brain like pinballs in an arcade game.

The first was that Spencer was far too cheap to order room service.

And the second?

The second was that, despite his protests to the contrary, she'd heard a female voice in the background, confirming what she'd suspected all along. Her husband was not alone in that hotel room.

But even more telling to Isabella was the realization that she really didn't care.

"This going upstairs, miss?"

Isabella raised her eyes from the clipboard to see the other mover, a young man with long, stringy hair and a goatee, pull a mattress to the lip of the tailgate.

"Yes. At the top of the stairs, make a right. It's the last room, the one with the white birchwood dresser. Do you need a hand?"

The man shook his head. "Nah, I'm okay. Dirk can help me."

*Dirk? You mean 'dead man walking' Dirk? Super!*

"Um, all right, then. I'll be right behind you."

She watched the man scoot by her, mattress on his back, before she moved to the driveway and peeked inside the van. Aside from some odds and ends, a few lamps, and her bedframe, the van was empty.

Isabella turned at the soft tap of tiny feet. Ellie, a buttercup clutched in her chubby fist, closed in on her. "Momma," she whispered, nudging Isabella's leg, "that guy looks just like Scooby's friend, Shaggy!"

"Shhh," Isabella whispered back, a finger to her lips. "We don't want to hurt anyone's feelings, Bug. I think his name is Alex, but I see what you mean." She set her clipboard on the grass. "Let's go inside and direct him to your room. I'm pretty sure that's your mattress he's carrying."

Ellie frowned. "But my room is still stinky, Mom."

"I know, and I promise we will figure out why." She scanned the yard until her eyes found her son. "Come on, Sammy," she called. "We need to go inside and show the movers where everything goes." Bending forward, she kissed Ellie's cheek. "Don't worry, El—you can sleep on the bottom bunk in Sam's room until we get rid of that funky smell, okay?"

"Okay. Can I bring my—" Ellie's words were cut off by a

terrified scream inside the house, followed by the thunder of running feet.

"What in the hell?" Isabella said, rushing for the entryway door.

Both shuttered front doors burst open before she'd touched either handle.

"Sorry, lady, but we're out!" Alex said, racing through the doors. He flew by her, taking the porch steps two at a time, and sped to the truck.

Dirk, arms pumping, face ashen, was right behind him.

"Hold on!" Isabella cried. "I don't understand!"

Alex hesitated before turning back to her. "Lady, there's something in that house!" he rasped, eyes wide as saucers. "I'm not sure what it is, but they don't pay me enough to find out!"

Isabella felt a shiver of fear run down her spine. "Wait! What are you talking about? What did you see?"

He shook his head and vaulted into the passenger seat of the van.

"Alex, wait!" Isabella cried out. "You still have some of our things!"

With gravel kicking beneath his feet, Dirk rounded the van to the driver's side door and hopped inside. He threw the truck into drive and, wheels spinning, yelled out the window, "We'll ship it to you!"

Stunned, Isabella, Sam, and Ellie stared stupidly after the moving van until it was out of sight, as if the answers to what had just happened could be found in its taillights.

Sam was the first to speak. "Well, you don't see that every day."

Isabella slowly shook her head but said nothing.

From behind, Ellie, voice high, responded to her big brother. "I bet they saw them! I bet they saw the people in the wall."

"People in the wall?" Sam asked.

"Yes, Sammy!" Ellie said. Then, looking around, she lowered her voice to a whisper. "You know, the ones who don't want us here. Martin says they are mad all the time and really scary. He hides when they come."

Sam looked at Isabella. "She thinks we have people living in our walls? Is she nuts?"

Isabella gave Sam a warning look.

"I'm not nuts, Sammy!" Ellie yelled, plugging a thumb in her mouth. "They aren't alive, dork. They're the ghosts of dead people."

"Oh, brother," Sam said, rolling his eyes.

One thumb still in her mouth, Ellie wrapped her free arm around Isabella's leg. "I'm not crazy, Momma. Bad things happened here a long time ago. Martin says the ghosts are stuck here forever."

Isabella, stomach roiling, ran a hand over the top of Ellie's head. "What else does Martin say, Bug?"

Ellie sniffed. "He says they watch us all the time. The ghosts do. He says they hate us and they want us gone."

After the movers abandoned the job, the kids sat in the kitchen munching on fruit slices while Isabella, deep in thought, debated what to do.

Her kids were looking to her for an explanation.

She had a few options. The easiest thing to do was to ignore what had happened with Dirk and Alex and say nothing. Option two was to go into an in-depth sermon about how a person's imagination could go wonky in an old house, manifesting images and voices that were not there.

Or, a third option—blame every noise and every creak they'd heard in that house on ghosts, hauntings, and the afterlife.

None of those choices appealed to her. Instead, she chose option 'D.'

And went with a semblance of rationality.

"Look, guys. I have no clue what spooked those two, but I'm willing to bet it has to do with the draft issue upstairs. We're all hearing doors slamming and weird banging up there, right?" She looked at Ellie. "Plus, Dirk and Alex were in your room before they tore out of here. We saw how that oak tree keeps tapping your window, remember? Truthfully, when the wind picks up, it's more of a steady thump than a tap, right? I bet they heard that and freaked out."

Sam and Ellie kept their eyes on their mother, occasionally nodding in agreement.

"Sometimes old houses make certain people uncomfortable," Isabella continued. "It's just a thing. They think if a place is older than a hundred, it has to be creepy."

"It *is* creepy," Ellie said quietly.

Sam gently tugged the back of Ellie's hair. "It's not creepy, squirt; it's just old. Old buildings make all sorts of weird noises, right, Mom?"

Isabella wanted nothing more than to hug Sam right then. She could tell he was nervous, yet instead of feeding on that anxiety and frightening Ellie further, he swallowed it.

All to alleviate his sister's fear.

"That's right, Sammy," Isabella said with a smile. "Any time there is a shift in the ground below it, a structure will creak and moan as it sinks further into the earth. It's called settling."

Ellie's eyes widened. "It sinks? Our house is sinking? Will we be buried alive?"

*Shit! That didn't go as planned!*

"No, no, of course not, Bug. It's a harmless and very common thing."

Weighing that answer, Ellie took a bite of a crisp apple slice. "That's good, because being buried alive is no fun at all."

Isabella chuckled. "No, I don't imagine it would be. Though, of course, having never been buried alive, I don't know for sure."

Ellie dropped her head. "I do. I heard it's awful."

Sam clucked his tongue. "You heard? Who the heck would tell you that?"

Ellie tucked her chin between her five-year-old hands and sighed. "Someone who knows someone who was buried alive."

Isabella felt her stomach, once again, plummet to her knees. "Who, Bug? Who were you talking to?"

"My friend Martin, Momma. I heard it from Martin."

While the kids continued to enjoy their snack, Isabella took the keys Spencer had left on the counter and started up the stairs to the second floor. Her footsteps were heavy as she climbed, Ellie's words bouncing around her brain.

*Martin. Again? Could Ellie be hallucinating, just like poor Uncle Jack? But how would that explain what happened with the movers? Or the voice in the blue room?*

When she reached the landing, Isabella turned left and headed straight to the last door on the west wing.

To the room that had been locked and where she'd thought she'd heard a child giggling.

Head on a swivel, Isabella moved cautiously, eyes sweeping the hallway, noting the closed doors and absence of sound. The atmosphere up here felt calmer now, the rooms vacant.

If something on the second floor *had* scared Dirk and Alex, it was long gone.

She reached the locked door and stood before it. Heart racing, hands shaking, she started to turn the doorknob but hesitated. Holding her breath, she placed her ear to the door and listened.

Silence.

Slowly, she turned the knob and met resistance. Body trembling, she looked down at the large metal ring in her hands. At one end of the keychain was a miniature replica of a home with a 'for sale' sign, the word 'sold' plastered atop the sign in red lettering. At the other end were dozens of keys in a variety of sizes.

*Christ, how many locks could this place have?*

Sighing, Isabella began trying each key, one by one. None of them fit.

"Well, isn't that a puddle of poo," she mumbled, annoyed. "Guess Spencer will be taking this door down after all."

She headed back down the hall to the east wing, keys jingling, astonished at how different each side of the house felt to her.

The west wing felt disconnected from the rest of the house. There was no sense of personality or character.

No sense of life.

Isabella recalled the realtor, Suzanne Johns, telling them about the style of the house and the symmetry involved in an English Regency design. She also remembered that the architect who'd built Rosemear had gone so far as to create several false doors to maintain that balanced look.

To that end, she wondered if the west wing was part of that need for symmetry that was a hallmark of the home's design. Essentially, the opposing side acted as a mirror image rather than providing a functional space for its residents.

It was a strange observation that made little sense, but there it was.

The east wing, however, was a different story. The air felt alive when Isabella entered that hallway, charged with some unknown energy.

An energy that was, at once, both positive and negative.

She stopped at the first door with the broken hinge—the 'Dr. Seuss' door—and gave it a jiggle. Metal scraped against metal, creating a groaning sound that continued to hum even after the door stopped moving.

"Will you look at that? A rational explanation!" she said, shattering the quiet of the hallway. Smirking, she channeled her inner Seuss by creating a nonsensical rhyme...

*The Prezibot gremlins*
*Put a creak in one ear!*

*Now, that would explain*
*All the noises we hear!"*
She smirked, her brain hanging on to the rhythm…
*Dang, that's not bad!*
*She said with a pucker.*
*As she tangled and fiddled*
*With a ghost motherfucker.*
"Jesus, girl, enough!" she said, smiling.

Making a mental note to move the hinge repair to the top of her list, she continued down the hall, trying to stay sharp and pull her head out of the clouds.

Because, for whatever reason, every time she came upstairs, she felt chaotic. Scattered.

Curiosity warred with trepidation as she reached the blue door, taking a defensive stance before it to prepare for what she might find on the other side. Steadying her breathing, she turned the knob.

The door opened easily, and a quick peek inside revealed nothing more ominous than the shadow play of the armoire against the opposite wall.

The room was empty.

"Hello, the house? I come bearing food, wine, gifts, and amazing conversation!"

Sam squealed and jumped out of his kitchen chair. "Aunt Luna!" he yelled. "Mom, she's here! Auntie Luna is here!"

Isabella smiled at the sound of their voices and headed downstairs.

When she reached the foyer, both kids were clinging to her best friend, arms around her legs, chattering excitedly.

"Auntie Luna!" Ellie cried. "We missed you!"

"Of course you did," Luna joked. "How could you not? I am, after all, the best auntie in all the lands! Why, there's talk of making a 'Luna Lake' holiday with fireworks, fabulous pastries, and custom-made country songs written just for me!"

Both kids giggled.

"A Luna Lake holiday?" Isabella said as she reached the bottom of the stairs. Raising a brow, she added, "Don't you think that's a bit, oh, I don't know, over the top?"

Luna threw her head back in laughter. "Over the top? Me? Have you met me? Everything I do is over the top!"

Isabella crossed the foyer and hugged her friend. "Man, girl, but you are a sight for sore eyes! I've so much to tell you! And show you! What do you think so far?"

Luna hesitated, her eyes sweeping the grand entrance. "I think," she said, "that you should ask me again when we're alone."

The shadow of a frown crossed Isabella's face before she wiped it away with a smile. "Hey, guys," she said, nodding at Luna's luggage, "how about you each grab a bag and take Aunt Luna's things to my bedroom?" She looked at Luna and smirked. "Until they deliver the furniture for the guest room, you and I will be bunkies!"

"Super," Luna said dryly. "Don't forget—we've shared a room before. I remember how badly you snore. And don't get me started on those cold feet of yours!"

Isabella laughed. "I do not snore! And I'll wear socks, okay?"

"Yeah, yeah," Luna teased. "And what about old what's-his-name?"

"Spencer? He's in Atlanta at a conference for the next week or so."

Luna smiled. "Aww, that's a damned shame."

"Are you talking about Dad?" Sam asked.

Isabella widened her eyes. "Dad? Of course not!" She shot a glance at Luna before clapping her hands. "Okay, my children, chop-chop! I'll make us all something to eat while you're gone."

"You got it, Mom!" Sam said cheerily, handing Ellie the smaller bag before hoisting the larger one over a shoulder.

"You little humans are the best!" Luna said. "Thanks! Now,

come right back because I have some delicious donuts waiting for you in the car!"

The children nodded enthusiastically before plodding to Isabella's room, the unwieldy luggage in tow.

The adults watched their progress momentarily before Isabella faced Luna again. "Okay, Cryptic Cathy. Why the mystery? What do you think about the place?"

Luna pursed her lips. "Okay, but you ain't gonna love it."

"Super," Isabella said dryly.

Luna put up a hand. "Just keeping it real, bud, like we always do. Don't take what I'm about to say the wrong way."

"Okay, quit pussyfootin' around and spill it, lady."

Luna sighed. "This house feels off to me. I felt it as soon as I got out of the car. And just now, coming through the front door, it felt like—oh God, this will sound insane."

Isabella's eyes softened. "Insane? You? Come on, girl; you're the sanest person I know."

"Maybe. It's just that when I climbed the front steps and stood at the entrance, I felt, I don't know, unwelcome? Such a strange feeling, like I had to be invited in, even though it's my bestie's house." She shrugged. "Or maybe it was more a feeling that I had to ask permission to enter."

Isabella smirked. "Ask permission? Are you a…" She bared her front teeth. "Are you a vampire?"

Luna squinted, displeased. "Ha, ha. Very funny."

"No, it's fine," Isabella continued, holding back a laugh. "Can you dance? I hear blood suckers are excellent dancers! *Fang*-dango, anyone?"

"Groan," Luna said, rolling her eyes. "Glad you are a talented artist 'cause your jokes suck."

"You mean 'bite.' My jokes bite. Sucking comes after the bite."

"Oh, my God!" Luna laughed. "Stop! Seriously, though, this house feels different from any I've ever encountered. It's like it knows something. About me, about you, about all of us. And the air feels charged, electric. It's as if…" She trailed off.

"As if?" Isabella prodded.

"As if it has a pulse. As if it's alive."

Isabella shivered, a chill sweeping over her body. What Luna had said was almost identical to what Ellie had told her the other day.

*Rosemear is alive. And it's not happy.*

# CHAPTER TEN
## *ABIGAIL*

*Rosemear*
*June 28<sup>th</sup>, 1859*

"Mr. Baldwin?" William Hawthorne stood at the entrance to the barn, calling into the darkness. "A word, if I might?"

Thunder rumbled in the distance; the air, heavy with moisture. Dark clouds hung low in the sky, an ominous black swath stretching to the horizon.

A powerful storm was brewing; William could feel it in every joint in his forty-nine-year-old body.

"Be right out, Mr. Hawthorne, sir," Clyde called from inside the depths of the barn.

William tipped his head back, closed his eyes, and inhaled. It even smelled like rain.

Clyde bounded out of the barn, sweaty and out of breath. "Somethin' I can do for ya, boss?"

William eyed the man with suspicion. "What, pray tell, has you so rattled that you're covered in perspiration and tripping on your own two feet?"

A blush crept up Clyde's face. "Oh, nothin' much. Checking the horses, doing some ironwork, that sort of thing."

"That so?"

"Yessir."

Narrowing his gaze, William said, "I see. So, tell me, Mr. Baldwin, do you have anything to report about that matter I tasked you with?"

Clyde bobbed his head. "I do, indeed. I was outside his chambers three nights this week. She was in there, canoodling with him. They was all lovey-dovey, neckin' and such. I can't be sure, but I think they was reading a book together as well."

William's face reddened in rage. "I knew he was hiding something from me! Reading together? Son of a bitch! It's not enough that my son is keeping the company of a Negro woman, but now he's also teaching that woman to read?"

Clyde, trembling at William's wrath, swallowed the lump in his throat. "I-I can't be sure, boss, but that's what it looked like."

William rubbed his whiskered chin before spitting tobacco juice onto the barn floor. "Well, then, I suppose I need to intercede. Teaching a Black woman to read is not only immoral, it's illegal around these parts. I need to protect my kin as well as my reputation."

"Sure, sure, Mr. Hawthorne. Why, Mr. Edward could find himself having to pay a mighty fine. Or worse, find himself locked up in a prison cell."

William nodded thoughtfully. "You are so right, Baldwin." He slapped the man on the back, inwardly recoiling at the overseer's offensive aroma. The man was disgusting, but William had always held his tongue about Clyde's hygiene and appearance.

Because very few men were willing to get their hands dirty performing acts that bordered on criminal.

But Clyde would. In fact, he enjoyed it.

"I'll need your help, Mr. Baldwin. We must formulate a plan to stop this ill-advised affair. I have some ideas to share with you, but first, I must know—can I count on you to do your part?"

Clyde grinned, displaying a gaping hole where his lower central incisors once lived. When he spoke, a spray of spittle flew from his mouth.

William ignored it.

"You don't even need to ask, boss," Clyde said, bobbing his head. "Whatever you need, I'm your man."

William smirked. "Excellent. Shall we begin?"

"Did you hear me? Abigail?"

Abby jumped and gave out a tiny squeal. She'd been deep in thought, walking the path to the river, and hadn't heard anyone come from behind her. "Mr. Edward, sir," she said with a small smile. "I apologize. My head is in the clouds today."

He smiled back. "Just Edward, please. After all, I am the man you kissed last night."

She blushed. "I seem to recall your lips were quite busy as well."

Edward laughed heartily. "Touché, my love. So, where are you headed?"

"I'm off to fetch some more water for Young Joseph. He still burns with fever."

Edward frowned. "Is that right? Well, perhaps it's time to call Dr. Coolidge."

Abigail shook her head. "Not necessary. Even though he is still warm, he is much cooler than before. I believe he's turned a corner and will be right as rain in a few days."

Edward raised a brow. "Perhaps you should be the medical advisor on Rosemear. You seem to know a lot about illness and even more about herbal remedies."

She looked down, flustered by his praise. "Oh, heck, Mr.... I mean, Edward. I just try to recall everything my momma taught me and hope for the best."

"Well, however you do it, it's impressive. Speaking of which...." Edward smiled slyly. "I would like to impress you this evening with a fine meal, after which I would serenade you with my Stradivarius violin. It has been said that I do a great rendition of Beethoven's 'Moonlight Sonata.'"

Abigail smiled shyly. "Mr. Edward, you wouldn't be flirtin' with me, would ya?"

"I would indeed, Miss Abigail."

She chuckled. "Well, whether you are or not, your idea sounds like a little bit of heaven."

Edward clapped his hands together. "Perfect! It's a date! Come to my room at the usual time. You can study your words while I prepare a feast. We'll eat while you read to me, and after our meal—when everyone is asleep—we can take a lovely stroll in the park." He bent forward and touched her lips with his. "What do you say, pretty girl?"

Abigail nodded. "Yes, sir. I-I mean, yes, Edward. That sounds fine." She brushed a hand over her dress nervously, smoothing out the folds. This romance, this flirtatious dance, was foreign to her.

She had no idea what the steps were or if she was even doing it right.

Smiling, she said, "You go on about your business now, and let me get back to my work. I'll see you in a short while."

"Yes, ma'am," he said, dipping his head for another kiss.

Following a forty-minute strategy session, William Hawthorne leaned against an old whiskey barrel in the barn, smoking his pipe and eyeing Clyde Baldwin. He'd always believed that you could take the measure of a man by his actions: a firm handshake, an earnest nod of the head, direct eye contact.

If that were all true, if a man's character could be measured by his actions, then Rosemear's overseer had the moral make-up of a slug.

Clyde's handshake was weak—a 'dead fish,' as William's father would have said—and his eyes moved from the walls to the floor to the rafters in the ceiling.

Landing everywhere but on William's face.

William hooked his thumbs over his leather belt. "You have the plan down, Mr. Baldwin? I'm counting on your allegiance and discretion here. Edward can never know where this correction comes from."

Clyde bobbed his head furiously, hoping to make clear his loyalty. He knew if William Hawthorne was pleased with how he handled Edward and Abigail's relationship, it could open doors he never thought possible.

Money, power, and prestige—all within his reach.

"Yes, sir, Mr. Hawthorne. I know exactly what to do. By the time I'm done with her, they ain't a man in the world who will want her, includin' your son."

William held up a hand. "Not interested in knowing the particulars, Baldwin. Just need to know the task will be completed." He studied the dirt caked beneath his nails. "I always seem to find myself in the unenviable position of cleaning up my family's messes, don't I? A difficult situation because, as you know, I detest violence."

A lie, one he'd been telling himself for years. In truth, he enjoyed the power of wielding a sword, of righting a perceived wrong.

And it was near-euphoric when lesser men quaked with fear in his presence.

"Yessiree, I know that much," Clyde said, wrapping an arm

around William's shoulder in familiarity. William stiffened. "Why, it ain't right that you gotta be the one to take that Negro woman to task, but there it is." Then, with a wink, he added, "And, truth be told, she's a handsome woman, so it ain't like this will be backbreaking work." Chuckling, he pushed a hip into William. "Although, if you gotta break your back, I can't think of a better way to do it, am I right? Besides, she's out of line. I'm pleased to do my part to help you teach her a lesson."

William tipped his head in assent, then extricated himself from the man's foul embrace and turned to leave the barn. "Oh, one last thing, Baldwin..."

Clyde playfully punched William's arm. "Whatever you need, sir."

Voice smooth as buttermilk, William said, "If my son finds out what we did here, you're finished at Rosemear."

Clyde gulped, his smile vanishing. "I understand. You can—"

William stuck his palm out, silencing him. "But that's nothing," he hissed, "compared to what I'll do to you if you ever touch me again."

Clyde watched, wide-eyed, as William exited the barn, back stiff, indifferent to the venom he'd just released.

A hot pool of rage began to bubble within Clyde's chest, and his eyes narrowed as it spread like lava through his veins.

And that rage would become the worst possible catalyst for the fate of Abigail Charles.

"Abigail? Are you ready to go?"

Edward stood outside Abigail's bedroom door and waited. After feasting on pheasant and roasted potatoes an hour ago, Abigail had sneaked out of Edward's room and returned to her own, waiting for him to give the 'all clear' to continue their evening with a walk in the park.

She rushed to the door, swinging it wide open. Her cheeks were flushed with excitement, her brown eyes now appearing honey-colored against the cornflower blue of her dress.

"I'm ready," she said, somewhat breathless. "Do I need a shawl?"

Edward smiled softly. "You look utterly stunning, my love. And yes, I think a shawl is wise. The air is chilly this evening."

After creeping down the stairs, they exited through the servants' entrance, climbed into a carriage near the barn that Edward had prepared earlier, and set off for the historic district and Savannah Square.

The park was deserted except for a flock of seagulls looking for scraps and two lovers walking in the distance. Abigail, attempting to conceal her race, covered her shoulders and head with her shawl.

Edward led her to a bench in Wright Square, and they sat side by side, admiring the full moon. He inhaled deeply and tipped his head back, studying the night sky. "I just love the sights and smells of Savannah, don't you? This park is just the tonic for whatever ails one. Whenever my troubles catch up, coming here makes everything right again."

He winked and took a swig from the bottle of bourbon he held against his chest.

He'd been sipping on that bottle—nestled inside a brown bag—all evening.

Tamping down Virgil's warning about the man sitting next to her and his excessive drinking, Abigail waited for Edward to finish his thought.

"The fresh air and beautiful landscapes here remind me of my mother and my wonderful childhood. Mother brought us here in the early evenings when my sisters and I were young. We'd run in circles for hours, chasing fireflies, pretending we were swashbucklers on a great adventure. Such fond memories."

Abigail stood and stretched before sitting on a patch of grass in front of Edward. "That sounds wonderful. Your mother must have been something special."

Edward smiled. "She surely was." He looked into her eyes and cocked his head, deliberating whether to share more. Decision made, he continued. "You know, Abigail, I've been thinking about what you said about my mother possibly being poisoned."

"Now, Edward, I told you not to pay me no mind. Sometimes, my mouth works faster than my brain."

"But that's the thing, my love. I agree with you. As a matter of fact, the more I think about it, the more I believe my mother's death seems a bit suspicious. I mean, I've not heard of severe abdominal cramping as part of yellow fever, have you? And everything I've heard or read about this cruel disease tells us that the hallmark sign of yellow fever is, well, a fever."

Abigail nodded. "Yes, that's true."

"Right. So, after much contemplation, I've thought of someone who would have liked nothing better than to see my mother dead."

Her eyes widened. "You did? Who? Who on earth would hurt your mother?"

Edward took a long swig from the bottle in the bag. "The bitch who took her place. I'm willing to bet that my stepmother and former governess, Lillian, is the type of person who'd try and take out the competition."

"Oh, Edward," Abigail said, shaking her head. "Truly? Your momma killed at the hands of another? Are you sure? That's a mighty big accusation."

After taking another pull from the bottle, Edward rose and sat on the ground next to Abigail. "I'm not sure of anything right now, truth be told." He reached for her hand and kissed her palm.

"Except how I feel about you. That fact is crystal clear." He momentarily held her hand to his face, then let go to take another swig of bourbon. "All I can say with certainty is that Lillian is a nasty woman. It wouldn't surprise me in the least to find out she'd had a hand in my mother's death. But, as we both know, suspecting that something nefarious has occurred is a far cry from confirming it." He shook his head. "But proof? Unfortunately, that I do not have. I can't prove any of it."

Abigail bit her bottom lip, indecisive. Finally, she spoke. "I could, uh, I could ask some of the menfolk who were here back then. Several have worked on Rosemear since the beginning—Abraham, Vincent, James." She chuckled. "Heck, I believe James was on this land even before your daddy bought it."

"Oh, Abigail," Edward said, his words slurred. "You would do that for me?"

Abigail nodded demurely. "Of—of course, I would. No trouble at all." She clucked her tongue. "Now, can I ask *you* something, Edward?"

He nodded. "Anything in the world, my love. I'm an open book."

She cleared her throat. "It's about the overseer. You know him, I'm sure. Clyde Baldwin?"

Edward nodded. "Ah, yes. The smelly fellow who tends the horses and such."

"He does. Plus, he sees to it that all the workers do what they are supposed to do. I expect he doesn't like me much, as I tend to speak my mind more than most."

Wobbling slightly, Edward stood, reached out a hand, and pulled Abigail to her feet. "Is he bothering you? If so, I can certainly have a chat with him."

She shook her head and brushed the grass from her skirts. "No, I don't suppose that would be wise. I believe if he is confronted, it would be like touching a flame to a stick of dynamite." She shrugged. "I just—I'd hoped that you could keep an eye on him, is all. He's made some downright vulgar suggestions, and while I don't expect he'll follow through, I could sleep a lot better knowing you were watching him."

Edward frowned. "Well, I don't like that. I don't like that one bit." He lowered his head and kissed her cheek. "Tell you what—I will feel him out, get a sense of his intentions. If I determine he is a lout and a danger, I will make sure he leaves the plantation for good. Fair enough?"

Abigail smiled. "More than fair. Thank you, Edward."

As they walked through the park back to the carriage, Edward had an overwhelming urge to hold Abigail's hand. He reached out and grabbed it.

She let go immediately.

"What are you doing?" she whispered. "It isn't safe, Edward. What if someone sees?"

He smiled crookedly. "Then I will tell them to mind their business. After all, how can I help wanting to touch the prettiest girl in Savannah?"

Abigail giggled.

They stopped before a giant oak tree, and Edward pointed to the thick branches overhead. "Do you notice anything different about this tree, Abigail?"

She shook her head. "Just that it's a big one, is all. Biggest tree around, it seems."

He smiled. "You're right! It is the largest tree in Savannah Square. Anything else strike you?"

She walked a slow circle around its trunk. Smoothing a hand over the bark, she studied the top branches and said quietly, "There's no moss. The other trees in the park are draped with Spanish moss, but I don't see any moss in this here square."

Edward clapped, giddy. "Good girl! Yes, the trees in Wright Square bear no moss, unlike the rest of Savannah. Legend has it that moss will not grow in an area that has spilled innocent blood."

Abigail's eyes widened. "Innocent blood? Was someone killed here?"

He nodded. "A woman called Alice Riley, a little over a hundred years ago. In the winter of 1735, Alice, an indentured servant from Ireland, and her lover, Richard White, were accused of killing their master, William Wise. Gossip was that Mr. Wise was a nasty fellow and beat Alice regularly."

"And they killed him?"

"Held his head under water and drowned him in a bucket, of all things. After they were apprehended, Alice and Richard were deemed guilty and sentenced to hang."

"Oh, my," Abigail gasped.

"Yes, it must have been something. Richard was hanged first, and after watching him swing, Alice claimed she was with child. As it happened, she was, and the authorities postponed the execution for eight months. Once the baby, James, was born, Alice Riley became the first woman to be hanged in Georgia."

Abigail sighed. "Tragic. What happened to the baby?"

"Died, I'm afraid, two weeks after his mother. People speculated that the infant was sired by William Wise rather than her lover, Richard. Although, it hardly seems to matter much now, does it? "

"No," Abigail said softly. "I suppose it doesn't."

When they arrived at the carriage, Edward helped Abigail into the coach box before settling behind the reins. "You know, they left that woman hanging for three days. Stories abound about whether she was left there to make a statement or whether it took her three days to die."

"Oh, that's dreadful!" Abigail gasped. "What a vile cruelty to inflict on a young body."

He shrugged. "Hard to pity a murderer, but I do agree it sounds like a gruesome end." He lowered his voice to a whisper. "They say such ghastly deaths are responsible for a spirit's unrest. So, tell me,

Miss Abigail Charles—do you believe in ghosts?"

She frowned. "Ghosts? Why, I never gave it much thought, Edward. I believe the living are given a soul on the day they are born and that our souls rise to face judgment when the good Lord calls them home. But no, I don't expect I believe in ghosts."

"Me either," Edward agreed. "But there are many who do. And, of those believers, some maintain that Alice Riley haunts this square, appearing every winter to look for her lost baby. Some folks swear they've seen her—even heard her—wailing as she pursues women walking here with their children. Some even say Alice's ghost has tried snatching babies right from their mothers' arms to claim as her own. Sad, isn't it?"

Abigail brushed a hand across her forehead, moving a stray hair from her brow. Smoothing her skirts, trying to avoid thinking about it too hard, she eventually answered. "Sad? Mr. Edward, I don't find that sad at all. I find it frightening as the devil hisself, terrifying enough to stop a body's heart."

"You aren't wrong," Edward said, flicking the reins until the horses moved forward. "But since we both agree there is no such thing as ghosts, we've nothing to fear, right?"

Abigail nodded but said nothing. Instead, she adjusted her shawl and settled back in her seat, taking in her surroundings. As sunset faded into night, the play of light cast an eerie glow, creating the illusion that the trees were moving, swaying like dancers on the darkening Wright Square. Abigail watched, fascinated, as countless shadowed limbs whipped violently above her despite the stillness of the evening air.

As if caught within an imaginary breeze, fighting to escape the wind, their origins, and their roots.

Hoping to find freedom.

Which, Abigail thought, was precisely what she was trying to do.

Cigarette smoke curled toward the heavens as the dark figure, clad in black and hidden behind a giant magnolia tree, watched Edward and Abigail pull away from the park. Fists clenched, anger building, he stomped his cigarette into the ground.

He knew he shouldn't be here, knew he shouldn't have come.

But he could no more temper his fascination with Abigail Charles than he could stop a rising tide or the setting sun.

She was no innocent. She was lustful and arrogant and smarter than most.

But soon, she would be dealt with. Soon, she would be schooled about her place at Rosemear.

And no one, not even Edward Hawthorne himself, would stop the chain of events Clyde Baldwin had already set in motion.

# CHAPTER
# ELEVEN

Isabella and Luna sat at the kitchen table, sipping hazelnut coffee and nibbling on chocolate chip cookies while discussing their plans for the day.

"What time are the delivery guys coming with your new furniture?" Luna asked.

Isabella shrugged. "Who knows? They told me 'Anywhere between noon and the second coming of Christ.'"

"Super," Luna said, voice dripping with sarcasm. "Glad they narrowed it down. So, in the interim, what shall we tackle first? Looks like you've got quite a bit done here already."

Isabella nodded. "The repairs have gone fairly well. No headaches, anyway. We've completed the major projects already—a new roof, an HVAC system, and replacement windows. And I have an exterminator scheduled for next week because Spencer thinks we have mice."

Luna lifted a brow. "Mice? I don't know about that, but you do have a rat in the general vicinity."

Isabella wrinkled her nose. "You're talking about Spencer now, aren't you?"

"Boy, nothing gets by you! Yes, I'm talking about that jerk you married. I swear, I have no idea why you stay with that jackass."

Isabella carried her mug to the sink. "Hopefully, I will be putting that 'jackass' out to pasture soon. You know, you gave me the best advice using a simple question a few years back. You asked if I thought I was better off with or without him. Do you remember that?"

"I remember."

"Well, I've asked myself that a dozen times since then, and I believe I've known the answer for a while. I just took the scenic route to get there."

"At least you got there. Might have taken you freakin' forever, but you made it!"

Isabella chuckled. "Indeed. Would you believe that after I found out about Spencer's affair with Julia, he had the nerve to ask me what I looked for in a relationship? Apparently, responding with 'a way out' was not the answer he was looking for."

Luna exploded with laughter. "Oh my God, that's priceless!"

"Yeah," Isabella smirked, "I found it funny; him, not so much. Not to sound like a drama queen, but it seems like forever since I felt valued and loved. I was always extending the olive branch, the only one to say, 'I'm sorry.' It was exhausting."

"I imagine it would be," Luna said gently. "If you ask me, Spencer and Julia Cocksucker deserve each other."

"*Julia Cox*, actually."

"Cocksucker, Cox—same difference. Bitch sucking her way to the top."

"You're not wrong. Spencer met her, flirted with her, and passed himself off as some hotshot pharmaceutical rep. I think he was exactly what she wanted—a sugar daddy. Her own freaking

Santa Claus."

"Yeah, well, I'd like to boot a lump of coal up Santa's ass. That way, he can shit a bowl full of diamonds to justify taking up air someone else could be breathing."

Isabella laughed. "Now, that I'd like to see!"

"Yeah," Luna said sourly, "I'll pass on that."

"Anyway, where was I? Oh, I remember. I was saying how tired I was of carrying the marital torch and how your advice made so much sense. So, I developed a solid plan to leave, even had a divorce attorney on retainer, and then…" She trailed off.

"And then Anna died," Luna finished for her.

"Yes. And I couldn't find the strength to file for a divorce back then."

"I get that," Luna said, walking to the sink. She stood next to Isabella and wrapped an arm around her shoulder. Voice barely above a whisper, she said, "But we are coming up on three years since we lost that precious baby, kiddo. How long are you going to punish yourself?"

Isabella looked hurt. "Is that what you think I'm doing?"

"I do. Look, Anna's death was an accident. A stupid, tragic accident, but it wasn't your fault."

"Wasn't it, though?" Isabella asked, scrubbing her hands over her face. "God, I remember that day like it was yesterday. You were visiting and wanted to take the kids to the park, but Anna was sick and couldn't go."

"Her temp was raging that day," Luna said gently.

"So, you took Sam and Ellie to the playground," Isabella continued, tone flat, "and I stayed behind with Anna."

"As I recall, you weren't feeling well, either."

"No, I wasn't. I think Anna and I had the same bug." She dipped away from Luna's embrace and mindlessly scrubbed the countertop. "Once you left with the kids, Spencer gave me a fever reducer and went out to get more while Anna and I cuddled on the couch."

"And you fell asleep."

Isabella's breath hitched. "Yes," she whispered. "I fell asleep, but Anna didn't. The next thing I knew, I was startled awake by, I don't know, something. I still don't know what pulled me out of that deep sleep."

Luna picked up a second sponge and wiped down the table. "Mother's intuition, maybe."

"Wish that intuition had kicked in ten minutes sooner," Isabella said softly. "When I went looking for her, the pool was the last place I thought to check. I mean, you know me—I've preached to my kids since they could walk about pool safety."

Luna sighed. "Of course you did. Like I said, it was an accident, Bella. Anna toddled outside, probably looking for her siblings, and got too close to the pool's edge. No one blames you for any of it."

Isabella shook her head. "But it's my job to protect my kids, Lune, and I failed miserably. So, yeah, I blame myself." She paused. "And I think Spencer does, too."

"Does he?" Luna snarled. "Well, I blame *him*! Instead of getting help immediately, he played the hero. He never called me, even though I was right down the road with the kids. Can you imagine? You don't call a medically trained person who is two minutes away?"

"To be fair, I didn't think to call you, either."

"And you didn't do substandard, shitty CPR like he did! Don't defend him on this, girlfriend. His ego got in the way of his common sense."

"He said he had it," Isabella said softly.

"And he was wrong. Again."

Isabella gazed across the room, seeing nothing but her devastating memories. "Yeah. He kept saying, 'Don't worry, I got this.' He must have said it twenty times while working on Anna. I was kneeling beside her, talking to her, telling her not to leave us. And he was… Honestly, I don't know what he was doing at that point. My focus was on my baby."

"He was being his typical, controlling, narcissistic self."

Amused, Isabella said, "What is it with you two, anyway? I get you don't like each other, but this is above and beyond general dislike."

Luna hesitated before answering. "Do you remember when I visited you in Florida? It was about two months before Anna died.'

"Sure. You made me take you and the kids out for ice cream cones almost every night. Think I gained ten pounds that week."

Luna smiled. "Same. Anyway, one day, you and I were talking about the sad state of your marriage. You told me what your attorney's advice was and were getting my take on it."

Cautious as to where this was going, Isabella nodded. "I remember."

"Anyhow," Luna said, "I agreed with everything your lawyer said. I even suggested that, on top of all he told you to do and document, you should hire a private investigator to follow Spencer and get photographic proof of his affair to bring to court. I believe I gave you the name of my cousin, Jed Devereaux. He started his business in Montana but now has investigators all over the country."

"I was in the process of contacting Jed when Anna drowned. I had a Zoom meeting set up with him on the eighteenth, two days after she died. Obviously, it never happened."

"It still can," Luna offered. "I can call Jed right now if you want."

"No, it's fine. Honestly, I don't even care anymore. I just want out."

Luna cleared her throat. "That's good to hear because that son of a bitch is dangerous."

Isabella laughed nervously. "Dangerous? I agree he is an asshat, but dangerous? I don't see it."

Luna sighed. "I know you don't, which is why I bring it up. That day, when we were chatting and discussing strategy, Spencer was in the other room, eavesdropping. I found out after Anna died and you were hospitalized. I was staying in your house—taking care of the kids until you were discharged—when the bastard cornered me in your kitchen. He was screaming in my face, yelling that he'd heard everything we'd said, and accused me of trying to wreck his marriage. Laughable, right?"

Isabella stared at her, stunned. "I hadn't heard any of this. What did you say?"

Luna lifted a brow. "What didn't I say is more accurate. I let him have it with both barrels, telling him that his stupidity and narcissism ruined his marriage, not me. I also said I would continue advising you to leave his ass. He wasn't happy, to say the least."

Isabella frowned. "Oh, Luna! I can't tell you how sorry I am. You shouldn't have to defend me or my choices to him. Did he— he didn't get physical, though, right?"

"Physical? No, other than blocking my path to prevent me from leaving. Joker was inches from my face and had just eaten penne pasta sauteed in onion and garlic. His breath smelled like the back end of a wolverine."

Isabella giggled.

"True story," Luna said with a smile. "When I refused to back down, he issued veiled threats, warning me he had doctor friends and could see to it I lost my reputation, my job, even my license as a nurse practitioner."

"Seriously? What did you do?"

Luna winked. "I told him to get the fuck out of my face. Then I kneed him in the nuts to prove my point."

Isabella grinned, eyes wide. "You didn't!"

"I sure as hell did. I'm only sharing this encounter because that peckerhead was willing to ruin my life for something he brought on himself. In my opinion…" Luna was cut short by the sounds of screaming.

"Ma!" Sam yelled from somewhere upstairs. "Ellie's bleeding!"

Isabella and Luna raced to the foyer and up the staircase to where the children stood. Ellie, tears streaming down her cheeks, had a hand clutched over her calf.

"Oh, my goodness, sweetheart!" Isabella said, crouching before her daughter. "What on earth happened?"

In full nurse mode, Luna crouched down as well, trying to assess Ellie's leg. "Move your hand, darlin', so Auntie Luna can have a look."

While she inspected the wound, which thankfully appeared to be superficial, Isabella wiped away Ellie's tears and turned toward Sam. "What happened, Sammy?"

Sam shrugged. "I don't know, Ma. We were playing soldiers, and Ellie went to her room to get her toy Jeep. You know, the one she uses for her Barbie dolls? We thought it would make a nice transport vehicle for the men."

Isabella tried not to smile. "The men, huh? Okay, so, what happened?"

Sam bit his lower lip. "I heard her scream, and by the time I jumped up, she was already in my room. I could see her leg was bleeding."

Isabella cupped Ellie's face. "Bug? What happened here? Did you fall or something?"

Ellie, calmer now, rubbed her eyes. Ignoring her mother's question, she looked down at Luna. "Aunt Luna? Is it...is it bad? Do I need to go to the hossible?"

Luna smiled up at her. "Hospital, you mean. And no, sweetie, it's not bad. We'll clean it up, dab on a little antibacterial cream, and find you a cool Band-Aid." She kissed Ellie's palm. "But you need to tell me what you cut it on, okay?"

Ellie sniffed and nodded. "I went to my room to get my Jeep but couldn't find it. It wasn't on my dresser, or in my toybox, or anywhere!" She pinched the end of her nose. "And it was extra stinky in there," she said nasally, "like, super-duper smelly. So, I held my nose, sat crisscross applesauce on the floor, and looked under the bed." Her eyes welled again. "And I saw something shiny, so I stretched my leg under the bed because I couldn't reach it with my hand. And something… something scratched me."

Luna frowned and looked up at Isabella. "Something like wires or metal pieces poking out from the bed frame? Or, maybe the movers damaged something in transit?"

Isabella bit her lip in thought. "Maybe. They sure were acting strange, but I'll tell you about it later." She glanced at her children. "Come on, kiddo," she said, rubbing Ellie's back, "let's get you cleaned up."

"El, you can use my trucks if you want," Sam offered helpfully. "Just until we find your Barbie Jeep."

"Thanks, Sammy," Ellie said quietly.

As the four walked to one of the upstairs bathrooms, Isabella ruffled Ellie's hair. "You know, Bug, there are many rooms in this house, and most don't smell like macaroni feet or doo-doo." Her attempt at making her daughter smile fell flat. "Any of them would make a neat bedroom if you'd like to change it up." She stopped and kissed Ellie's forehead. Luna and Sam stopped as well. "I'm just saying you aren't locked into 'stink central.' It would be easy enough to move your stuff."

Ellie thought for a moment. "You said that you and Auntie Luna were going to find out where the smell was coming from, that maybe it's in the walls, right?"

"That's right," Isabella said. "I think a bird or other animal got trapped inside a wall. Luna and I will demo everything, have a look-see, then repair the holes or replace the plaster walls with sheetrock." She glanced at Luna and said, "I hate to punch holes in the original walls, but we gotta find the source of that funk."

"Agreed," Luna said.

Ellie thought the offer over. "I think I'll keep the same

bedroom."

Isabella ushered Ellie toward the bathroom again while Luna and Sam stayed close behind. "You sure, Bug?"

"Yeah, I'm sure. Besides, it makes Martin happy."

"Martin?" Luna asked.

"Martin is Ellie's imaginary friend," Sam whispered.

"He's not pretend, Sammy! And he wanted me to have that room!"

"How come?" Isabella asked, tamping down a prickle of alarm. "Why did Martin want you to take that particular room?"

Ellie stopped walking and looked up at Isabella, confused. "Well, um, because it was his room, silly. My bedroom used to belong to Martin."

Once Ellie's cut was cleaned and bandaged, Isabella sent both kids outside to play while she and Luna explored 'stink central.'

"Pew!" Luna said when they entered Ellie's room. "Boy, that kid wasn't kidding! It smells like something took a 'Spencer,' curled up, and died in here."

Isabella snickered. "Took a Spencer? What are we, twelve?"

"Get it? 'Cause he's a shit? Come on, it's funny!"

"Toilet humor," Isabella joked. "Outstanding. You should've been in stand-up."

"I'm glad you finally recognize my talents."

Isabella rolled her eyes. "Well, you're not wrong. He *is* kind of a shit."

"Kind of?" Luna said wide-eyed. "Girl, his face should be on Porta Johns nationwide! Anyway, enough about him. What's the first order of business?"

Isabella put her hands on her hips. "I thought we should first check the bed and floor area for jagged metal or something. I don't want Ellie to get cut again."

Luna, arms folded, leaned against the wall. "Speaking of... I assume her tetanus vaccination is up to date in case it *was* metal that cut her?"

"Yes, ma'am. Since school starts here in a month or so, I made sure she was all caught up during her last physical."

"And what about this Martin dude?" Luna asked. "Do I even want to know?"

"Well, um, Sam thinks it's an imaginary friend," Isabella explained. "Ellie, on the other hand, says he's real and that Rosemear was his home. Truthfully, when I first heard the name, I assumed she'd overheard us talking about your brother and conjured him up as a friend."

"But not now?"

"No, not so much. Ellie claims he's a little boy who died and is interred on this land. Not only that but apparently, this Martin knows someone who was buried alive. Ellie has even described this kid in detail as if she's seen him more than once." She shook her head slowly, trying to absorb the meaning of her words. "But Jesus, Luna—ghosts? Ghosts hang out in other people's homes, believers' homes, not mine. They haunt people who hear a bang in the middle of the night and immediately conclude it's their dead grandmother with a message from beyond. Or new-agers who sip girly drinks with tiny umbrellas instead of shooting whiskey and blame everything on karma rather than looking for an alternate explanation." She groaned into her hands. "There is a logical reason for what's going on here. We just have to find it."

Luna tapped her chin. "So, you're saying you don't believe there are any circumstances where the dead choose to return to the land of the living?"

"I wish I did. Truly. I'd give anything to see my Anna Rae again.

But I've always believed that when you're dead, you stay dead."

"Ghosts aren't zombies, toots," Luna said with a smirk. "It's not like *Night of the Living Dead* out there. They're simply departed souls who cannot rest."

"Well, whatever they are, they aren't real to me. It's a trick of the mind or shadow play or…or mental illness." She was quiet for a moment, then gently asked, "How about you, Lune? You're a believer. Have you seen your brother at all?"

Luna shook her head sadly. "No, but not for lack of trying. I've had psychics come in, conducted countless seances, and prayed to anyone who would listen to bring me Marty. All I'm left with is the assumption he was so dearly loved that he had no unfinished business."

Isabella smiled warmly. "That's a lovely way of looking at it. As for me, while I admit to witnessing some spooky stuff here, once I get out of that 'it's gotta be paranormal' headspace, I know I can find a rational explanation for all of it."

Luna quirked a brow.

"Okay, for *most* of it," she conceded. "But the thought that Ellie could be ill frightens me more than any ghost ever could. All I keep thinking about is my family and our history."

"You're talking about Uncle Jack," Luna said.

"Among others, yes."

"Have you ever considered that maybe Jack was telling the truth? That he really was 'special'? Gifted?"

Isabella looked torn. "Not really. Honestly, if I did, it would crush me to think that when he died, he died knowing no one believed him. But no," she said, standing straighter, "I know the stories. My family has an extensive history of mental illness."

"And what makes you so damned special, ma'am?" Luna joked. "My friend, we all have assorted fruits and nuts dangling from our family trees. That doesn't mean my little Ellie-bell has copped the crazy gene and is suffering from delusions." She walked to the closet and opened it, scanning the inside without really seeing. "You're afraid she's developed, what? Schizophrenia? Sorry, but I'm not buying it. I've known your kids all their lives, and neither gives off a skewed mental health vibe. Besides, it is exceedingly rare to see schizophrenia in anyone as young as El."

"I suppose," Isabella said. "So if that's not it, what gives?" She tossed her head, flipping her hair behind a shoulder, and joked, "And what is it with this Martin character? He doesn't call, doesn't write. It's like he just, I don't know, *ghosted* us or something."

Luna chuckled. "Now, who's the comedian?"

Isabella shrugged before looking around. "Find anything dangerous in that closet, Hoss?" she asked.

"Does an old shoe and a bag of mothballs count?"

"Depends on how old the shoe is."

Luna laughed lightly. "Nothing super suspect in here. At least, nothing sharp enough to draw blood. How about you?"

Isabella got down on all fours at the side of the bed and peeked underneath. "Nope, I don't see anyth—" She stopped suddenly and then squealed as her torso was yanked toward the dark void beneath the twin bed.

"Iz!" Luna screamed, racing across the room. "Oh, God!"

She dropped to the floor and, heart pounding, looked under the bed.

And found Isabella with her hand slapped over her mouth, trying to hold in a giggle.

"Are you kidding me right now?" Luna yelled, pissed as hell.

Wriggling from beneath the bed, Isabella straightened, then bent forward and, laughing hysterically, placed her hands on her knees. "Oh, my God," she wheezed, "did you ever fall for it! I can see the headlines now! 'Local woman attacked! Friend fears the monster beneath the bed is responsible! News at eleven!'"

Luna gave her an icy stare.

"I'm sorry, but you gotta admit that was funny!" She paused, still snickering, a sly grin on her face. "Anyway, I did find this," she extended her hand, palm up, "before the under-the-bed gremlin tried to snatch my soul. It's one of my emerald earrings. They've been missing since the move."

"Great," Luna said, voice clipped. "Happy for you."

Isabella gave her friend an over-the-top pout. "Aw, come on. Don't be upset with me." She pressed her lips together, holding in another round of giggles. "I'm sorry you were afraid the bed was eating me."

"I wasn't afraid the bed was eating you," Luna deadpanned. "I was cheering you on. I haven't seen that kind of action in a long time."

Isabella laughed harder.

"Anyway," Luna continued, "while we all agree you're a hoot, could you back off on the scares for now? I about shat my bloomers, and there's enough stench in here already!"

"Hah! You think my prank just now was scary? Wait until I show you the blue room and tell you what happened there. It's enough to scare the pants off a virgin."

"Then it's a damn good thing I'm not a virgin, ain't it? Seriously, do you remember me saying it felt like I needed to ask permission to enter this house? The whole vibe here is, I don't know, off or something. Like the setting of a psychological or supernatural thriller. Have you ever heard of the Biltmore? Franklin Castle? The Hill House?"

"Isn't Hill House that new club in Manhattan?"

Luna clucked her tongue. "Girl, you need to get out more. Bottom line? This place gives me the heebie-jeebies."

"Okay, okay, I get it. Message received. A little more charm, a little less 'yikes!'"

"Less 'yuks' would be good, too," Luna said dryly.

"Impossible!" Isabella cracked, looking around. "So tomorrow, let's start knocking down some walls in here. I need to find the source of that funk." She started toward the door. "Come on," she said, wrinkling her nose. "As my dad used to say, let's blow this popsicle stand."

Luna, following closely behind, muttered, "Good call. If I have to smell that irresistible combination of rotting cabbage and un-washed assholes much longer, I may toss my cookies."

Isabella snorted, and they walked, arm in arm, down the hall-way, away from Ellie's room.

And never heard the gentle hum of rubber tires nor saw the flashing lightbar of Ellie's Jeep as it rolled out of the closet and across the bedroom floor.

# CHAPTER
# TWELVE

"Well, you weren't lying," Luna said as her eyes roamed over the bedroom door. "That bitch is blue."

"I know, right? Wait until you see inside, though," Isabella said. Holding her breath, unsure whether the door would even open, she grasped the knob and turned.

It opened easily.

"Well, that's a first," Isabella said over her shoulder. "Come on, Lune. Check it out."

Warily, Luna followed Isabella into the room. Her eyes scanned everything, from the fireplace and speckled mirror above it to the bay windows and the armoire. Tipping her head back, she peered at the ceiling and whistled.

"Told ya," Isabella whispered. "Freaky."

"Totally," Luna whispered back. Then, voice still hushed, she added, "Remind me again—why are we whispering?"

"Because it… Oh, hell, I don't know. It seemed like a good idea at the time. Before, when I was exploring, I heard a voice. And then something touched me."

Luna, mouth agape, stared at Isabella. "Um, ex-squeeze me?"

"I know, I know. Scared the crap out of me, too." She eyed Luna uneasily.

"Well?" Luna planted her hands on her hips. "Do I hafta beat it out of ya?"

Isabella took a deep breath. "I was up here exploring and couldn't open the door at first. Once I gave up and walked away, it opened by itself."

Luna shrugged, unimpressed. "Happens sometimes. Don't you remember my parents' house? It was built in the late 1800s, and the doors always swelled in the heat of the summer. I bet that's what happened. But tell me more about this voice and the 'phantom toucher.'" She made a rolling "go on" motion with her hand.

Isabella took another deep breath. "Yeah, the swollen door was my first thought, too, until I stood inside the room. I heard shuffling noises behind me, and then something grabbed me and an angry voice told me to get out. After that, I flushed the notion of sticky wooden doors." She shuddered.

"That *is* freaky," Luna said. Then, frowning and lifting a brow, she added, "You sure it wasn't douchebag Spencer?"

"I wish. No, although the voice was masculine, it was older and ordered me to leave. Just before it spoke, I could actually feel its breath on my ear. It squeezed my shoulder, said 'Leave this place!' and then said *'Get! Out!'* Of course, I was already wigging out by that point, so maybe my fear conjured the touch. Hell, maybe fear conjured the whole episode. Over the last few years, I've learned that the mind is a powerful force."

"Yeah, but holy fucking Hannah—what if?" Luna mumbled.

"Exactly. So, I hightailed it downstairs and told Spencer."

Luna rolled her eyes. "Lemme guess… His Highness was less than supportive."

"He thinks I'm relapsing," Isabella said quietly. "Which, I won't lie, scares the shit out of me. That's just the thing Spencer would use to get custody of the kids."

"That prick couldn't handle custody."

"Probably not. But I'd be forced to pay child support, which would be substantial considering the size of my bank account. Enough so he could hire a full-time nanny and not break a sweat."

"Oh, fuck that asshole!"

Isabella's lips curled into a slow smile. "As my biased best friend, you have to say that."

"Maybe. Look, every oddity in life has an explanation, whether natural or otherworldly, right? Scary sounds can—but don't necessarily have to—have a supernatural slant." She lifted her hand and, using her fingers, began counting off the possibilities. "Number one—the whine of pipes through the walls. The plumbing in this old girl has to be ancient, right? Hell, I imagine when a faucet runs or a toilet flushes, it can sound like a screaming banshee up in here. Number two on our list of possibilities could be the groaning of wood as the wind pushes against the exterior, or the creaks and grunts of the house settling further into the soil."

"Is there a number three?" Isabella asked.

"Have you ever known me to stop at two with anything? Food, wine, shoe shopping, lovers. I believe in 'go big or go home.'"

Isabella snorted.

"Anyway," Luna continued, "number three is that it could be a neighbor's voice carried on the wind. This house is on a hill, after all." She picked up a hardcover classic, *To Kill a Mockingbird*, from the bookshelf beside the mantel and smoothed a hand over the cover. "And finally, we have option four."

"What's option four?"

"That this house *is* haunted as fuck," Luna joked. "But what is *not* happening is that you're relapsing. I'm one hundred percent sure of that."

"And the hand on my shoulder? What's your explanation for that?"

"Like I said… your house is haunted as fuck," Luna said with a laugh. "Seriously, I'm not sure. What do you think it was?"

Isabella, hands on her hips, scanned the room. "I think," she said, drawing out the words, "that this is an extraordinary house filled with many memories of the people who once lived here. Maybe we need to do a little research into the history of Rosemear; maybe the voices, strange noises, and flickering lights are just memories created long ago and absorbed into the structure itself."

"Lingering energy?" Luna said. "That's called a residual haunting."

"Okay, let's pretend I have no idea what that is."

Luna reached a hand out to the speckled mirror over the fireplace, then pulled it back, afraid to touch it. "A residual haunting is like a video playing on repeat. The 'actors,' or ghosts, play a situation or memory on a loop. It's like they can't escape the past. Most say they aren't even aware of the living."

Isabella's face dropped. "Really? How sad. I wonder if you can have a residual haunt along with one where the ghosts interact with people?"

"An active haunt? Wow, you've changed your tune pretty quickly! What happened to the whole 'ghosts haunt other people's homes' and 'the dead stay dead'?"

"Well, if the spook fits," Isabella joked. "Honestly, I'm grasping at straws here. If I can prove all of this," she waved her hand around the room, "is supernatural, then Ellie is not mentally ill. Instead, she's some kind of psychic or spiritual medium."

Luna nodded. "Which would create the possibility that Uncle Jack was, in fact, not a fry short of a Happy Meal but a gifted psychic himself." She glanced at her watch. "Okay, it's a little after one right now. Let's go downstairs, pour a glass of wine, and create a fabulous charcuterie platter. We can do our online research while we eat and drink. I don't know about you, but I can't think straight when I'm hangry."

Isabella winked. "Need a Snickers bar?"

Luna laughed lightly. "Maybe just the 'bar' part." She grabbed Isabella's hand. "Come on, mon amie. We'll eat and look up the history of this joint."

"And with any luck, the remaining furniture will be here by the time we finish eating."

They were almost at the staircase when Luna snapped her fingers. "Wait, that reminds me… You wanted to tell me about the moving guys and their weird behavior."

Isabella hooked an arm through Luna's as they descended the steps. When they reached the bottom, she turned to her friend. "Oh, I have a bunch to tell you. First, though, is that we have company coming for dinner tonight. It's a neighbor, Nathan Decker, and his nephew, Matthew. He is also bringing his dog, Midget, with him. Sweet pup."

"Midget? What is it? A chihuahua?"

"Oh, you'll see," Isabella said cryptically. "As far as Nathan goes, he's a police officer who transferred to Savannah PD from another department to be closer to his family. His sister, Marnie, lost her husband six months ago, and Nate thought Matty could use a male role model in his life right now."

Luna grinned mischievously. "You sure seem to have discovered an awful lot of personal information about Mr. Nathan Decker." Still smiling, she added, "Tell me he's a hottie."

"Is that all men are to you, Lune? A piece of meat?"

Luna winked. "With gravy and a side of taters."

"Well, for your information," Isabella said, holding back a laugh, "he isn't just hot… he's on fire."

"Yes! I can use a bit of eye candy about now."

"Can't we all? Anyway, I expect them at six and have yet to make the meatballs or toss a salad."

"Okay," Luna said. "I'll check on the kids while you pull out the ingredients for the salad. Then, I'll toss the bitch, you roll those meaty balls, and between slicin' and dicin', we can start our research, okay?"

"Sounds like a plan," Isabella said. Throwing an arm around Luna, growing serious, she added, "I truly don't know what I'd do without you, my friend. You keep me sane."

Tilting her head, Luna quipped, "Good damned thing, too. With your family history, you'd be in a padded room about now."

"Funny. Now come on, wise-ass. I have some juicy tomatoes dying to meet you."

"Sammy, do you believe in ghosts?"

Ellie and Sam sat on the gazebo floor, sorting through their Pokémon card collection.

"Geeze, Ellie. What is it with you and ghosts all of a sudden? It's like all you think about. Ghosts, and this Martin kid."

Ellie stood and stomped her foot. "I do not!" Tears welling, she said softly, "I just don't know what I'm supposed to do. I-I don't know what Martin wants."

Sam gathered the cards and stood. "What makes you think this Martin dude wants something? Maybe he's, like, lonely. Or," he continued with a gleam in his eye, "maybe he likes you! Maybe he wants to be your boyfriend!"

Ellie stomped her foot again. "You take that back, Sammy!"

Sam grinned and puckered his lips, making a kissing sound. "Eww, Martin loves you!"

"Mom!" Ellie yelled.

"Hey!" Luna called from the back door. "What's going on over there?"

Ellie trotted to the house, tears in her eyes. "Sammy's making fun of me!"

Luna bent down and hugged her. "You go on inside, Bug-a-boo. I got this."

She watched Ellie enter the house, turned to Sam, and wagged a finger. "You, Mr. Smarty Pants…front and center."

Sam, head down, walked solemnly toward Luna. "I'm sorry, Aunt Luna, but she keeps talking about this Martin kid. Freaks me out."

Luna folded her arms across her chest. "Look, kiddo. I get that Ellie can sometimes be… intense. But she's just a little girl, and she's scared." She ruffled his hair. "You are the one she most looks up to, Squirt Doodle. Did you know that?"

Sam slowly shook his head.

"Well, it's true. So, when the person she most admires makes fun of something very real, at least to her, it's hurtful. Do you understand that?"

He nodded, glum.

"Good boy. So, we're clear, right? No more bustin' your little sister's onions."

"I promise."

"Good man. Now, I've got to help your mom with dinner prep. How about you stay here and watch for the furniture guys?"

"You got it!" Sam said enthusiastically.

When Luna turned to go back inside, Sam stopped her. "Wait! Can you ask El to come back outside? I promise I won't be mean."

Luna winked. "You got it, Sammy."

An hour after the furniture she'd purchased was delivered and set up, Isabella entered the kitchen wearing a teal V-neck summer dress. She stood there momentarily, watching Luna stir the meatballs in a pot, and smiled.

With her trim figure, olive complexion, and long black hair pulled into a messy bun, Luna was impossibly gorgeous, even while performing such a mundane task.

"Why are you staring?" Luna asked, still facing the stove. "Do I have a booger or something?"

Isabella laughed. "Well, with your back to me, I wouldn't know. I'm just incredibly jealous that you can look amazing stirring meatballs." She smoothed down her dress. "So, your opinion, ma'am... Does this Aztec print make me look fat?"

Luna faced her and smiled. "Come on, lady. We all know a burlap sack and fifty additional pounds wouldn't make you look fat." She nodded approvingly, "You look amazing, although it's quite a fancy dress for spaghetti and meatballs, isn't it? You wouldn't be trying to—I don't know—impress your new neighbor, would you?"

Heat rushed up Isabella's face. "Uh, no, no, of course not," she stuttered. "On the other hand, I don't need to look like a slob, do I? This dress is cool, comfortable, fun."

"Flirty?" Luna asked, brows waggling.

"Oh, puh-*lease*!" Isabella said with a laugh. "Channel change— how are those meaty balls looking?"

"Are we talking about the ones on the stove or the ones in your neighbor's pants?"

Isabella gasped. "Luna!"

"Fine, we'll leave that alone. For now. And everything looks amazing. The dining room table is set—love the design, by the bye—and the salad is chilling out in the fridge, cozying up to a bottle of Pinot. What time is this dreamboat coming again?"

Isabella chewed a thumbnail. "Soon, I think. Since we couldn't find much info online about Rosemear's history, I'm hoping Nate can relate some of his experiences. As a teenager, he hung out in the cemetery behind the house with his friends."

Luna frowned. "Creepy place to hang out, isn't it? Especially,"

Luna held the slotted spoon under her chin as if it were a flashlight and spoke in a ghoulish voice, "when ghostly spirits roam the grounds. Muahahaha!"

"Knock it off!" Isabella laughed. "Oh, before I forget… Midget is, um, not exactly pint-sized. She's big."

"How big? Like fifty pounds big or 'holy shit, that's not a dog, that's a freight train' big?" Luna asked. "

Before Isabella could answer, the doorbell chime reverberated through the house. Immediately afterward, her cell phone rang. "Shoot, that will be our guests, but Spencer is calling. Can you get the door and show them inside?"

"Okay, but if Nate falls instantly in love with me, don't say I didn't warn ya."

Isabella rolled her eyes and watched Luna leave the kitchen before answering the phone.

"Hello, Spencer."

"There's my girl! How are things going over there?"

"Fine." She could faintly hear music playing and people laughing in the background. "Where are you?"

"Oh, uh, just in the hotel lobby. They have a local band playing here for the week. What are you up to?"

"Just getting ready for dinner." She cleared her throat. "How is the conference going?"

"Good, good. We are heading to Charleston tomorrow to meet with MacMillan's East Coast vice president. I figure a day there, and then I'll head home." He clucked his tongue. "Babe, I think this Atlanta-to-Charleston thing will be a regular occurrence for me. According to Bob Murphy, the marketing rep I met here, most of MacMillan's conferences and sales meetings happen in Atlanta."

"I see," she said. "Glad it's working out for you."

"What's wrong? You sound weird or something. Are you feeling okay? Any more, um, noises?"

Isabella leaned against the counter. "We'll talk when you get back. We have a lot to discuss."

"Sounds serious," Spencer said, his words clipped.

"It's important, but I'd rather not do it over the phone."

Spencer said nothing.

Ignoring his silence, she continued. "I will tell you that Luna doesn't think I'm relapsing. I just wanted you to know that in case you were worried. Actually, if I'm being honest, I've felt more clear-headed the last few days than I have in a long time."

"What's that supposed to mean?" Spencer snapped. "That when I'm around you, your mind is mud?"

Isabella chose her words carefully. "I'm saying that having Luna here to validate my feelings and experiences is cathartic. She genuinely cares about me."

"Wow," Spencer said, jaw clenched. "You know, just because I don't feed into your delusions doesn't mean I don't care about you."

Isabella sighed. She should never have brought this up over the phone. "Let's not get into this now, Spencer. When you get back, we'll have a long talk."

"With or without Luna in the room?" he asked, voice tinged with contempt.

"Oh, for fuck's sake, grow up!" Isabella said with equal disdain. "Luna is leaving to return to work in two days, anyway. She'll be gone before you get home."

"Fine."

"I have to get dinner on the table. Talk soon?"

Spencer grunted into the phone. "Sure. Talk soon."

*Four Seasons Hotel*
*Atlanta, Georgia*
After speaking with Isabella, Spencer sat in the posh hotel lobby, eyes closed, and rubbed his temples with his fingers.

"Fucking bitch," he murmured under his breath.

Sensing a presence, he cracked one eye open and looked up.

"Hey, Jules," he said wearily.

"Hey, boss," she replied, looking down at him with a smile. "Where'd you disappear to? I thought we had dinner plans." She placed both hands on his shoulders and raised a brow. "Is your gloomy puss a result of the 'fucking bitch' you just hung up with?"

"How astute of you." He circled her waist with an arm and pulled her onto his lap. "The bitch I was talking to is the lunatic I married. God, I can't stand her. I've tried to figure a way out of this nightmare marriage for years. The only reason I haven't kicked her to the curb is her big, fat bank account." He nuzzled Julia's neck. "I wish…"

Julia stroked his head. "You wish what?"

He lifted his head and searched her face. "I wish she were you, Jules."

She kissed his forehead. "Don't worry, lover; we'll figure out what to do."

Spencer kissed her hand. "I already have an idea—a good one, too. I've started by putting some key pieces in motion, but I'll need your help to implement my plan."

She nodded. "And you can tell me all about it over dinner, my love. I'm famished."

Spencer's hand traveled from her waist to her ass. "I was thinking," he growled, "of appetizers first."

Julia giggled. "You're a dog, Spencer Boyd! We had 'appetizers' before lunch!"

He leered at her. "And I plan to have them several more times before the day is through." Setting her on her feet, he stood. "Come on, gorgeous. Let's go to my room, and you can rock my world."

"And then will you feed me?"

"Yes, ma'am. And over dinner, we can discuss creating the perfect plan to eliminate Isabella Boyd from our lives, once and for all."

# CHAPTER THIRTEEN
## *ABIGAIL*

*Rosemear*
*July 1st, 1859*

Abigail stood outside the barn and called through the doors to the man tossing hay bales into the loft.

"Vincent? Can you stop a spell and come here, please?"

Vincent wiped his neck with a stained kerchief and tipped his straw hat back. "Yes'm, Miss Abigail. Be there in two shakes."

He hefted the last hay bale, pitching it effortlessly into the barn loft, before removing his hat and hurrying outside. "You needed something, Miss Abby?"

Abigail smiled at him with genuine affection. Vincent Brown was among the first to comfort her when she'd arrived at Rosemear, devastated after being ripped away from Prophet, terrified by what awaited her in her new home. Vincent had taken her under his wing, teaching her how to stay out of the way of the big boss.

And, until recently, she'd done just that.

She studied Vincent's scarred, calloused hands and weathered face. He was somewhere in his late sixties, though no one—not even Vincent himself—knew his age with certainty. Abandoned as a child, he, nonetheless, grew up to be a courteous, sweet, and tireless worker who kept up with most of the younger men working on the plantation.

Abigail gave a quick nod. "Just needing to ask you a few questions, Vincent Brown. I find myself helping Mr. Edward solve a mystery."

Vincent twisted his hat in his hands before brushing a droplet of sweat away from his forehead. The temperature was already nearing triple digits, and it was only noon. "Ma'am?"

She cleared her throat. "Um, yes, well, Mr. Edward and I was wonderin'," she stopped and corrected herself, "I mean, we *were* wondering if you recalled the days before Mr. Edward's momma died? His actual momma, I'm speakin' of."

Attempting to pull the memories of several years ago to the forefront, Vincent rubbed a hand over his mouth. "Ms. Sarah, you mean? No, I don't suppose I do recall that, Miss Abby. But I surely do remember the day she was called home. I'd gone to town to fetch Doc Coolidge, but the poor woman had already passed by the time we got back. Can't say as I recollect the days before she died. If'n she was sick, well, that ain't somethin' the Hawthornes would likely tell us workers."

Abigail's shoulders slumped. "No, I guess not. I appreciate the help, though, Vincent." She turned to walk back to the house.

"Um, Ms. Abigail? You might check with Abraham. James, too. Could be they seen something amiss as they done more work inside Rosemear's walls than the rest of us."

"Thank you, Vincent," she said, turning back to him. "I believe I'll do just that. Can I ask you something else?"

"Ma'am?"

"When you saw Mrs. Hawthorne for the last time before you went to get Doc Coolidge, did anything seem odd to you?"

"The whole affair seemed odd, Miss. I recall being especially taken aback by how she looked. Ms. Sarah were always a striking woman, but when she got the sickness…" He stopped, searching for the right words.

"When she got sick, what?"

He looked away, uncomfortable. "Now, understand, it's bad business to speak ill of the dead, and that ain't my intention. But Ms. Sarah's hands and feet had somethin' fierce growing on 'em, and a couple of them sores lay open, festering on her limbs, too. Ain't never seen the likes in all my years, truth be told. She were all kinds of yellow, too. Even her eyes."

"Must have been terrible for her," Abigail said, digesting the information. "One last thing, Vincent—would you know where I can find Abraham or James?"

He nodded. "They was going to the fields to check on the crops. We heard tell of a nasty mold growing on some tobacco plants over in Effingham County." He searched her eyes for a moment. "Now, I know I ain't your keeper, Miss Abigail, but you be careful. These old bones sense a change 'round here. Sure as I stand here, the winds have shifted, bringin' evil on they backs."

"Oh, Vincent, I don't believe in such things," she said, patting his hand. "Evil needs a portal to enter the body, and all the doors leading to my soul are shut tight. But I thank you for the warning and the help."

Vincent nodded slowly. "That be all, then, Miss?"

"Yes. Go on back to your chores, and I'll attend to mine. Mr. Baldwin is nearby, and we don't want him finding us dilly-dally-ing, do we?"

Vincent donned his hat, nodded, and walked back to the barn. Abigail watched him leave while chewing a thumbnail, his words swirling around in her mind.

*The winds have shifted, bringing evil on their backs.*

She'd felt it, too.

The air at Rosemear was thicker, the atmosphere charged

with an unseen force. She'd found herself on edge, jumpy, waiting for something huge to sweep in, change her life, devour her whole.

It was an unrest, an apprehension, that had arrived without cause. Something was coming.

She only prayed that, whatever it was, she was strong enough to handle it.

Abigail stood at the edge of the tobacco field, shielding her eyes from the sun's glare. "James? Abraham? You boys out here?"

A rustling sound to her left momentarily startled her. Yelping, she clutched her chest.

"Didn't mean to startle you, Miss," Abraham said, emerging from between two large tobacco plants. "Hard to make a ruckus between these soft tobacco leaves."

Abigail patted her chest, trying to calm her racing heart. "No, no, it's fine, Abraham," she said, taking a deep breath before dropping her hand. "Is James with you?"

"I'm here, Miss," James said from behind Abraham.

"Good. I wanted to ask you both about the former mistress of Rosemear. Mr. Edward is tryin' to make peace with his mother's dyin' and such. You remember Mrs. Sarah Hawthorne, don't you?"

Both men nodded in tandem. "Surely we do," James said with a slight wheeze. He was a middle-aged man with a quick smile, a muscular physique, and scarred lungs from an ugly bout of tuberculosis as a child. "Ms. Sarah was a fine woman. Handsome and kind, too. She never took to no name-calling or beatin' workers like…" He trailed off.

Abigail smiled softly. "Like who? Please, James, you can speak freely."

He glanced nervously at Abraham. "It's just we don't be wantin' any trouble, Miss. Speaking ill of the boss's missus could cause us all manner of troubles."

"I swear he'll never hear of it," Abigail promised. "So, you were saying?"

James stepped closer. Lowering his voice to a whisper, he said, "Ms. Sarah was the kinder of the two, is what I mean. Ms. Lillian don't seem to like us much. Why, once I saw her order a man beaten for just lookin' her way. He didn't mean no disrespect, mind you. Just curious."

Abraham joined the discussion. "It's true, Miss Abigail. That one got a fierce temper."

"And she pokes around in sorcery or some such nonsense," James added. "Even had a witch come here after Master Martin died."

Abigail frowned. "A witch? For what?"

James shrugged. "Dunno for sure. Heard tell it was somethin' to do with protecting the house from evil. Ms. Lillian believe her young'uns died 'cause Rosemear is cursed."

Abraham bobbed his head. "That right. Why, one day, she had us diggin' up bones from the back graveyard just to bring 'em inside."

Abigail gasped. "What? Why on earth would she do that?"

"It was that witch that told her. To protect her kin, I imagine," Abraham responded. He looked sheepishly at James. "We didn't wanna do it, but when the missus gives you a task…" He shrugged. "Terrible thing digging up the dusty old bones of folks passed. Most of them we dug up died from the fever of '54. Ain't rightly sure what Ms. Lillian and that witch did with them, but if you ask me, it ain't proper. Dead need to be left alone, I say."

"I agree," Abigail said. "Tell me, did Ms. Sarah think the same? About Rosemear being cursed, I mean? Is that where Ms. Lillian got the notion?"

James shook his head. "No, ma'am. Ms. Sarah didn't cotton to such foolishness."

Abigail chewed her lip. "And when Ms. Sarah got sick… Do

you recall how long she was ill, or how it started?"

James and Abraham cast wary glances at each other. After a moment, James finally spoke. "Me and Abraham don't need no whuppin', but, if'n you sure what I say don't get back to Mr. William…"

Abigail nodded. "I promise."

Resigned, James said, "Ms. Sarah were a healthy woman before Ms. Lillian came to Rosemear. Hardly recollect a day she weren't out walking the grounds or tendin' to her herbal garden. Then, soon after Ms. Lillian came to Rosemear to look after the young'uns, Ms. Sarah got awful sick."

"For sure," Abraham said, taking over the story. "Real sickly. I recall one time she came to the barn, just skin an' bones, huffin' and puffin' like one of them steam locomotives. She told me her hair was fallin' out, just comin' out clump-like, all of a sudden. I expect she were hoping one of the womenfolk would have a salve or a cure for her. No one did, though. Not a one."

"Doesn't sound much like the fever," Abigail said, eyes hard. "Sounds more like someone poisoned Ms. Sarah."

"Yes, ma'am," Abraham said with a frown. "Same thought we had, though I don't know why. Ms. Sarah never hurt nobody."

Abigail rubbed her arms, suddenly chilled. "Thank you, gentlemen. We best get back to work."

She turned to leave, and James grabbed her forearm. "We…we got your word, Miss Abigail? None of this business getting back to Mr. William?"

Abigail nodded. "No one will ever know how you feel about Ms. Lillian or that you suspect her of poisoning Sarah Hawthorne. I swear to you… I will take it to my grave."

"Hello, love," Edward whispered, aware others were nearby.

Abigail stood at the slop sink in the scullery, wringing out the stockings she'd just washed. Turning, she wiped her hands on her apron and smiled. "Hello, Mr. Edward. How is your day going?"

"Better since I've seen you." Discreetly, he checked his surroundings. "Of course," he mumbled near her ear, "it would be even better if you were in my arms right now."

Abigail bent her head demurely. "That sounds lovely, but…" She gestured toward the other two women in the room. One, a domestic servant named Tessa, was sorting clothing for the laundry, while Gertie, a cook, was washing pots. "I, um, I learned some information that may be useful to you. Perhaps when I'm done here?"

Edward winked. "You know where to find me." He dipped his head closer to hers. "I'll wait for you by our spot near the oak tree. Fifteen minutes?"

She nodded, her heart light. "Yessir, Mr. Edward. See you then."

Fifteen minutes later, as daylight edged toward dusk, Abigail and Edward huddled beneath the old oak tree, discussing everything she'd learned about Sarah Hawthorne's bizarre symptoms and her ultimate death.

Twenty minutes after relaying the information from Virgil and Abraham, Abigail returned to the main house to help prepare the evening meal, a spring in her step, oblivious to the cruel fate that awaited her.

And unaware that she would never, ever return to that majestic tree again.

# CHAPTER FOURTEEN

Isabella passed the stoneware dinner bowl across the table to Nathan.

"Please, Nate—mangia! My husband will be home the day after tomorrow and will not love having these leftovers in the fridge!"

Nate grabbed the bowl and chuckled. "I know you said he doesn't like meatballs, but…"

Luna chimed in. "Oh, trust us, Nate. Spencer looks for reasons to melt down."

Isabella gave Luna a warning glance, dipping her head toward the kids. "But everyone has a food group they hate, right?"

Sam, a strand of spaghetti stuck to his chin, bobbed his head. "Yeah, I hate broccoli. Yuck!"

Isabella found Sam's eyes before discreetly tapping her chin. The last thing she wanted was to embarrass him in front of his newly found friend.

Sam wiped his mouth with a napkin. "How about you, Matty?"

he asked between mouthfuls of noodles. "What food do you hate?"

Matty expertly twirled some pasta around his fork. "I guess peas?" He shrugged. "I don't know—I'm not too picky about food. I'll try anything once."

Nate laughed. "And there's nothing wrong with that, my man. Life is full of choices, and being open to trying different things leads to a sweeter life."

"True," Isabella agreed. "How about you, Bug? What is your least favorite food?"

Ellie thought for a moment. "Black pudding."

Fork halfway to her mouth, Isabella chuckled. "Black pudding? Ellie, you've never had that in your life! I'm not even sure what's in that dish."

"Blood, Momma. They use pig blood and fat and everything gross."

"She's right, you know," Nate said. "Black pudding, aka blood pudding, is fairly popular in Ireland. My great-grandmother used to make it for my mom. She hated it, too."

Isabella frowned. "How do you know you wouldn't like it, Bug? I mean, if you've never even tasted it?"

Ellie, head down, remained quiet.

"Come on, munchkin," Luna nudged Ellie's arm. "Why do you think you wouldn't like it?"

"Promise not to get mad?"

"Not in a billion, gazillion years," Luna said.

Ellie's lower lip trembled. "It's just that I'm sure I won't like it because my best friend says it tastes like fro-up."

Isabella swallowed hard, as if trying to push a sinewy piece of meat down her throat. "Your best…" she rasped, "your best friend? But you haven't made any friends yet, Bug. Do you mean your new friend, Martin?"

Ellie nodded.

"Who's Martin?" Nate asked.

Isabella shook her head imperceptibly. "Later," she mouthed to him.

"Hey," Luna said a bit too loudly. "I spotted some ice cream sammies in the freezer. Why don't you guys grab a few and hunt for lightning bugs while we clean up these dishes?"

Sam jumped to his feet. "Yeah! I have a glass jar in the garage we can use to catch them!" He raced to the kitchen, grabbed three ice cream bars, and the trio headed toward the front door.

Sam stopped suddenly. "Mr. Decker, can we bring Midge with us?"

Nathan peeked under the table. Midget looked bored to tears, her immense head resting on her paws. "Sure. Just keep an eye out for her, okay? She thinks she's a daring explorer but doesn't have the stamina or smarts to get anywhere but lost. I don't have the heart to tell her."

Luna glanced at Midge. "You know," she teased, "I think she can hear you. She looks sad."

"You give her too much credit," Nate joked back. "She's sad because I won't give her a meatball."

"We'll watch her! Promise!" Sam said excitedly. He slapped a hand to his thigh. "Come on, girl! Let's go outside!"

Midget jumped up, knocking her massive body into a leg of the dining room table, and, tail wagging, trotted over to Sam.

"Sorry about that," Nate said, steadying a teetering bottle of wine. "She moves like a bull but thinks she's a swan."

"My last boyfriend was like that," Luna joked. "Most uncoordinated, ungraceful human I've ever met, but, boy, could he cook!"

Nate chuckled.

Rising, Isabella called after Samuel. "You're in charge, Sammy boy. Keep everyone in the yard, okay?"

"Will do, Ma!"

She watched as they tore through the plantation doors, then

turned back to Luna and Nathan, still seated at the table. "Shit!" she said, frustrated. "So, Martin—the kid only Ellie can see— doesn't like black pudding. What the hell do I do with this, Luna?"

Nate raised his hand as if he were a student in a classroom. "Um, excuse me, but…who is Martin again?"

Isabella sat heavily in her chair. "We aren't sure yet. Either Martin is her recently created imaginary friend or…" She stopped.

"Or?" he asked, taking a sip of wine.

"Or he's a fecking ghost!" Luna said, unable to mask her excitement.

Nathan coughed into his napkin, choking on surprise and Pinot Noir. "A ghost? Wow! So, you've, uh, you've seen them too?"

Dumbfounded, Isabella stammered, "T-too? You're saying you've seen ghosts here?"

"Breathe," Luna soothed, grabbing Isabella's empty wine glass and pouring her another. "Here—drink and be merry."

"Sounds like I might need it. Maybe just leave the bottle."

Luna winked and topped off her own glass.

"You sure you want to hear all the gory details?" Nate asked, laying his napkin on his plate. "After all, I get to sleep at Marnie's tonight, but you guys have to sleep here. Maybe this is an 'ignorance is bliss' type of situation."

Isabella shook her head. "Tempting, but no. I have to find out what I'm dealing with. I can't fix whatever it is if I don't understand it."

"Uh,' Luna said, eyes wide. "What if…have you considered that it could be something other than Ellie's mental health or the supernatural, Bella? That there might be a third option?"

"Like what?"

Whispering, Luna said, "Like someone is living here, hiding here, without your knowledge! I've read about cases where intruders break in and secretly live in another person's house. It's called phrogging, and it's creepy as fuck."

Isabella gasped. "Jaysus, Luna! Do you want me to never sleep again?"

"Of course not! I'm just saying it might be a good idea to search this joint from top to bottom." She smirked. "In the daylight. With Officer Decker and his big, fat gun."

Nate laughed heartily. "I can look around tonight if it will make you both more at ease."

Isabella shook her head. "No, we'll all do it tomorrow. Demo day, right? For now, I'm dying to hear about your spooky experiences, Nate."

He drained his glass, then thanked Luna when she refilled it. "It happened back in high school. Remember when I told you my friends and I would come here to party? It was late October, only four days before Halloween. We were out here—doing stuff we weren't supposed to be doing—when we spotted the shadowy figure of a man in one of the upstairs windows. I swear that I was sober as a judge, too."

"You're joking," Isabella said.

"About the ghost or being sober?"

Isabella smiled. "Maybe both."

He smirked, holding up three fingers. "Scout's honor… Someone, or something, was standing at that window. We'd been running around the place, roughhousing and being obnoxious. One of the guys, goofing around, pushed me. I lost my balance and ended up flat on my ass, counting the stars in the sky. That's why I was looking up in the first place."

"And you saw a man?" Luna asked. "Short or tall? Ugly or cute?"

Isabella frowned at her.

"What? I'm single. So sue me."

"But they're dead, my nutty friend."

Luna snorted. "Oh, come on! Half of the men I've dated were iffy in the pulse department."

Nate smiled and shook his head. "Well, tall, for sure. Older,

I think. As for the rest, I can't say—he was kind of see-through."

"Yikes!" Isabella gasped.

"I know. It scared the crap out of my sixteen-year-old self. It was so bizarre, being able to see the intricate molding on the ceiling as I looked through the window. And—boy, this sounds wild to say out loud—I saw that molding *through* him, not around him."

Luna grimaced. "Well, you don't hear that every day!" She took a swig directly from the wine bottle, wiped the back of her hand across her lips, and stood. "Shit, we're for real gonna need another bottle of Pinot."

Isabella tilted her head, perplexed. "Wait a damned minute, Luna Lake. Aren't you the same best friend who believes in all things supernatural? I mean, you're into crystals, tarot cards, even palm reading, and seances. How is it this surprises you?"

Luna strolled to the cabinet in the corner of the dining room and took out another bottle of wine. Returning to the table, she said, "I'm more shocked than surprised. I've been looking for proof of the paranormal for years. Blind faith only takes you so far." She opened the bottle and poured herself a generous drink. "But if we could capture real evidence of life after death? Man, that would be amazing!" Rolling the stem of the glass between her fingers, she grew serious. "I've witnessed hundreds of deaths in my career. Some people just…go. No fanfare, no cloud-like mist shooting toward the heavens. But others? Others seem to interact with something or someone right before they pass. They'll point or whisper at a corner of the room and, suddenly lucid, claim that one relative or another has come to take them home."

Isabella nodded. "I've heard of that. It's like they rally and interact with family right before they die. I've always thought about how comforting that must be to those left behind. Not everyone gets the opportunity to say a last goodbye."

"Very true," Luna said. "I did a six-month stint working in hospice one year. I'll tell you—hats off to those nursing angels who work in that field."

"I remember that," Isabella said. "That rotation wrecked you for a while."

"It did. Anyway, I spent countless hours with people waiting for death's door to open. But during that time, I never felt a cold chill or heard a 'whoosh' as life left the body and the soul traveled to," she shrugged, "wherever. Still, I'm certain something is out there waiting for us, and I'd love to validate that belief."

"Is that why you're into the paranormal?" Nate asked.

"Yep. That and my baby brother. Knowing Martin was up there, happy and pain-free, would provide so much solace."

"So, Ellie's friend Martin is your brother?"

"No. Martin is…" Luna stopped and looked at Isabella.

"Much younger," Isabella said. "Luna's brother died of leukemia when he was twelve years old. Ellie's 'Martin' seems to be about four or five."

Nate rubbed his chin. "Hmm. Well, it sounds like we do a little snooping into Rosemear's background to find answers about Ellie's new friend."

"Agreed," Luna said. "And I have someone I would love to bring out here to do a walk-through."

"A walk-through?" Isabella asked, skeptical. "As in a psychic or something?"

Luna nodded. "Or something. Her name is Roma Lee, and she's quite gifted."

Isabella frowned. "I don't know, Lune. I'd still like to find a non-spooky reason for all of this. I say we gather the history of this place—previous owners, extended family members, deaths on the property—before we bring in a ghost whisperer, okay?"

"All right, but I would like to call her and give her the heads-up that we may be reaching out. Roma is so good that she's usually booked several months in advance."

"No problem."

Nathan stood. "Well, I hate to cut the evening short, but I have an early shift in the morning." He gave them a devilish smile. "Because crime waits for no man, even if that man is enjoying his current company immensely."

"Oh, of course." Isabella rose, somewhat flustered. "We didn't mean to keep you so late."

"Nonsense. You'd have to kick me out if I didn't have work tomorrow. Now, how about I wash and you ladies dry?"

Luna's eyes widened in mock surprise. "Shut the front door! A man who is not only cute but does the dishes? Be still, my beating heart!"

Isabella clucked her tongue. "A rare find, indeed. Luna and I will take care of the dishes, though. I'll be working you hard enough when we start tearing down walls!"

Nate snapped his fingers. "Oh, yeah—about that. I can be here around three, provided I don't encounter murder and mayhem during my shift. Why don't you text me a wish list of any supplies we'll need, and I can pick it up on my way home from work. I think Gibbon's Hometown Center has most, if not all, of what we'll need."

Isabella clapped her hands. "Oh, that would be amazing! I met the owners, Sid and Claire, and they seem lovely. Happy to give them my business!"

"Okay, then. Until tomorrow, ladies."

"Come on, we'll walk you out. I have to get the kids into the tub anyway."

When they stepped outside, Nathan called out, "Matthew! Midge! Come on, guys, time to head home!"

Sam, Matty, and Ellie ran to the front steps with Midget trudging behind them. Sam held a glass jar full of lightning bugs under one arm. "Look, Mr. Nate!" he said, holding up the container, "look what we caught!"

Nate whistled. "Great job, Sam. I don't think I've ever seen so many in one jar!"

Isabella bent forward. "But you have to let them go soon, honey, or they'll die."

"I know, Ma. Just wanted to show you guys." He looked over his shoulder at Matty. "Um, Mom? Can Matthew sleep over tonight?"

"Sure, I'm fine with it," she said, glancing at Nate, "but it's really up to his mom and Mr. Decker."

Nate frowned. "I don't know, kiddos." His eyes found Matty's. "Your mom will be sleeping tomorrow morning after her shift, and I won't be back until the afternoon. Asking Mrs. Boyd to watch you all day is a big ask."

Sam, eyes pleading, looked at Isabella. "That's okay, right, Mom? We'll be super good, I promise!"

Isabella ruffled his hair. "Really," she said to Nate, "it's no problem. And Marnie can sleep without one eye open, wondering if Matty is okay. Besides, he'll be good company for the kids while Luna and I explore the house." Winking, she added, "You know… looking for phroggers."

Luna groaned. "You understand I'm standing here, right? Like, right here!"

Nate laughed. "Okay, then. Guess I better go get his toothbrush and jammies."

Isabella shook her head. "No, it's okay. I have dozens of T-shirts he can wear and too many extra toothbrushes to count."

"Okay, then," Nathan said. "Behave yourself, my brother. Mind Mrs. Boyd and Ms. Lake, and remember your manners. I'll be back mid-afternoon."

"Yes, sir," Matty said.

Ellie snuggled beside Isabella, hugging her leg as they watched Nathan and Midge walk down the driveway.

Isabella tilted Ellie's chin up and gazed into her eyes. "You okay, Bug? You look concerned or something."

Ellie's mouth turned down at the corners. "I was just thinking about the fireflies. They must feel sad, stuck in the jar like that, kind of like…" She stopped and rubbed her eyes.

"Like what, baby?"

Sniffing, she replied, "Like how the people in the wall feel. Trapped and scared with no way out."

Sneaking a worried glance at Luna, Isabella pulled Ellie closer. "Oh, El, honey," she said, "Aunt Luna and I are going to figure all this out, I promise. In the meantime, why don't you and the boys go out back and let those fireflies have their freedom, huh?"

"Okay, Momma."

"Sam? Matty? Take Ellie outside and let those lightning bugs go, okay? It's time for them to fly!"

With the jar firmly in both hands, Sam nodded and raced to the backyard, Matty and El close behind him.

"Jesus Christ," Luna whispered. "Trapped people in the wall? What the actual fuck is going on here?"

"I wish I knew, Luna. I wish I knew."

Hours later, after the kitchen was clean and the kids asleep, Isabella and Luna sat in the gazebo out back, stargazing and making plans.

"Okay, so, first things first," Luna said. "I think tomorrow we need to start researching the history here. I suggest we scour the internet for any mention of Rosemear, its tragedies, or the previous owners. Oh, and I'll call Roma and see about her availability."

"Great," Isabella said. "I also think a trip to the public library is in order. We can look through old newspaper articles, property and land deeds, and obituaries that mention this house." She groaned and rubbed her temples.

Luna noticed. "Hey, you okay? You want an ibuprofen or

something?"

Isabella shook her head. "Already took one. It's so strange. I've been consistent with my meds, yet over the last few months, I've had this constant throbbing in my head and I've felt like I did when Anna died."

"How's that?" Luna prodded gently.

"I don't know… Scattered? And although I feel clearer than last week, it still seems difficult to focus. On top of that, these headaches come almost daily, and I'm not sleeping very well lately."

Luna cleared her throat. "But you're, uh, on point with your anti-anxiety meds, right?"

Isabella nodded. "I am, but maybe I need something else, something stronger. Nothing seems to be working like it has in the past." She smiled. "Except for you. You have a wonderful, calming influence on me when you're here, Luna Lake."

"I'm glad," Luna said, humbled. "So, have you found a doctor here yet? Your symptoms may resolve just by tweaking the dosage. If that doesn't work, we can revisit your prescriptions. There are tons of effective treatments out there, many without nasty side effects. It's not like it was twenty or thirty years ago."

"I know, and finding a new doctor here is at the top of my list. But my point is that it's been three years since Anna died, and I'm still walking that same tightrope of paranoia, afraid to breathe and constantly looking over my shoulder." Isabella picked at a fingernail. "It's like I'm biding my time, waiting for a strong gale to blow through my life and knock me off that tightrope, sending me into the deepest hole yet."

Luna nudged her shoulder into Isabella's. "There isn't a hole in the world so deep that we can't climb out of it. Together."

"Kind of cheesy, but I love you for it."

"Hey, I love cheese!"

Isabella tipped her head back and closed her eyes. "I can't tell you how frightening this is for me. Since moving in, I've felt like someone is watching me. Not only that, but I've heard phantom voices and snippets of conversations all through the house."

Luna kept her tone neutral despite the alarm bells ringing in her head. "Um, do these…do these voices speak to you?"

Isabella chuckled. "Not yet."

Luna whooped. "Thank you, Jesus! Man, I was worried for a minute there!"

Isabella sneered. "You're not out of the woods yet. It could be they're talking to me, but the volume is too low to understand what's being said. And I swore I heard a baby crying upstairs last week, so I tore through the second floor, searching for the source. The cries sounded feminine, like a little girl." Her voice cracked. "Like Anna Rae."

Luna patted her hand. "Oh, Izzy-B, I'm sorry. That must have been painful."

"Painful," Isabella agreed, "and scary as hell. What if everything happening here is a figment of my imagination? What if all I've experienced is not the result of an old house settling or even the terrifying prospect that Rosemear is haunted?"

"What are you saying?" Luna asked, frowning.

"I'm saying, what if it's me? What if the voices I hear, the creaks and groans and phantom wails, are a result of delusions conjured within the walls of an ill mind? A mind still mourning? And what if Ellie is picking up on my level of crazy and, I don't know, creating monsters where they don't exist?"

Luna placed her head on Isabella's shoulder. "I don't believe that, Bella."

"I pray you're right. I hope my symptoms—the hallucinations, the lost time, the panic attacks—I suffered before aren't coming back. I don't think I could bear it again."

"Let's not jump—" Luna stopped suddenly, lifting her head from Isabella's shoulder. Eyes squinting toward the house, she asked, "What the hell is that?"

"What?"

"That," Luna said, pointing to an upstairs window. "See? It looks like someone is standing beside the curtains on the sliding doors upstairs."

Isabella flicked her eyes to the second floor and stiffened. "Too tall for one of the kids. Could it be a shadow from the chandelier?"

Luna stood and stretched out her hand. Hoisting Isabella to her feet, she said, "Let's go find out, shall we?"

"Okay, but I warn you…if we find Casper up there, we'll both wish I *was* delusional!"

# CHAPTER FIFTEEN

Hearts pounding in tandem, hand in hand, Isabella and Luna crept wordlessly up the staircase. Halfway up, Luna released Isabella's hand, leaned against the wall, and wiped a sweaty palm on her jeans.

"Jesus," she whispered. "Hold up. What's the plan if we find something, human or not?"

Isabella winced, whispering back. "Plan? Damn, I don't know. I thought you knew."

Despite her fear, Luna nearly laughed out loud. "Me? Girl, my only plan right now," she said, voice still hushed, "is to avoid shitting my pants!"

Isabella stifled a giggle. "Okay, well, clench those cheeks, and let's keep moving. Chances are it's just a trick of the light we saw. Unless…"

"Unless what?"

"Unless that phrogger of yours has come out of hiding."

"You understand that none of what you're saying is making me feel better, right?"

Isabella smirked, and they continued climbing, eyes sweeping the top of the staircase.

Nothing was there.

"Okay, then," Isabella said, relieved. "I suppose it was just shadows. But since we're here, let's peek in on the kids."

"Right behind ya."

After ensuring the children were safely in bed, Isabella and Luna stood outside Sam's door, debating what to do next.

"Well, if it's up to me," Luna said, "I vote we go downstairs and devour a few pints of maple walnut."

Isabella smiled. "Now, that's a plan I can get behind. But first, come with me down the west wing. I want to check that locked room again and get your feeling for that side of the manor."

Luna pouted. "Now?" she asked, peering down the shadowed corridor ahead of her. "It's darker than a witch's a-hole down there."

"Seen a lot of those, have ya?"

"A lot of what?" Luna said absently, still eyeing the darkened hallway.

"Witches' a-holes."

"Seen my fair share."

"I'm sorry," Isabella joked.

"Don't be. It brings perspective to my profession."

"Perspective? Are we still talking about assholes here?"

Luna wiped a drop of sweat from her brow. "Yep, mad respect for 'em. Without them, we'd all be full of shit."

Isabella chuckled. "Interesting take. Look, I know it's dark over there, but we have lights. Besides, aren't you the one who always says nothing exists in the dark of night that isn't present in the light of day?"

"Do I? Well, I sound like an insufferable blowhard. Why the

hell do you tolerate me, anyway?"

Isabella chuckled, took Luna's hand, and tipped her head toward the west wing. "Come on, let's see if that door opens. Promise I'll be in and out."

"That's what he said."

Groaning, Isabella pulled Luna down the hallway. She flipped a wall switch near the hall entrance, bathing the space in soft light.

Luna tensed and sucked in a breath.

"It feels bad, right?" Isabella asked.

"Bad? Oh, honey, this is creepy as fuck! I keep expecting to see twin girls with blank faces waiting at the end of the corridor."

Isabella nodded. "It does feel a bit Stephen King-ish. The architect of Rosemear designed everything to be symmetrical. When I first laid eyes on this side of the house, my knee-jerk reaction was that it wasn't really there. It felt like looking at a mirror image of the east side of the house. Like," she struggled to find the right words, "like a vision without substance."

Luna let go of Isabella's hand and crept forward. "Like a mirage."

"Yes, exactly like that."

Luna clucked her tongue. "What are your plans for this side of the house? I mean, Sam and Ellie's bedrooms, plus the extra master, are on the other side. It looks like," she silently counted, "four rooms on this wing?"

"Three bedrooms, a spacious hall closet, and a Jack and Jill bathroom. I want to make the largest bedroom my art studio. The lighting in there is phenomenal. The remaining rooms could be a second guest room and a study or office. I thought I could get a daybed for the office to provide an extra sleeping area if more than a few guests stay over. That would give us two private guest rooms on the second floor—the one here and the blue room on the other side—plus the daybed in the office and the guest room you're staying in downstairs."

"Guest room? Um, no. It's Auntie Luna's room," Luna teased.

"I stand corrected." Isabella stuck out her tongue playfully. "So, *two* guest rooms and a sleeper sofa in the office. Not that I expect many overnight guests besides you and my brother."

Luna waggled her brows. "Danny! How is that gorgeous brother of yours, anyway? I keep waiting for him to wake up one day, discover he's madly in love with me, and sweep me off my feet."

Isabella winked. "Still got the hots for him, huh? Understandable. After all, it's only been about twenty years."

Luna nudged Isabella's arm. "That's enough out of you, Boyd. Come on, let's check that locked room and get the flock outta here. An obnoxiously big bowl of ice cream is calling my name."

Together, they walked to the last door on the right. Isabella reached for the doorknob, then stopped suddenly. "You want to hear something weird?"

Luna rolled her eyes. "You mean aside from the myriad of weirdness we've already experienced in this house? Sure, shoot."

"It's just that, during the walk-through with the realtor, I don't remember seeing this room or the blue one on the east side. But we *had* to see them, right? We'd never buy a home that we hadn't fully inspected. So, why can't I remember?"

Luna frowned. "Not sure, but you've had a lot on your plate, toots—all the crap with Spencer, Anna's death, planning this move. Maybe your mind was elsewhere during the tour."

Isabella shrugged. "Perhaps, but we also had the final walk-through a few weeks after the initial tour. Surely, my mind wasn't so preoccupied both times."

"What are you saying?"

"Just wondering," Isabella said, rubbing her brow, "or worrying, to be more precise. What if I'm missing blocks of time again?"

"And what if I'm the bloody Queen of England?" Luna said. "Look, worrying doesn't fix tomorrow's troubles, sweet-cheeks. It only ruins today's peace."

"Wow, profound. Dalai Lama?"

"Nah, I think it's Mr. Rogers," Luna deadpanned. "Or maybe Pinterest. Now, can you quit it with the looney bin talk while I check this door?" She reached out and jiggled the doorknob. "Still locked. Got the key?"

"Nope."

"Super."

"Yeah. I'd hoped it would magically open, like the door to the blue room did. Oh, well. Guess we take it down tomorrow and check out the interior."

Luna smacked her lips. "Aces. We done here?"

"Yes, ma'am. First one to the—" Isabella's words were cut short by a series of thumps echoing through the locked door.

"What the…?" Luna whispered. "You heard that, right?"

Isabella, heart racing and throat dry as dust, could only manage a nod.

"Wind?"

"May-maybe," Isabella offered with a half-hearted smile. "It *is* pretty windy tonight. Or it could be a mouse."

"Uh, sure," Luna said, doubtful. "Not Minnie or Mickey, though. That shit sounded like the biggest fuckin' mouse in the world."

Isabella nodded, linking arms with Luna. "Let's get to that ice cream."

They made it only a few feet before a crisp hiss, followed by a pop, plunged the house into total darkness.

"Oh, for fuck's sake!" Luna groaned. "You have your cell phone?"

"Nope, I left it on the dining room table. You?"

"Nope."

"All right. Well, the stairs are straight ahead and to the right," Isabella said. "The fuse box must be somewhere downstairs."

They inched toward the staircase, backs against the wall, feeling for solid ground with the tips of their toes. When they arrived at the top of the landing, a piercing scream ripped through the entire floor, turning their blood to ice.

"Eleanor!" Isabella gasped, sprinting blindly down the hall, Luna right behind her. They reached Sam's bedroom door and threw it open. Inside, the glow from a battery-operated Batman clock offered a scant amount of light.

"Mom!"

"I'm here, baby!" Isabella shouted, running to Ellie's cot in the corner of the room.

Sam, on the top bunk, was leaning over the safety railing, clearly confused.

Beneath him, snoring softly on the bottom bed, Matthew slept on.

"Bug, what is it?" Isabella said, reaching the bed and cradling Ellie in her arms. "What's happened?"

Luna squatted next to the cot. "Bad dream, kiddo?"

Ellie's eyes filled with tears. "So bad. I dreamed I was falling, and then I couldn't breathe."

Luna looked at Isabella. "Maybe a night terror."

"You okay, El?" Sam asked, rubbing the sleep from his eyes.

Ellie, limbs trembling, stared at his shadowy form but said nothing.

"Oh, honey," Isabella soothed, pulling her child closer. "It was just a dream. Everyone has those 'falling' dreams from time to time." She patted Ellie's back. "You're fine, Bug."

Ellie shook her head. "But it was so real, Momma! I was falling, and then my head hit something, and it was *really* hard! And then I was in a box, under the ground, with no air to breathe!"

Isabella's heart skipped a beat. "Under the ground? Like, in a cave or something?"

Ellie burst into tears. "No, it wasn't a cave—it was a grave! And it was cold and dark, and I could smell the dirt and everything! I was buried so deep, and I screamed and screamed, 'I'm alive!' just like she did, but nobody came!" She sniffed, wiping her nose with the back of her hand. "No one came, Momma. Nobody saved her!"

Isabella's stomach lurched, and she thought she might vomit. "Saved who, sweetheart?"

"Abigail!" Ellie cried. "No one saved Abigail!"

"Abigail?" Isabella cast a worried glance at Luna. "Honey, where did you hear that name?"

Ellie stared straight ahead, eyes on the far wall, reliving the nightmare. "From Martin. He told me Abby moved here after he...." She trailed off.

Luna frowned at Isabella. "Maybe she overheard us talking?"

Isabella shook her head. "No, I don't think so." Standing, she held a hand out to Ellie. "Come on, Bug. How about you sleep with me in the big girls' bed? Auntie Luna will be in her own room tonight, and I can use the company."

"It's so dark, though," Ellie said, trembling.

"I know. I think we blew a fuse. Let me help you downstairs, and Luna will stay with you while I find the fuse box."

"Yeah," Luna said with a smile, "you can hang in my room until your mom gets the lights back on. You hear what I said? *My* room! Not another guest room, but Auntie Luna's very own room! Pretty cool, huh?" When Ellie failed to react, Luna added, "Don't worry, Shortstack. I'll protect you."

Ellie got to her feet and slowly headed toward the bedroom door, dragging her blanket and a stuffed bear behind her. "Okay, but it still won't be safe," she mumbled, a tear sliding down her cheek. "They're coming soon, Aunt Luna, all of them. And they're not happy."

Early the following morning, while the kids slept, Isabella and Luna discussed their plans for the day over coffee and homemade cheesecake.

"You know," Isabella said with her mouth full, "I could eat this every day for the rest of my life and never tire of it. What's your secret?"

"Extra cream cheese, a water bath, and the souls of the damned," Luna said with a wink.

"And here I thought you would say something corny like your secret ingredient was love."

"Love? Yeah, nope. It's definitely souls and, on occasion, Bailey's Irish Cream."

Isabella chuckled. "Well, it works. So, I was thinking—maybe after this, you could take a ride to the library and town hall to do a little research on Rosemear? They'll be closed tomorrow and Sunday, and I'd like some info to chew on over the weekend. No sense dragging three kids all over town." She took a sip of coffee. "Or, if you'd rather, I can do the research, and you can mind the rugrats?"

"Sweet Jesus!" Luna gasped. "Not that I don't love your kids, but…." She faked a shiver. "There's a reason I'm childless."

Isabella smirked. "You're childless because you're still waiting for Mr. Right."

"Who probably doesn't exist," Luna said dryly. "Okay, you stay here, and I'll go poke around. When I get back, we can start ripping up floors and taking down walls." Steam rose from her coffee cup, and she blew on it before taking a sip. "What do you think Ellie meant last night? Who is coming?"

"Damned if I know. I assume it was part of her nightmare. She was pretty shaken up."

"Part of a nightmare?" Luna said, raising her brows in mock horror, "Look, as your BFF, I wanted to spare you the truth, but in the interest of saving your ass someday, I'll give it to you straight."

"Uh-oh."

"Uh-oh is right. If this were a horror movie, you'd be the first to die. You'd be the dope hiding in the shed with the power tools—"

"Oh, come on," Isabella interrupted. "I'm not that bad!"

Ignoring her, Luna continued. "Or the one who runs into a remote cornfield to escape a machete-wielding maniac wearing the skin of his last victim."

"Ouch," Isabella teased, miming a dagger to the heart.

"I'm serious, Iz. Something possibly dangerous, definitely spooky, is happening in this house. 'They're coming'? Dang, when Ellie said that, my stomach dropped, and my heart just about stopped. And a woman named Abigail being buried alive? How in the fuckety fuck did El know that name?" She scrubbed her hands over her face and side-eyed Isabella. "How are you so calm, anyway? Jesus, that child seems to know shit she shouldn't know and talks about stuff no kid her age ever would—stuff she didn't talk about before ya'll moved in. I don't know about you, but I think we need to get Roma here sooner rather than later."

Isabella was quiet for a moment, staring into her coffee mug. "No, you're right, of course. Things have gotten more intense in the last week, but as far as Ellie knowing about Abigail Charles? Maybe she did hear the realtor talking about it. We were so focused on the tour that I honestly can't recall where the kids were when Suzanne brought it up. Regardless, you have a valid point, so see what you can set up with your ghost-whispering friend. You head out tomorrow, right?"

Luna nodded. "Right. I leave in the morning, then work Sunday through Wednesday, pretty much non-stop. But afterward, I get a nice five- or six-day break and can return to help with the renovations."

"Perfect. Spencer comes home tomorrow afternoon but leaves for Charleston again on Wednesday or Thursday. You'll never even see each other." She carried her plate to the sink. "Could you get Roma Lee here while he's gone? I prefer not to deal with his mockery and snarky comments."

"And I'd prefer to put my boot up his ass, but as the song says, you can't always get what you want."

Isabella chuckled. "True story, Mick."

"Greatest band that ever lived! Anyway, I'll see if she can come a week from tomorrow," Luna said, bringing her dishes to the counter. "That way, Mr. Asshat will be gone, and I'll be back. In the meantime, let me get dressed and get moving. The sooner I get the research done, the sooner we can start the demo. I'll start at the tax office, then check the courthouse for property deeds. After that, if there's time, I'll hit the library for any news articles mentioning Rosemear. Sound good?"

"Better than good," Isabella said, giving Luna a squeeze. "Thanks so much for being here for me. You always are, though, aren't you?" She kissed her friend's cheek with a resounding smack. "I've no idea what I would do without you, Luna Lake! Don't you ever die on me!"

Luna raised a brow. "Um, sure, sure. In the interim, though, while I'm over here *not* dying, do me a favor and write down the address for the library."

Isabella put up a thumb. "You got it!"

"Oh, and don't forget to ask Nate about a security system," Luna said. "I think we'll all feel better with eyes on this place."

Thirty minutes later, Luna left the Savannah Public Library with a fistful of printouts and a healthy respect for librarians.

The librarian, Kristin Marx, was a pretty woman with a heart-shaped face and a brilliant smile. Her suggestion to check the Library of Congress for local history provided much information about Rosemear's checkered past. She also offered Luna the contact information for Harrison Rogers, a local historian for Savannah.

"Now, if y'all are so inclined," Kristin had said, "besides Harrison, there's an older gentleman in town who has traced his family back to the 1850s. His great-great-grandfather was enslaved on plantations in Georgia and South Carolina."

Luna frowned. "Okay, but I'm looking for history on the Rosemear plantation."

Kristin nodded. "I know, but this man, Atticus Jones, has information about the people of several different plantations, including yours. I warn you—he comes off as a bit irritable, but deep down, he's a sweetheart. I can even tell you where to find him."

Twenty minutes later, Luna was walking through Savannah's Historic District, heading toward Oglethorpe Square while searching for a card table facing the stately Owens-Thomas House.

She found it in under a minute.

Studying the elderly gentlemen sitting across from each other, a scarred metal table and a chessboard between them, Luna was struck by just how 'Norman Rockwell' the moment appeared to be.

On one side of the table, a Black man with a severe expression and a salt-and-pepper beard scowled at his opponent.

On the other side, a White man with rheumy eyes, a faded straw hat, and the bulbous nose of a heavy drinker scowled right back.

"Your move, Jones," she heard the White man say.

Tentatively, she approached both men, stopping a couple of feet away. Her eyes traveled over the table's surface, beyond the steaming cups of coffee and the steel chess clock, to the gleaming ivory and ebony chess pieces, before finally landing on her target.

"Excuse me, sir," Luna began, pinning her gaze on the man with the sad eyes, dark complexion, and denim shirt. "Are you Atticus Jones?"

"Last time I checked," the man said gruffly, never lifting his gaze from the chessboard.

"Great! You're just the man I wanted to see!"

Atticus slowly raised his head and stared blankly at her. "That so?"

"Yes, indeed it is. The town librarian, Kristen Marx, gave me your name. She thought perhaps you could help me."

Atticus stared, saying nothing.

"Yes, well, I'm searching for historical information regarding previous residents of an old plantation named Rosemear. I'm researching it for a friend."

The man snorted before looking across the table at his companion. "You hear this, Herbie? Lady wants information from me!" He took a noisy gulp of coffee. "Don't that beat all? Like I was the damned Google or something."

Herbie snickered. "Aw, hell, Jonesy, this is the most attention you've gotten from a lady in forty years. Why not listen to her?"

Atticus grunted. "Because I'm old, numbnuts. At my age, I gotta conserve my minutes. Can't be wasting the precious time I got left on foolishness." His eyes drilled into Luna's. "What do you say, Missy? What will you give me to answer your questions? Ain't nothing free in this world."

Luna narrowed her eyes. "Holding a person's feet over the coals while their heels are already smoking? That's savage, Mr. Jones." Smirking, she added, "But I like your style. How's this? You tell me what I need to know, and I'll tell you how to avoid hearing ol' Herbie here say 'checkmate' within the next three moves."

Herbie busted out laughing. "She's quick, Jonesy. And she ain't wrong, although I expect to have your ass in two moves."

Luna held back a smile.

Atticus stood. "Fine. Walk with me a minute, chess lady. You have until we reach the Colonial Park Cemetery and back to tell me exactly what you want and why I should help you. That'll be about," he checked his watch, "fifteen minutes, depending on whether my rheumatism acts up."

Luna smiled. "Fifteen minutes? Hell, I can do it in ten."

# CHAPTER
# SIXTEEN
## *ABIGAIL*

*Rosemear*
*August 10th, 1859*

For the last five weeks or so, ever since Abigail had divulged what she'd learned from Vincent, James, and Abraham about Sarah Hawthorne's illness, Edward had been pensive, withdrawn, and quiet.

Eerily quiet—and perpetually drunk.

In truth, Edward's alcohol use had increased almost two-fold, crossing the imaginary line between 'social drinker' and 'pour me a double and leave the bottle.'

All in the last month.

As for Abigail, she'd been walking a thin line of her own during those last few weeks of summer. Tensions were high as, according to Young Joseph, a large group of people from the North were determined to end slavery.

"Honest, Ms. Abigail," Joseph had told her, "they say these White folk, these abolitionists, want to help free us. They got a secret underground tunnel or some such to sneak people out, all quiet-like. A'course, the Hawthornes surely won't like that much."

His words, spoken weeks ago, still resonated; the excitement, the fear, and the hope were still palpable.

But Abigail Charles was nothing if not practical.

Life had taught her that the best way to manage the disappointment of failed expectations was not to have any expectations at all.

She believed wishes and hopes were for the gullible and the young. And now, in her eighteenth year, Abigail felt neither the naivety of the inexperienced nor the innocence of youth.

She just felt tired.

Pushing all of Young Joseph's theories about freedom aside, and with afternoon waning, Abigail rushed toward the barn to finish her chores. She was looking forward to seeing Edward that evening. It had been weeks since they'd been on a walk, had a meal together, or met secretly beneath 'their' oak tree. He'd been either busy with plantation work, impossibly drunk, or preoccupied with potential scenarios regarding his mother's death.

To his credit, Edward acknowledged he'd been an "inattentive" beau to Abigail and swore to do better, starting with dinner and a moonlit walk that evening.

She was thrilled.

Entering the barn, swinging an empty bucket in one hand, she hummed a happy tune and headed for the drum of chicken feed near the back wall. After caring for the chicks, she would complete her final job, one she detested—mucking out the horse stalls.

Halfway to the feed container, she stopped, trying to grasp the sight in front of her. Young Joseph, in a stained, yellowed shirt, face streaked with tears, was pinned against a wooden wall by a beefy forearm.

A forearm that pressed against Joseph's throat.

"Lord almighty!" Abigail gasped. "What is this now?"

The owner of the scarred, meaty arm turned from the frightened man trapped against the far wall and faced her.

"What it is ain't none of your concern, Missy!" Clyde Baldwin snapped, spittle erupting from his mouth. His lips were drawn back in a sneer; his eyes were glazed, manic.

Feral.

They were the eyes of a dangerous man.

"Me and the boy are just having a conversation," Clyde continued, turning back to Joseph. "Ain't that right, boy?"

Joseph, gulping for oxygen like a fish out of water, could not speak. Instead, he pulled at Clyde's forearm, trying to relieve the pressure on his windpipe.

Unsuccessful, his eyes met Abigail's in a silent plea for help.

Mind working frantically, legs shaking, Abigail walked closer to the duo. Not only did she need to get Young Joseph safely away from Clyde Baldwin, but she had to do it without becoming a target herself.

"Um, I do apologize for interrupting, Mr. Baldwin. Perhaps I can offer some assistance? Lord knows Young Joseph can be a bit hard-headed at times, but he generally minds me. If it pleases you, I can take him off your hands, maybe set him up to tend the horses."

Clyde, arm still pressed against Joseph's throat, spat on the ground. "You think I'm needing your help, Missy? You suggestin' I need the 'assistance' of a Negro woman to keep my men in line?"

Abigail swallowed her fear and tried to maintain a neutral expression, ignoring the droplets of sweat forming on her forehead. "Oh, no, sir, not suggesting that at all. Of course, you can discipline your men how you see fit, but Young Joseph here hasn't been himself lately, what with the fever and all. As you are such a wise man," she said, despising herself for her bootlicking, groveling tone, "I'm sure you know such an illness can make folks mad for a spell. I just thought—"

"You *thought*?" Clyde yelled. "That's your problem, then!" He lowered his voice to a whisper, enunciating his next words. "You. Don't. Get. To. Think. Not ever." He spat on the ground again. "You ain't allowed to think or speak or," he hesitated, "or fuckin' *learn* unless I give the okay. Hawthorne may have bought you at that auction, but you work for me!"

Abigail, eyes wide, wrapped both arms protectively around her waist, attempting to hide her shaking hands.

Clyde released his hold on Joseph's throat and faced Abigail. Although his muscled body blocked Joseph from her sight, she was comforted by the sound of Joseph's coughs.

"And speaking of learning," Clyde said, voice low. "You seem to have picked up quite a few fancy words, ain't ya, Abigail? Been talking all smart-like around here, acting high and mighty." Disgusted, his eyes raked her up and down. "Call me loco, but it's like you been readin' or some such."

Abigail's heart pounded in her chest.

Smirking, he moved to stand beside Joseph. "Say, boy," he began, clasping Joseph's shoulder, "you wouldn't know anything 'bout that, would ya? About if Miss Fancypants here has been schooled in reading and writing and such?"

Abigail's eyes met Joseph's. Suspicion was one thing, but if Clyde ever found out the truth about what she'd been doing with Edward, her life, such as it was, would be over. It was bad enough that she, an enslaved Black woman, was eagerly partaking in a forbidden activity—learning to read and write.

Worse was that she was also keeping company with her owner's son.

Her owner's *White* son.

"You hear me, boy?" Clyde snarled at a cowering Joseph. "What do you know about this treachery? What have you heard? And don't even think about lyin' to me, or it will be *your* ass instead of hers getting' shipped off this plantation!"

Abigail fidgeted nervously with her skirts. "Mr. Clyde, sir. I'm not sure what you are implying…"

"Exactly my point!" Clyde said, punctuating his words with a clap of his hands. Then, in a sing-song voice, he mocked her. "'I'm not sure what you are implying.' Nobody talks like that 'less they been studying their learner books! You didn't talk like that when you come here!"

Seeing Clyde's reddened face and clenched fists, Abigail stepped backward. "I'm sure I-I just heard folks talking like that. I have," she stopped, switching tactics, "I gots a good memory, sharp as a whip. One of them brains that recall all kind of stuff."

She held her breath, hoping he would second-guess himself when she reverted to her previous speech patterns.

He did not.

Strutting up to her, his hands tucked into the front of his pants, he squinted. "You lying to me. Know how I know that? On account of you got a twitch," he reached out his index finger and pushed it, hard, into her temple," right here, next to your eye. It's what we poker players call a 'tell.'"

Joseph cleared his throat, wanting nothing more than to be out of the barn and away from the overseer. "Um, excuse me, sir," he rasped, throat raw, "I don't know nothin', honest. So, if it's all the same to you, I best be getting back to my chores."

Clyde stared him down and simply said, "No."

"Um, beggin' your pardon, sir?"

In two strides, Clyde reached Joseph, hooked him by the back of the shirt, and yanked him over to Abigail. "I'll get the truth outta you, one way or another. You look at her, boy, really look," he said, shaking Joseph's body. "Spill your guts, or risk your own neck."

Tears filled Joseph's eyes.

"Now," Clyde whispered into the frightened teen's ear, "who is learning this woman to read?"

Joseph's eyes avoided Abigail, moving from the splintered ceiling rafters to the overhead loft, currently empty and sprinkled with pale strands of straw. Beads of sweat formed over his top lip as his eyes scanned the recesses of the barn, looking for something.

Something like salvation.

Or redemption.

"Joseph?" Abigail said softly. "Tell him, now. Tell him I ain't done anything wrong."

Joseph coughed into his hand, shifted his stance, and finally looked at her. His face was pained, his eyes wet with tears. He loved Abigail with all his heart, but his body had become frail after his recent illness and would not survive a Clyde Baldwin beating.

Nor would he survive being dumped on a far worse plantation, exiled from Rosemear. He had family here. Friends, too. And most times, even if he did get whipped, it wasn't so bad. He'd heard tales of men on other plantations getting beaten until bones broke, blood ran, or skulls cracked.

Just recently, Patrice, one of the scullery maids, had told him about a young man two states over who, at the moment, remained unconscious after being beaten with a wooden club weeks ago.

Joseph understood that, in his current condition, he would never survive such physical abuse.

"Well?" Clyde said, tightening his grip on Joseph's shirt and lifting him higher, forcing the boy to stand on his toes or risk getting choked by his own collar.

Joseph glanced at Abigail once more, shame telegraphed in his eyes.

And in that glance, that instant, she knew he would betray her.

"This-this is all just what I hear, mind you, Mr. Clyde," Joseph said softly, hating himself. "Can't rightly say if'n it's true facts or not."

Abigail's stomach lurched. *Dear God, no!*

"Fine, fine, boy," Clyde said placatingly. "What'd you hear?"

Joseph kicked his boot at a random piece of straw on the dusty floor. "I, um, I heard tell she been keeping company with Mr. Edward

Hawthorne. And that she got some learning books from him."

Clyde grinned, displaying gums speckled with black shreds of tobacco leaves. "That so?"

Joseph nodded. "What I heard tell. As I say, no tellin' if it's true. Could be just gossip among the womenfolk."

Clyde narrowed his eyes at Abigail. "Oh, it's true. What I heard, too." He waggled his brows. "Heard other things, as well. Stuff even worse than a slave learnin' to read."

Abigail looked back and forth between them both. Finally, addressing Joseph, she whispered, "Why are you doing this? I've been nothing but kind to you! I saved your life!"

The young man's face reddened with shame. Although angry at himself for betraying her friendship, he'd deal with the sleepless nights and the self-loathing later.

What he couldn't deal with was the possibility of being sent away from Rosemear and his family.

"That be all, then, sir?" Joseph asked, working to keep the bitterness from his tone. He and the other plantation workers despised Clyde Baldwin for his cruelty and abuse, but that loathing couldn't hold a candle to how badly Joseph hated himself for sacrificing Abigail.

"Yeah," Clyde mumbled. "You go on now. I believe Miss Charles needs a different kind of lesson today. One that'll stick with her good."

Terrified, Abigail watched as Joseph, with one last apologetic look, slipped past her and exited the barn.

"Now, then, Missy," Clyde sneered, "it's about time for that lesson." He reached for his belt buckle, opened it, and pulled. The leather slid easily from the belt loops, making a hissing sound as it went.

Abigail tensed. "Now, just hold on, Mr. Baldwin," she started, attempting to keep the fear from her voice. "I don't expect Mr. William or Mr. Edward would be happy if you were to damage me with a beating!"

Clyde snorted. "A beating? What makes you think I'm fixin' to beat you?"

Abigail frowned, confused. "Well, the uh—the belt. You took it off as if…"

Clyde cackled, interrupting her. "Are you stupid, girl? Don't you know there is another reason a man takes off his belt?"

Fear ripped through Abigail's young mind as comprehension dawned. Heart thumping, she raced toward the barn door.

She had to get out, had to get help.

Had to get Edward.

Still screaming, and with the overseer just steps behind her, Abigail reached for the handle of the closed door.

Suddenly, she was yanked backward, arms flailing and feet scrambling.

Twisting and turning to escape Clyde's grasp, she struggled as he half-dragged, half-carried her to a large mound of hay in the corner of the room. Throwing her carelessly onto the makeshift bed, he bent forward, his bear-like hands pawing at her skirts.

"Stop! Stop!" she cried, tugging at the fabric clenched in his fists. "Please! Don't do this!" And then, desperate, she added, "Mr. Edward and I are in love! If you do this, he'll kill you!"

Ignoring her, Clyde snapped open a pocket knife and began slicing at her clothing.

"And Mr. William!" she sobbed, fighting with all her strength, trying to roll out of his grasp. "Mr. William will be furious as well! He paid good money for me!"

Clyde paused, his grin chilling. "Mr. William?" He lay across her and brought his face within inches of hers, his rank breath turning her stomach. "You think Mr. William will be mad?" he whispered. "Hell, who do you think set this up, sweetheart?"

Fists flying, Abigail pounded Clyde's upper body and pushed at his chest, trying to escape from beneath him.

Grunting, he adjusted his grip on her, wrapping one thick hand around her wrists and holding them above her head. He made quick work of her remaining clothing, slicing and slashing until she lay beneath him, panting and naked.

He wiped the back of his mouth with his free hand and leered at her. "You ready for the ride of your life, bitch?"

"Nooooo!!" she screamed again, trying to buck him off her body. "Someone, please!"

But no one came.

Minutes later, as Clyde violated her in the most intimate ways possible, Abigail ignored the pain, ignored the overseer's animalistic grunts and fetid breath, and let her mind take her away.

Because the brain has a remarkable way of shielding itself from trauma.

Her journey took her to a grassy patch of grass in Wright's Square. There, beneath the stars and under her favorite oak tree, she and Edward sipped champagne from fancy glasses while he read to her.

It was a pleasant place to be, and Abigail was content to stay there.

An intake of breath—so subtle she nearly missed it—pulled her back to reality. Straining to hear above Clyde's rhythmic 'uh, uh, uh' groans and disgusting 'yeah, give it to me!' whispers, she turned her head just in time to see the shadow of a man peeking through the now-ajar barn door.

The familiar silhouette hesitated a moment before, shoulders sagging, he wordlessly closed the door again.

Leaving Abigail in a world of hurt that far surpassed the physical pain she endured now.

It was the soul-crushing pain that followed a trusted friend's betrayal.

Joseph's betrayal.

# CHAPTER SEVENTEEN

*You may break my body,*
*Or you may take my life.*
*But you can never crush my soul.*
*For I am stronger than the chains that bind me,*
*and I fear no one.*

*——Abigail Charles, 1859*

# CHAPTER EIGHTEEN

Luna, respirator mask in place, dropped her safety glasses over her eyes and hefted the sledgehammer with both hands. Aiming at the back wall in Ellie's room, she wiggled her butt like a ball player at bat and yelled, "Fire in the hole!"

"Hey, Joe DiMaggio!" Isabella said with a laugh. "Pretty sure 'fire in the hole' is meant for an impending explosion."

Luna shrugged. "Sounded better in my head."

The pair had been doing prep work since Luna returned from her research mission. They'd moved Ellie's furniture to the west wing, then lain down tarps to protect the parquet floor. The plan was to punch holes in the non-load-bearing plaster walls, search for the source of the awful stench permeating the space, and then insulate and repair the walls if possible. If fixing them wasn't possible, they would need to be replaced with sheetrock.

Dealing with the exterior walls, most likely load-bearing,

would have to wait until Nate arrived.

"Hold up!" Isabella shouted, moving quickly to Luna's side. "I forgot to measure the room for the drywall. Nate will need the dimensions if we can't repair the existing walls."

"Oh, right," Luna said sheepishly. "Sorry. I have a bad habit of getting ahead of myself." She leaned her forearm on the sledgehammer and looked around the room. Most of the plaster was painted, but a side wall was covered with floral wallpaper. "Think we can peel that off? Just curious if there is anything underneath it."

Isabella tapped her chin. "Hmm, well, let's see." She walked over the tarp to the papered wall, running a hand over the surface. "Must have been a bitch to get this to stick. I've heard it's tough to paper a plaster wall. The surface is too rough or something."

"True, but it can be done—just a pain in the ass to do it. My Great-Uncle Walter hired someone to wallpaper a bedroom in his old Victorian. Took a three-person crew a few days for sure."

Isabella smiled and began measuring the room. "How is Great-Uncle Walter, anyway? I haven't seen him in years."

"Ornery as ever," Luna said, grabbing the end of the measuring tape. "I had to play peacemaker when his physician dared to suggest Walter stop with the vodka. His liver function is shit, and the doc thought cutting back on the booze would help. Needless to say, Walter was not amused."

Isabella wrinkled her nose. "I bet. He does love his Tito's."

"And his Grey Goose. And his Smirnoff."

"Aww, give him a break, Lune. Uncle Walter has been around the block a few times and earned his vices. He's what now? Ninety?"

"Just turned ninety-two in May."

Isabella snapped the measuring tape back in place. "Good for him," she said absently. Moving closer to the wall, she inspected the surface, flicking a fingernail over a jagged corner of paper. "Hang on, I think I can peel some of this off." She gripped the tiny edge and slowly pulled. "Yes!" she said excitedly. "Oh, this is fun!

Just like peeling skin after a sunburn!"

Luna laid the hammer on the floor and walked across the room to Isabella. "Which is why sunscreen is your friend. See anything?"

Isabella continued to tug gently, removing the decorative covering in thin strips. A moment later, she stopped. "Holy crap," she said over her shoulder. "What fresh hell is this?"

Luna bent forward and peered over Isabella's head. "Fucked if I know!"

Transfixed, they stared at the faded drawing halfway up the wall. The image was done in dark ink or charcoal and depicted a six-petaled flower within a circle. Next to it, the words 'beware' and 'save us,' along with a date, were written with a shaky hand.

Luna squinted. "Pretend I'm not blind as a bat and tell me what that says. I can't read the date."

"I think it's 1858." Isabella moved her face closer to the wall. "It also says 'beware' and 'save us.' Save us from what? And what's with this flower thing?"

Luna studied the image. "I can't be sure, but I think it's a daisy wheel."

"Um…okay?"

"It's also called a hexafoil. If I'm right, it was a popular symbol in medieval England. See how it seems to be a continuous line? As if there is no beginning and no end?"

Isabella nodded.

"That trick is supposed to confuse evil spirits so they can't find an opening to enter the home." She straightened. "In a nutshell, it's a protection spell."

"A protection spell? Like witchcraft? Jesus Christ, what have I gotten us into?"

Luna frowned. "First off, you haven't gotten anybody into anything. It was your douche canoe of a husband who found this place, remember? And secondly, just because a hexafoil is associated with witches doesn't make it bad. In this case, whoever put this here was trying to put a security blanket over the house. We can ask Roma about it next week." She leaned forward once again. "Is that a letter next to the word 'beware'?"

Isabella ran a hand lightly over the lettering. The writing was faded and difficult to make out. "Could be. If so, it looks like an 'M.'"

"As in Martin?"

"Maybe?" Isabella said. "Is this an 'A' near it?"

"No clue. My near-vision sucks donkey ass."

"Unfortunate," Isabella quipped. "Well, hopefully, Roma can tell us. Meanwhile, I'll get the reciprocating saw from the garage so we can cut this out and hang onto it."

"Good idea," Luna said. "Maybe bring the circular saw, too. And grab me a Pepsi on the way back, will ya? I could use the caffeine."

"Okay. I'll check on the kids, too. They're supposed to be watching a movie, but it seems awfully quiet down there."

Isabella turned to leave when a sudden tap-tap-tap coming from outside caught her attention.

Luna's head spun toward the sound as well. "Is there nothing in this place that don't pucker your red eye?"

"Hah! True, but this one might have a logical explanation. There's an old tree beneath the window, and I think one of the branches keeps hitting the house."

Luna walked to the bay windows lining the turret tower and glanced down. "If'n you say so. But from this angle, there doesn't seem to be a rogue limb that close to the exterior."

Isabella joined Luna at the windows. "Huh, strange. I could swear there was one before." She scanned the yard. "Tapping stopped for now, anyway. I'll have Nate take a look when he comes over."

Luna smirked. "Nate? Not Spencer? Oh, what a tangled web we weave!"

Isabella wrinkled her nose. "Cute. Come on, my silly friend. You can grab the saws while I check on the kids and fetch your soda."

"Sounds like a plan, Stan," Luna said. Wiping her hands on her jeans, she moved close to Isabella and started singing softly. *"Bella and Nathan, sitting in a tree..."*

"Oh, shut up!" Isabella said with a grin.

Halfway down the hall, when they were too far away to hear, the knocking started again.

*Tap. Tap. Tap.*

Thirty minutes later, after feeding the kids lunch and setting them up with a board game, Isabella and Luna returned to work.

"I think rain is coming," Luna said, setting up a large trash container in the center of Ellie's room. "I can feel it in my bones."

Isabella dragged a Shop-Vac across the floor, setting it beside the trash can. "Then you have good bones. They're forecasting some nasty weather, so I'm keeping the kids inside for now. The storms here can be quite dangerous."

"Yep," Luna agreed. Looking around, hands on her hips, she said, "So, you want to start cutting out the hexafoil while I punch a hole in the back wall?"

"That works," Isabella said. "Don't forget your mask. There has to be mountains of asbestos in here." Connecting a Bluetooth speaker she'd stored in Ellie's closet to her phone, she queued up her 'classic rock' playlist.

Immediately, the haunting strains of a harmonica filled the room.

"Jesus, Boyd," Luna said. "Is that Springsteen's 'Nebraska'? Little gruesome, don't you think? Please tell me you don't listen to this every night before bed."

"As a matter of fact," Isabella said, clearly confused, "I don't."

"Good, because that song is about a couple of killers."

"Yes, I know. Charles Starkweather and Caril Ann Fugate, serial killers who operated in fifty-eight." She frowned. "But what I don't get is how it ended up on my playlist."

"Gulp. So, in a house creepy as fuck—one that may or may not be haunted—a song written about the murders of almost a dozen people just hops onto your playlist?"

"No, it's worse than that," Isabella groaned. "It couldn't 'hop' on my playlist because it isn't on my phone. I've never downloaded this song. Like, anywhere. Too dark for my tastes."

"Double gulp."

"What the hell could it mean?" Isabella asked. "Is there a link between the Rosemear murders and the Starkweather homicides? Maybe the house is trying to tell us something by playing that song."

"Or maybe the house is just fucking with us, trying to scare us."

"Well, it's working."

"Okay, let's not panic," Luna soothed. "Knowledge is power, and we've learned a few things so far."

Isabella nodded. "Right. We know that a young woman named Abigail Charles was accused of killing the original owners here. We've also discovered the strange markings on the wall and that the last owners ran out of here with just the clothes on their backs." She chewed her thumb. "What we don't know is why. Hell, what we don't know could fill an ocean."

"True, but I learned some history when I went to town this morning. Some of it comes from a local gentleman by the name of Atticus Jones, who spoke of Rosemear and its enslaved people." Luna glanced toward the bedroom door and lowered her voice. "I wanted to make sure the kids were occupied before we discussed what I uncovered. From the little I read, this joint's checkered past could make tragedy a national pastime."

"Super," Isabella said dryly. "Okay, when Nate gets here, we'll review what you've found." She sighed. "I guess Rosemear was a slavery operation. I wonder if that's what the small graves outside are about. What if Rosemear is the final resting place for those poor people forced to be here? Christ, Luna, do I even want to know about this stuff?"

"I think you have to if you ever want to find peace here. And, honestly, it's the respectful thing to do. Learning about Rosemear's dark past validates the souls who bore so much misery and hardship here."

"You're right, of course. It's just so sad to think a place I am coming to love could have harbored such evil years ago."

"But it's their past, not yours. We can't control what happened more than a century ago. All we can do is acknowledge and learn from it."

Isabella smirked. "Okay, Dr. Phil. Geesh, you've been so insightful lately. I'd think you were running for office if I didn't know better."

"Hey, don't act so shocked! Once in a blue moon—or, as I like to call it, a 'blue Lune'—your friend comes up with some pretty prophetic shit. Just be glad I let you ride on my magic bus of wisdom."

Isabella bent forward, laughing. "I'm sorry," she said, "but Blue Lune? Your 'magic bus of wisdom'? Where do you come up with this stuff?"

"I'll have you know," Luna said before picking up the sledgehammer, "that the name 'Luna' stems from the chariot-riding goddess of the moon. So, yeah, I'm kind of a big deal in Roman mythology." Adjusting her safety glasses and mask, she turned to Isabella. "You ready to make some noise?"

Isabella revved the circular saw and grinned. "Right behind you, Blue Lune."

*Charleston Inn*
*Room 402*

"I don't know, Spence," Julia said, sitting on the bed as he laid out his plan. "Seems like a lot could go wrong with this. I get that your wife is neurotic, but what if this other chick, this moon girl, figures it out?"

"Luna? Fuck her. She's a bitch, anyway."

"A bitch that could put us in prison! What you are suggesting is…"

"Is what, exactly?" he said, anger flaring. "Look, Julia, that cunt I married killed my daughter! She deserves any bad shit that comes her way!"

"But I-I thought you said that the day Anna died, you—"

Spencer cut her off. "Doesn't matter now. Look, it's not like I'm planning to kill her or anything. Although, honestly, that would be a shit-ton easier, and I'd still get her money."

"We are *not* killing your wife, Spencer!"

"No, I know, I know. I just want my life back, Jules. I want a life where you and I can do anything, buy anything, and not break a sweat."

Julia chose her next words carefully. Her grandmother used to say that criticism was a sandwich best served between two slices of praise. "I want that, too. Look, you've put a ton of thought into this idea, and I appreciate your vision. I know your wife has given you nothing but grief and heartache. It's an interesting plan, but where do the kids fit here?" She chewed the inside of her cheek. "You know I love you, Spence, I do. But a ready-made family? I'm too young to play stepmom."

"And I'm not asking you to. But they're my children, Julia. Once Isabella is out of the way, we'll get a live-in, someone to take care of them."

"I don't know," Julia said, wheels turning in her mind. "Can I think about it? I'd still like to start fresh, just you and me, but I get it." She stood and tugged at his hand. "Come on, stud. We have forty minutes until the meeting starts. Take a shower with me and shoot me to the moon."

Spencer grinned. "You're insatiable, Jules."

She licked her lips suggestively. "Only with you, lover. Only with you."

"Well, that was an adventure," Luna said, removing her mask. "Remind me next time to tell you to hire someone. Damn, but this stench is unreal! It's gonna be embedded in my nostrils for weeks!"

"Yeah, I hear that," Isabella said. "The good news? We're definitely on the right track. The smell in here increased tenfold once we opened the walls."

Luna nodded at the drop cloth on the floor before them. "And these wonderful things we found behind the plaster? What do you make of them?"

Isabella shrugged, eyes roaming over the dozens of bones they'd laid out neatly on the tarp. "No clue. Some sort of animal for sure, but what kind? Not that skeletonized remains could be the source of that revolting smell."

"Not hardly. Unless…" Luna paused. "What if there are fresher carcasses we haven't found?"

"Lovely thought. Nothing inside the wall you opened?"

"Nope. Just dust and some wooden laths on life support. How the hell did these animals get in?" Tense, Luna rubbed the nape of her neck. "And, once in, why couldn't they get out? I fucking hate mysteries, Bella. You know this."

"I do," Isabella said sympathetically. "I'm sorry to drag you into this, but since you're already uncomfortable…" She winked. "I have another mystery guaranteed to give you a bellyache."

"Oh, I'm all a-tingle over here, waiting."

Isabella shrugged. "It's just that, judging by the different skull shapes, it seems these bones are from various animals. I doubt they all entered the house simultaneously."

"Uh…okay?"

"So, if that's true, why were they huddled in one spot when we found them? I doubt they all decided to party together."

"True," Luna said. "And it kind of looked like they were deliberately stacked on top of each other."

"Agreed. So, how does that happen naturally?" Isabella asked.

"No idea. Maybe they wanted to keep warm?" She studied the assorted bones. "I think the smallest bones belong to a rodent. That one," she said, pointing to the edge of the drop cloth, "could be a squirrel."

Isabella raised a brow. "Who are you? Dr. Doolittle?"

"Hah! For your information, wise-ass, my dad took me hunting a few times. Occasionally, we would come across a dead animal or two. This carcass reminds me of a squirrel we found one day. Poor thing was facedown, with his little arm stretched out as if pleading for help."

"That sounds awful."

"It was. And talk about gross? It was still decomposing."

"Yuck. How old were you?"

Luna tilted her head. "Hmm, eleven or twelve? And, although I'd seen dead animals before, this little squirrel got to me. I couldn't get that scene out of my head for weeks. It was the last time I went hunting with my father."

"I bet." Isabella checked her watch. "Okay, I don't know about you, but I'm famished. The kids ate, but how about I fix us something? Tuna sammies?"

"Sounds good. After that, we can—"

She was interrupted by a knocking sound somewhere near the window.

*Thump. Thump. Thump.*

"Oh, come on!" Luna said. "Now it's not a gentle tap but an insistent thump?"

Creeping to the window, they stood side by side and peeked at the ground below. The skies were dark, nearly black, and thunder rolled in the distance.

"See anything?" Isabella asked.

"Not sure. It's darker than my ex's heart out there."

Isabella pressed her forehead against the glass to better view the yard. "So strange. There are, like literally, no branches that even come close to the house. At least none that I can see through the blackness out there."

"So, what, then? Maybe the sound isn't coming from that tree at all?"

Isabella nodded. "That's what I was thinking. I wonder if the noise could be traveling from another room. Like a reflection of sound waves from a distant area of the house or the grounds?"

Luna shrugged. "As good a guess as any."

"Okay, let's check out the other rooms before making lunch. I wanted to move that armoire in the blue room anyway so we can get a look at that closet."

"Lead the way, mon amie."

After checking Sam's room and finding nothing of note, they moved to the blue room, unsure again whether the door would open.

It did.

Entering, Isabella scoured the floor, ceiling, and fireplace for potential sources of the noise they'd heard while Luna peered through windows, looking for rogue tree limbs bashing against the house.

They found nothing.

"Well, there goes that idea," Isabella said with a frown. "At least upstairs, anyway. Help me move the dresser away from the closet?"

They each took a side and, finding the armoire too heavy to lift, slid it along the floor and away from the closet door.

"Why do I feel like opening this closet will be like opening

Pandora's box?" Luna said uneasily.

"Yeah, that's all we need!" Isabella placed her hand on the closet doorknob and said over her shoulder, "Cover me. I'm going in."

"Wait!" Luna said, grabbing Isabella's arm. "What if it's like a portal or something? Should we tie a rope around your waist so I can pull you back?"

Isabella chuckled. "Girl, you gotta quit with the spooky movies—this isn't *Poltergeist*!" Opening the closet door, she looked up and spotted a long chain suspended from a ceiling light.

She tugged on the pull chain. Nothing happened.

"Shit, it's too dark to see anything." Taking her cell phone from her back pocket, she shone a light on the closet's interior.

"Anything?" Luna asked, straining to see over Isabella's shoulder. "Monsters? Gremlins? Jason Momoa?"

"None of the above. Although there's this…" Isabella lifted a framed picture leaning against a side wall and backed out of the closet. Holding the picture up, she inspected the portrait.

"Wow!" Luna gasped from behind. "Looks old as hell. Who are they?"

The painting, encased within a square wooden frame, depicted a family posed around a Victorian sofa. A man and woman sat on a teal settee, four children of various ages surrounding them. The youngest child looked no older than two.

"I recognize this room," Isabella said. "The high ceilings, the molding. It's the den of this house. And, judging by their clothes, it could be the Hawthorne family."

Luna lightly touched the image of the youngest child. "A little boy." She shivered. "Man, this gives me the wicked chills. Could this be Ellie's friend, Martin?"

"Well, Christ, Lune…if we admit that, we acknowledge this house really is haunted." She moved her face closer, studying the subjects in the picture. "Do you see their eyes?"

Luna frowned. "What about them?"

"Don't they seem, I don't know, off somehow? Especially eerie or something."

"This whole thing is eerie, girl," Luna said. "These people are creepy as hell. It's almost like…"

"Like they're watching us?" Isabella finished for her.

"Exactly right. So, what are you going to do with it?"

"For now, I'll take it downstairs and see if it grows on me. Maybe casually show it to Ellie and gauge her reaction."

"Huh. I'd go with 'burn the bitch,' but that's just me. What happens if El identifies the kid as her pal Martin?"

"Not sure. We'll cross that terrifying bridge when we get to it."

After checking the remaining room, the one with the Dr. Seuss door, they moved to the rooms on the other wing but came up empty.

The smallest room on the west side, the locked one, remained secure.

As they headed down the stairs, a nagging thought hammered into Isabella's brain.

*If the only thing that closet contained was an old picture, why did someone feel the need to barricade that door with an armoire?*

# CHAPTER NINETEEN

Sam and Matty dove into their snack of cheese and crackers, munching happily and laughing between bites. Ellie, on the other hand, silently picked at her plate.

"Not hungry, Bug?" Isabella asked.

Ellie sighed dramatically. "My tummy feels weird."

Luna reached for Ellie's forehead. "No fever. Anything hurt, love?"

Ellie slowly shook her head.

"She's just worried about that nightmare she had," Sam said casually. "The one from last night, right, El?" He shrugged, unperturbed. "That, and the shadows on the wall she keeps seeing."

Isabella frowned. "Well, we know about the awful dream, but what's this about shadows?"

Ellie pushed her chips around her plate. "I dunno. Just shadows that look like people. Sometimes, they're moving so fast I can hardly see where they go! I think they're trying to get away."

Isabella pressed her lips together. "Get away from what?"

Ellie shook her head emphatically. "I don't know, but it's something bad. Yesterday, when me, Sam, and Matty were playing in the front yard, I had to go potty."

Sam snorted. "She almost peed her pants!"

"Did not!"

"Samuel!" Isabella scolded.

"Sorry, Ma."

"What happened next, El?" Luna asked softly.

After one last scowl aimed at Sam, Ellie continued. "I came inside to use the bathroom, and a shadow man was standing in the upstairs hallway, looking at me."

Luna clutched her throat. "Christ on a cracker, I knew it!"

"Luna!" Isabella admonished with a subtle shake of her head.

Ellie's eyes widened. "Are you—are you scared, Aunt Luna? 'Cause if you're scared, I'm scared more!"

"Nah, don't mind me, Bug," Luna said, tapping the tip of Ellie's nose. "I didn't get enough sleep and I'm grouchy today. I'm not scared at all!"

Ellie narrowed her eyes.

"Okay, well, maybe just a smidge," Luna said with a wink. "We thought we saw a shadow up there, too, Bug," Isabella said. "Aunt Luna and I were sitting outside and thought we saw something, but it was nothing. I think the crystal chandeliers and the unique trim create dark shadows." Turning to the boys, she asked, "Have you seen strange shadows here?"

Sam peeked at Ellie, then shook his head.

Matty, suddenly uncomfortable, changed the subject. "Why do you call her Bug?" Then, embarrassed by his boldness, he added, "I'm just wondering, is all. I'm always curious about the origins of nicknames."

Luna nearly spat out her soda. "Excuse me? The 'origins of nicknames'? You sound like a forty-six-year-old man! I had no idea you were so smart, Matt!"

The boy shrugged. "I guess. I get straight As, and the teachers in my gifted and talented program wanted me to skip two grades, but my mom said no. She said there's more to school than just learning."

"Your mom sounds pretty great," Isabella said, smiling. "As to your question, when Ellie was a baby, she was a snuggler. I used to rock her in my arms and sing to her—Nat King Cole's 'Snug as a Bug in a Rug' was always her favorite, so..." She shrugged and began clearing the table. "Now, let me ask you a question, Matthew. You've lived in Savannah all your life, right?"

Matthew nodded. "Yes, ma'am."

"Have you heard any stories or local legends about Rosemear?"

He shrugged. "Rumors, mostly. Did you know you have a graveyard way back on your property?"

"Yep. Your uncle told us, but we haven't been back there yet. Nate thinks it's where the original owners are buried."

"Yeah," Matty said softly, "my mom said that, too. I've been back there a few times." Suddenly, he looked horror-stricken. "But—but not when anyone lived here. That would be trespassing. Yeah, I'd never do that." Face growing red, he traced a finger over the lines in his palm.

"No worries, kiddo," Luna said. "You wouldn't be a kid if you didn't explore, am I right?"

"Besides," Isabella winked, "now that we live here, you can explore whenever you want!"

"Okay," Matty said. "Well, a few times when I was back there, I heard a lady humming a song I didn't recognize." He looked at Isabella sheepishly. "And I heard people talking. It wasn't a nice conversation, either. Sounded like arguing."

"And that was in the graveyard?" Luna asked.

Matty nodded.

"Okay. Anything else?" Isabella asked gently. "Anything inside the house?"

"Just the shadow guy," Matty said. "I saw him through an up-stairs window once. He kept walking back and forth, peeking out, like he was waiting for someone."

"Or something," Luna said ominously. Turning to Sam, she said, "Hey, little man. Can you find your old aunt a piece of paper and a pencil?"

Sam jumped up. "Yes, ma'am. Be right back!"

"What are you thinking?" Isabella asked.

"I'm thinking we jot down everything that's happened here and see if we can make sense of it."

"Good idea." Isabella lifted Ellie's plate. "You finished, sweet-heart? If so, I'll put your snack in the fridge in case you get hungry later."

"Okay, Momma."

Sam raced back into the kitchen, waving a notebook and a pencil case. "Got it!"

"Good man," Luna said, reaching for the notebook. "Okay, let's see…"

Isabella stopped her. "These guys don't need to hear the boring details. We've tortured them enough."

Understanding flashed in Luna's eyes. "Oh, of course. No need to hang with the old people! Go! Have fun!"

"Come on, guys!" Sam said. "Let's find another game to play!"

"Sorry," Luna said once they'd vanished down the hall. "Your kids are so mature that sometimes I forget they're still kids."

"You and me both!" Isabella agreed. She nodded toward the notebook. "So, where do we start?"

"Where we always start," Luna said, flipping the pad open and picking a pencil from the case. "At the beginning."

Fifteen minutes later, Luna stared at the list they'd created, dumbfounded.

"Damn!" she said. "There's a ton to unpack here."

Isabella, at the sink finishing up the lunch dishes, spoke over her shoulder. "Okay, well, read me what you have so far."

Luna scanned the nearly full page. "Stop me if I'm missing anything. For now, I've tried documenting everyone's firsthand experiences while leaving out rumor and innuendo." She looked up from the paper. "Nothing scary ever happened to Spencer, right? I mean, besides being born a douchebag?"

Isabella chuckled. "Not that he's mentioned. Although he's so busy getting laid and trying to convince me that I'm relapsing, who knows."

"God, I hate that prick!" Luna growled.

"Never mind him. What you got?"

"I started with your experiences. In the blue room, the door, which appeared locked, opened on its own for you. Then, when you stepped inside, a creepy voice warned you to get out, and someone grabbed your shoulder."

"Right. And don't forget the armoire blocking the closet, the portrait left behind, and the antiseptic-type smell in there."

"Gotcha. Adding that to the list," Luna said, scribbling furiously. "Next, we both witnessed a shadowy figure on the stairs, flickering lights, and that God-awful stench in Ellie's room."

"Oh, and my missing earrings, sunglasses, and pencil." Isabella remembered, snapping her fingers and sending soap suds flying.

Luna giggled.

"Smooth, right?" Isabella joked, drying her hands on a dish towel. "What else? Oh, the unexplained tapping near Ellie's window. We still haven't figured out what's causing that."

"Or who this Martin kid is and why only Ellie can see him."

"Am I crazy, or…" Isabella stopped, putting up a hand. "Wait!" she quipped. "Don't answer that!"

Luna waggled her brows. "My momma didn't raise no fool."

"Hah, funny girl! But seriously, I'm wondering if Ellie could be the nexus of the activity here in Spook Central. She and her bedroom seem to be the center of what's happening."

"True," Luna said, scrubbing fatigue from her face. "Martin, being scratched, the animal carcasses, and the pissed-off 'people in the wall.' Oh, and her night terror last evening. Dreaming she was buried alive? I mean, she's a kid, for Christ's sake. How the hell would she even know about that?"

Isabella sighed. "I have no clue, which scares me to death. I think I'll hold off on showing her the portrait we found."

"Because?"

"Because I'm afraid she'll latch on to the idea that it's Martin in that picture, even if it isn't. Studies I've read say the mind can create false memories to verify an individual's perceived 'truths.'"

Luna pursed her lips. "Which reduces my confidence that Andy Gray, the most popular boy in school, really did ask me out in the eighth grade."

Isabella chuckled. "Andy Gray? Do you mean the asthmatic kid with trust issues who always smelled like fried bologna? Believe me… even if your mind conjured the memory, you aren't missing much. I heard he hasn't worked in years and still lives with his mother."

"Damn! I knew he was trouble!" Luna joked. "Where were we? Oh, yeah. We have Nate and Matty's experiences with shadows, and the taps and bangs we've heard in Ellie's room. Oh, and the witches' mark on the wall and the writing beside it."

"And the creepy vibes we feel," Isabella added. "Ones that might have caused the movers to sprint out of here as if…"

"They saw a ghost?" Luna finished for her.

"Yeah, like that." She checked the wall clock. "We still have a little time before Nate gets here. I'd like to wait until he arrives to review what you uncovered in town. In the meantime, Doc, high-ho, high-ho, it's back to work we go."

Luna saluted. "Right behind you, Dopey!"

Two hours later, Isabella and Luna sat cross-legged on the floor, prying up random portions of the herringbone-shaped parquet flooring.

"Try not to mar the surface if you can help it," Isabella said.

"I hate to dig up any of this gorgeous floor," Luna grunted as she tried to remove a particularly stubborn piece near the corner. "I understand why we have to, but it still sucks."

"It does, but those animal bones don't explain the stench here. I'm hoping we find the answer beneath the floorboards." Isabella tilted her head back and sighed. "Because I really don't want to have to fuck with the ceiling." She popped a piece of wood loose from the joist it was nailed to. "No wonder this floor squeaks. At least half of the pine subfloor is missing and hasn't been replaced. Someone just nailed the finished floor to random joists."

"The lazy man's way out!" Luna said. "I'm surprised no one put a foot through the floor."

They worked the flooring piece by piece, listening to a classic rock station and occasionally breaking into song.

"Hey," Luna said, inspecting a section she'd uncovered beneath the parquet. "Think I found something."

"What you got, Slim?" Isabella asked.

Luna pointed to a weathered box nailed between two joists. "Not sure, but someone went through a ton of trouble to hide this here."

Isabella moved to Luna's side and took a hammer from her tool-belt. Working to pry the box from the joists, she grunted, "Man, it's really on here. Hang on to the bottom, Lune—I can't tell how heavy it is yet, and we don't want to damage the first-floor ceiling."

A few moments later, following a sharp crack, the box fell into Luna's hands. "Gotcha, bitch!" As soon as she spoke, an icy breeze blew through the room. "Okay, now they truly are just fuckin' with us!"

"It's probably just, um, just the air conditioner kicking on," Isabella said uncertainly.

"Right. The AC, not *Annabelle* or *Damien*. Got it."

"Okay, lady," Isabella huffed. "What's going on? What happened to your 'ghosts are people, too' theory? You seem to have jumped that ship and boarded the 'lock the doors and save the children' vessel instead. What gives?"

Luna lifted a shoulder. "I've no fucking clue. I do know that I've felt uneasy and exposed ever since arriving here. It's a constant sense of being…"

"Watched?" Isabella finished for her. "Yes, we said that earlier."

"No, I think watched is the wrong word. Scrutinized, maybe?"

"Studied?"

"Or hunted." Luna groaned. "I'm going to have Roma do a cleansing when she comes. Burning sage is supposed to smoke out bad energy."

Isabella rubbed the chill from her arms. "Can't hurt." She gestured across the room. "Let's put the box on that sawhorse and try to open it."

Luna frowned. "Have you heard nothing I've been saying, woman?"

"How do you mean?"

"Remember what I said when we moved the armoire? About how opening the closet door behind it felt like we were opening Pandora's box?"

"Yes, but…"

"This," Luna said, raising her hands, "is a box, Iz. Maybe my feeling wasn't about the closet in the blue room but about this box."

Isabella swallowed back her unease. "Nonsense. Greek mythology aside, and throwing no shade at Pandora, nothing bad ever came from opening a box."

"Are you serious?" Luna said, eyes wide. "Forgetting Pandora's stupid ass for a moment, how about the wife in the movie *Seven*? Her head was stuffed into a box and left in the desert for her husband to find! Or those psychopaths who mail explosives or deadly poisons to unsuspecting people? They open the box, and bam! Lights out!" She took a shaky breath. "Grave robbers, kidnappers who mail body parts as 'proof of life,' the terror of opening a birthday box from my grandma, only to find another knitted sweater!"

Isabella grinned. You've put a lot of thought into this."

"Yeah, yeah, mock me all you want—just don't come crying to me when your walls start to bleed."

"Bleeding walls? Oh, brother! And, for the record, I loved the knitted sweater your nana made for me!"

"Please—she was nearly blind by then! The left sleeve was three inches longer than the right!"

"It was a fashion statement, and I adored her for it. Now, if you're finished, Sally Doomsday, hand me that flat-headed screwdriver. We need to pop the lock."

Luna handed her the tool and leaned over the sawhorse. "You want to put it on the floor? Might give you more space to work with."

"No, I think I have it," Isabella said, threading the screwdriver through the rusted lock. After a quick, upward pull, the lock cracked in half and fell to the side. "Well, that was easier than I thought." She carefully lifted the box and sat on the floor, placing the box in front of her. Looking up at Luna, she palmed the lid and joked, "Get ready to run…"

"Very funny. I'll have you know that King Tut's tomb—another box, by the way—is allegedly protected from intruders by what's known as the 'Curse of the Pharaohs.' It's said that anyone who helped open Tut's tomb would die an early, horrible death. And many did!"

Isabella raised a brow. "Geesh, I never knew how superstitious you were! Okay, in that case, stand back. I'll take the hit."

Luna took a not-too-subtle step backward, turned her head,

and squeezed her eyes shut.

Isabella flipped open the lid. "It's papers," she said, rifling through the contents. "Letters, I think."

Luna opened one eye. "That's it? No severed head or evil talisman?"

"Nope. Just letters." Isabella picked up a yellowed page. "Specifically, it looks like love letters. There are dozens of them."

"Letters to whom?"

"Abigail. I think all of these are love letters to Abigail Charles, written by someone named Edward."

"Edward?" Luna said. "But didn't the realtor say she was in love with the plantation owner, William Hawthorne? And when that love was not reciprocated, she killed him and his wife in a jealous rage?"

"That was the rumor. Perhaps William went by his middle name? My grandparents did that. I was in my twenties before I realized my grandmother's first name was Catherine, not Elizabeth."

"Mine did that, too," Luna offered. "Tripped me up when I was tracing my family history."

"I bet. Anyway, whoever Edward was, he obviously had access to the house and this room. Maybe he's one of the Hawthorne kids?"

"Maybe. Read me one of the letters."

Isabella scanned the delicate page in her hand. "Some of the ink is smeared and the words are blurred, but I think I can figure it out."

Luna sat down beside Isabella. "You know, I took a class in college about the origins of invention or something. It was a blow-off elective class, but I learned a few things despite myself." She nodded to the letter. "In the mid-nineteenth century, quills were replaced by steel-nibbed pens. Still, they both required using an inkwell. I assume the ink could easily smear if it wasn't completely dry before someone handled the page."

Isabella smiled. "It's incredible that after all these years of friendship, of sharing secrets and heartaches and triumphs, there are still things I don't know about you."

"Mystery is what keeps our love alive."

Isabella chuckled, held the letter closer to her face, and began reading.

*May 22, 1859*

*Dearest Abigail,*

*Yesterday, I was reborn! Seeing your kindness and compassion with an ailing Young Joseph touched me to the core. You are a uniquely strong woman, and I am ashamed it took me so long to recognize that strength.*

*Your sweet smell, gentle smile, and unparalleled beauty have captured me with a ferocity I'd not experienced in years past. In fact, I've never felt this way about a woman, any woman, in my life.*

*That day in the barn, when I discovered how perfect you are, is a day I'll not forget. It was as if a thief rushed in, stole my heart, and placed it within your chest.*

*Two hearts, beating as one.*

*You've gotten under my skin, dearest Abigail, invading my mind and senses.*

*If I were given one wish, it would be that you felt it, too. The excitement, the possibilities, the raw need that demands to be fed, consequences be damned!*

*I have decided to journal our relationship within these letters. Truth be told, these are words you may never see because, for now, they are for my eyes only.*

*Perhaps, one day, I will read them to you when we are old and gray. Until then, I remain faithfully yours.*

*Edward*

Isabella gently folded the letter and, teary-eyed, placed it back in the box.

"Wow!" Luna gasped. "They don't make them like that

anymore! How sweet was he?"

"I know. It makes me sad to think how their story ended."

"Agreed," Luna said, standing. "Sort of a 'Romeo and Juliet' feel to it, right?"

Isabella nodded. "Yes, very much so."

"I wonder if she killed the Hawthornes or was wrongfully accused?"

"Not sure, but maybe we'll find the answer in these letters."

"Come on, girly," Luna said, stretching out a hand. "Let's take this box downstairs and put it with the information I found in town. When Nate gets here, we can go through it all."

Isabella clasped Luna's offered hand and stood. "Is it just me, or did this letter tug at your heartstrings more than it should have?" She wiped her eyes." It's so bizarre."

"Not bizarre. Human," Luna said, throwing an arm over Isabella's shoulder. "Come on!" she said, playfully pulling Isabella down the hallway. "I'm here, so be happy!"

"Don't I look happy?" Isabella teased, wiping her eyes again.

"If that's your 'happy' face, I'd ask the good Lord for a refund!"

As they descended the stairs, Luna started singing, "Don't worry, be happy," in an exaggerated soprano that had Isabella roaring with laughter.

And somewhere on the west wing, in a voice too soft to hear, a little boy laughed with her.

# CHAPTER
# TWENTY

Isabella and Luna were in the dining room, organizing Edward's letters and the information Luna had discovered, when Nate arrived.

"Knock, knock," he said, partially opening the front door and peeking in from the porch.

Isabella greeted him in the foyer. "Hello, there," she said with a wave. "Come on in. Luna and I are in the dining room."

Nate shook the rain from his umbrella and leaned it against the side of the house. "Sorry to let myself in," he said apologetically. "I tried knocking, but I'm sure you couldn't hear it above the storm. It's nasty out there."

The overhead chandelier lights flickered as if to validate his claim about the weather.

Isabella looked up. "Might be a good idea to take out some flashlights and lanterns, huh?"

"I would. In the short time I've been staying at Marnie's, we've lost power three times." He held up a bag. "I come bearing nachos, cheese fries, and an excellent bottle of Chardonnay. Figured you girls could use a pick-me-up after working upstairs all day." He hesitated a moment. "But before you dive in, any allergies to know about? I only ask because the place I bought these uses peanut oil in other dishes, so cross-contamination is always possible."

Isabella snatched the bag from his hands. "Yummy! And, to answer your question, Luna is deathly allergic to penicillin. Not only does she carry a few lifesaving EpiPens in her purse, but I keep a couple for her here, too. Can't be too careful, you know?"

Nate raised a brow. "That bad, huh?"

"Yep. Awful." She handed him back the bag of food and smiled. "But, fortunately, neither of us has a food allergy, and we will happily devour these nachos and fries. You can join her in the dining room while I grab plates, napkins, and wine glasses. We have a lot to talk about!" She glanced behind him. "Wait, no Midget?"

He shook his head. "She doesn't seem to be feeling well. Her appetite has been wonky, and she's tossed her cookies a few times. I'm afraid she might have eaten something she shouldn't have at the pet-sitter's recently."

"Oh, poor baby."

"Yeah, I need to find a new doggy daycare, I think. The lady I use takes care of a half-dozen dogs without help, and she's already lost my dog a couple of times. Since Midge is an unapologetic scavenger, she gets in trouble on occasion."

"Hold up a sec," Isabella said. "Just how in the blazes do you 'lose' a gazillion-pound dog?"

Nate shrugged. "No clue, but she did. When she lost Midge last month, it took me four hours to find her."

"Well, that is unacceptable. And, honestly, we've grown very fond of that 'Clifford' dog of yours."

Nate smiled. "It's pretty obvious the feeling is mutual."

"That's what I mean. Until you find another pet-sitter, Midget is welcome to hang out here as long as you need."

He chuckled. "Oh, I don't think so. I could never do that to you." Then, with a wink, he added, "I like you too much."

Isabella's cheeks grew hot. "Um, we… we like you, too."

Nate's upper lip quivered as he held back a smile.

"Uh, okay, you can go on into the dining room. I'll grab what we need and be right back," she said, willing her heart to slow down. His words, innocent as they were, had rattled her.

*I could never do that to you.*

*I like you too much.*

Five minutes later, the three were huddled around the table, munching on fries and insanely good nachos.

Isabella bit into a gooey chip. "Talk about ruining your supper, but who cares! These are so good, Nate!"

"Yes, dangerously good," Luna said between bites. "Officer Decker, I fear I've fallen for you. Where did you get this, anyway? It's like the cheese is making love to my tongue."

Nate laughed. "There's a new food truck in town. The man who runs it is a former Marine named Devin Walsh. I go there once or twice a week on food runs for the guys at the station." He peeked at Isabella and shrugged sheepishly. "Low man on the totem pole has to buy lunch."

Isabella winked. "Goes without sayin'."

"Anyway, we've become kind of friendly. Devin's a great guy, and," he waggled his eyebrows at Luna, "he's single. Good-looking and financially stable, too."

Luna narrowed her gaze. "Sounds too good to be true. What's wrong with him?"

"Luna!" Isabella said with a laugh. "Not nice!"

Nate chuckled. "Nothing is wrong with him. He was married, and it didn't work out. His ex-wife is sort of, um, difficult."

"So, she's a bitch then," Luna said bluntly.

"Well, if the term fits," he said with a wink. "Anyway, something good came from the marriage. He has sole custody of an adorable four-year-old daughter named Skye." He popped a fry in his mouth. "I know you leave tomorrow, but next time you're in town, I can take you both to meet them if you'd like."

"If he's that good, sign me up," Luna cracked.

Isabella nodded. "Yes, we're always up to making new—"

The lights flickered once more before the room was bathed in total darkness.

"Well, shit," Isabella said. "Maybe there's a tree down or something."

"Mom!" Sam yelled from somewhere upstairs. "Power's out!"

"Coming!" Isabella said, rising.

Nate touched her arm. "No, I'll go. Matty doesn't even know I'm here yet. I'll fetch them up and herd them back downstairs."

"Thanks," Isabella said. "I have a few lanterns here if you need one."

Nate stood. "That's okay," he said, toggling the switch for his phone's flashlight. "This light is pretty bright. Be right back."

Isabella moved to the dining room entryway, grabbed a flashlight, and aimed it toward the staircase, following his progress and lighting his way.

Once he was out of earshot, Luna murmured. "Jesus, what an ass."

"Excuse me?" Isabella said, turning to face Luna, surprised at how offended she'd become. "Are you nuts? Nate is probably the kindest man I know!"

Luna stuck out her tongue. "Not 'ass' as in jerkoff, Bella. I meant, like literally, what an ass!" She sighed dramatically. "Honestly, I could watch that man walk away all day, every day."

Isabella chuckled. "Hah! Well, I'll make you a deal. You can watch Nate leave," she clucked her tongue, "as long as I can watch him come!"

Luna doubled over with laughter, dangerously close to spitting out a mouthful of expensive Chardonnay.

The electricity was back on when Nate returned with the kids.

"That was quick," he said, peeking through the dining room's bay window. Outside, a clap of thunder shook the house as if to remind them that the storm still raged.

"Mommy, I'm scared!" Ellie said, rushing into Isabella's arms. "I don't like thunderstorms!"

"I know they're scary, Bug, but you're safe. Besides, thunder is just the sound the clouds make when they kiss."

Sam rolled his eyes. "Mom, that's not true! We learned about it in science last year. When lightning strikes, it makes a hole in the cloud. Thunder is the sound we hear when the hole closes."

Matty stood taller. "Um, actually, it's more complicated than that. Thunder is created by the sudden expansion of air made by a bolt of lightning. The heat from the electricity explodes within a rain cloud, causing a shockwave we know as thunder." He looked down at his shoes, suddenly uncomfortable. "It's all about the static electricity produced when positive and negative electrons collide."

Nate smiled. "I'm gonna start calling you Einstein, kiddo."

Matty blushed.

"How is it that two little kids can make me feel like an idiot," Luna quipped.

"Yeah, no kidding!" Isabella said. "Well, whatever causes it, you guys are safe. Right, Nate?"

"Absolutely!"

Isabella clapped her hands. "Okay, come on, gang! While we grownups do some paperwork, you can watch a Disney movie in the living room."

"Can we have popcorn?" Sam asked.

Isabella frowned. "Sorry, bud. I think we used the last of it the other night. How about some pretzels instead? Not too many, though. Dinner is right around the corner."

"Deal!"

While Isabella set up the children, Luna stood near the dining room window, occasionally peering into the storm. "Man, it is black out there. How is Midge with thunder?"

Nate tucked his hands into his pockets. "Well, she isn't a fan, but neither is she off-the-wall neurotic during a storm. I'm sure if she had her choice, it would be blue-sky sunny every damned day."

"Girl after my own heart," Luna joked.

"Mine, too. So, tell me," Nate nodded to the box in the center of the table, "what's in the box? Buried treasure?"

"You could say that," Luna replied. "We found it under some floorboards in Ellie's room. It's filled with love letters to an enslaved girl who used to live on the plantation."

"Abigail Charles? Isabella mentioned the name before."

Luna nodded. "Yes. It looks like maybe one of the original owners wrote them." She chewed the inside of her cheek. "Hey, can I ask a favor?"

"Of course."

She eyed the entrance to the room, ensuring Isabella wasn't nearby. "What I am going to tell you must be kept in the strictest confidence," she said, her voice low. "I'm only sharing it because I'm worried about Isabella. Without going into too much detail, she's had a rough time over the past few years. Her husband has only added to her stress with his infidelity and arrogance."

Nate frowned. "Well, I haven't met Spencer yet, but—and don't take this the wrong way—asshole or not, he and Isabella are married. I'm not one to get between a man and his wife."

"You might change your tune when I tell you that, besides

being a fat bag of dicks, I'm afraid he might be dangerous."

Nathan's jaw clenched. "Dangerous? Like physically? You think he might hurt Isabella or the kids?"

"Honestly, I'm not sure about physical abuse, but emotional? Hell, he's already done it." Wearily, she rubbed her hands over her face. "Ellie had a twin sister, Anna Rae. Three years ago, she and Isabella were home sick with the flu while Spencer was out doing God knows what. Sam and Ellie were at the park with me."

"This sounds bad," Nate said.

"Horrendously so. Anyway, long story short, Bella fell asleep on the couch, and somehow Anna got the back door open and made her way to the swimming pool."

Nate looked like he'd been sucker-punched in the gut. "She drowned?"

Eyes filling at the memory, Luna nodded.

"Christ, that's awful," Nate said. "Worse than awful. She must have been what? Two years old?"

Luna nodded sadly. "Yes, two years old and unable to swim. The accident pushed Bella over the edge. Grief ate at her by day, and guilt assaulted her by night. One day, she finally broke."

"My God. I don't even know what to say."

"Not much *to* say, really. Nothing will change the past. Anyhow, I took a leave of absence and stayed in her house for weeks, tending to the kids while she was recovering in a mental hospital."

"Was Spencer in the house with you?"

"Unfortunately," Luna said sourly. "And, although you could never call me a fan of his, even I was shocked to see another side of him. A very ugly side."

"How ugly?"

"Mega ugly. I discovered that the bastard blamed Isabella for Anna's death and intended to have her committed. Like long-term."

Nate raked a hand through his hair. "Seriously? What a scumbag."

"That's not all. Whenever we were alone, Spencer would toss out wild accusations, accusing me of sabotaging his marriage. He'd overheard Iz and me talking about her plans to leave him. She knew he was cheating on her, knew he'd only married her for her wallet. One day, he cornered me, threatened to have my nursing license revoked."

"Jesus, I hate this dude already. Could he do that? Mess with your license?"

"Nah, I doubt it. But he did back me into a corner to try and scare me." She laughed mirthlessly. "Imagine that—a preppy, self-righteous prick like him trying to intimidate me. Obviously, he doesn't know me very well."

"What did you do?"

"Let's just say I wouldn't be shocked to learn he needed to ice his balls for weeks," she said, smiling. "Anyway, it's not about me. My Izzy-B is still healing, still fragile. It wouldn't surprise me if Spencer used that to his advantage."

A crack of lightning, too close to the house for Luna's comfort, flashed outside. Right behind it, the ensuing roll of thunder told them the storm was right on top of them.

"I think I get the picture," Nate said, scowling. "Unfortunately, I deal with men like him way too often. What can I do to help?"

"Just be aware, look out for her. Maybe bring Matty and Midge by for a visit while I'm gone."

Isabella's approaching footsteps caused Luna to lower her voice even more. "I hate to put you in the middle of this, Nate, but I don't know who else to turn to."

Nate whispered back. "Don't worry. I've got her."

When Isabella entered the dining room, Luna and Nate were huddled in the corner.

"Okay, what'd I miss?" she asked. "You two look like you're

planning something."

"The only thing I'm planning on is eatin' me some more of those nachos," Luna quipped.

Dubious, Isabella cocked her head. "If you say so." She nodded at the folder and box on the table. "Let's see what you found, Luna, and then we can dive into Edward's letters."

Nate, hands in his pockets, didn't move. He stood still, staring at a painting hanging in one corner of the dining room.

"Uh, hello? Earth to Nathan," Luna said. "Are you planning on joining us?"

"This is a beauty," he finally said, nodding to the painting. His eyes found Isabella's. "Is it Rosemear? Did you do this?"

Isabella blushed. "I did. I painted it almost five years ago and long before I set eyes on this house. Even stranger? I almost always do landscape paintings, so I have no idea what pressed me to do this. Honestly? If I hadn't signed and dated it, I couldn't swear it was my art. I don't even remember painting it."

"Sweet Mother McCrarey!" Luna whispered. "It's like Rosemear knew you'd end up here!"

"Like it was calling to me, but I couldn't hear." Isabella shook her head in wonder. "Like it was calling me home."

Once they were seated at the table, Luna reached for the folder and opened it. Flipping through the pages inside, she said, "Okay, I've tried to organize it as best I can. This first pile of papers includes the former owners of Rosemear and anything I could find out about them." She lifted another stack of paper-clipped pages. "This section is information I learned about the land, any deeds, and what is known about the graves out back. And this last part," she waved a third stack of papers, "contains copies of newspaper articles, research done by the town historian, and what Atticus Jones told me regarding his ancestors, the murders here, and Abigail Charles."

Nate whistled. "Wow, looks like you got a lot of information."

"Unfortunately, I didn't. While it looks like it, much of the info is fluff and kind of redundant. There are a few deeds, some plot maps, a couple of obituaries and brief newspaper articles, and my handwritten notes after interviewing Mr. Jones."

"Well, it's certainly more than we had," Isabella said. "And it's more than the realtor led us to believe was out there. She told us any historical information about the crimes here was lost in a fire."

Luna nodded. "Much of it was. This history," Luna tapped the folder, "is pieced together by several sources. A lot of it is based on suspicion and assumption." She grinned. "So, unless Martin decides to tell us what *he* knows, it's all we got."

"I'm not volunteering for that job," Isabella said. "Can you imagine what Spencer would do if I told him I was communicating with a ghost? With intel like that, he'd have me committed and throw away the key."

"Let's not talk about him—it gives me indigestion. So, how do you want to do this? There are three piles of papers and three of us, so shall we each take a section?" She handed Nate the second pile and Isabella the third, keeping the first in front of her."

They read quietly, with only the occasional rustle of pages breaking the silence. Nate was the first to speak.

"I'm reading a surveyor report done on the property in 2014," Nate said, rubbing his chin. "How many acres of land do you have here?"

"A little over fifteen, I think," Isabella answered.

"Okay, according to this survey guy, Rosemear used to have much more than that—like five hundred acres more. Its main crop was tobacco, but it also had several cotton fields."

Isabella's eyes widened. "Five hundred?"

"Yep. I assume that over the last one-hundred-seventy-plus years, acres of property were sold off. The land was prime real estate back in the day and, I'm sure, only grew in value." He took a sip of wine. "Savannah has transformed over the years, and now what was once Rosemear land probably stretches downtown and beyond."

"Weird to think of how big this place was," Luna said. "Can you imagine how much five hundred acres would be worth in Savannah today? I wonder wh—"

The sudden slam of a door, followed by the thump-thump-thump of running feet, cut off Luna's words. Startled, she shrieked, then covered her mouth with both hands.

Isabella and Nathan jumped to their feet.

"Sounds like it came from upstairs," he said unnecessarily. All three were in the same position—heads tilted back, studying the dining room ceiling.

"Yep," Isabella answered in a whisper, eyes traveling the ceiling length. "Only problem is the kids are down here, watching a movie. There's no one up there."

"Nope," Luna murmured, rubbing the chill away from her arms. "Not a one."

Nate stuck his cell phone in his back pocket. "Okay, well, we won't know until we check it out, right?" He bent forward and lifted his pant leg, discreetly checking the holster at his ankle.

Despite his attempt at discretion, Isabella noticed. She nodded toward the gun. "You don't expect to need that, right?"

"I don't. But as a former Boy Scout, I like to be prepared." He smoothed out his pants leg and winked at Isabella. "Don't worry. It's probably just a ghost, not a phrogger."

"Not funny, mister!" Luna growled.

"Hey, I'm just messing with you. And while I'm sure it's nothing, it doesn't hurt to look, right? Plus, I can check on your progress in Ellie's room."

"Then I'm coming with you," Isabella said.

Nate frowned. "Uh, until I look around, I'd rather you stay

downstairs with Luna and the kids."

"And I'd rather be taller and blonde, but it is what it is." She squinted at him. "I'm coming with you, Officer Decker. Besides, I wanted to show you where the problem doors are upstairs."

"I'm sure I can find them."

"And I'm sure things would go faster if I were there to guide you."

Frustrated, Nate threw his arms out to the side. "What if there *is* an intruder, though? While we're standing here wasting time, some jamoke could be upstairs committing all kinds of felonies."

Isabella giggled. "A jamoke?" she said, looking at Luna. "Why do I feel like I've just jumped back in time?"

"You'd make a fabulous Lucy. Remember, everyone loves Lucy."

"I don't think I have the proper skin color for red hair. And I look absolutely horrid with red lipstick."

"Oh, very true. Positively freakish."

"Is comedy hour over?" Nate asked, rubbing the back of his neck. "Look, it's dumb to argue about this. Just let me do a quick sweep upstairs, okay?"

"Nate," Isabella said, brows raised. "I wouldn't have to argue if you'd hand in your 'savior' card and listen to me."

"Savior card? I've been called a lot of things, but savior ain't one of them."

Isabella squinted at him. "Well, if the cross fits."

Luna snickered.

Nate slowly shook his head. "Tell me, Mrs. Boyd," he said, trying to hide a smile, "are you always this difficult?"

Luna huffed. "Dude, you don't know the half of it!"

"You call it difficult; I call it determined," Isabella said dryly. "Now, if we are done here, can we go look for the monster, please?"

"It's not a monster, Bella. It's a lost soul with unfinished business or a demon wanting to steal our souls." Luna tilted her head.

"Could be the creaking of an ancient house or the wind against the eaves." She paused, then snapped her fingers. "Or—and this is where my money is—it's a homicidal maniac waiting for the perfect moment to chop us all up into fun-sized pieces." She patted Isabella's arm. "But rest assured, Sis. It's not a monster."

"Comforting," Isabella said. Her eyes found Nate's, and she swept out an arm. "After you?"

"Super," Nate grumbled, slipping past Isabella and heading toward the stairs. "Just stay close, will ya?"

Isabella grabbed the back of his shirt. "Like bees on a honeycomb, Officer Decker. Like bees on a honeycomb."

# CHAPTER TWENTY-ONE
## *ABIGAIL*

*Rosemear*
*August 10th, 1859*

Abigail had no idea how long she'd lain there.

Tears slid down her cheeks as she stared at the barn rafters, willing herself to move. Silently, she struggled, her muscles betraying her mind's commands to stand.

Her body's deceit was the second betrayal she'd experienced this warm summer evening.

The first breach of faith—and the one that stung the most—sat squarely on Young Joseph's shoulders.

His disloyalty hurt more than any physical pain she'd ever experienced.

Ignoring the dull ache crushing her heart, Abigail pushed all thoughts of Joseph's actions from her mind and focused on the task at hand.

Survival.

Ten minutes passed before she could roll to her side; after

another five, she sat up, wincing at the burning pain blazing a path between her legs. Head on a swivel, she checked for any signs of her rapist.

Satisfied that Clyde Baldwin was gone and she was safe for the moment, Abigail searched the floor, looking for her clothes.

Instead, she found blood.

Rivulets of red trailed from her thighs to her calves, keeping beat with the throbbing between her legs.

She gasped, gawking at the crimson flow, mortified by the stain of sin thrust upon her.

As if she needed a reminder of the horrors that had occurred and the cost of what had been taken.

Ignoring her budding panic, she resumed the search for her clothes, finally spotting them in a pile beneath the loft ladder.

Dragging herself painfully across the barn floor, Abigail made her way to the crumpled heap of clothing and sat before them. One by one, she inspected the garments. Her intimates, a cotton shift and petticoat, were shredded; her calico dress wrinkled and stained.

She pushed aside the tattered undergarments and, moaning softly, lifted her dress over her head.

Every inch of her body felt raw, bruised, battered.

When she got to her knees, the barn began to whirl.

Ignoring the sensation, she stood.

Nausea choked her as her vision blurred and the room spun faster. Panicked, she tried to keep her legs under her, shuffling her feet while swiping at empty pockets of air. Unable to regain her balance, she collapsed backward, landing with a thud on her right hip.

A vile laugh, dark and wicked, reached her ears.

Then, a leisurely clap as Clyde Baldwin emerged from the shadows.

"Well, now, ain't that a sight to behold," Clyde said, still clapping slowly. "Might be a tad more fun to see you flat on your back with your skirts hiked up, though." Snickering, he added, "Oh, wait! That's a sight I seen before, ain't it?"

Abigail feared he could hear the thunder inside her chest as her heart galloped like wild horses beneath her filthy clothing. "You've taken all I have to give, Mr. Baldwin," she whispered, holding back a sob. "I have nothing left."

"Nonsense!" Clyde's voice boomed at her. "Why, it's surely been an hour since we last enjoyed each other's company! What do you say? Want another go-around?"

He licked his lips as his gaze traversed every inch of her body.

Anger flared from somewhere deep within her, and Abigail struggled to stand. She refused to let him see her fear, even if that meant risking a second attack.

Because she'd rather die fighting on her feet than helplessly on her knees.

Upright at last, Abigail said, "Do what you will, Mr. Baldwin. You can't hurt me anymore."

His face grew red with rage. Clenching his jaw, hands fisted, he took a step forward. "That what you think, little one? That I can't hurt you anymore?" He clicked his tongue in disapproval. "Honey, they all kinds of pain and sufferin' out there. Just you wait and see."

He charged her, and Abigail screamed, scurrying back while lifting her arm to stop him.

Still driving forward, Clyde swiped a hand near her midsection and found a fistful of fabric. Abigail stumbled but was able to stay on her feet.

Before Clyde could yank her toward him, a booming voice ricocheted off the barn walls.

"Stop! Stop this immediately!"

Clyde froze, and Abigail—arm held protectively over her bosom—lifted her gaze to see who had spoken.

*Thank you, Jesus!*

Clyde released his hold on Abigail's dress and leisurely turned.

Edward Hawthorne, body shaking in fury, stood glaring at him.

"Evenin', Mr. Hawthorne," Clyde said coolly. "Somethin' I can do for you?"

Appalled at the overseer's flippant attitude, Edward staggered forward until he was inches from Clyde's face.

"Some… something you ca…can do," Edward slurred. "Unbelievable! Yes, Baldwin, there is something you can do for me!" He grabbed Clyde by the neck. "Step away from Miss Charles right now before I break you!"

Clyde raised both hands in surrender, then stepped backward when Edward released him. "You got it, boss. Don't see why you getting all hot and bothered over a Negro woman, though."

Edward, jaw clenched and eyes still on Baldwin, said, "Abigail? Are you all right? Did this flea-infested mongrel harm you?"

Abigail took a calming breath, trying to hide her disappointment. Edward's unsteady gait, his mumbled words, and the reek of bourbon permeating the air told her he was, once again, intoxicated. "He attacked me, Mr. Edward," Abigail said, eyes downcast. "He… he violated me. Took liberties with me no man has taken before."

Edward, eyes black with rage, reached for the overseer's throat once again.

Gasping, Clyde tugged at the hand around his neck. "Violated you?" he wheezed, gaze pinned on Abigail. "Hell, I rode you hard, Missy. And you loved it. You ain't never had such pleasure before!"

"Shut up!" Edward thundered.

Winking, Clyde whispered, "Wanna know how I could tell she was havin' fun, Edward? It was on account of how wet she was. Yeah, she was good and wet for ol' Clyde."

"You shut your filthy mouth, Baldwin!" Edward roared, hurling him to the floor.

Clyde rolled into a ball and waited for the onslaught he knew was coming.

"Damn you!" Edward screamed, kicking blindly at the man on the ground, punctuating each word with a vicious strike. "What. Gives. You. The. Right. To. Take. What. Isn't. Yours?"

"Ahh, but I made her mine," Clyde smirked, "I fucked her good."

A primitive cry escaped Edward's lips, and his foot flew forward, savagely connecting with the overseer's mouth.

Blood and saliva sprayed into the air as, trying to maintain his balance through a haze of whiskey, he began a concentrated assault on the overseer's midsection. "Answer me! Who told you that you could take what is rightfully mine? Who gave you permission?"

Clyde, arms wrapped protectively around his abdomen, cackled like a hyena. "Permission? You really don't know, do you?" His eyes found Abigail's. "None of ya know, do ya?" Supporting his injured ribs with a forearm, he sat up. "Jesus, man, think! Who on this plantation has the power to let me take what I want?"

Edward's brow dipped, and his forehead wrinkled. "What are you going on about? No one at Rosemear would condone such a cowardly act upon a defenseless woman!"

Anxiety building, Abigail took a deep breath but remained silent. She had no intention of disclosing the ugly lies Clyde had told her about Edward's father and his complicity in her attack.

She didn't believe any of it.

In her estimation, any man who had helped create a soul as sweet as Edward Hawthorne could never be that cruel.

Clyde sneered, displaying a row of rotting teeth bathed in blood. "That what you think, is it?" he lisped, the gash in his lip slurring his words.

Edward curled his hands into fists. "You're stalling. Make your point, man!"

"My point is… oh, never mind. Let me ask you a question

instead," Clyde said, rubbing his chin as if deep in thought.

Abigail tensed, waiting.

"Come on, then," Edward said, planting a boot in the center of Clyde's chest and pushing him to his back, pinning him to the ground. "Ask me this question of yours so I can get to the business of beating you senseless."

"I will if you let me up," Clyde huffed. "I can't hardly breathe with your foot on my chest."

Edward released him. "You have thirty seconds," he growled.

Clyde struggled to his feet. "Here's the thing. Did you ever wonder," he said, placing a finger in his mouth and wiggling a loose front tooth, "what your pappy would do if you were to be caught up tight in a scandal? A scandal that, say, involved canoodling with a slave girl and teachin' her to read?" He pulled his finger away from his mouth and studied the streak of blood surrounding his cuticle. "Not for me to say, but if it were me, I'd be madder than a wet hen. In fact, I might be so mad as to enlist the help of someone trustworthy."

"Don't listen to him, Edward," Abigail pleaded. "It's all lies. Your daddy wouldn't do this."

Edward, neck veins pulsing, said nothing.

"Yes sir, that's what I'd do, and that's what your pappy did," Clyde said, sweeping his arm in an arc. "Did you know I followed you to the park? Yes, sir. Hid there behind a tree, just watching you. How do you think your daddy found out about all this? After I set him straight, he concocted this plan, this 'reminder,' to teach you about keeping to your kind." He spat a clot of blood onto the ground. "He wants you far away from this woman."

"You're insane! You expect me to believe that my father sanctioned this vile attack against one of his people to teach me a lesson? What lesson would that be?"

Clyde wiped a hand under his nose, spreading blood across his cheek. "As I say, he's learnin' ya to stay away from those beneath you. This person," he pointed angrily at Abigail, "ain't nothin' but trouble. And you ain't just tryin' to learn her, you trying to bed her!"

Edward took a step forward, but Abigail grabbed his arm. "Wait," she said softly. "Let him finish and be done with it."

Clyde squinted. "You want to know what his instructions was? Your daddy say, 'I need that girl out of my son's life, and I don't particularly care how you do it.' Then, he clapped me on the back and said some powerful words. 'Clyde,' he said, 'the devil comes in all forms to tempt and tease the weak: A kindly old man, a snake coiled in a tree, a beautiful woman with a black heart. Our job, as Christian men, is to stop the devil in his tracks.' Now, ain't that deep?"

Edward paled. As a child, he'd heard William Hawthorne's warning that 'the devil comes in all forms' ad nauseum throughout his school years. Still, family loyalty told him to dismiss Clyde's words.

"Liar," Edward said, voice cracking.

"Nah, you know it's true. I can see it in your eyes that you believe me. Your daddy set this up; may the Lord strike me dead if he didn't." He grinned wickedly. "Oh, and I'm of the mind that Miss Lillian knew about our plans, encouraged them, even. She turns green with envy whenever a pretty lady like Abigail here walks by."

"Hold on." Abigail jumped in, fire in her eyes. "You're saying Lillian Hawthorne is part of this?"

Clyde leered at her. "You know, you're awfully brave, Missy. I'm thinking you ain't learned your lesson about respect yet." He dragged a thumb over his bottom lip, noted a droplet of blood at his fingertip, and licked it off.

Abigail's eyes widened, and she started to shake.

"But don't you worry," he continued, fidgeting with his belt buckle. "Good ol' Clyde here is gonna keep on poundin' sense into you. And I reckon to keep ridin' you silly until you learn your place. Now, come on over here, sweet thing."

Abigail gasped and took a step backward.

Hot, blind rage overtook Edward, surprising him with its ferocity. Growling, he leaped forward, tackling Clyde and throwing him to the ground.

Fists flew as the duo rolled on the barn floor, trading punches. Clyde landed an uppercut to Edward's jaw; Edward, in turn, blackened Clyde's eye with a powerful jab.

"Stop, please!" Abigail cried out. Frantic, she looked around, searching for a savior. Her eyes lit upon the back barn door. It was slightly ajar, a sliver of waning daylight peeping through the tiny opening.

And behind that cracked door, a shadowed figure watched them through impossibly wide eyes.

"Please!" Abigail yelled. "Help! They're going to kill each other!"

She heard a muffled sob and the shuffling of feet before the beam of light vanished with the closing of the door.

Abigail fell to her knees. "Oh, Lord," she sobbed. "Save us!"

Work done for the day, Abraham laid down his trowel and mopped his brow with a kerchief.

He'd been repairing the exterior bricks on the cook's cabin for days. The high temperatures inside the cookhouse, combined with the poor quality of materials used to build the structure, made crevices and cracks inevitable.

Bone-tired, Abraham sat back on his haunches and squinted at the man before him. "Tell me truly, Virgil... You saying you done leave them in there? Fightin' like wildcats?"

Virgil, hands laced behind his back, studied the ground. "Well, yeah, I reckon I did. Nothin' I could do that ain't leadin' to a whooping."

Abraham nodded. "A Black man getting in between two White

men's business means trouble for sure. Still, our Miss Abby is in there."

Virgil frowned. "I know. And it look like she been hurt, too."

"Hurt? Hurt how?"

Uncomfortable, Virgil shrugged. "Only thing I know is Mr. Clyde did…something. Miss Abigail's dress were dirty, and her underthings…" His face grew hot. "They was in a pile, all tore up."

Abraham ground his teeth. "This news don't please me, Virgil. No sir, it don't please me at all." Eyes narrowing, he said, "We be needin' a conversation with Mr. Clyde Baldwin. What else you know?"

Virgil shook his head. "Nothing else. But I think I know some-one who do."

"Who?"

"Young Joseph. I saw him sneakin' out the barn earlier, a shake after Miss Abigail went in. Ashamed to say I kept workin' and minding my business."

Abraham took in the information. "Keeping Miss Abigail safe *is* our business. But that don't matter now, Virgil." He stood, stretch-ing his back. "All in the past, and ain't nothin' gonna change that. What we do now is what matters."

"You got a plan?"

"I do. First, we find Young Joseph and see what the devil is goin' on here. If we gonna act, we need to be sure we doing what's right. Can't help no one if we set up a fox trap in the wrong henhouse."

"And after we find Joseph?"

Abraham cracked his knuckles. "After that, we find Miss Abigail and keep her from harm, whatever the cost."

Virgil nodded solemnly. "Yes. Whatever the cost."

After an endless barrage of punches and kicks, Clyde Baldwin lay still on the barn floor.

"Is he dead?" Abigail whispered.

Edward reached a bloody, battered hand to Clyde's neck. "No, he's alive. I believe I just knocked him out."

"I'm indebted to you, Edward. No telling what would have happened if you didn't…"

"You're welcome, love." He dropped his head. "Abigail, I don't think Baldwin was lying. I'm afraid my father had his hand in the attack on you."

She moved closer, finding his familiar scent of tobacco and bourbon comforting. Placing her head on his chest, she listened to the galloping rhythm of his heart, fearing it might soon burst. "Hush, now," she soothed, running a hand over Edward's shoulder. "Clyde Baldwin is a wicked man, and evil folk tell no truths."

"Abigail," Edward slurred, exhaustion and the last three glasses of bourbon suddenly catching up with him, "will you be okay here for a little while? I must speak to my father, bring him here before Baldwin regains consciousness and can change his story."

Uneasy, she looked at the crumpled form of Clyde Baldwin. "Maybe I should come with you. I need to fetch a new dress anyway."

Edward shook his head. "No, I think it's safer here. Baldwin should be out for a while, and if my father is behind this, I want him to see you, tattered dress and all." He smoothed a hand over her back. "Until I learn the truth, I fear I can't protect you. I am but one man, and my father has many spies among his poor laborers. Any one of them would like nothing more than to curry favor by doing his vile bidding. Staying hidden, for now, is safest for you."

Abigail nodded into his shoulder. "If you think that's best."

"I do," Edward said, kissing her forehead. "I will confront Father, bring him back here to challenge Baldwin's claims. Stay near the door. Should this filth awaken before I return, run for help." He broke off his embrace and headed toward the exit. "I should be back in less than fifteen minutes, Abby. I promise I'll get to the bottom of this."

After Edward left the barn, Abigail focused again on the man on the ground. Clyde remained motionless, angry welts and purple bruises dotting his face and hands.

Remembering his assault, recalling every disgusting word he'd said, she felt an emotion she seldom allowed herself to experience.

Rage.

She moved closer—her eyes never leaving Clyde's face—until she was inches from his feet.

Mustering up the courage, she kicked his calf. Hard.

He didn't flinch.

Satisfied he remained unconscious, she stepped around his legs, stopping at his torso. Bending forward, she stared into the face of the man who had brutalized her.

"You're an evil, evil man, Clyde Baldwin," she hissed, "and you will pay for what you did to me. Edward Hawthorne doesn't cotton to rapists! He will see you never step foot on this plantation again!"

The corner of Clyde's mouth twitched.

Unnerved, not entirely trusting her eyes, she bent closer and studied his face.

This time, his lips curved into an unmistakable grin.

Abigail shrieked and, heart pounding, she threw herself backward.

What happened next happened in a blink.

A growl began in Clyde's belly, growing louder as it rumbled to his chest. Through half-opened eyes, he snarled and shot out a hand, clamping her right arm at the wrist.

Abigail screamed again, wincing as he adjusted his hold and squeezed harder. The tiny bones in her wrist cracked and popped, sending shards of pain over her hand to her fingers.

Cackling, Clyde yanked Abigail's arm and she fell to her knees beside him. "Not so fast, woman," he breathed, his fetid breath gagging her. "You and me got some unfinished business." Still holding her wrist in an iron grip, he rolled to his side.

Frantic, twisting and pulling to free herself from his control, Abigail looked around for a weapon. She spotted a hoe and a rake in one corner of the barn and a bucket and shovel in another.

All adequate weapons. Unfortunately, they were at least fifty feet away and useless to her.

Out of options, she quickly scanned the room again, silently praying for a miracle.

And found it seconds later, half-buried beneath some loose straw less than five feet away. Unwieldy, but it would have to do.

She held her breath, planning her next move.

Clyde started to rise.

# CHAPTER TWENTY-TWO

O nce they reached the upstairs landing, Nate put a finger to his lips and mouthed, "Ellie's room? Right or left?"

"That way," Isabella mouthed back, pointing to the east wing.

Nate's lips quirked. "Directionally, that'd be a right," he whispered.

"Nobody likes a wise-ass," Isabella whispered back. "Come on, it's the last room." She waved dramatically, indicating the right side of the hall. "The last room on *this* side."

Nate smiled and gave a tiny salute.

They worked through the east wing bedrooms, checking behind doors and peeking inside closets. Finding nothing, they moved to the west side of the house, inspecting all the rooms except the one with the locked door and no key.

They returned to the upper landing, where Nate said, "Okay, in my line of work, we call that a cursory look. Now, we retrace our steps and spend more time looking around."

Isabella nodded. "Right behind ya."

Silently, they crept back down the east wing hallway, stopping at the first room on the left.

The room with the "Dr. Seuss" door.

"Interesting," Nate said, grabbing the edge of the open door and rocking it back and forth on its hinges. "Well, it definitely creaks." Peering into the room, he asked, "What was this used for, anyway? Seems on the smaller side for a bedroom."

"It is. I was thinking nursery, maybe? Big enough to fit a small bassinet or crib and a dresser."

A sudden tingle kissed the nape of her neck before a blast of cool air rushed by them.

The unexplained breeze was followed by the faint wails of a woman in mourning.

Isabella gasped. "Holy Hannah," she whispered, edging closer to Nate's shoulder. "Did you hear that?"

"Hear?" Nate said, frowning. "No, I didn't hear anything, but I did feel that draft. Why? What did you hear?"

Isabella glanced down the west wing hall. "I don't know. It sounded like a woman crying."

"Down there?" Nate nodded toward the opposing hallway.

Isabella hesitated. "I'm not sure. I think so. Sound seems to carry up here."

They stood still for several moments, listening. All was quiet.

"Okay, well, whatever it was has stopped for now," Nate said softly. "Let's continue a detailed search. Keep an eye out for an open or broken window. Sometimes, even the slightest crack can cause a pipe to rattle or set off a sudden whoosh of air."

"Which could sound like a moan," Isabella said quietly. "Or a woman crying."

Nate shrugged. "Maybe."

They moved further down the hall, stopping before the blue

door. "Damn," Nate said. "You don't see that color every day."

Isabella nodded, distracted. Somehow, her hand had found its way into his. And worse, he either didn't notice or didn't care. "Uh, no, quite right." She pulled her hand back, mortified, and twisted the doorknob. "And see?" She gestured at the ceiling. "Same color as the door."

Nate crossed the threshold and looked up. Whistling, he said, "This is incredible! I've read about this but have never actually seen it. Do you know the story behind this color?"

Isabella shook her head.

"Well, from what I've read, the practice began centuries ago. Back then, superstition and a healthy dose of fear ruled the masses. To combat negative energy, folks used this color, called 'haint blue,' hoping to trick malevolent spirits into thinking the room was surrounded by a sea of water or a blue sky. They believed that entities couldn't cross over either of those."

"So they painted the doors and ceilings blue for protection? Protection from what?"

"Could be anything," Nate said. "Bad luck, wandering ghosts, disease."

"Disease?" Isabella said. "I wonder if that's why this room smells like antiseptic or bleach or something. Maybe someone doused it with cleaner after a serious illness? Hopefully, Luna's medium friend can tell us more about it."

Moving to the far wall, Nate rounded the armoire and opened the closet door. He clicked the dangling chain overhead, but the space remained black.

"Yeah, sorry about that," Isabella said. "Luna and I found out earlier that it doesn't work. I'll have Spencer fiddle with it when he gets home tomorrow."

Nate clenched his jaw. "About that," he said, shining his phone's light into the darkness. "I just wanted to say I'm around if you need me."

Isabella stared at him blankly.

"You know," he continued, uncomfortable, "in case you or your husband need more muscle or something."

Isabella smiled. "That's very kind. I may take you up on it!" She headed to the hallway. "Shall we check the remaining rooms?"

Nate followed, softly closing the door behind him. Sliding closer to her, he whispered into her ear. "Okay, but stay behind me. We all heard something moving around up here, so until we know for sure, safety first, right?"

Isabella waited for him to move ahead before sliding her fingers into the back of his belt. "Not to worry, Officer. My momma didn't raise no fool."

"Hello, my pretties!" Luna called from the living room doorway.

"Hi," Sam said, voice low. "Ellie fell asleep, so we're watching monster trucks!"

Sam and Matty were huddled on the couch while Ellie, right thumb securely in her mouth, snored softly on the living room floor.

"Monster trucks, huh? Okay, but dinner is in about thirty minutes, my wee friends. Hamburgers and my famous mac and cheese." She grabbed an afghan from behind an easy chair and moved closer to the sleeping child.

"Hey, Sammy," Luna asked as she tucked the blanket around Ellie. "What's this?"

Sam leaned forward. "What?"

"This," Luna answered, pointing to Ellie's left hand. "Looks like she has a death grip on a journal or something. And, since I'm confident my favorite five-year-old does not journal…" She gently pried the leather-bound book from Ellie's fingertips and waved it in the air. "It begs the question…where did she get it?"

Sam and Matty looked at each other and shrugged. Matty was

the first to speak.

"There are lots of secrets here, Miss Luna—and even more secret hiding places."

Luna grimaced. "Ohh-kay." She drew out the word. "Creepy much, kid?"

Matty rolled his eyes. "I'm serious, though. There are all kinds of concealed nooks and crannies here. For instance…" He jumped off the couch and strolled across the room. "See this?" he said, pointing at one of the many bricks that made up the fireplace. "This is a false brick. You can tell because there is no mortar, right?" He wiggled the brick, freeing it from its position. "It's light," he tossed it in the air, "and hollow, too. And there is a latch right here," he turned the brick on its side, "which opens the box up. I'm pretty sure this is where Ellie got the book."

Sam nodded. "Yeah, she was messing around by the fireplace a lot today."

"Really?" Luna said, mind racing. Speaking to Matty, she said, "What else have you uncovered with your remarkable abilities of deductive reasoning, little man? Secret passageways? Dungeons or catacombs below the house? Trap doors?"

Ellie sat up, rubbing the sleep from her eyes. "Have you found them yet, Matty? The dead people?"

An instant later, several things occurred simultaneously.

First, a frantic buzzing sound—like a swarm of angry bees—blanketed them. As the whirring grew louder, two propane lanterns adorning either side of the fireplace flickered, and the TV over the mantel began scanning through random channels.

As the speed of the channel changes increased, the volume on the television grew louder. The clipped voices of various announcers and actors became a deafening, rapid-fire chattering.

"What the hell?" Luna yelled, turning a slow circle, palms covering her ears. "Who has the remote?"

Sam and Matty had moved next to Ellie on the floor, the

afghan draped over the trio's shoulders.

"I think it's on the end table, Aunt Luna," Sam shouted over the din.

"Got it!" Luna said, lifting the device and powering down the television.

Immediately, the obnoxious chatter stopped, although the buzzing, swarming noise droned on.

"Thank God!" Luna said. "That was driving me cuckoo! Gotta love technology, right?"

"It's not the remote, Aunt Luna," Ellie said softly. "I think it was them. I think they, um, they want us to notice them."

As soon as Ellie spoke the words, a loud series of knocks reverberated off the walls, lamps flashed on and off, and the temperature in the room plummeted.

"Jesus Christ!" Luna whispered, shivering as a blast of cold air, honeysuckle sweet, seemed to grab her, its icy fingers pinning her to the spot.

Holding her, paralyzing her, as a predator paralyzes its prey.

Unable to move, helpless in its grasp, she held her breath and waited to be devoured. Instead, it let her go.

As if whatever or whoever it was merely wanted her attention, just as Ellie had said.

The hair on her arms lifted, and Luna swallowed the nasty taste rising in her throat.

"Are-are you okay, Aunt Luna?" Ellie whispered. "You look sick."

Luna smiled and nodded, trying to slow the hammering in her chest. The rational side of her brain told her they were in a room with a chimney on the outside while a storm was raging, the wind howling.

*Drafts are always a consequence of owning a fireplace*, she thought. *Storms make strange noises and mess with electricity.*

The other side of her brain, the side that had just experienced a paralyzing and unknown force, told the rational side to shut the fuck up.

When she trusted her voice, Luna, teeth chattering, opened her mouth to speak. "El, where…" She stopped, stunned, as her words left her mouth in a visible mist.

"What the hell?" she muttered. "Where are we? Siberia?" Then, noting the three terrified faces peeking up from beneath the afghan, Luna grinned. "Oh, come on, guys! It's an old house! Tons of electrical issues and sucky insulation, right?"

Three pairs of dubious eyes squinted at her.

"But just in case…" Luna said, rubbing the chill from her arms. "Can you lay off the 'I see dead people' stuff, Eleanor? Whenever you start talking about the people in the wall, I have to check my shorts!"

No one laughed.

"Wow," Luna said, clucking her tongue. "Tough crowd."

"Sorry, Aunt Luna," Sam said. "It *is* weird, though, how stuff happens whenever Ellie talks about them." Brushing the blanket off his body, he turned to his sister. "Remember yesterday when you started talking about being buried alive again? And how the people in the wall call to you, ask you to free them?"

Ellie nodded but said nothing.

"Well, after you said that, you went to see Mom while me and Matty stayed in my room."

Luna, gaze fixed on Ellie, asked, "What happened, Sammy?"

Sam looked at Matty. "You tell it. You do it better, anyway."

Matty shrugged. "Well, okay. So, a few minutes after El left, we were playing Sam's Nintendo when we heard footsteps running in the hall. Sam got up from the floor, intending to prank Ellie and lock the door."

Luna scowled. "Not cool, Samuel."

"Sorry," Sam said sheepishly.

"Anyway," Matthew continued, "no one was there when he peeked down the hallway. At first."

Luna's heart kicked up a notch. "At first?"

Matty nodded. "Yeah. But then he saw something." He lifted both hands in a 'stop' position. "Now, I didn't see it, but I *did* hear someone running, so I believe him. I know he saw something."

Luna looked at Sam. "Okay, what did you see, Bubba?"

Sam fidgeted, playing with his fingers. "I saw—well, I thought I saw—a lady. She was sort of, I don't know, gliding down the west wing hallway."

"Gliding," Luna said, keeping her voice neutral.

"Uh, yeah. Like, not walking regular? Then, when she got to the end of the hall, she disappeared. I think she went into that last room down there."

"The locked room?" She looked at each of them in turn. "Are you sure? We haven't been able to open that door yet. No key."

"Pretty sure she doesn't need a key," Matty mumbled.

Luna crouched down and placed her hands on Sam's shoulders. "You're sure about what you saw up there? It's important we have all the facts for my friend Roma. She, um, investigates old homes, tries to find explanations for stuff."

Sam's head bobbed up and down. "I'm sure something was there, Aunt Luna, like a dark outline or shadow of a person. The figure wore a long dress, so I think it was a lady. She moved down the hall lightning fast, too! That's why Matty didn't see her."

"Gosh, that must have been scary, Sammy."

He nodded, eyes wide. "Very!"

"So, why'd you keep it a secret then, sweetheart? Why didn't you say something earlier?"

Before he could respond, Ellie, her expression worried, chimed in.

"It's not Sammy's fault. It's because I told him not to tell."

Despite their current circumstances, Luna snickered. "You *told* him not to?" She smirked at Sam. "Since when do you do what your little sister tells you to do?"

Sam, face reddening, shrugged. "It seemed important to her."

"Good answer, kid," Luna winked, sitting cross-legged on the floor in front of them. "Okay, Shortstack, what's the skinny? Why did you ask your brother to keep quiet?"

Ellie, elbows on her thighs, rested her face in her hands. Whispering, she said, "Because Martin asked to keep it a secret. He's worried that if we talk about seeing the lady, the others will hear and get really mad. They don't like her because she protects us, so she hides a lot."

"Protects us?"

Ellie nodded. "Yep. Us and Martin. She protects him from the bad ones, the others." She leaned in closer, her voice barely audible. "Martin calls them the 'Meanies' on account of them playing dirty tricks and stuff."

Luna brushed away a stray hair from Ellie's eye. "Who are the Meanies, baby?"

"The bad ones. The ones who buried the people in the wall long ago." Ellie inspected every corner of the room before continuing in a whisper. "Martin says that the Meanies like to scare people away from Rosemear. And if that doesn't work, then…"

"Then what?" Luna asked, fearing the answer.

Ellie's face fell. "Then they hurt people. They hurt them," she pointed to her temple, "up here. Make them think they are crazy and stuff. And Martin says sometimes, if the people still won't leave, the Meanies make them stay here forever." She shook her head sadly. "Martin's been at Rosemear for a long time. He doesn't like it here, but the Meanies won't let him leave. He says there are a lot of people trapped here."

Luna closed her eyes and concentrated on breathing. She could hear the thunderous beat of her heart echoing off every bone, taste the bitterness of bile from her churning stomach, and feel the shiver and shake of adrenaline-fueled muscle. It was taking everything she had not to grab the kids and Isabella and run as far away from

Rosemear as possible.

*Pull it together, Lake! Think! What is it they say? That somewhere between healthy skepticism and blind faith lies the truth?*

"Yeah," Luna muttered. "Whoever said that never stayed at Rosemear."

"Huh?" Sam asked.

"Just talking to myself, Sammy." Taking another deep breath, sounding much calmer than she felt, Luna focused again on Ellie. "What about the lady, sweetie? Who is the lady Sammy saw?"

"Oh, she's one of the good ones! I like Abigail! Remember I told you about her? About her being buried alive?"

Luna could only nod.

"Abigail protects us," Ellie said with a smile, oblivious to Luna's distress. "Us and Martin."

Luna studied her hands, choosing her words carefully. "She helps Martin with the Meanies, and I get that. But what does she protect us from?"

Ellie looked up, her eyes suddenly filling with tears. "From it all. Abigail told Martin we are surrounded by danger, and not just by dead people. He said there are alive people who…"

"Who what? I'm not sure I follow, El. Who else wants to hurt us?"

"Martin didn't tell me that. All I know for sure is the bad ones, the Meanies, aren't alive anymore." She shook her head. "And that they chased away the families who lived here by making them scared, or sick, or even worser! Some of them died here and are not supposed to leave."

"Did she…did she say anything else? Any more detail on the type of danger we face?"

"No. All I know is that the dead…."

Ellie made a strangled sound—somewhere between a sigh and a hiccup—before her lashes fluttered, and her eyes rolled behind her lids.

Luna feared she was about to seize.

"Ellie!" she yelled, shaking her shoulders. "Eleanor Boyd, are you okay? Answer me!"

In a voice not entirely her own, Ellie, eyes closed, croaked, "Martin is worried. He says to tell you no one is safe here." A single tear rolled down her cheek. "Especially Mommy. Mommy isn't safe anywhere."

When Isabella and Nate returned to the first floor, Luna and the children were sitting at the dining room table, each with a sheet of white paper in front of them.

In the center of the table, between two unlit kerosene lanterns, stood a large container holding various crayons and markers.

"Great rainy-day idea!" Isabella said, a bit too cheerfully. A flash, followed by a loud crack, startled her. "Geesh, close one!" she said, rubbing her neck. "Hate those! Anyway, what's everyone working on?"

Luna was hunched forward over Ellie's shoulder, admiring her work. "Come take a look. Judging by the paired animals, I think it's Noah's Ark."

Ellie scribbled furiously. "Not animals," she said through gritted teeth. "It's people. Pairs of people." Mindlessly, she ground the crayon back and forth, pushing until the paper tore and the crayon snapped in two. "Because none of us should be alone in Rosemear. It's the only way to stay safe, see?"

Isabella, wide-eyed, flicked a worried glance at Luna.

At a loss, Luna could only shrug and shake her head.

"You're safe, Bug," Isabella said, trying to keep the fear from her voice. "Momma and Aunt Luna won't let anything happen to you."

Ellie continued to scribble.

Desperate to lighten the mood, Isabella pointed at two figures Ellie had drawn. "Um," she said, trying to sound calm and composed. At the moment, nothing could be further than the truth. "Is that you and Sammy?"

Ellie started working on the top corner. "No," she said, pointing to two people near a tree. "This is Sam and Matty. This," she touched the figures Isabella had pointed to, "is me and Martin. I still have to draw you, Auntie Luna, Mr. Decker, and Midge."

"And Dad," Sam said. "Don't forget Dad."

Ellie ignored him.

Nate cleared his throat. "Well, you're excellent at drawing, Ellie. I assume you've gotten that talent from your mom. I must say, you've really managed to capture Matthew here." He studied the picture closely. "Is that the small headstones out back? Good eye for detail."

Ellie shrugged. "Even though we don't know them, they were somebody's someone once. It's important not to forget."

Luna clucked her tongue. "Not even sure what to say to that except, uh, eek?"

When Isabella gave Luna a warning shake of her head, Luna threw her hands up. "Well, for criminy's sake, Iz… She's five!"

Ignoring that argument for now because she knew Luna was right, Isabella attempted to change the subject. "Okay, who's hungry? We have a table to set and burgers to grill!"

"But it's still raining, Mom," Samuel said.

"It is. Lucky for you, Aunt Luna and I moved the grill beneath the portico last night."

Nate clapped his hands together. "Great! I flip a mean burger and would be happy to man the grill." He turned to the kids. "Come on, guys. Behind every good cook stand some darned good assistants!"

"Try not to set anything on fire!" Isabella teased.

"Or anyone!" Luna added.

Ellie took Nate's offered hand, and they headed to the back

door, Sam and Matty right behind them.

After they were out of sight, Isabella said, "Oh, my freaking God! What in the hell is going on here?"

Luna draped an arm over Isabella's shoulder. "So much more than we'd imagined, mon amie." She peeked behind her, assuring herself they remained alone. "I'm not sure if you and Nate found anything, but I can say with one hundred percent certainty that what me and the kids just experienced in the living room was…"

She stopped and shivered, remembering.

"You know," Isabella said, her voice dripping with sarcasm, "this whole thing you've got going where you just stop speaking mid-sentence? Yeah, it's kind of annoying. As my best friend, I think you should know this."

"Hey, just be glad I'm not standing in a puddle of piss on your gorgeous carpet! But the good news? You're not crazy."

"Super. So, what's the bad news?"

Luna rubbed her eyes and groaned. "The bad news is… you're not crazy."

# CHAPTER TWENTY-THREE
## *ABIGAIL*

*Rosemear*
*August 10th, 1859*

When Edward burst through the doors of the main house, an eerie silence greeted him.

There was none of the usual hustle and bustle that went along with running an estate, no hushed speaking among the servants, no doors clicking closed or hurried footsteps.

Just an unnatural quiet.

Staggering to the den, he stopped before the bar cart, poured himself two fingers of scotch, and downed it in one gulp.

Then he poured two more.

"Courage in a bottle," he mumbled, vision fuzzy. "Isn't that what you taught me, Father?" he yelled, voice echoing throughout the room. He filled the glass once more, brought it to his lips, and drained it. Looking around, he swayed a bit before tugging at his waistcoat.

Then, Edward Hawthorne went searching for his father.

"Let me go!" Abigail cried, pulling against Clyde's fierce grip. "Please! You're hurting my wrist!"

Clyde, reeling from a probable concussion, squeezed Abigail's wrist harder. "What makes you think I give a shit, woman?" He tugged her arm, trying to bring her closer, and she shrieked.

"No, no, no! I'll not let you hurt me again!" Yanking with all her might, she pulled her wrist from his grasp and scrambled to the weapon she'd spotted beneath the hay. Bending forward, she snatched the tool into her hands and turned to him.

Clyde chuckled. "And what are you plannin' on doing with that, Missy?"

Abigail brandished the pitchfork. "Whatever it takes to keep you away from me!"

Clyde snickered, taking half-hearted swipes at the tool. "If'n I get ahold of it, I'm gonna stick it up your ass!"

"Stay back!" Abigail warned, tightening her grip on the handle.

Growing weary of the game, Clyde feigned surrender, raising his hands. "Fine, go on. I ain't gonna stop ya."

Abigail, body trembling, moved back, daring to hope.

Her hope, as it turned out, was short-lived.

With a growl, Clyde lurched forward. "Now you're dead!"

Abigail watched in horror as two bear-sized hands grabbed the tines of the pitchfork and pulled, trying to wrestle it away from her.

Shrieking, she kicked wildly at his legs, pushing and pulling for control of the weapon, before both of them lost their footing.

The momentum forced Clyde to drop his end of the pitchfork, and he staggered backward, his head and torso connecting with a thud against the barn wall.

Abigail, off balance, stumbled forward, the pitchfork's handle still gripped snugly in her hands.

An instant later, mid-scream, she was jolted to a stop. Wide-eyed, she stared, trying to digest what she was seeing.

Clyde Baldwin, heels off the ground, was pinned to the wall behind him by the perfectly honed tines of the pitchfork.

She started to scream again.

Impaled through his belly, Clyde had one hand on the pitch-fork handle while the other reached for Abigail. "What the fuck you do?" he whispered.

Abigail's hand flew to her mouth as she stared in horror. Blood bubbled from his lips now, and a trail of crimson ran from his abdomen to the floor below. Unable to speak, she took several steps back, away from the awful sight, before she collided with a sturdy, immovable object.

Abraham.

"Oh, Abraham!" Abigail cried, turning and burying her face in his chest. "What have I done? They will hang me for sure!"

Abraham set her firmly in front of him and looked her in the eye. "Now, Miss Abby, you know I ain't gonna let that happen. You had no choice but to do this." He eyed the man currently skewered against the wall, blood still dripping from his mouth but very much alive.

"But it—it was an accident!" Abigail whispered. "I fell."

"Don't matter how it happened, lady," Clyde spat out. "You get me a doc right now, or you'll hang for this for sure. But if you help save me, I'll see to it you're spared."

Abigail, mind whirling, caught movement to her right. "Virgil!" she gasped.

Hat in his hands, Virgil stepped behind Abraham. "Yes'm." Twisting the cap he held, he frowned. "Miss Abby, you know you can't trust a snake like Mr. Baldwin. Doubt he'll live, but if'n he do, he'll tell the boss, for sure."

"Virgil's right," Abraham said softly. "Only one way to make sure he don't tell."

"Stay back!" Clyde hissed. "I'm warnin' you!"

Close to hysteria, Abigail croaked, "Oh, no, I can't do it, Abraham. I can't just kill a man!"

He sighed, a long, weary sound, as though he were bone-tired. "I know you can't." Looking at Virgil, he asked, "You ready to do this?"

Virgil nodded.

"Do what?" Abby asked, suddenly panicked. "What are you going to do?"

"We are fixin'," Abraham said, "to make sure no one knows who exactly did this." He walked closer to Clyde, Virgil right behind him. "Don't expect folks would hang all three of us." He gripped the end of the pitchfork. "Apologies, Mr. Baldwin, but you done brought this on yourself."

"No! Wait!" Clyde croaked, putting up a hand.

Abraham launched himself forward in one swift move, digging the pitchfork further into Clyde's belly.

Clyde screamed. "I-I'll fuckin' kill you!" Both hands on the pitchfork handle now, he yanked hard, a feeble attempt to remove the tines impaling him. It moved slightly, and a quick look of relief passed across his blood-smeared face as though he thought maybe, just maybe, he would get out of this.

Until Virgil emerged from beneath the shadow of a much larger Abraham.

"Forgive me, Lord," Virgil said quietly.

"What the fu…" Clyde coughed, blood spraying from his mouth. "Just what the fuck you think you're doin', man?" He kicked a leg toward Virgil, wincing at the pain in his belly when he moved. "Go on! Get away from me!"

Mouthing the words 'I'm sorry,' Virgil positioned his hands at the tip of the wooden handle and pushed, turning the tool as he went. A wet, slurping sound reverberated through the barn as the pitchfork burrowed deeper into Clyde's flesh.

"Lord, have mercy!" Abigail sobbed. "What have we done?"

Abraham yanked the pitchfork from Clyde's abdomen, stepping

to the side as the overseer's body fell to the floor. "I expect the only thing we could have done, Miss Abigail. We set things right."

Abdominal artery severed, Clyde Baldwin—overseer, brute, rapist—bled to death on the dusty barn floor.

Blind drunk, Edward swayed in the center of the parlor, blinking furiously at the sight before him.

The strong scent of copper assailed his nostrils as he searched his mind, trying to recollect how he'd gotten here. His last memory was of entering Rosemear and taking the stairs, two at a time, to his father's bedroom.

He slapped himself across the face, hoping the pain would awaken him from an alcohol-induced hallucination.

But the scene remained unchanged.

And the man sprawled on his back on the parlor floor, surrounded by an ocean of blood, was very, very real.

Bile clogged Edward's throat as he studied the as-yet-unidentified male on the floor. The victim had countless wounds covering his body, but it was his face that had borne the brunt of the attack.

The man's nose was nearly severed; his cheeks slashed to ribbons. One ear was missing, as was his right eye. The remainder of his face was spongy and raw, like chunks of flesh dripping off bone.

Leaving him unrecognizable to most.

Most, but not all.

In an instant of clarity, Edward knew the familiar silk suit, the golden watch in the dead man's pocket, the costly calfskin shoes.

"Father!" he screeched.

Squatting down, suddenly sober, Edward placed two shaking fingers on William's throat.

As he'd expected, there was no pulse.

"Jesus Christ," Edward gasped. Lightheaded, knees shaking, he attempted to stand.

Almost immediately, his toe slid in a puddle of blood, and he rocked forward. Screaming, he locked his arms in front of him, attempting to break his fall.

And found himself, wrist-deep, in a hole in William Hawthorne's belly.

Horrified, Edward ripped his hands from his father's entrails and shook them, spraying blood and flesh through the air. Dazed, he plopped down on his behind and scrambled backward, on his ass, through a river of blood, intestinal tissue still dripping from his hands.

Several feet from William Hawthorne's body, Edward's stomach revolted. He coughed once, twice, before finally retching all over his father's brand-new calfskin shoes.

Then, he started to howl.

"What do we do now, Abraham?" Virgil asked, eyes never leaving Clyde Baldwin's crumpled form.

"Now, I expect we clean up," Abraham said. "But we do it fast. If Mr. Clyde's body is found, the law will pay a visit right quick."

Virgil nodded. "Yes, sir. Savannah's Guard and Watch will come out for sure."

"But where will we put him?" Abigail asked, chewing on a nail. "Surely someone will see if we carry a body out of this barn. We need...we need help."

"You got someone in mind?" Abraham asked, knowing the answer.

"I do. Can you carry Mr. Baldwin to the back corner near that empty stall? He'll be hidden if you cover him with hay. I'll be back in a little while."

"Where you goin', Miss Abby?" Virgil asked.

Abigail pulled her ripped sleeve over her shoulder. "I'm going to the only man besides you two I trust. I'm going to Edward."

Margaret "Maggie" Hawthorne was in the backyard picking strawberries when she heard her brother's blood-curdling screams.

Following his cries, she raced through the side door and into the parlor, skidding to a stop at the vision before her. Her father, or what was left of him, lay still on the gleaming floor.

Even from ten feet away, Maggie could see he wasn't breathing.

Her eyes snapped to her brother, Edward, weeping in a corner, covered in blood and vomit. It took a moment before she finally found her voice.

"Edward?" she croaked. "What-what is this? Good God, did you do this?"

Edward's eyes flashed. "Me? Are you daft, woman? Do you honestly believe I could kill Father?"

Maggie shook her head. "Of course not. It's just that, well, look at yourself, Edward! Have you been drinking again?"

Ashamed, Edward lowered his head.

"Bloody balls! Would you even know if you did this, given your inebriated state and your history of alcoholic blackouts? Not to mention, you're covered in blood!"

"Of course I'm covered in blood!" Edward screamed, angry and on the verge of hysteria. "How could I avoid getting contaminated while checking his condition? Every square inch of this space is painted in blood! And, yes, I've been drinking. But I don't think…" He straightened and rubbed the nape of his neck. "Scratch that. I *know* I could never do this, drunk or not!"

Maggie closed her eyes briefly. "Fine. Then who did? And where the hell is Lillian?"

Giving his father's body a wide berth, Edward moved closer to Maggie. "I haven't seen anyone else besides you. I've no idea where Lillian or any of the staff could be."

"Well, we'd best find them," Maggie said. "Someone here is a killer, and unless you want to be accused of this crime, we'd best figure out who."

Edward stared at her, horrified. "But-but I told you! I didn't do this!"

Maggie clucked her tongue. "Tell that to the authorities, little brother. As the primary heir to a very wealthy man, you have the most to gain from Father's death."

"Christ, Maggie!" Edward screamed. "I did not kill him! And, since we are speaking of the most to gain, how about you? You know as well as I do how conniving you can be."

"So?"

"So, Father's will stipulates that I be a citizen in good standing to inherit his fortune. But if I were to, I don't know, be found guilty of murder? In that case, the estate would go to his only other living child." He raised a brow. "Which would be you, dear sister. Now, do you still want to talk about the person who has the motive to not only kill William Hawthorne but to frame his son for murder?"

Maggie, face growing red, remained silent.

"That's what I thought," Edward said, regaining control. "I'm going to wash up in the kitchen, and then I suggest we locate Lillian. I've learned that she and Father may be responsible for shockingly brutal crimes against our family and our most loyal workers."

"Fine," Maggie said icily. "And what of the authorities? Should we not send a worker to fetch Savannah's Guard?"

"We will, once we've located Lillian. I want a full report of what she knows and may have heard so we can pass on that information to the law." He headed toward the kitchen. "I'll only be a minute."

Maggie watched him walk away for a moment before calling

after him. "And what if we can't find Lillian?"

Without stopping, Edward called back. "Then I think we may have found the number one suspect in Father's murder."

Ten minutes after Clyde Baldwin took his last breath, Abigail walked through the back door of Rosemear into the kitchen.

"Hello?" she said softly. "Is anyone here?"

Silence.

She looked around, alarmed at what she saw. The immense room was uncharacteristically cluttered. There were empty grocery boxes near the pantry, a counter full of vegetables yet to be washed, and spilled sugar on the floor near the sink. Abigail couldn't recall a time when the kitchen wasn't spotlessly clean.

"Hello?" she said again. "Mr. Edward?"

She kept moving, calling out as she walked through the foyer and into the den.

That room, too, was empty.

"Edward!" she yelled louder. "Mr. William? Is anyone here?"

Greeted by more silence, Abigail continued through the house, eventually reaching the bloodied man without a face stretched out on the parlor floor.

"Oh, Lord!" she cried. "Edward?"

Heart racing, she padded closer to the figure, tears in her eyes. "Edward?" she said again, eyes roaming over the body.

When her gaze landed on the man's feet, she breathed a sigh of relief.

Edward had no interest in flashy shoes.

But his father did.

A loud bang from above startled her, and she moved from the parlor to the foyer, stopping at the foot of the elaborate staircase.

Hearing nothing, she crept up the stairs, momentarily forgetting about the dead man in the barn.

Clyde was gone and no longer a threat. He meant nothing anymore.

Her biggest fear now was that William Hawthorne's killer could still be lurking about, putting them all in danger.

She reached the second-floor landing and froze. Two hushed voices, male and female, were coming from the main bedroom. Holding her breath, she tiptoed to the door and peeked inside.

Edward and Maggie, their backs blocking her view, were standing over the bed, staring down at something.

"Mr. Edward? Miss Margaret?" Abigail whispered.

Edward and Maggie turned as one, allowing Abigail to view what held their fascination.

Lillian Hawthorne was face down on the bed, unmoving, her hair and clothing saturated in blood.

"Oh, sweet Jesus!" Abigail said, blessing herself. "What has happened here?"

Maggie studied Abigail's bruised face, torn dress, and blood-soaked hands. "Perhaps we should be asking you that question, Abigail. You look a fright. Where have you been, anyway?"

Confused by the implication, Abigail said, "Why, I've been in the barn. There's been some trouble there. It's what I came to see Edward about."

Edward sank to the floor. He rubbed his face with his hands and looked up at her. "I'm afraid it will have to wait, Abigail. A horrendous crime has been committed here. My father and his wife have just been murdered!"

Abigail rubbed a chill from her arms. "I feared that was Mr. William in the parlor. Oh, I am sorry, Mr. Edward, Ms. Margaret. This is… simply awful!"

"Yes, it is, but our grief must wait. We need to get the law out here right away."

Abigail drew a steadying breath, ignoring the urge to run. "Uh, the law, Mr. Edward?"

"Why, yes, of course. A serious crime has been committed, and the guilty party is on the loose."

Abigail wiped her damp palms on her skirt. "Before you send for them, though, can I speak to you? It's about the barn."

Maggie's eyes narrowed, and she plastered on a fake smile. "What could you possibly have to talk about that is more important than finding my father's killer? Unless you know something about it?"

"Oh, Maggie! Enough!" Edward snapped, getting back to his feet. Addressing Abigail, he said, "I'm sorry, Abby, but I must take care of this first. We could have a lunatic living among us."

"I understand, but…" Abigail pushed. "About the barn? Something bad has happened."

"Worse than this?" Edward said brusquely, waving a hand over Lillian's body. "Look, you're safe right now. Just stay close by until this gets sorted."

"Yes, sir," Abigail sighed. "I'll be in the kitchen, tidying up, if you need me."

"Interesting," Maggie murmured once Abigail had gone. "She seems very familiar with you, Edward. If I didn't know any better, I'd say she was sweet on you."

He dragged a hand down his face and groaned. "Oh, what are you going on about, Margaret Jane?"

Maggie grinned. "Just saying. Someone like that, pining after a White man? I expect Father would have something to say about that."

Edward froze.

"No sir, he wouldn't be pleased at all," she continued, enjoying herself. "Let's say he were to, I don't know, forbid her from acting on those feelings? Why, that would take away any chance she had at a better life, wouldn't it?" Maggie inhaled dramatically. "Wait a minute! Do you smell that?"

Edward scowled. "I've no time for your games, Margaret.

Right now, all I smell is blood and death."

"Sure, there's that," she agreed, "but that's not what I'm talking about. I'm talking about the underlying stench here."

"What stench?"

Margaret sneered. "The reek of a desperate whore."

Edward's jaw ticked. "You know, if you were a man, I'd beat the piss out of you! Abigail is no whore! She's as genuine and sweet as the day is long!"

"And she's the best suspect we have. Well, except for you. What is it the Bible says? The love of money is the root of all evil? And, as you are the sole heir to a fortune, your name would surely come up in an investigation. Just my opinion, mind you, but if I were you, I'd think long and hard about shielding her from this."

Gritting his teeth, Edward said, "Abby is not a killer."

"Probably not. Truthfully, I myself would hate to point a finger at Abigail to the authorities. Lovely girl. It's just that I'm not sure my conscience could let this go." She studied a fingernail. "Of course, if I were gifted, say, half of Father's fortune? Well then, I could leave here and start over without reminders of this terrible day."

"You cannot be fucking serious!"

"As the God-damned plague, Edward. Paying me off is option one. Option two is that I tell Savannah's Guard and Watch that you got into an awful fight with Father over your affair with a slave girl."

"That's a lie, and you know it!"

Maggie patted his back. "But you'd never prove it. Look, just throw Abby's name out there. It will take suspicion away from you, and you'll make sure nothing happens to her. If she is innocent, the investigation will show that. Even if they accuse her of murder, you know enough people. You could clear her name and live happily ever after with your share of Father's money."

Unable to stay in the room with either Lillian's mutilated corpse or his traitorous sister any longer, Edward moved into the hallway. "You're out of your mind. I'd never do that to anyone, let alone Abigail. I love her."

"But if you don't accuse her," Maggie warned, "you'll lose a fortune and most likely your freedom. It won't take long for them to figure out you two are having an affair, Edward. You'll be charged with conspiracy at the bare minimum. And Abigail will hang."

Edward rested his head against the wall in the hallway. "You're forgetting the most critical piece of this puzzle, Margaret. If neither of us did this, and if Abigail is without guilt, then who committed these atrocities?"

Margaret squinted at him. "Whoa, not so fast. I never said I believed you and your little strumpet were innocent of these murders."

Edward clenched his fists. "And *you* never claimed to be innocent either!" he barked, storming away from her and hurrying toward the staircase.

"No," Margaret whispered to his retreating form, "I never did."

# CHAPTER TWENTY-FOUR

Isabella was placing a vase of flowers back on the dining room table when Sam bounced into the room.

"Hey, Ma? Do you think Matty can stay over again? Please, please, pretty please?"

Nate stood nearby, organizing the folders Luna had put together. "Gee, I don't know, Sam," he said. "You know what Ben Franklin said about visitors who overstay their welcome, right? Just like fish, they start to stink after a few days."

Isabella laughed. "I don't expect he meant that for a child, Nathan. Besides, it's fine. School will start soon, and these sleepovers will be few and far between." She tilted her head. "How about a trade? I was going to ask if my two could stay at your house tomorrow night. My husband is coming home, and, well, we have a lot to discuss."

Nate looked at Sam. "Okay, go tell your friend he has another night here. But I'm going to get him some clothes and stuff. Since you're only nine, you might not know this, but ten-year-olds can't wear the same clothes for more than two days in a row. It's illegal."

Sam's eyes widened. "Really?"

"No," Nate winked, "but it should be."

When Sam ran upstairs to tell Matthew, Nate addressed Isabella. "I have to work tomorrow, but Marnie has the next two days off. You can bring the kids over anytime."

Isabella smirked. "Maybe you should ask Marnie before you commit. Anyway, if she can, I would appreciate it. If not, no biggie. I'll find something entertaining for the kids to do while I speak with their father."

Flipping through the pages inside one of the folders and not seeing the words, Nate coughed into a fist. "So, um, obviously, the state of your marriage is none of my business, and I'm not asking you to betray any confidences. That said, if you're ever, um, uncomfortable in his presence, you have my number. Call me any time, day or night, and I will be here."

Isabella folded her arms across her chest. "You're a lovely man, Nathan Decker," she said, smiling. "One day, you'll make some woman the luckiest girl in the world."

His cheeks flushed, and, eager to change the subject, he skimmed the page in his hand. "Uh, thanks. So, it looks like a previous owner did a survey out back but couldn't find any information about the headstones the kids found. Maybe the gentleman Luna spoke to—"

"Someone mentioned my name?" Luna asked, drying her hands on a dish towel as she entered the dining room. Addressing Isabella, she said, "Everything is cleaned up in the kitchen, toots. Since I just heard a stampede of little feet going up the stairs, I assume we have some privacy to talk?"

"That bad, huh?" Isabella joked.

Luna clucked her tongue. "You've no idea. What happened is so freaky that I didn't want to rehash it in front of the munchkins.

They've lived through it once already."

"Yikes. Should we be sitting down for this?"

Before Luna could answer, an enormous boom shook the house.

"Christ!" Luna jumped back. "Will this storm ever end?"

"In about twenty minutes," Nate said. "This is the second line of storms coming through, but it's moving quickly."

"Thank you, Jim Cantore," Luna deadpanned.

Nate chuckled.

"Well, at least the power is still on," Isabella said. "Come on, let's grab a seat and exchange info."

Isabella and Luna each took a paper-clipped pile of papers and sat down. Nate, staring out the window, didn't move.

"Uh, you coming there, Jimbo?" Luna cracked.

Nate snorted. "Funny," he said, turning to them. "No, I am, but something suddenly hit me. What if we did our own investigation? You know, like actual ghost hunters? I have a few voice recorders and a video camera at home, packed up but easily accessible. We could do a question-and-answer session and take random pictures." He shrugged and turned back to the window. "Or is that too weird?"

"Not weird at all," Isabella said. "But I wouldn't have the slightest idea where to start. Luna? What say you?"

"I say it's a great idea! We just have to be careful not to push."

"Push?" Isabella asked. "As in?"

"Confrontation. The only thing challenging a spirit does is piss it off." Luna snapped her fingers. "We could use one of the kids' toys as a trigger object! If Martin really is here, maybe we can get him to play with us."

Isabella chewed a nail. "I don't know, Lune. Sounds dangerous for three 'jamokes' who don't know a damned thing about ghost hunting."

"Well, I'm not completely green," Luna said defensively. "Roma Lee has taught me lots of tricks. And if we do get some evidence, she can use it when she cleanses the house."

Isabella glanced at Nate, still studying the storm. "What do you think, neighbor?"

"I think it will be difficult to look for ghost activity with the kids around," Nate said, his back to them as he continued to look out the window. "You leave tomorrow and return Friday, right, Luna?"

"Yeah, mid-afternoon. Roma is coming Saturday night."

Nate walked to the table and rested a hand on Isabella's chair. "What if we did an investigation Friday night? Spencer will be on the road, and if Marnie's schedule holds, she has next Friday and Saturday off. We can have the kids stay there Friday night while we do our thing."

"Wait," Isabella said, hand up. "That would mean Marnie has the kids tomorrow and again next weekend? Oh, that's a terrible thought. I haven't even met the lady, yet I'm handing off my kids to her? No way. I want her to like me, after all."

Nate chuckled. "Oh, she'll like you, trust me. And since Matty has basically moved in here since we met you, fair is fair." He bent down and tapped the end of her nose with a finger. "No worries, pretty lady."

It was Isabella's turn to blush.

"Well, I, for one, love this plan!" Luna said excitedly. "Any evidence we find will be fresh when we show Roma. It also gives us time to find other equipment, like spirit boxes, EMF meters, and REM PODs. Heck, they even have a paranormal music box now."

Isabella lifted a brow. "I have no idea what any of that is, but get whatever you think we need, Luna, and I'll pay you back. Just don't get any security-type cameras. Spencer already has them all over the house and grounds but hasn't hooked them up yet. I don't need a gazillion extra cameras here."

"Check," Luna said with a salute. "No cameras shall be purchased. In the meantime, let's finish our conversation about

'Rose-weird' before the little tykes invade us again."

"Clever," Isabella said. "Why don't you go first? Your story seems more intense than what Nate and I experienced on the second floor."

Luna rubbed her temples. "It was horrifying but, at the same time, undeniably cool. Check this out—Sam and Matty were on the couch, and Ellie was asleep on the floor when I first looked in on the kids. She was holding a book the boys said she'd found inside a false brick in the fireplace."

Isabella frowned. "My five-year-old discovered a false brick? Who is she, Nancy Drew? How on earth did she even find it?"

"It seems her pal Martin led her there."

"Whoa," Nate said softly. "Now you've got my attention."

"Oh, that's not even the scariest part, weather-boy," Luna quipped. "When Ellie woke up, the first thing she did was ask Matty if he'd found the 'dead people' yet. Not sure if you've noticed, but shit gets real every time she mentions the people in the wall."

Isabella paled. "What kind of shit?"

"The kind of shit that would make your toes curl, and not in a good way. It was the most intense paranormal experience I've had to date. It started with a low, drone-like buzzing in the living room, followed by the overhead lights and table lamps turning on and off."

"Swell. Maybe instead of a psychic, we need an exorcist."

"Wait," Luna put up a hand, "it gets better. A moment after the lights went bonkers, the television began changing channels by itself, the volume increasing as it scanned. Do you have any idea how embarrassing it is to have a KY-Jelly commercial blasting in the background with a room full of kids?"

"I can honestly say I don't," Isabella said.

"Well, it ain't pretty. Not as bad as when the Trojan commercial was blaring, but..."

"Oh, now you're just teasing!"

"Maybe. But I'm not joking about the frigid air that blew

through me and nailed me to the spot—middle of summer, yet I could see my breath. And I was immobilized where I stood. If the house caught fire, I would have burned to death."

"Even if Jason Momoa was waiting across the room?"

"Okay, let's not get crazy here."

"Noted," Isabella said with a wink.

"We've experienced the temperature drop, too," Nate chimed in. "Anything else?"

Luna leaned forward, whispering now. "Did you know we had 'Meanies' in the house? According to Ellie, who got the scoop from Martin, Meanies are the nasty ghosts who haunt Rosemear. Martin says they trap the 'good' spirits still living here." Her brow wrinkled. "Can I say 'living' here if they're all dead?"

"Good God," Isabella whispered back. "Bad *and* good entities? Just how many ghosts are here?"

"No clue, but the bad ones sound like assholes. They fuck with people's minds, make them go cuckoo so they'll leave. If that doesn't work, they do worse, whatever that means."

"Super," Isabella said. "Any more good news before I share our experience?"

Luna nodded. "Just one more thing. Samuel says he saw a woman upstairs. She wore a dress and 'glided' down the hall before entering the locked room on the west wing. Matty didn't see her but did hear the sound of running. At first, they expected to see Ellie."

"It's like when Isabella heard crying upstairs," Nate offered. "I heard nothing, but we both felt the temperature drop."

"You heard crying?" Luna asked Isabella.

"I did. It started like your experiences, with a swift, cold breeze that appeared out of nowhere. Then, a wretched wail came from somewhere down the hall. It was as if the person, a woman, I think, was suffering unimaginable pain. That's how it felt, anyway."

"And you would know, having gone through such pain," Luna

said sympathetically.

"Unfortunately, yeah. But that doesn't rattle me as much as what you just told us about Samuel. Why on earth wouldn't he say something?"

Luna shrugged. "Believe it or not, it's because Ellie asked him not to. She said that Martin told her when we mention the dead in this house, it ramps up the Meanies. And they especially dislike the lady Sam saw because she tries to keep everyone safe."

"This lady have a name?" Nate asked.

"She does. Abigail Charles."

Isabella reached for Luna's hand. "Holy shit! This is real, isn't it? You, Nate, the kids—you couldn't all share in my hallucinations. Which means if ghosts are real, if this is a true haunting, then…" She stopped, choking back tears.

Luna smiled. "Then hand in your tin-foil hat, woman, cause it's official. You ain't cray-cray."

"I'm—I'm not, am I?" Isabella said, wiping a tear from her cheek. "I'm not crazy, not relapsing. I'm good."

Nate winked. "Yeah, you are. Better than good."

Two hours later, with the kids asleep and Nathan gone, Isabella and Luna sat at the kitchen table reading about Rosemear's history.

Flipping through papers, Isabella sighed. "You know what I keep thinking about?"

"Jason Momoa?"

Isabella laughed. "What is it with you and that guy anyway?"

"Um, have you seen him? Makes my ovaries tingle just looking at him."

"Good to know, but that's not what was on my mind," Isabella said with a smile. "I was thinking that, until now, at least in my mind, ghosts were a figment in someone else's imagination. Same with UFOs, Bigfoot, or parallel dimensions. I've always believed that if I can't touch it, feel it, or see it, it isn't real. But now…"

"Now we've both felt, heard, and seen things paranormal. And we can't put that genie back in the bottle. Changes the perspective, doesn't it?"

"Oh, a thousand times over. And, truthfully, if it was just a lost spirit attached to this place, I could share Rosemear with them. It might freak me out and take some getting used to, but I would be okay with it. But all the other stuff? The disembodied voices, the shadows, the phantom cries at night? And for God's sake—who the fuck are the 'Meanies'?"

Luna shrugged. "Every ghost here with a stick up their ass? Who knows. Not to be dramatic, but everything we've experienced—the weird symbols on the plaster upstairs, the horrible smells, the bones in the gosh-dang wall—all scream 'evil' to me. Maybe even satanic."

"You know," Isabella groaned, "sometimes I wish you'd blow sunshine and unicorns up my ass instead of being so damned honest all the time."

Luna huffed. "Hey, I've seen your ass, and it ain't big enough for a unicorn. Now, *my* ass, on the other hand…"

Isabella rolled her eyes before glancing down at the papers she held. "So, when Martin says the house doesn't want us here, does that mean all the ghosts, or just the bad ones?"

"No clue," Luna answered. "I suppose we'd need to know who's here before we can answer that." She read from the notes in front of her. "Let's start with the history of people who lived at Rose-weird."

"Can you not call it that? Gives me the willies!"

"Fine, ya big baby! So, according to the town historian, five people owned Rosemear before you, and most left under mysterious circumstances." She raised a finger to halt the conversation before sneezing into her elbow a half-dozen times.

"Allergies acting up? Not Midge, I hope!"

"Nah, it's pollen or ragweed or some such nonsense," Luna said. "Happens every summer. I have some prescription antihistamine capsules that work great. I'll leave the bottle in the drawer with my EpiPens. That way, I'll have them here next week."

"Good idea. So, you were talking about the previous owners?"

"Right. The OG, as we know, was William Hawthorne. He and his first wife, Sarah, had three children—Margaret, Elizabeth, and Edward. Sarah Hawthorne died at the age of forty-one from yellow fever."

"So young."

"She was. William married the children's nanny a year after Sarah's death."

"Fast worker."

"Indeed. During their marriage, William and his 'nanny bride' Lillian Bouchet, had two children. The firstborn, an infant named Rosemary, died at birth."

"Rosemary? I wonder if that's where 'Rosemear' came from?"

"Could be. After Rosemary's death, they had a second child. This time, it was a boy."

"Martin," Isabella said softly.

"Yes. Four-year-old Martin died in 1858 of diphtheria. It was a disease with a high fatality rate among the young. But even worse, William's second child from his marriage to Sarah, little Elizabeth, died of the same thing six months earlier."

"Losing three children in five years? I can't fathom that kind of pain," Isabella said.

"Me either. Anyway, in 1859, after the murders of William and Lillian, the surviving male heir, Edward, took possession of the home. He never married and was rarely seen in public. He died in 1923, isolated and alone, at the age of eighty-five."

"Just shows that money can't buy happiness."

Luna agreed. "True story. After Edward died, the house

remained vacant for four years until James and Clara Taylor pur-chased it." She shuffled some papers. "They stayed until 1941, a year after their only child, twelve-year-old Harry, succumbed to some unknown disease."

"Sad. Where did they move?"

"They didn't. Unable to cope with the loss, James went off the rails and shot Clara in the face before turning the gun on himself."

"Christ!" Isabella gasped. "That's horrible! Did they...did they do it in the house?"

Luna shrugged. "It doesn't say, but the next owner's luck was just as awful. Henry and Mary Douglas moved in sometime around 1948. A young couple, they lived alone until, after trying for years, Mary finally became pregnant. She gave birth to a little girl they named Alice in 1959."

Engrossed in the story, Isabella whispered, "What happened to her?"

"She died of a febrile seizure at eighteen months."

"No way!"

"Yes way. Of course, Henry and Mary were devastated. One day, while curled up in sorrow with a bottle of scotch, Mary turned on the gas to the oven but never lit the pilot light. Both she and Henry were found dead of carbon monoxide poisoning. They never knew if Mary did it deliberately."

Isabella rubbed her forehead. "Sweet Jesus, so much suffering here! Please tell me that's it with the tragedies?"

"Well, the next couple fared much better. Arthur and Pearl Lewis were childless and used Rosemear as a second home. They bought the house in 1974 and lived here, part-time, for almost thirty years until Arthur died in 2002. Pearl never returned to Rosemear after Arthur died but didn't sell the place until 2014. Those buyers, John and Macy Cates, were the ones who ran out of here faster than the devil can fly."

"So, how long did those folks make it before they bolted?"

"Not long. Illness struck again, unfortunately. The Cateses had six-year-old twins, Noah and Lily. Just months after the family moved in, Noah began experiencing mysterious symptoms and became deathly ill."

"Wow. I don't even know what to say about all this. Does it say if Noah made it?"

"Unfortunately, it doesn't."

Isabella drained her glass. "Well, if I only do one thing this weekend, it will be to track down the Cates family. I need to speak to them and find out if my kids are in danger here."

"I agree." Luna gnawed at a cuticle. "There is one more thing I noticed that caught my eye as a numbers nerd."

"Uh-oh."

"Well, it could be nothing. It's just that every adult male who lived here, except for Edward Hawthorne and John Cates, died at age forty-nine."

"Wait. What?"

Luna nodded. "Yeppers. When they checked out, William Hawthorne, James Taylor, Henry Douglas, and Arthur Lewis were all forty-nine years old. Edward, of course, was in his eighties, and John Cates was thirty-eight when he ran out of here. So, it could be coincidental, but…."

"But that's a hell of a coincidence," Isabella finished for her.

"Exactly. So, what have you got there?"

"It's an article from the archives of an old-time newspaper called the *Savannah Republican*. Must be something Kristen Marx, the librarian, printed out for us."

"I'm really starting to like that gal. So, what's it say?" Luna asked.

"The date of the piece is August 12th, 1859. It looks like the murders of William and Lillian, committed two days before the article came out, made front-page news. Hang on a sec," Isabella said, scanning the page. "Holy Hannah!"

"What?"

"There were three murders committed that day, not two. How did we not know this?"

"Three? Who was the third victim?"

"Clyde Baldwin, overseer of Rosemear. He was—gulp—killed with a pitchfork."

"That's something you don't see every day," Luna said, frowning. "Say, what was the date of the murders again?"

"Um, the article is dated August 12th, 1859, but the killings happened on August 10th."

"So, the anniversary of these murders is this Saturday, which happens to be the day Roma is coming to do her thing. Spooky, right?"

"Uh-huh," Isabella said, distracted.

"Yep. Another mighty big coincidence, don't you think?"

Isabella's eyes never left the page she was reading. "Hmm, I suppose so."

"But the craziest thing," Luna teased, knowing Isabella was only partially listening, "is the severed toes they found. All of them nasty buggers just strung together like Christmas lights or a Hawaiian lei or something. I've got a set here if you wanna take a look." She started digging around her pocket.

Isabella finally looked up. "I'm sorry, were you saying something?"

"Nothing as interesting as what you're reading, apparently."

"Sorry, Lune. I'm reading about the crime now, and it mentions an enslaved girl being found guilty of all three murders."

"Abigail Charles?" Luna asked.

"Right."

"Well, that tracks with what Atticus Jones shared with me. He said his great-great-grandfather, Prophet, was Abigail's sweetheart for a time. Family information passed down from generation to generation changed a bit through the years, with folks peppering the story with their own versions of events, but the gist remained the same. Abigail and Prophet were separated during a slave auction. Atticus said they were sold by a man named Pierce Mease Butler to settle a debt."

"Guy sounds like a dick."

"No kidding. Four hundred thirty-six people were sold over two days. Abigail was sent here, while Prophet was taken to a plantation in South Carolina. According to Atticus, they never saw each other again."

Isabella shook her head sadly. "Poor Abigail must have been devastated."

"I'm sure," Luna said, nodding toward the paper Isabella held. "Does it say what happened to her? Mr. Jones' family believed Abigail was sold to another plantation after being punished for her alleged crimes."

"No," a small voice said from the kitchen doorway, "Abigail wasn't sent away. She died here, at Rosemear."

"Ellie?" Isabella said, greeting her daughter. "Good grief, what are you doing up so late, Bug? You and your furry friend should be in bed."

Ellie squeezed her teddy bear, Mr. Jingles, tightly to her chest. The movement sent a soft, melodic chime throughout the room as the bells decorating the bear's overalls jangled. "I couldn't sleep with all the noise up there."

Isabella flicked a glance at Luna. "Noise? What noise, sweetheart?"

Ellie tucked the bear under her arm and rubbed her eyes. "All kinds of noises, but mostly stuff from Mr. Jingles. Even when I put him in Sammy's closet, his bells keep ringing."

Melodramatically, Luna made the sign of the cross.

Isabella rolled her eyes.

"What...what is making his bells jingle, Ellie?"

She shrugged. "Martin, I think. But I don't think he's making the thumps and stuff coming from my room." Voice hushed, she added, "I think it's the Meanies, Momma. They stomp and cry and talk in whispers. And they're mad, like, all the time."

Isabella, throat dry, tried to ignore the icy fingers of dread racing down her spine. "I, uh, well, Aunt Luna and I are talking kinda low, so maybe that's what you hear."

Ellie stuffed her thumb in her mouth. "But what about the crying and the bangs? And Mr. Jingles?"

Luna flicked a bell on Mr. Jingles' leg. "This is an old house, El. Drafts and odd noises are all part of the package. And you said it yourself—Martin is probably playing with Mr. Jingles."

Ellie placed the bear in one of the chairs at the table and plopped down next to him. "I don't think he's playing, Aunt Luna. He seems super-duper upset lately. I think he's trying to tell us something bad is coming."

Isabella felt every hair on her body stand up. "What's coming, sweetie? What is Martin trying to tell us?"

"I'm not sure, Mommy," Ellie whispered. "But I think he's telling us to run."

# CHAPTER TWENTY-FIVE

*Saturday, August 3rd*
*Present Day*
*8:30 am*

An hour after Luna left for Hilton Head, Isabella, coffee in hand, tiptoed down the hall to her bedroom.

Leaning a shoulder against the doorjamb, she watched the tiny figure snoring softly in her bed. After last night, she didn't have the heart to send Ellie back upstairs to Sam's room.

To the phantom whispers, the eerie knocks, and the percussion section of Mr. Jingles' orchestra.

After a moment, Isabella left her sleeping child and returned to the kitchen and the laptop she'd left open on the breakfast bar. Before Luna left, they'd been scouring the internet for contact information for John and Macy Cates using a locating service Isabella had paid for.

Within minutes, they'd found four couples named John and Macy Cates living in the United States. Two were decades older than the people who had once occupied Rosemear and not a viable option. A third John Cates resided alone in Manhattan, a widower following the death of his wife, Macy, in 2012.

The fourth and final couple lived in Charlotte, North Carolina, with their two children, Macy's mother, Claire, and a black and tan German Shepherd named Thor.

Isabella took a moment to process what she'd discovered. The amount of detailed, personal information that could be found for a small fee was unsettling.

*Christ!* she thought. *Even the dog's name is public!*

A cloak of guilt settled over her shoulders. She was invading the Cateses' privacy, poking into their personal lives. She also realized she had little choice.

She would move heaven and earth—barter and bicker with the devil himself—if it meant keeping her kids safe.

Just as she began to jot down the Cateses' contact information, her cell phone rang. Recognizing the caller ID, she smiled.

"Miss me already, Officer Decker?" she answered, shocked by her flirty tone.

"You've no idea, Mrs. Boyd," Nate replied playfully. "How are you this morning? Rugrats behaving?"

"Sam and Matty are still asleep. Ellie slept with me last night. Some strange goings-on here after you left scared the bejesus out of her."

"Can't say I like the sound of that," Nate said. "You can tell me about it when I come over. Speaking of which… My shift doesn't start until two today. I thought I could grab the kids and bring them here before I go in, to give you some privacy with your husband."

"How thoughtful of you. Truly. As far as Spencer goes, though, there's no hurry. He phoned earlier and said he had a last-minute client or something and wouldn't be home until after six. Worst case is I drop the kids at Marnie's after dinner."

"No, you've had more than your fair share of kid duty, but…" Uncomfortable, Nate hesitated a beat. "Um, not my business, but will Spencer be upset when he returns and the kids aren't there? I know he hasn't seen them for a few days."

"Upset? No, I doubt it. Spencer is, how shall I put it, old school? He believes children should be seen and not heard. I've always wondered if he actually wanted kids or was just looking for bragging rights. Nothing breaks the ice in sales like whipping out a wallet full of kid pictures, you know?" As soon as she said it, she felt an unexpected stab of regret. Even though she intended to divorce Spencer, she still felt a particular loyalty to him as the father of her children. "But that's not to say he doesn't love his kids. He does, I'm sure. It's just difficult for him to… parent."

"I see," Nate said, although he didn't. In the short time he'd known them, he'd found Sam and Ellie to be easygoing kids. "So, what's on your agenda today besides speaking with Spencer?"

Isabella checked her notepad. "My top priority is to reach out to John and Macy Cates, the last owners of Rosemear. We know from the realtor that their son got deathly ill very soon after they moved in, and I need to know if they blame their son's condition on this house." She sighed. "I hate to intrude, but I need to protect my kids."

"Of course you do. Look, how about if I swing by around noon? I can bring the kids back here and feed them a delicious lunch of—you guessed it—franks and beans. Then, while I make a living locking up bad guys, the gang will be in Marnie's capable hands."

Isabella chuckled nervously. "Ah, hotdogs are your specialty, after all."

Nate smiled. "Indeed they are, ma'am."

There was an uncomfortable silence, a lull in the conversation, and Nathan felt a tug of worry in his gut. Until now, speaking with Isabella had never felt awkward. "Um, are you still there? You got quiet all of a sudden."

"I'm here. Sorry for momentarily checking out, but it hit me when you said 'locking up bad guys' just how dangerous your job truly is. If I were your wife, I don't know if I could live with the worry that you wouldn't come home one night."

After a pause, Nathan murmured, "If you were my wife, there'd be no need to worry. I'd make damn sure to come home to you every night."

Shocked at his sweet candor, Isabella touched a palm to her flushed face. "So, um, noon, then?" she stuttered.

"Yes, ma'am. It will give us a few minutes to discuss what happened with Ellie last night before I bring the kids back here."

"And you're sure Marnie is okay with it?"

"Perfectly. She's happy to do it since you've been amazing helping us with Matty."

"Nonsense," Isabella said. "We love having him here. So, see you in a few hours? And Nate? Thanks for being such a good friend."

"You bet. See you soon."

After Nate ended the call, a soft smile touched his lips. Everything about Isabella Boyd intrigued him.

Her schoolgirl giggle, her beautiful smile, the way she tilted her head and bit her lip when deep in thought.

Sure, she was drop-dead gorgeous, but it was her tender heart and fierce loyalty that drew him in. She had an uncanny ability to make you feel like you were the most important person in the room.

The woman was on his mind constantly, as were the kids. And the more he learned about her, the more he wanted to know.

"Decker," he mumbled, scrubbing a hand down his face, "you're a fucking idiot. She's still a married woman, and you..."

Then, as if acknowledging his attraction to Isabella for the first time, he finished the thought in his mind.

*And you, my moronic friend, are in serious trouble.*

After speaking with Nate, Isabella jogged upstairs to check on Sam and Matty. The room was silent; the bedroom door shut.

She stared at the closed door, perplexed. Samuel never closed his door.

Because, even at nine years old, despite his claims to the contrary, Samuel still believed that monsters dwelled in the dark.

And lately, Isabella wasn't entirely sure they didn't.

"Knock, knock," she said, tapping the door. "You guys up?"

No answer.

She knocked once more and waited for a reply. When she heard no movement from within, Isabella turned the knob.

The beds were empty.

"Sam?" she called out. "Matty? Where are you guys?"

Again, no answer.

Satisfied the room was empty, Isabella explored the second floor, calling their names as she walked. "Samuel? Matthew? Olly olly oxen free!" After no response, she said, "Not funny, dudes! Nate is coming to get you in a few hours, and you haven't had breakfast yet."

After she checked the east wing, she headed down the opposing hall to the west side. When she reached the end of the hallway, the locked door stood wide open.

Peeking inside, she found Sam and Matty standing silently in the center of the room.

"Sam?" Isabella said, startling both boys. She crossed the threshold and looked around the space, seeing it for the first time. The quarters were cramped, almost as small as the room with the Dr. Seuss door. "Boy, it's a good thing I'm not claustrophobic. How'd you get that door opened, anyway?"

The boys looked at one another before Samuel spoke. "We didn't, Ma. It was open when we woke up." Sam nervously played with his fingers. "See, we heard noises and went to investigate. We thought maybe Ellie was playing down here."

Matty was nodding enthusiastically. "That's right! Except, when we went to find her, she wasn't here. No one was." He paused. "Well, no one we could see."

"But we heard stuff," Sam said, picking up the story. "At first, it sounded like singing."

"Or humming," Matty offered helpfully.

"Right," Sam continued. "But as we got closer, it sounded more like moaning or crying."

"Crying?" Isabella asked. "Last week, I thought I heard a little girl crying. And then, when Nate and I were up here, I heard what sounded like a woman sobbing. Ellie heard crying last night, too."

"What do you think it means, Ma?" Sam asked. "Are they sad? Do ghosts cry?"

"Oh, sweetie," she said, swallowing the lump in her throat. "I'm not sure how to answer that one. I suppose since they were alive once, it stands to reason those thoughts and feelings stay with them."

"I guess," Sam said. "Anyway, it doesn't feel scary in here. Not really. Not like in the blue room or El's room. It just feels depressing."

Isabella rubbed her upper arms. "Cold, too. Why don't you boys go downstairs and check on Ellie? She was asleep in my room but should be up by now. Then, I'll make some breakfast. How do pancakes sound?"

Matty's stomach rumbled loudly. "That sounds awesome! I'm pretty hungry!"

Isabella laughed. "I can tell." She addressed Samuel. "After we eat, we'll need to pack an overnight bag for you and Ellie. You guys are sleeping over at Matty's tonight."

"Woohoo!" Sam hollered, fist-bumping Matthew.

"And you'll be on your best behavior for Matty's mom, right?" she added, voice rising with mock severity. "Otherwise, you and I are gonna have a problem, my friend."

"Okay, Momma."

"Good boy. Off with you, then. I'll be down in a minute after I check on this door lock to see why it's been malfunctioning."

"Come on, Matty!" Sam said with a grin. "Race ya!"

She watched them tear down the hall, laughing and sprinting to the upstairs landing. "Slow down!" she yelled at their backs.

When they'd disappeared around the corner, she turned back to the door and fiddled with the knob, turning it back and forth, flipping the lock on and off.

She met no resistance.

"Okay," she said softly, "I'll bite. If everything works, why haven't we been able to get into this room?"

Ignoring the door for now, she wandered around the small space. A round window on the north side provided the only natural light. She imagined there was enough room for a twin bed and a chest of drawers, nothing more.

A glint from one of the corners caught her eye. A coin? Jewelry?

She moved closer and picked it up. It was a rose gold bangle-type bracelet with a snake coiled around the front, its eyes embellished with what looked like emeralds. Isabella had seen photos of a similar piece while reading a magazine highlighting the Victorian era. Serpent jewelry in those days was often given to a loved one as a symbol of eternity.

"And where did you come from?" she murmured, turning the piece in her hand. "Who did you belong to?"

Making a mental note to dive deeper into its meaning, she looked around once more before stuffing the bracelet into a front pocket and heading to the kitchen.

When Nate arrived at Rosemear, looking devilishly handsome in his police uniform, Isabella did her best not to swoon.

She wasn't convinced she'd pulled it off.

"You wear that uniform well, Officer Decker," she said as

they stood near the front door. Then, smiling widely, she teased, "I bet you have a fan club in town; I bet the women around here intentionally run red lights and ignore the crosswalk just to see you up close."

He laughed heartily. "Oh, yeah. I got 'em lined up. I call them my 'lead-footed ladies' because they're forever jumping curbs and rushing down Main Street to feast on my charm and good looks."

Isabella grinned. "I don't doubt it." She closed the front door and ushered him inside. "Come on in. I appreciate Marnie doing this."

"She's happy to do it."

"Hey, kids," Isabella shouted. "Nate's here!"

"Be there in a minute, Mom!" Sam yelled back. "Just looking for Ellie's toothbrush!"

"Looking for?" she muttered. "Where the hell would it go? It's a toothbrush."

Nate chuckled. "A mystery, for sure, but while we wait, you can tell me what's happened since last we spoke."

"Sounds good," Isabella said. "Follow me to the kitchen, and I'll put on a pot of coffee."

Nate bowed slightly. "After you, ma'am."

Ten minutes later, Isabella carried two steaming cups to the table and sat beside Nate.

"Sorry, fresh outta donuts," she quipped, placing the coffee in front of him.

"Hah, funny! I'm actually more of a cheesecake guy."

"Oh, then you have to try Luna's recipe! Pure heaven on earth. I'll ask her to make it next weekend." She blew on her coffee. "So, since your shift starts soon, I'll give you the SparkNotes version of what's happened since last we spoke."

"SparkNotes?"

"Yeah. Like CliffsNotes, only trendier."

Nate smiled. "Trend away."

Her stomach did a little flip when Nate smiled at her, and she tried to ignore it. "I suppose the biggest 'oh, crap' moment was that we discovered there was another person killed the day of the Hawthorne murders."

"No kidding? Who?"

"An overseer of the property. He was stabbed to death with a pitchfork."

"Ouch. Same perpetrator?"

"I haven't delved that far into it yet. I can tell you that we've found five previous owners of Rosemear. The original owner, William Hawthorne, was married twice. He and his first wife, Sarah, had three children—Margaret, Elizabeth, and Edward. You with me so far?"

"Yep."

"Okay, so, in 1851, Sarah Hawthorne died of yellow fever. A year later, William married the children's caregiver, Lillian."

"Sounds like a *Lifetime* movie."

"If not, the producers should look into it," Isabella joked. "Anyway, six years after Sarah's death, their daughter, Elizabeth, succumbed to diphtheria."

"That's rough. How old?"

"Twenty-one."

"Damn." Nate rubbed his chin. "Where's Martin in all of this?"

"After William and Lillian married, she became pregnant right away. Baby Rosemary, born in 1853, passed away at birth. A year later, Lillian gave birth to a son."

"Martin."

"You got it. That poor kid died at four from the same illness that took his half-sister, Elizabeth."

"So, Rosemary, Elizabeth, and Martin. Three kids in one family. Talk about shit luck," Nate said.

"And a parent's worst nightmare. I don't know, Nate. It's like this house has a black cloud hanging over it. There have been countless tragedies here in addition to the Hawthornes. If I were superstitious, I'd say this place is cursed."

"Not surprising," Nate said, "given its history with enslaved people. The despair and heartache those folks must have experienced had to leave an imprint here."

"Of course, but I think it might be more than that," Isabella said. "Not to sound overly dramatic, but I wonder if other forces are at work here. Forces that will do anything to keep this house bathed in the shadows of the dead rather than in the light of the living."

"Comforting," Nate said dryly. "Anything else?"

Isabella nodded. "Did you know the anniversary of the Hawthorne murders is this Saturday? It coincides with the only date Luna's psychic friend had available to visit here, which is kind of eerie." She stood. "More coffee?"

"Please."

After refilling their mugs, Isabella continued. "Some other interesting things to note. We discovered that almost every male who has died in this house did so at age forty-nine. How's that for coincidence?"

Nate whistled. "I don't believe in coincidence, but I'm happy to be miles away from forty-nine right now." He stirred his coffee. "And last night? What happened with the kids?"

Isabella started to answer when Sam called from somewhere upstairs. "We're ready, Ma! Just getting my guitar!"

Cringing, she turned to Nate and whispered, "He's not very good. Hope Marnie doesn't hit him on the head with it."

Nate howled with laughter. "Not likely. Matty has been learning to play the trombone, and if his mother hasn't clocked him yet, I think Sam is safe."

"Poor Marnie," Isabella sighed. "So, before the kids come

down…" She lowered her voice. "I'll tell you about last night, but I must warn you—the creep factor was off the hook."

Nate winked. "Don't worry. I'm starting to get used to it. It's part of the charm and allure of Rosemear."

She lifted a brow. "Charm and allure?"

"Hey," he grinned, "I read Marnie's decorating magazines. I know stuff."

"Okay, but remember my words of caution!" She smacked her lips, gathering her thoughts. "Ellie has a stuffed teddy bear named Mr. Jingles," she whispered. "She's had him since she was a baby and sleeps with him every night. His name comes from the half-dozen or so silver bells he wears on his overalls."

"Sounds like an interesting fellow."

"Under ordinary circumstances, probably. But Ellie says those bells began to ring by themselves last night, right after she heard a series of bumps, thumps, and hushed talking."

"Christ."

"Yeah. That's not all, though," Isabella continued. "Ellie also walked in on a conversation Luna and I were having about the fate of Abigail Charles. According to Atticus Jones, after she was accused of the Hawthorne murders she was sold and sent to work on another plantation."

"That's rough."

"Yeah, except according to my daughter, Abigail never left here. She died on the property."

A chill raced down Nate's spine. "How the hell could she know that?"

"Martin, maybe?" Isabella felt like she was spinning out of control and couldn't get the words out fast enough. "Then, this morning, the boys thought they heard a woman singing, or possibly crying, in the locked room at the end of the west wing. When they went to check it out, the door was wide open. I've been unable to open that door since we bought the house."

Nate frowned. "I remember you saying. I figured you'd have to take the door down."

"I did, too. But I checked the lock and the doorknob, and Nate, everything works fine." She bit her thumbnail. "It sounds bizarre, but it's almost like the room was waiting to see if we were worthy to enter the space."

He shook his head. "After everything that's going on here, I believe it." He carried his mug to the sink, then turned to face her again. "Isabella, do me one favor, okay?"

"Of course."

His brow wrinkled. "Not playing the 'savior' card, but I would be lying if I said I wasn't concerned about you being here alone. Just call if you need me, okay? I can be here in twenty minutes."

Her face flushed, touched by his kindness. "I said it before, and I'll say it again… You are a sweet man, Nathan Decker."

He winked. "Not according to my fourth-grade teacher, Mrs. Szamreta."

The sound of small feet hitting the stairs interrupted them. "We're ready, Uncle Nathan!" Matty yelled.

Nate checked his watch, hating to go. "Well, guess that's my cue."

Isabella wrinkled her nose, feeling the same pang of sadness in her chest. "I guess it is. See you in a few days?"

He smiled. "Yes, ma'am."

She watched from the front porch as the four jogged down the steps and piled into Nate's truck before disappearing down the driveway.

"Go get those bad guys, Officer Decker," Isabella whispered. "Stay safe, and see you soon."

# CHAPTER TWENTY-SIX

*Saturday, August 3rd*
*Present Day*
*1:00 p.m.*

Isabella, a notepad and pencil nearby, was punching in the number for John Cates when she received a text from Spencer.

Sighing, she abandoned the call and checked his message.

"Oh, goody," she muttered sarcastically. "You think you're still 'on point' for a six p.m. arrival. Well, no rush, Spence. Why not treat Julia Cocksucker to dinner first? I'm sure she's earned it."

Closing the text without responding, Isabella rechecked the Cateses' phone number and made the call.

On the third ring, a young girl answered. "Hello?"

"Yes, hello," Isabella said. "My name is Isabella Boyd, and I am looking for a John or Macy Cates who recently lived in Savannah, Georgia. Do I have the correct number?"

There was some shuffling, followed by the dull muffle of a hand covering the phone's receiver.

"Dad, telephone!" the little girl said, her words smothered.

In a moment, a masculine voice said, "Can I help you?"

"Mr. Cates?" Isabella asked.

"In the flesh, as they say."

She smiled, remembering how often her father had used those exact words. "That phrase brings me back," she said into the phone. "My dad used to say that all the time."

John grinned. "It's a keeper for sure. So, what can I do you for?"

*Do you for*, Isabella thought warmly. *Another Dad-ism.*

"Well, what I have to say will sound strange, but…" She doodled on the notepad, devising the best way to start without scaring him off. "My name is Isabella Boyd. My family and I recently purchased your former home here in Savannah."

Silence.

"Mr. Cates? Are you still there?"

"I'm here," he said gruffly.

Flustered by the change in his tone, Isabella continued. "Um, yes, well, I seem to have run into some…" she hesitated, "…issues here at Rosemear, and I was reaching out, hoping you could clarify them for me."

"Look, Mrs. Boyd," John said, "I wish I could help you, but we weren't there that long."

"Oh, yes, I understand that," she said hastily, "and I apologize for disturbing you. I just have a few questions I'm hoping you can answer."

"Fine," he said, resigned. "But I'm in the middle of something, so if we could hurry this up…"

"Understood," she said. "The thing is, I'm at my wits' end here, Mr. Cates. My daughter, Ellie, seems to believe this house has some supernatural—"

"Yeah, well, I don't believe in that stuff," he said, cutting her off. "Sorry, can't help you."

"Wait!" she shouted into the phone, fearing he would hang up. "Please, I need help. I'm terrified something will happen to my kids."

He sighed heavily. "What do you need to know?"

"I can't thank you enough," she said, relieved. "Recently, I've uncovered some disturbing details about the history of the home and several deaths that took place here. I understand your son, Noah, became quite ill while you were here?"

"Noah was a very sick little boy for a while. He was so sick, in fact, that we moved to Charlotte to be closer to Duke Children's Hospital in Durham. Macy and I truly feared we'd lose him."

"How frightening. Is he okay now?"

"Right as rain. Noah and his twin sister, Lily, are back to their old shenanigans."

Isabella smiled. "Wonderful to hear. If you don't mind my asking, was it cancer or something?"

"No, nothing like that. It was just some random, unexplained illness. Noah's temperature spiked to over 104 degrees for days, and he developed a yellowish tint to his eyes and skin. By the time we got him to the hospital, his organs were failing."

"Oh, my gosh," Isabella said softly. "You and your wife must have been scared to death."

"We were. The triage nurse at Duke kept asking us if we'd traveled to Africa or South America. She said his symptoms mimicked dengue fever."

"That's yellow fever, right? How bizarre."

"For sure. The doctors ran all kinds of tests, but, in the end, Noah recovered within a week of being hospitalized. Truthfully, he was on the mend twenty-four hours after we left the house."

Isabella frowned. "So, you... what? Think Rosemear was making him sick?"

"Crossed my mind, but not in the way you're thinking. My first thoughts were not of something supernatural or unearthly but something more mundane—a contaminated water supply, lead paint, asbestos in the ceiling. All I know is that we were told it was some quirky virus that came out of left field and disappeared as quickly as it came."

"Still upsetting for a parent, though."

"It was the most frightening time of my life."

"I would imagine," Isabella said, wheels turning. "Say, can I ask which bedrooms you used?"

"Of course. My wife and I took a room downstairs, and the kids slept upstairs. Lily's room was on the west side of the house, while Noah's bedroom was on the opposite side. His was the last room on the right."

*Ellie's room!*

Isabella's stomach flipped. "That's my daughter's room. We found papers hidden beneath the floorboards, dead animals inside the walls, and strange symbols etched into the plaster. Oh, and there is a God-awful smell in there that we don't believe has anything to do with the animal remains. Do you know anything about these things?"

"Can't say as I do, but we weren't there long enough to experience much, except for that smell. I planned to rip out the walls to find the source, but we left before I could."

She tapped her pencil on the table. "And how about the blue room? There was an armoire blocking a closet door. When we moved it, we found a portrait inside the closet depicting a family of six. Have you seen it?"

"I haven't," John said. "But like I told you, we only used two rooms upstairs. We weren't there long enough to explore. Hell, I was still getting the downstairs set up."

"I see. So, nothing else, then? No random sounds, phantom whispers, cold breezes?"

"It's an old house, Miss," John replied. "Old homes are notorious for creaks, moans, and drafts."

Disappointed, Isabella said, "Okay, well, thanks for your time.

I appreciate your speaking with me."

"If I think of anything else, I have your number."

Dejected, Isabella was about to end the call when John spoke up again.

"You know, there are many nooks and alcoves in that house," he said, clearing his throat. "So, even if I did witness something that seemed, uh, off, I chalked it up to the architecture interacting with light."

Isabella's pulse quickened. "Are you saying you *did* see something supernatural here, Mr. Cates?"

"I'm not sure what I saw, frankly. A shadow or movement in the periphery? A flicker of light where no light should be? As I said, it's a uniquely designed home, Mrs. Boyd, so I don't consider anything I saw to be a result of ghosts or goblins."

Isabella sighed. Whether he had experienced it or not, the man would never admit to the possibility of paranormal activity in Rosemear.

"Well, thanks again for your time. I hope you enjoy the rest of your weekend."

John hesitated, seemingly debating whether to tell Isabella something more. "Just a moment, ma'am. In the spirit of full disclosure, I will tell you something odd that happened there, something out of the norm that may interest you. I'd forgotten because it seemed so out of character for our daughter, Lily."

Isabella's ears perked up. "Oh? And what was that?"

"Well, while we lived there, Lily kept bringing up someone we'd never heard of. Strangest damned thing, since we knew no one by that name. It only lasted a few weeks, and she stopped speaking of him soon after we moved."

"Him?" Isabella croaked, fear filling her belly. "Who was Lily talking about?"

"Before I tell you, you must know something about my

daughter, Mrs. Boyd. Lily is neurodivergent and doesn't talk much. The fact that we're getting her to answer the phone is, quite honestly, huge. So, when she relayed her experiences from the house, she didn't kill us with details."

"I understand," she said. "What did Lily tell you?"

"She told us she'd made a new friend, a little boy who played with her in Noah's room."

"So, a boy, not a man?" Isabella asked, anxiety building. "Did you—did she tell you his name?"

"She did. Does the name 'Martin' mean anything to you?"

Isabella's eyes fluttered, warmth flooding her body. John had just confirmed that Martin was, indeed, real.

Meaning her sweet Ellie was not delusional.

She was psychic.

Several hours after the call with John Cates, Isabella was curled up on the sofa in the den, reading from Edward Hawthorne's diary. She'd already read his letters, and aside from learning he'd gifted Abigail with that serpent bracelet, she'd found that they were mostly just love letters.

The journal, on the other hand, seemed to offer more information about Rosemear's history. Isabella learned that Ellie's room had, indeed, belonged to Martin Hawthorne.

And the last room on the west wing, the one with the perpetually locked door where ghost children giggled and the serpent bracelet was found, had been Abigail Charles' room.

Keeping a finger on the page she was reading, Isabella flipped through to the end of the book. The final entry was dated August 5th, 1859. Judging by the jagged pieces of paper near the spine, someone had torn out the closing notations.

*Why would they do that? What were they hiding?*

She scanned the room thoughtfully, her eyes landing on the oil painting of the family they'd found upstairs. Its back to her, the framed canvas leaned lazily against a rolltop desk as if it had always been there.

As if it belonged not just in Rosemear but in this particular room.

Laying the journal on an end table, she stood, studying the raw wood slats that formed the back of the portrait. The edges of the canvas were stretched taut over the frame, then crudely secured at each corner with a thin tack. It seemed a primitive and amateurish framing job for such a detailed, professional piece of art.

When she'd brought the painting downstairs yesterday, she'd turned it to the wall to hide its face. She didn't want Ellie to see it just yet. If the child in the picture was Martin, her daughter needed to be prepared.

*Oh, who am I kidding?* she'd thought at the time. *It's not just Ellie who needs to be prepared!*

Suddenly jumpy, she moved closer to the painting, wiping her hands across her jeans as she walked. Her fingers brushed over something hard, and she froze.

*The serpent bracelet!*

Pulling it from her front pocket, she studied the intricate pattern etched around the sides of the piece. While the rose gold color attracted the eye, and the lace-like etching was gorgeous, the coiled snake in the front—with two tiny diamonds at the edge of each emerald eye—made it a stunning piece of jewelry.

The row of sparkling rubies circling the serpent's tail didn't hurt either.

Isabella decided she would get the bracelet appraised. If it was as valuable as she assumed, it belonged to the relatives of Abigail Charles, not her.

She reached for the portrait and flipped it around, studying the subjects in the painting.

Something seemed off, though she couldn't put a finger on what.

A fleeting thought dangled at the edge of her consciousness, promising an answer, before slipping back into the recesses of her brain and obscurity.

*Think, dammit! What's different?*

A loud bang coming from somewhere on the second floor startled her. "Oh, come on! What now?"

She laid the bracelet on the desk and crept toward the staircase. Although the skies outside were overcast, the many windows at the home's entrance allowed snippets of natural light to bathe the foyer. The second floor, with several windows of its own, would be just as well-lit.

But knowing that did little to slow her racing heart or tame the butterflies in her stomach. Taking a calming breath, she replayed Luna's words in her mind...

*Nothing exists in the dark of night that isn't there in the light of day.*

Ghosts were simply ordinary people, taken too soon, who had unfinished business. They weren't ghouls or demons hell-bent on scaring someone to death; they weren't evil entities plotting to capture our souls.

They were just people, albeit dead people, trying to connect to the living.

*There's nothing to fear here.*

Isabella rolled her eyes. "Nothing to fear, huh?" she muttered, shaking her head. "We're over here ass-deep in boogeymen and bullshit for weeks, but there's nothing to fear. Very prophetic, Boyd."

She scanned the upper landing, pulse pounding in her ears.

Nothing was there.

"Of course, this would happen now," she said, the sound of her own voice comforting. "It's like they know when I'm alone." Throwing her shoulders back—as if being a quarter-inch taller would slay the dragon—Isabella called up the stairs. "Okay, I'm coming up! If there's something you want to say to me, now is the time!"

She started to climb, counting as she ascended, anticipating the fourth step's groan of protest.

"One, two, three, *creak*," she smirked. "Just like clockwork."

Pausing at the top of the stairs, legs quaking, she squinted at the menacing corners of the extra-wide landing. It was darker than she expected, and she flipped on the ceiling lights.

"Hello?" she asked, blinking beneath the chandelier's brilliance while marveling at the insanity of her plight. She didn't know if she would laugh, cry, or throw up if someone actually answered. "Is anyone there?"

The house was eerily quiet, seemingly asleep; the groans and clanks had stopped.

Even the air was stagnant.

Suspended, as she was.

Then, she heard it.

"Momma?" a voice whispered. "Momma, is that you?"

Startled, she jumped back, heels landing on the edge of the top step. Seconds away from tumbling down the staircase, Isabella scrambled forward until she regained her footing.

Heart pounding, she basked in a momentary wave of relief before two unseen hands wrapped around her shoulders and pushed.

Screaming, arms flailing wildly, Isabella searched for something to grab onto.

Something that would save her.

But there was only air.

An image flashed through her brain of Sam and Ellie, giggling with glee as they burst through the front door before screaming in terror when they found her bloody and broken body at the foot of the staircase.

Panicked, feeling her feet leave the floor, she screamed, "No!"

And felt five slender fingers wrap around her wrist and yank. Hard.

Before she understood what was happening, Isabella was jerked to safer ground, several feet away from the top step and a potentially fatal fall. She bent forward, hands on her thighs, adrenaline still pumping, and tried to steady her racing heart.

All the while noting the lingering scent of lavender in the hallway.

"Abigail?" she said, voice quaking. "Abigail Charles? Was that you?" After a moment, she added, "Or was it you, Martin? Did you just help me, buddy?"

Nothing.

Sighing, she said, "Okay, but you know, if we want to live in harmony, we have to communicate. Agreed?"

When there was no response, Isabella began heading toward where she thought the little girl's voice had come from.

Abigail's room.

As she walked, her mind kept poking her, forcing her to face a fact she'd tried to ignore.

Because, although she'd come to accept the tragedies of her past, there was no denying that the child-like voice Isabella had just heard, the one who'd whispered "Momma," sounded comforting, easy, familiar.

And an awful lot like Anna Rae Boyd.

The door to the little room on the right was still open when she reached it. Cautiously, Isabella entered.

She felt small in this room, inconsequential, and wondered if that was what William Hawthorne had intended—to make Abigail Charles feel small. The thought made Isabella's blood boil.

"Mission accomplished, asshole!" she said through gritted teeth.

She had no idea where this sudden rage came from but understood that if William miraculously appeared before her, alive and well, she would likely end up in handcuffs.

Pacing the small space, she scanned the room for loose floorboards or false walls that could conceal the missing pages of Edward's journal. The floor appeared intact, but there was an odd gap in the wall's wainscoting that should not have been there.

Running a hand over the panels, she pushed on the slats every few inches. On the third push, the wall moved, and a hidden door swung open, revealing a set of steps going down.

"Hmm, servant stairway to the kitchen or highway to hell?" she mumbled, squinting into the darkened stairwell.

After purchasing the house, Isabella had read that older Victorians, like Rosemear, often contained a hidden staircase for servants. The secret passageway allowed workers to travel directly from their bedrooms to the galley or kitchen, bypassing the home's main living areas.

She assumed these steps led to the kitchen and not to the raging fires of perdition.

She hoped she was right.

Hands shaking, she withdrew her cell from a back pocket and turned on the flashlight. At best, the wooden stairs were ancient and worn. At worst, they were completely unreliable and would never hold her weight.

Silently praying the nachos she'd had yesterday didn't add an extra five pounds, she grabbed the wobbly handrail and started down.

At the bottom of the stairs was a shuttered door.

Anxiety building, Isabella slowly pushed it open and walked through.

And found herself standing in the kitchen pantry.

"Thank you, Jesus," she muttered.

Satisfied that at least one mystery was solved, she climbed back up to Abigail's room and sat cross-legged on the floor. Turning on the recording app on her phone, she began to speak.

"Abigail? Are you here?" she asked, immediately feeling foolish.

*Are you really doing this, Boyd? Talking to air and invoking spirits as if you know what the hell you're doing?*

"I'm—I'm not sure if what I've experienced is you, Abby, or another spirit," Isabella said softly, ignoring the alarm bells ringing in her head. She was entering a territory she had no business exploring without Luna or Roma. "But whoever just saved me, thank you."

The room remained still.

"Or," Isabella continued, speaking more to herself than any ghostly presence, "perhaps it's not supernatural at all. Maybe it's just me, free-falling into another mental breakdown." She scanned the room. "Or maybe it's a sign I need to up my meds because, honestly, what sounds nuttier? That I've inherited the family's 'cuckoo' gene and need medication to remain sane, or that I have a house full of pissed-off dead people from a century and a half ago fucking with my mind?"

She heard a rustling from behind, followed by the unmistakable giggle of a child.

"Oh, hell, no," Isabella whispered, fighting the urge to run. "Uh, hello? You can come out if you want," she said, voice cracking. "You—you don't have to be afraid."

Nothing.

After continued silence, she took a different approach. "Is our being here upsetting you? Do the renovations to restore Rosemear make you angry? Hey," she said, laughing nervously, "help me out here! This is my first haunting, and, unfortunately, I never got the rule book!"

No response.

"Martin? Was that you giggling?"

After a moment, Isabella unraveled her legs, stood, and headed for the door. Immediately, a rhythmic pounding—like the thunder of running feet—rushed up from behind her, and she spun.

Frigid air brushed over her body, causing the hairs on her arms to spring up. There was a kind of warping of the space in front of her, like a vortex or door opening from another plane. The air seemed to vibrate, pulsing and humming at a steady tempo, until a portal appeared.

And a translucent form stepped through.

She was a young African American female with kind eyes and smooth skin, clothed in nineteenth-century garb.

"Abigail?" Isabella croaked. "Is that you?"

The woman smiled and nodded.

Feeling a sudden and overwhelming sadness, Isabella whispered, "Are you trapped here?"

Smile fading, Abigail pointed toward the open bedroom door. Her sad eyes met Isabella's, and she began to fade.

"Abigail, wait! Don't go!"

But the ghost of Abigail Charles shook her head, mouthed the word 'danger,' and vanished as quickly as she'd appeared.

Leaving only the scent of sweet lavender behind.

Stunned by what she'd just seen, Isabella backed out of the tiny room. Once in the hallway, she watched, fascinated, as the bedroom door started to close on the heels of one more voice.

"Momma?" a little girl whispered from somewhere inside. "Momma, are you here?"

Isabella froze.

The voice grew louder, reverberating throughout the upper floor. "I miss you so much, Momma! Where are you? I can't find you!"

Isabella felt her heart pounding in her ears before her soul—just beginning to repair itself—shattered into a million pieces.

*It's not possible!*

She knew that voice better than she'd known her own.

And it didn't belong to Martin.

Before Isabella could reply, the voice grew angrier. "You were my mother, and you let me die! Mothers are supposed to protect their children!"

*Oh, my God, no! I'm so sorry, baby! Please!*

A rush of fear, adrenaline, and regret assailed Isabella all at once. Her mind folded into itself, cocooning her from the pain of loss, and her vision faded to gray as she was swept into the sweet abyss of nothingness.

Just as she hit the ground, the entity's last words reached her ears.

"Why, Momma?" the ghost that was not Anna Rae cackled, its voice strangely guttural. "Why did you kill me?"

# CHAPTER TWENTY-SEVEN
## *ABIGAIL*

*Rosemear*
*August 10th, 1859*

Abigail was wiping down the kitchen cabinets when the man she had come to love plodded into the room.

Nose reddened from alcohol and feet firmly planted, Edward swayed, piercing her with his steely gaze.

"Abigail," he growled, "we must discuss what happened here and your role in it."

Stomach queasy, she hung the rag over the sink's edge and turned to face him. "I'm not sure what you mean, Edward. I had no part in this." She waved a hand, voice cracking. "No role in this awful business. I only came here to talk about the crime I *am* responsible for. The one involving Mr. Clyde Baldwin and what happened in the barn."

Edward leaned lazily against the counter, watching her. His posture was non-threatening, detached.

She wasn't sure if his casual stance was meant to put her at ease or if he didn't trust himself to stand without wobbling.

He continued to stare, offering nothing.

Troubled by his silence, Abigail rushed on. "After you left the barn to find your father, you see, Mr. Clyde attacked me again."

Edward, eyes never leaving her face, said coolly, "Go on."

"Well, yes," she said, flustered. "Mr. Clyde grabbed my wrist, threatened me with all manner of vile things. Things that, as a proper woman, I dare not repeat." She took a shaky breath, eyes filling with unshed tears. "Anyway, sir, he went after me just like before, and I feared for my life. As God is my witness, I feared for my life."

Eyes half-closed, Edward burped softly into his closed fist. "Um, I see," he said, his voice trailing off.

"Edward?" Abigail said, annoyed. She was in a life-or-death situation, and he appeared to be dozing. "Did you hear me?"

Snapping to attention, he barked, "Of course, I heard you! I was merely thinking! For the love of God, can't a man think?"

Abigail wisely let the question hang in the air.

"Now then," he said with a smirk, "judging by the look on your face and the blood on your clothing, things did not go well for Baldwin, huh?"

Abigail looked down at her blood-covered dress. "No, sir, it did not."

"So, what happened? Is he still alive, or did he die like my father? Alone, covered with a dozen stab wounds, and left to bleed to death?"

Abigail gasped, shocked. "You-you think I did this? You think I killed your parents?"

Edward sighed and slid down the front of the counter, landing with a plop on the kitchen floor. Raking a hand through his hair, he said, "No, love, of course not. I'm just trying to figure this all out." He looked up at her. "Is he dead, then? Baldwin?"

Abigail gave a brief nod. "It was an accident. I was holding the pitchfork up, just trying to keep him away," she said, teary-eyed. "But he… he grabbed the handle and pulled. I fell forward, still holding onto the pitchfork, and stabbed him. It happened so fast."

She purposefully left Abraham and Virgil out of her explanation. She would not punish her friends for transgressions that rested solely on her shoulders.

Edward stood, wobbling a bit. He grabbed the counter with one hand and raised the other to Abigail's face. "We need to figure this out, my love," he said, stroking her cheek. "We've already sent for the law. Margaret says, well, she says when the law gets here, they're likely to charge me with murder. They will say you and I were having an affair and that my father forbade it."

"That's not—" Abigail started before he cut her off.

"And," Edward said, his voice growing louder, "there will be speculation that we conspired to kill both Father and Lillian, leaving us wealthy and free."

"But that's not true!" Abigail said, nearly shouting herself. "They must know you could never do this! And I… well, I was otherwise occupied by an evil, evil man!"

"Agreed, but we have to be smart here," Edward said, lowering his hand from her face. "If I'm arrested, who will save you? Baldwin, although a coward and a cad, was White. The masses will see you hang for his death." He smiled gently. "But I have an idea that can spare us both. My plan may seem extreme, but it really is for the best. You have my word that I will do everything I can to protect you."

Panicked, Abigail scoured her mind, trying to understand Edward's meaning.

*What extreme plan?* she thought, suddenly queasy.

Multiple murders had visited the plantation in a single day. And, while she couldn't imagine what Edward's plan could be, she *could* imagine the dozen possible ways she would die if blamed for killing three people.

Three important people.

Three important *White* people.

Disheartened, fearing Edward's plan might involve sacrificing her to an angry mob, she began formulating a plan of her own.

Because Abigail Charles had seen a lot of ugly in her short life.

She'd seen how betrayal, arrogance, and greed could blacken a person's heart. She'd stood in the presence of underhanded, self-serving men who manipulated the naïve with their promises and their lies.

Edward's words carried the weight of those memories, reminding her she had no voice here at Rosemear.

No status.

She was just an uneducated, enslaved Black woman trying to survive in a White man's world. She would never be Edward's equal, never bear his children, never claim the title of "Lady of Rosemear." She'd been deluding herself into believing they had a future together.

They did not.

Sighing, bracing herself for his answer, Abigail asked, "What did you have in mind, then?"

Edward pursed his lips. "Well, for starters, we'll need alibis for both of us. It's best to add some truth to our story to appear legitimate." He snapped his fingers as if he'd just created an ingenious plan.

Abigail saw right through his theatrics.

She believed he'd devised this plan long before their conversation started, probably the instant he'd found the Hawthornes dead.

Edward droned on, unaware of the crushing weight on Abigail's chest. "Well, we can say you'd just been attacked by Baldwin on my father's orders, which is true. You were out of your mind, consumed with anger, fear, and pain."

Abigail swallowed the bile lodged in her throat. "And I what, Edward? Killed them all? Is that your extreme plan? To blame me for all three deaths?" She covered her mouth with both hands. "I'll be hanged without a trial!"

Edward brushed off her concern. "Nonsense! I would never let that happen." He broke off for a moment and a strange look came into his eyes. "Actually, with Father's death, I own you now. You're my property, and the authorities can't very well take away my property, can they?"

For the first time in her young life, Abigail genuinely felt stupid. Stupid and forsaken and very, very small. "I-I'm your property now? You own me? I thought..."

"You thought what?" Edward asked.

"Never mind. It doesn't matter now anyway." She straightened her spine and threw back her shoulders. "You do what you must to protect yourself, Mr. Hawthorne," she said stiffly. "I'll do the same." Gathering her skirts in her hand, she turned to leave. "I hope you get all that you deserve. Good day to you, sir."

Panicked, Edward shot out a hand and grabbed her by the arm. "Wait! What do you mean? Are you angry with me, Abigail? I love you! I simply want to do what's best for both of us!"

Abigail sighed. "No, you don't. You want to do what's best for you, despite what that means for me. And that isn't love, Edward. It's power and control and... ownership. Now, please let me go. You're hurting me." She jerked her arm, and he released her.

"I'm sorry," he said, genuinely contrite. "I didn't mean to hurt you, but you must listen!"

Abigail shook her head. "I've heard enough. I'm going upstairs to gather my things. If the authorities come searching for me, they'll find me in the cabins. I'll not hide, but I will not sacrifice myself for anyone, either." She dropped her voice. "Even you."

Stunned, Edward watched her retreating form as she headed to the stairs. It took him a moment to grasp what had just occurred, how everything between them had suddenly changed. Unable to accept it, he chased after her, stumbling in his drunken haze, his only thought to make her see reason.

To stop her before she did something foolish and ruined them both.

Abigail felt, rather than saw, Edward right behind her. Adrenaline coursed through her veins as she sprinted up the staircase, feet pounding the steps, keeping rhythm with her heart.

She was terrified.

Terrified of the man she thought she knew, thought she loved.

"Abigail, wait!" Edward yelled, clawing for her, his fingers brushing over the back of her dress. "I just want to talk! We can figure out this whole thing together!"

Arching her spine to escape his grasp, she rounded the top of the steps and started to turn, wanting only the safety of her bedroom.

But before she could move, a shadowy figure dressed in black appeared on the landing, stopping her with a firm hand.

The motion halted Abigail's momentum, and she rocked backward. Panicked, she flailed at the railing to her left.

But it was too late.

With a laugh that could only be described as sinister, the shadow pushed.

Abigail screamed—arms windmilling and feet scrambling for purchase—as she tried to maintain her balance.

The last thing she felt as she flew backward was the air beneath her feet as she tumbled helplessly down the staircase.

And the last thing she heard was Edward's shriek of horror as she sailed past him, head and torso slamming against the wooden risers, until she landed with a sickening thud against the foyer floor.

After that, Abigail Charles heard no more.

# CHAPTER TWENTY-EIGHT
## *ABIGAIL*

*Rosemear*
*August 10th, 1859*

"Jesus, get ahold of yourself!" Margaret shouted, slapping her brother on his head as he crouched above the body on the floor.

Pulling his gaze from Abigail, Edward lifted his tear-stained face. "What did you do?" he croaked. "For the love of God, Margaret! You've killed her!" He returned his attention to Abigail and brushed a strand of hair from her bleeding scalp. Pools of blood collected beneath her head and snaked around her body.

A small river of crimson wound its way to his feet and, sickened, he shifted his position.

"Listen, jackass," Margaret spat, "instead of crying like a woman, why don't you check to make sure she's actually dead?"

Edward sniffed and wrapped his fingers around Abigail's wrist, checking for a pulse.

He felt nothing.

Wiping the back of his hand over his snot-stained upper lip, he shook his head. "No, there's nothing. She's…she's gone."

Margaret blew out a breath. "Well, unfortunate, but stairs can be dangerous. People die from accidental falls all the time."

"Accidental?" he gasped, standing to face her. "There was nothing accidental about this! I watched you push her!"

"Oh, please, don't be so dramatic! I didn't push her. I merely braced her, holding her up so she didn't fall. Maybe you would recognize that if you hadn't been imbibing all damned day!"

Fire flashed in his eyes. "Drink or not, I know what I saw, Maggie. And soon, the authorities will know as well."

Margaret cackled. "Ha! We all know you don't have the stomach for that, little brother! And what do you think will happen when I'm questioned? If I get nervous, I might start singing myself." She got closer, whispering in his ear. "You know, all about how you and the 'help' have been having an affair? One that Father disapproved of, and now, surprisingly, he and his wife end up dead? Yes, I think Savannah's Guard and Watch would be very interested in that news."

Edward paled. "You wouldn't! I-I told you that I didn't kill… good God, I *couldn't* have killed them!" He stepped away quickly, as if being too close to the blazing tongue of his sister would set him afire.

"So you said," Margaret snapped. "But we both know about your temper, Edward. And about your alcohol-induced amnesia and missing blocks of time. What if you committed these crimes but have no recollection?"

Squinting at her through misty eyes, resignation in his voice, he added, "I may be a drunk and a cad, Margaret, but I'm not a murderer." He looked back toward Abigail and started to tremble.

"Edward," Margaret said sternly, "you need to get yourself together. Act like a man instead of a weak little boy!"

Openly sobbing now, he covered his face with his hands. "Oh

my God, I can't believe this is happening! My beautiful Abigail! Please come back to me!"

Margaret rolled her eyes. "Are you done?"

Outraged, Edward snapped, "What the hell happened to you, Maggie? Where is your compassion? A woman is dead, for Christ's sake!"

"Yes, and wringing my hands and snotting all over myself won't change that." She shrugged. "I am who I am, Eddie. And right now, I'm your best friend."

Edward started to pace. He stepped around Abigail, breath hitching, and faced his sister again. "Fine," he sniffed. "What-what do we do?"

Margaret nodded toward the body on the floor. "We bury her. When the Guard arrives, we tell them she ran off after killing Father and Lillian. They'll be hunting a ghost for weeks, giving us time to tidy up any loose ends."

"Such as?"

Margaret studied her hands, their ragged cuticles a testament to her character. She'd been unconcerned about clear skin, frilly dresses, or painted lips all her life. Instead, her joys were horseback riding, hunting, and drinking smooth whiskey straight from the bottle. "Abigail is—*was*—a respected figure among the staff and her peers. If the authorities speak with her friends here at Rosemear, they may doubt our story."

Edward frowned. "I've no idea what you're on about. How does telling them she ran off help us?"

Margaret shook her head, disappointment at odds with disgust. "Christ, Edward, think! While the authorities spend days tracking her, we can dispatch anyone who disputes our version of events."

"Dispatch? What the hell are you talking about?"

"You let me worry about that," she said, patting his cheek. "For now, I need you to find a tarp or blanket to wrap her in. We will take her miles away and bury her."

"But wha-what about a coffin?" Edward stuttered. "We can't just drop her underground without protection from the elements or…or insects! And I want her close to me, not miles away!"

"She's dead. I highly doubt she'll know the difference."

Edward's jaw clenched. "But *I* will know the difference! There's no way I am burying my love without a coffin. If you want me to do this, we need to give her a proper burial."

"Have it your way, then," Maggie said with a dismissive flick of her wrist. "There are empty coffins out back. Lillian ordered the bones of some former servants to be unearthed and placed in the walls of Martin's room." She cackled mirthlessly. "Bitch listened to that crazy spiritualist and believed her when she said the house was cursed."

Edward gathered a blanket from the settee and gently draped it over Abigail's still form. "I'll carry her to the kitchen and place her in the broom closet by the back door. After I've," he hesitated, "after I've found an empty coffin, I'll come get her."

Margaret nodded. "You'd best hurry, though. Be dark soon. I'll stand watch, making sure no one…" Her words trailed off, and then, perplexed, she said, "Wait a minute. Where the hell is the staff? The cleaners? The cooks?"

Edward bent forward and scooped Abigail into his arms. Straightening and adjusting his grip, he shook his head. "Not sure. They were gone when I found Father and Lillian."

Margaret chewed her lip. "Then either one of them killed Father, or someone in authority sent them away."

Edward slid past her, holding Abigail's body against his chest, and, his heart impossibly heavy, headed to the kitchen. "Doesn't matter now. Just keep watch. I'll return as soon as possible."

Forty minutes later, Edward returned to find Margaret sitting on the kitchen counter, an apple in her hand.

"How the hell can you eat at a time like this?" Edward hissed.

"Have you no decency?"

"My starving to death ain't gonna bring your girl back, Eddie," she said, taking a large bite and chewing noisily. "So, did you do it?"

"I said I would, didn't I?" he shot back. "But if we want to finish this tonight, we must hurry. It'll be nightfall in less than an hour."

Jumping down from her perch and opening the door, Margaret gestured with a wave. "After you."

"No," he countered, "after you. I'll be carrying Abigail, so you must keep watch."

Margaret clapped her hands. "Bravo! And to think—minutes ago, you were bent in half, sniveling like a coward. There's hope for you yet, Eddie." With a wink, she slipped out the door.

Scowling at her retreating figure, Edward removed Abigail's body from the closet and held her close. Face pressed into her hair, drinking in her scent, he whispered, "I am so sorry, love. My only desire was to protect you, and I failed miserably." He gently kissed her forehead. "I swear to you, Abigail Charles, that from this day forward, and as long as I shall live, I will never love again!"

And Edward Hawthorne kept his word.

Fifteen minutes after placing Abigail in the coffin and burying her in a shallow grave, Edward returned to the house, downed half a bottle of his finest bourbon, and passed out, face down, on the kitchen floor.

Unaware that, at that precise moment, Abigail Charles was regaining consciousness.

Because the pretty girl with the sweet disposition was not dead.

Instead, she had awakened in her underground prison three feet beneath the earth's surface, disoriented, terrified, and gasping for breath.

Howling, slowly suffocating, Abigail kicked and clawed at the pine box that held her prisoner beneath the earth.

And she kept at it—screaming, hitting, pounding the wood above her—until exhaustion won, her limbs stilled, and her eyes closed.

And there, among people who would never be family and on soil she would never call home, Abigail Charles breathed her last.

# CHAPTER TWENTY-NINE

*Saturday, August 3rd*
*Present Day*
*8:00 p.m.*

When Isabella opened her eyes, she found herself on Sam's bed, a light blanket draped over her legs. The room was dark, with only a sliver of moonlight slipping through the curtained window. Confused, she shot up in bed, desperate to recall the last few hours.

Or had it been days? She couldn't be sure because, under stress, time was a fickle thing.

Searching her mind, she tried to revisit the last memory stored there, but it was as if her brain had erected a barrier. Frustrated, she rose, wandered into the hallway, and was greeted by the faint smell of lavender.

Suddenly, she remembered.

"Anna?" she croaked. "Baby, are you here?"

A shuffling noise from the first floor startled her, and she strained to hear. Walking on tiptoes, though she didn't understand why, she went to the top of the landing and looked beyond the railing to the foyer below.

All was quiet.

Head on a swivel, ears perked, she moved lightly down the stairs. The distant echo of footsteps, followed by the subtle click of a door closing, startled her. Heart racing, she checked her pockets for her cell phone, intending to call Nate. When last she'd used it, she'd been shining its light on the steep slant of the servants' stairs.

It was gone.

*Fuck!*

Reaching the bottom step, she held her breath and followed the soft taps and bangs down the first-floor corridor, stopping before one of the bedrooms.

Whoever, or whatever, was creating those noises was on the other side of that closed door.

The door to Luna's room.

Stomach sour, Isabella pressed an ear to the wood. Someone was opening and closing the dresser drawers.

Hands trembling, she reached for the doorknob and slowly turned.

Seconds later, the knob was wrenched from her fingers as the door swung open from the inside.

Isabella screamed.

"Christ, you nearly scared me to death!" she gasped, staring at the man before her.

Spencer smiled stupidly. "Sorry!"

"'Sorry'? I thought someone broke…" She trailed off, eyes narrowing. "Hey, what are you doing in here? This is Luna's room."

He frowned. "Luna has her own room now? In my house? Well, ain't that grand."

"It *is* grand, Spence," Isabella said, growing annoyed. "Besides, not to beat a dead horse, but last time I checked, I paid the bills around here."

Spencer struggled to maintain a neutral expression. "Yeah, so you keep reminding me." Clearing his throat, he added, "Anyway, I'm glad you've finally rejoined the living. I found you on the floor and haven't been able to rouse you." He smiled sadly. "I was worried you'd slipped so deep into your mind you'd never find your way back."

"That so?"

"It is. I came in here looking for smelling salts or something."

"Smelling salts? What is this? 1975?"

Spencer chuckled mirthlessly. "Okay, okay, but she's a nurse, and I was desperate. How are you feeling, by the way?"

"Strange." She rubbed her temples. "I'm exhausted, I have a killer headache I haven't been able to shake, and I think I…" She stopped.

"What?"

"No," Isabella corrected herself, "I *know* I heard Anna upstairs. She was talking to me, asking me why I've not come for her."

Spencer sighed heavily. "Oh, my poor, poor Isabella."

She shot him an angry look. "I'm not crazy, Spencer. I know what I heard!"

He put an arm around her shoulder and led her down the hall. "Or what you think you heard, right? Because the hard truth is that Anna is dead and buried. She died under your…" He stopped, leaving the unspoken accusation to hang in the air. "Look, it doesn't matter why she died. What's done is done, and as much as we'd like to, we can't bring her back." He held her at arm's length. "Come on. How about I make you something to eat and draw you a bath? It will help you relax."

Isabella stopped suddenly, shrugging his arm off her shoulder. "I'm not a child, Spencer. I'm not hungry, and I don't need a bath."

He rested his hands on his hips. "Okay, well, what *do* you need? Because, honestly, I'm concerned about your being here alone. I have to leave early Wednesday morning, and you don't seem…

okay. Maybe we should hire someone to help with the kids, just until you feel better."

Initially, his words made her heart drop as old insecurities trickled in.

But soon, her subtle doubts turned into a raging storm.

"Oh, for fuck's sake! You—the one who is gone for days or weeks at a time, rubbing elbows with CEOs and screwing your assistant— are questioning whether or not to trust *me* with the kids?"

"Whoa, hold on!" he said, voice growing louder. "I never said I didn't trust you with Sam and Ellie! And as far as Julia is concerned, I'm fucking tired of repeating myself! She and I are finished, got it?" His fist shot out, and he punched the wall behind her. "You're twisting my motive and my meaning!"

"No, Spencer, I'm not. I know exactly what motivates you," Isabella snapped back, ignoring her pounding heart. His jab to the wall had landed dangerously close to her head. "And I know what you meant."

"Enough!" he said, jaw clenched. "None of this is doing any good. Look, it's late, and the kids are probably hungry. How about we make some grilled cheese and soup or something?"

Isabella blinked rapidly. "The kids? The kids are at a sleepover next door. How long have you been here, anyway?"

"I don't know. A few hours, maybe?"

Her gaze pinned him to the spot. "Hours? And you didn't realize the children were gone?"

Spencer's eyes flashed. "Don't start that shit with me, Isabella! I was concerned about you and didn't have time to go looking for them!"

She laughed bitterly. "So, home for what? Two or three hours? And, in that time, you never thought of finding the kids? Never thought to call an ambulance when I didn't regain consciousness? What if I'd had a stroke or something?"

"Oh, for God's sake! I work in the clinical field every damned day! I think I'd recognize a medical emergency if I saw one!" He shook his head vehemently. "No, the only thing I saw was an ill mind in collapse, unable or unwilling to handle the real world!"

"Go fuck yourself, Spencer!" she shouted. "I've handled the 'real world' quite nicely while you've been off spending my money and playing house with your mistress. And I think I've done a damned good job over the years, parenting alone. My kids are healthy, happy, and thriving!"

He studied the floor as if what he would say next greatly pained him.

"Except for Anna Rae," he said softly. "Except for her, right? Because she isn't thriving anymore, is she?"

Isabella simply stared at him, stunned by his words and the venom behind them. "You're such a fucking asshole, Spencer! Just when I think you can no longer shock me with your cruelty, you prove me wrong."

"Hey, she was my kid, too!" he yelled. "Just because she died on your watch doesn't give you license to take ownership of the pain!"

Isabella scrubbed her hands over her face. "I'm exhausted. Exhausted and out of patience with your greed, vile words, and arrogance."

"You call it arrogance, but I call it truth. For three years, people have indulged your brand of crazy by rewriting the script of what *really* happened the day Anna died. Well, it stops here. It's about time you accepted your role in her death."

A few months ago, his words would have sent her back down that self-hating rabbit hole and into the arms of a bottle of Valium. Now, they meant nothing. "I had no idea how deep your hatred of me ran. So, let's put our cards on the table, shall we?" She headed toward the kitchen, Spencer on her heels. "I'm going outside to the gazebo. While I'm gone, you need to pack your things and leave Rosemear for good. We, and this sham of a marriage, are over."

His face reddened, and his jaw clenched. "You can't be serious."

"As a fuckin' heart attack," she snapped. "But I guess you'd know that, right? I mean, since you hang out with doctors and can recognize a medical emergency and shit?"

His eyes narrowed, and his fists clenched, but he said nothing.

"Anyway, I'll be contacting my attorney on Monday morning. I suggest you do the same."

Back stiff, she brushed by him and out the back door.

And never saw the fury in his eyes as he watched her leave.

After a moment of red-hot anger, he composed himself and smiled. He would never need an attorney because there would be no divorce. Soon, if his plan worked, Isabella would know only solitude within the padded walls of a psychiatric facility.

Or she would be dead, driven mad before dying by her own hands.

Spencer didn't care either way, as long as she was out of his life. Permanently.

An hour after she heard Spencer race out of the driveway, gravel crunching beneath his tires, Isabella returned to the house, an eerie silence greeting her when she entered the kitchen.

Determined to find her phone, she took the stairs to the second floor and headed for Abigail's room, where she'd last had it.

She needed to find it, needed to call Luna.

And Nate.

Isabella felt an overwhelming urge to let Nathan Decker, a lawman and a friend, know what had just occurred. She'd known Spencer for a long time and didn't believe he'd just walk away from what he loved most.

Money.

Attempting to anticipate his next move, she decided he'd do one of two things—return to Rosemear begging for forgiveness, or return angry, looking for revenge.

Her money was on the latter.

Feeling strangely calm, proud of herself for having the courage to finally end her marriage, Isabella reached Abigail's room and found her phone lying on the threshold.

"How'd you get here?" she muttered, picking it up and scrolling through her contacts. Since Luna was working a double shift, she decided to text rather than call.

*Hey, girl, I did it! Kicked Spencer's ass out and asked him for a divorce! Details to follow when you get here Friday! Miss you!*

She ended the text with a heart emoji and hit send. Looking around, she said, "Is anyone here? Anna? Abigail?"

The only answer was the night wind whistling against the ancient windows of Rosemear.

Feeling foolish, Isabella headed toward the landing. With each step she took, the lights winked and flashed before finally flickering off, leaving her in total darkness. Heart in her throat, she switched on her phone's flashlight and turned a slow circle, scanning the hall from floor to ceiling.

A loud crash from the west wing shook the plaster walls and echoed throughout the house.

Then, a woman's scream.

"Jesus Christ," Isabella croaked, wiping her damp palms on her thighs. Flooding the corridor with light from her phone, she whispered, "Abby? Is that you?"

In her periphery, an undulating black mass drew her attention. Shapeless and silent, it started to move, gaining speed as it came, heading straight for her.

Isabella screamed, intuitively throwing an arm up to protect her face before turning to run.

Heart racing, inches from the top step, she dared a backward glance before tripping over something solid near the top of the stairs.

Sprawled face down on the floor, cell phone still in hand, she shone the light over the object she'd tripped on.

Ellie's toy Jeep.

The car was turned on its side, two wheels furiously spinning.

And stuffed inside the toy, caught in the beam of the phone's flashlight, were Isabella's missing sunglasses.

Stunned, she sprang to her feet and raced down the stairs.

The lights were back on when Isabella reached the first floor.

Despite that, as she stood beneath the brilliant glow of the foyer's chandelier, Isabella's heart still pounded, and her knees still quaked.

She tucked her phone into her back pocket and moved quickly toward the kitchen. Her stomach roiled as the shot of adrenaline that always accompanied fear coursed through her.

She was convinced that whatever had come at her upstairs was still there, watching her.

Ready to pounce.

She'd experienced that level of terror before—climbing the stairs out of a bleak, darkened basement in her former home, convinced someone was chasing her. But this felt more threatening, more ominous.

After what seemed like an eternity, she reached the relative safety of the kitchen, thankful that the feelings of impending doom had subsided.

Needing to do something 'normal,' she grabbed a beer from the fridge before emptying a can of soup into a saucepan. Leaning over the counter while the soup heated, she took a long pull of beer and began her text to Nate.

*Good evening, neighbor! I hope your shift is going well and you haven't received any SOS messages from Marnie! I just wanted to let you know I asked my husband to leave tonight. He said some horrible, unforgivable things, and it was time to show him the door.*

*That said, I've no doubt he will return to try and convince me to take him back. Spencer is nothing if not determined. If he returns, I intend to have him escorted off the property. Just wanted you to know in case you heard my address over the radio and panicked! Lol.*

*Also, more strange (ghost-like) events occurred this evening, leaving me stunned but grateful for our planned investigation and Roma's visit this weekend. Anyway, looking forward to telling...*"

An eerie, scraping sound behind her—as though the kitchen chairs were being dragged across the floor—echoed off the tiles, and she jerked, her finger pressing 'send' before her text to Nate was completed.

Clutching her necklace in a sweaty palm, she turned slowly, a scream locked in her throat before escaping her lips as a high-pitched squeak.

Because five of the six chairs usually gathered around the dinette table were no longer nestled snugly beneath it.

Instead, they were lined up, one in front of the other, against the kitchen wall.

Like the seating on a bus or passenger train.

Her gaze was glued to the third chair, where a boy of about eleven or twelve was mindlessly spinning the wheels of the toy Jeep he held in his lap.

Shocked at the image before her, Isabella initially missed something even more terrifying—a sixth kitchen chair, precariously balanced on one leg, twirling furiously in the center of the room.

Taking it all in, forcing herself not to run, Isabella took a swig of beer and finally found her voice.

"Mother of God," she whispered, mouth dry as dust. "What the hell is happening?"

The phantom boy continued to spin the Jeep's wheels, one at a time, oblivious to her presence. Isabella closed her eyes, gathering courage and praying her sanity would hold.

She laid her phone on the counter and took a steadying breath. "Hel-hello," she said softly, averting her gaze from the chair still twirling in the middle of the room. "My name is Isabella. What's yours?"

She wrapped an arm around her middle, waiting for an answer while pinching her abdomen to ensure she wasn't dreaming.

*I'm losing my damned mind! This can't be real!*

The child's finger dropped from the toy's wheels, and he turned his head to face her. Their eyes met, and his brow furrowed before he silently mouthed a single word.

It was a word every woman who has ever raised a child would recognize.

*Momma?*

Suddenly, Isabella recalled Rosemear's history and believed she knew who this child was.

Harry Taylor, twelve-year-old son of James and Clara.

Luna's research had shown that one of the previous Rosemear owners, James Taylor, overwhelmed by grief at his son's sudden death, had shot his wife before turning the gun on himself.

"Harry?" Isabella whispered. "Sweetheart, is that you?"

The child nodded, despair behind his eyes.

"Oh, honey," she said, heartbroken for the boy, "don't you worry. We'll fix this and get you where you need to be, somewhere safe where your parents are waiting for you."

The chair in the center of the room suddenly stopped rotating and crashed to the floor.

A moment later, Harry Taylor vanished, leaving the Jeep and Isabella's sunglasses on the seat of the chair he'd occupied.

And leaving Isabella dazed, emotionally drained, and in tears.

Forty minutes later, her feet tucked snugly beneath her on the couch in the den, Isabella was studying the Hawthorne portrait, trying to discover what was different about it.

She was sure there was something.

Turning the painting, attempting to see it from another angle, she held the canvas closer to her face and scrutinized each subject.

"Holy shit!" she gasped as clarity struck. "The eyes! Jesus Christ, the eyes!"

When Isabella had first discovered the portrait, the people in the painting were looking straight ahead.

Now, all eyes stared to the right.

She jumped up and hurriedly leaned the picture against the desk, shaking her hands as soon as it left her grasp.

As if the mere act of touching it had singed her fingertips.

Once she had cast it aside, though, her old nemesis—doubt—snaked through her mind. "But maybe I'm wrong," she mumbled, chewing on a hangnail. "Maybe their eyes were always looking to the right."

The clang of the doorbell startled her, and she glanced nervously at the grandfather clock against the wall.

It was after ten p.m., and Nate was working until at least eleven.

Luna was still in Hilton Head.

It had to be Spencer.

"Shit, shit, shit!" she whispered, her mind going through several options: ignore the bell, shout out to whomever it was to go away, or peek outside to identify her visitor.

Creeping to the den window, she pulled back the lace curtains.
*Nate!*

Quickly checking her image in a wall mirror, she smoothed a

hand over her hair and moved to the door. "Nathan Decker!" she gasped. "You nearly gave me a coronary!"

"Sorry for dropping in so late, but when I got your text..." He hesitated. "Are you okay, Isabella? I was afraid something had happened. I tried calling you, but you didn't answer, and I got a little worried."

"Come in," she said, grabbing his arm and ushering him inside. "Sorry, I must have left my phone in the kitchen. It's been a little intense here this evening." She tucked her hands into her pockets, afraid she would wrap her arms around him and pull him close. She needed the comfort of another being.

A drop-dead gorgeous being who actually had a pulse.

"So, you were worried about me? That's very sweet, Nate," she said, smiling shyly and wiping an imaginary line of drool from her chin.

He looked especially enticing in uniform.

Studying his features, Isabella prayed he didn't notice her near-swoon as she devoured him with her eyes.

He noticed.

Eyes darkening, nostrils flaring, Nate moved closer.

Reflexively, Isabella took a step back. "I, um, thought you were working until eleven tonight," she stuttered.

"I am. Well, I was," he corrected. "I had some personal time, and it was pretty quiet tonight, so I asked my supervisor if I could leave a little early to check on you."

Isabella beamed at him. "You did that? For me?" Touched and unable to stop herself, she put her arms around his neck and hugged him tightly. "That's probably the sweetest thing any man has ever done for me."

Nate buried his face into her neck, breathing her in. "If that's true, you've been hanging with the wrong kind of man."

"You're right," she said, reluctantly letting him go. "Hopefully, I've rectified that tonight by asking my husband for a divorce." She took his hand and led him to the den. "Come on. I'll fix us a drink and fill you in on everything that happened here this evening."

Nate followed, ignoring the pit in his stomach and the alarm bells ringing in his head.

Isabella had given her husband his walking papers tonight, and from what little Nate knew about Spencer Boyd, he wouldn't take that lying down.

The man would return here at some point—while Isabella was still raw and emotionally vulnerable—to plead or argue or, God forbid, do something worse.

Nate was sure of it.

*And if I'm on patrol twenty minutes away, who will protect her?*

# CHAPTER
# THIRTY

*Friday, August 9th*
*Present Day*
*1:00 p.m.*

"Ding-dong!" Luna yelled, entering Rosemear, a black bag in each hand and a bottle of wine beneath her arm. "Queen Luna has arrived! Where are my subjects?"

Isabella came out of the kitchen, drying her hands on a towel. "Your Majesty!" she said with a mock bow. "I wasn't expecting you until four or so."

Luna moved to the middle of the foyer and placed her bags on the floor. Handing the bottle of wine to Isabella, she said, "I wasn't expecting to be here until after four either, but since my last patient couldn't make his appointment, I got out early."

"That's awesome! Thanks for canceling, patient!"

Luna clucked her tongue. "Well, he didn't exactly cancel. Frank was an eighty-year-old sweetheart with end-stage renal disease who didn't wake up this morning."

"Oh, no. I'm sorry to hear that."

"Nah, it's all good. Frank was an exceptional person, but he'd been living a shitty life for years. Honestly—and I seldom say this—his death today was a blessing. For the last eighteen months, he wasn't actively living because he was too busy dying. Anyway, the appointment before Frank's *was* canceled, so I told the boss I was skipping lunch and heading out early." She frowned. "Unfortunately, in my haste, I left my purse in my office at work." She smiled. "No driver's license! Good thing I know a cop!"

"Dang. You should have gone back. Your meds…"

"Nah, it's fine. I have what I need here. Besides, I was worried about you."

Isabella smirked. "You know, you're the second person this week who's said they were worried about me. I could get used to this."

"Poppycock! You would never get used to being fawned and fussed over! Too headstrong and independent."

"Touché," Isabella said with a tiny salute. "Still, it's nice to know some people care if I live or die."

"You mean Spencer? Oh, fuck him!" Luna growled. "That weasel wouldn't know a good thing if it crawled up his skank ass, tap-danced through his intestines, and came out the end of his microscopic wiener."

Isabella chuckled. "That wiener got his walking papers on Wednesday, so soon my marriage will be nothing but an unhappy memory!"

Luna squealed and ran in place. "Yes! Finally! Man, I'd love to have been a fly on the wall when he got served! Piece of shit probably cried like a bitch!"

Isabella laughed. "Probably. Anyway, it's like the weight of the world is off my shoulders." She studied her hands. "I feel like the old me again, Lune. I think the kids feel it, too. My soul is, I don't know, lighter since Spencer has been gone. Hell, I've even started painting again."

Luna hugged her. "As you should. Do you know how proud I am of you, Izzy-B? You've slain a dragon!"

"I did, didn't I?" Isabella said with a soft smile. "Anyway, come on, my lunch-skipping rebel. I'll make you a BLT on rye, and we can discuss the plans for this evening's investigation."

"Fine, but only if you fill me in on all the deets of your ghostly encounters over the weekend. Sending a five-sentence text doesn't work for me!" She looked around the foyer. "Why is it so quiet? Where are the kids?"

"With the microscopic wiener. After I kicked him out, I didn't hear from Spencer for days. He finally called yesterday, asking if he could have the kids for the weekend."

Luna grabbed her chest in mock surprise. "He did? That sperm donor, that poster child for why women need birth control, is actually caring for his kids all by his lonesome this weekend?"

"No," Isabella said, rolling her eyes. "I'm sure Julia Cocksucker is playing stepmom about now."

"You think that piece of shit is living there now? With her?"

"Don't know, don't care," Isabella said briskly. "That man is no longer my problem, which reminds me—can you give me your cousin Jed's contact info again? If Spencer decides to play dirty, I might need a private investigator to gather ammunition for court."

"Hah!" Luna shouted. "Of course, he'll play dirty. It's the only act in his playbook!"

"True," Isabella said as they started toward the kitchen. "Anyway, it makes our lives easier this weekend. Nate's sister was going to keep the kids at her place tonight and tomorrow while we did our investigations. Now, she won't have to."

Luna stopped walking and faced Isabella. Cocking a brow, she teased, "Was she now? And was this all arranged by a certain hot police officer?"

Isabella blushed. "Well, yeah, Nate set it up, but…"

"But nothing!" Luna said, linking arms with Isabella as they continued walking. "Pay attention tonight to his signals. He's sweet on you!"

Isabella groaned. "What a mess, huh? Haunted house, rotten husband, gorgeous neighbor who invades my dreams. Maybe I'll take the vow, become a nun."

Luna giggled. "A nun? Oh, that's rich!"

"Hey, I can be as holy as the next guy!"

"Yeah, okay, Sister Mary Margaret. But maybe you can feed the hungry before you do your devotions?"

Isabella winked. "You want cheese on that BLT, my child?"

An hour later, Isabella and Luna sat in the den, sipping Cabernet from crystal glasses.

"I gotta tell you, Izzie-B, I am so glad you are finally giving that prick the boot. What the fuck was he thinking anyway? Leaving you unconscious for hours?"

"Who knows? After the horrid things he said to me, things about Anna's death…"

Luna growled. "What things? Is that what's wrong?"

Isabella smiled, but it was a sad smile. "That transparent, huh?"

Luna nudged her shoulder. "Not to anyone but me, sweet-cheeks. So, what gives? Please tell me you haven't let that slug get under your skin."

"No, not just him. I find myself questioning everything lately. This past week, the disembodied voices, the banging and scraping noises, the cold spots? They've increased tenfold."

Luna drained her glass and poured another. "Then it's a good damned thing Roma is coming tomorrow. Sounds like the activity is escalating."

"Is it, though? What if Spencer is right? What if the apparitions and cries and whispers telling me to…"

Luna froze. She slowly pulled the wineglass from her lips, eyes searching Isabella's face. "Telling you what?" she asked softly. "Is there any danger… Bella, are you thinking of harming yourself?"

"I didn't think so at first," she said, voice raw. "But the last few days, I've heard Anna begging me to 'find' her, listened to the shrieks of a female screaming like a banshee, and tried to block out a male voice telling me suicide is the only way to be with my daughter."

"You listen to me, girlfriend," Luna said, squeezing Isabella's hand. "You need to stop doubting your sanity. These ghosts, these *Meanies,* are just fucking with you. Don't you think I'd know if the cheese was sliding off your cracker? Do you think all of us could share the same hallucinations or delusions?" She pointed toward the foyer. "Every single person who has come through those doors has experienced something here. Hell, even the movers got spooked by something. Or someone." She reached for the bottle of wine and topped off Isabella's glass. "Fun fact… Did you know that the dead feed off the energy of the living, be it positive or negative?"

Isabella shook her head. "No, I didn't know that."

"Well, it's true. And the ghosts of Rosemear are fat and happy, feeding off the bad juju Spencer sprinkles wherever he goes."

Isabella bit her bottom lip so hard she tasted blood. "It's just that… Oh, God, Luna. It's like I'm tiptoeing through life on a tightrope without a net. A strong wind could knock me off any minute now, hurling me hundreds of feet to the ground below."

"But the winds have died down, love," Luna said softly, "and the cyclone that was Spencer has been banished from the kingdom."

"You're right," Isabella said, sighing. "I'm just so terrified of slipping back into that mental nightmare."

"Never gonna happen," Luna said. "I won't let it, but more importantly, you won't. I suspect that shedding that parasite you married will get you off that high wire and onto stable ground." Winking, she added, "And if not, I'll throw you off myself. You're so damned depressing when you're like this."

Isabella chuckled. "Sorry. Anyway, I'm sure you're right. And as for the parasite, I'm just glad to be rid of him."

"Me, too! You rock! It can't be easy for you, even if he's a foot-licking Barbie fucker."

Isabella laughed. "He is, isn't he?"

"For sure. On another note, your texts about what's gone on this last week made my skin crawl! Man, what I wouldn't give to have seen an actual ghost!"

Isabella bit her lip. "Yes, well, be careful what you wish for. It was amazing, terrifying, and unbelievable all at once. And dangerous. When I first heard what I thought was Anna Rae calling out to me, I was at the top of the stairs."

"You heard Anna Rae? You're shitting me!"

"I shit you not. I was on the verge of falling but was able to catch myself before it got ugly."

"Thank God! That would've left a mark!" she said wryly.

Isabella shook her head. "I'm not done. Just when I was out of danger, someone on the landing pushed me."

"Jesus, Iz! Way to bury the lead! Who was it?"

"No idea," Isabella said, moving to the desk. "But I started to fall, for real, and someone, or something, saved me. I—I think it was Abigail."

"I think I love this girl."

"Same. Anyway, after that happened, I was poking around in Abigail's room, looking for the missing pages in Edward's journal, when I found this."

She picked up the serpent bracelet and handed it to Luna.

"Wow, gorgeous!" Luna said with a whistle. "So, this is the eternity bracelet you texted about?"

"Beautiful, right? I also discovered a hidden staircase in her room that leads to the pantry. It's old and worn but safe enough to use."

"Might be a good place to investigate tonight." Luna stood and stretched her back. "So, let's recap. You told me about seeing

Abigail come through a portal, the dark blob that rushed you and tried to steal your soul, and tripping on Ellie's Jeep that held your sunglasses." She studied the ragged corner of a cuticle, destroyed by years of constant handwashing. "Oh, and how Martin's room was the one Ellie and the Cates kid chose. But what I'm dying to know is, what's with the kid in the kitchen? Just saying it out loud causes my ass to pucker."

"Lovely," Isabella quipped. "I will in a minute. But first…" She went to the portrait leaning against the desk and held it up, facing Luna. "Do you notice anything different about this picture?"

Luna squinted and leaned closer. After studying it for a moment, she gasped. "Holy Hannah! Their eyes! I could swear they were looking straight at the camera before. Now, every damned one of them is looking to the left!"

"To the right, you mean," Isabella said, still holding the portrait before her. "They moved from staring dead center to looking right."

"Um, no, silly. I know my left from my right."

Puzzled, Isabella flipped the frame to look for herself. "This— this can't be!" she cried.

Because in front of her, six pairs of eyes, previously fixated to the right, had reversed course.

And were now all staring vacantly to the left.

Nate arrived for the investigation around six p.m. wearing a brilliant smile and a camera around his neck.

Isabella gave him a brief hug and playfully tugged on the camera strap. "Come prepared, have ya?"

Nate smirked. "Boy Scout, remember? This camera can record or take digital photos. Figured we might need both options."

"Good thinking," Luna said.

After filling him in on all he'd missed—and showing him the ever-changing portrait—they ordered a couple of pizzas and gathered around the kitchen table to examine the equipment Luna had brought.

"Impressive gear," Nate said, raising a brow. "You seem pretty comfortable with this ghost stuff, Luna. Me? I'm still trying to wrap my head around the 'eyes in the portrait' thing."

"Not comfortable as much as accepting." Luna nodded at the assorted devices. "This equipment is fairly basic but should be fine for our needs." She held up a puck-shaped item. "Behold, the REM POD. It detects shifts and fluctuations in the air around us."

"How does it work?" Isabella asked, taking the device from Luna to inspect it.

"Easy peasy. A spirit has energy, right? A REM POD detects that energy and will signal if anything comes near. Like so..."

She took the device from Isabella and laid it on the table. Turning it on, she waved her hand over the antenna, and immediately, an alarm sounded. "Voila! I've also seen it used to communicate with the dead. You ask a yes-or-no question and see if it lights up with an answer."

Nate smiled. "Pretty cool. How about this?" he asked, picking up a small ball from the table. "Looks like a cat toy."

"Indeed it is!" Luna said excitedly. "It flashes when disturbed. I'm not sure how reliable it is, but if it starts moving by itself, we'll know something propelled it. I thought we could see if Martin wanted to roll it to us."

"Great idea!" Isabella said. She picked up another device from the table. "Oh, I've seen this contraption before. An EMF detector, right?"

"You got it!" Luna said.

Nate frowned and raised a hand. "Excuse my ignorance, but..."

"It stands for 'electromagnetic fields,'" Luna answered.

"Yeah, I know what they're used for in the earthly world. I'm just not sure how it's a ghost-hunting tool."

"Gotcha. Okay, the theory," Luna explained, "is that since spirits are made up of energy, they can absorb, alter, or otherwise change the electromagnetic waves around us. The EMF detector will light up, signaling the potential presence of a ghostly form."

"Sounds intense," Nate said.

"It can be. These tools, plus a voice recorder I purchased, will be a great start. And we can use your video camera and our cell phones to record and take pictures."

The doorbell rang, and Isabella stood. "Must be the pizzas. Be right back."

When she left, Nate whispered, "She told you about the kid in the kitchen, right? And the spinning chair?"

Luna nodded. "She did. Fucking scary as hell."

Nate was loath to verbalize what he was thinking. "I, um… It's not that I don't believe her. It's just that, well, a ghost kid lining up chairs? Spinning one in the middle of the room? I don't know, Luna. It sounds…" He stopped, unwilling to complete the thought.

"What?" Luna said, slightly annoyed. "Crazy? Jesus, Nate, don't you dare say that to her!"

Chagrinned, he shook his head. "I would never."

"Good, because let's be real here. The weird noises and cold spots, the bells clanging on Mr. Jingles, the changing portrait? These are things we've all seen and heard! Not to mention that you've admitted to having some experiences here as a kid." She blew out a breath. "Do I wish nothing was happening here? Of course, I do. Mentally, Bella is in a tough place right now. She's dealing with Rosemear's renovations, a failed marriage, and a house full of unwanted entities. And let's not forget she is still reeling over Anna Rae's death three years ago and her parents' murder a year before that."

"That's right," he said sadly. "Isabella mentioned her parents were killed in a home invasion. Did they ever find the perpetrators?"

"Unfortunately, no," Luna answered. "Her parents were the sweetest people, too. Treated me like a daughter. One of the promises I've made to myself is to find the bastards who did it and see them fry. Of course, it's a hump in the ass not having access to the investigatory details…"

Nate nodded. "If you give me what you have, I can ask around if you want. The department handling the investigation might be more forthcoming with a fellow cop."

Luna's heart squeezed. "Would you? That would be amazing, Nate! Let's keep it to ourselves, though, okay? I don't wanna get Bella's hopes up."

"Of course," Nate said. "And about what I said before… I'm an idiot, Luna. I should never have questioned her mental health."

Luna softened. "Aw, hell, you aren't an idiot. It's a ton to absorb, and I get that. But ghost children playing poltergeist with the kitchen furniture after all we've witnessed? Is that such a leap?"

The sound of footsteps drew near, and Luna put a finger to her lips.

"Pizza delivery!" Isabella shouted as she entered the kitchen carrying two boxes. "We can chow down and discuss where to set up the equipment. Oh, and Nate," she said, "before we do, can you check a wall in the upstairs hall for me? It looks like I have a hole in the plaster, but it's too high up for me to see."

Luna grinned. "Well, you are on the short side, half-pint."

"Hilarious," Isabella deadpanned, placing the equipment Luna had brought back inside the black bag. "I just want to make sure the scratching and clawing sounds I heard aren't due to a furry critter breaching the fortress."

Nate smiled. "Sure. I'll take a look after we eat. You have a ladder up there?"

Isabella nodded. "In Ellie's room. I was using it this week to take down the remaining walls."

Luna grabbed a napkin, held it to her nose, and sneezed. "Fuckin' allergies suck ass!"

"You okay?" Isabella asked.

"Yeah. I'll take one of my antihistamines before we start

investigating. So, did taking the walls down to the studs help stink central?"

"Unfortunately, no," Isabella replied, picking up the black bag. "How about I put this stuff on the other table while we eat? Lune, can you grab the plates and drinks? Be back in a flash."

Isabella walked to the dining room and gently laid the gear bag on the table. Tossing up a silent prayer that they caught some objective evidence tonight, she turned and hurried back to the kitchen and her friends.

Unaware that timing, in death as it was in life, was everything.

If she'd waited a moment longer, Isabella would have witnessed something genuinely paranormal.

The frantic beeps and flashing lights as every device within the canvas bag went off in tandem.

"Hey, Isabella? Luna?" Nate called from upstairs. "Can you guys come here for a second?"

The pair jogged upstairs to the second-floor landing, where Nate, still on the ladder, was frowning at the wall.

"What up, Hoss?" Luna asked.

Nate descended the ladder. "Did you know there's a camera behind the wall?"

"Behind it?" Isabella said, dumbfounded. "I know Spencer put up several cameras in the corners of the house, but no. I had no idea."

Luna sneezed again. "Why the fuck would that shit-stain put a camera behind the wall?"

"Yeah," Isabella said. "Why, indeed. It makes no sense."

Nate frowned. "It does if he's been watching you."

"Son of a bitch!" Luna yelled.

"Why?" Isabella asked. "What does he hope to find?"

Nate tipped his head back. "Not sure. Ammunition, maybe?"

"For what, though?"

Luna snapped her fingers. "That sneaky snake! He's spying on you, Bella, recording your response to each paranormal event. And he's documenting your reaction to use against you in court." She held back another sneeze. "I have to get some relief from these allergies. Be right back!"

Nathan watched her race down the stairs before turning to Isabella. "I think Luna is right about your husband spying on you. If you'll allow me to remove the camera, we can examine it. Unfortunately, it means putting a bigger hole in the wall."

"I can't believe this," Isabella said, astounded. "Who does that? What could he possibly..." She stopped, a sinister thought popping into her brain. "Nate, do you think Spencer could talk through the camera, as well as record things?"

"It's possible, but I can't know for sure until I look at it. Why? What are you thinking?"

"I'm thinking that he is so low, so demented, he could be trying to make me think I'm losing it."

Disgusted, Nate said, "Gaslighting you? Is he that much of a scumbag, given your painful history?"

"You bet he is. Admittedly, I don't know how he could conjure apparitions, but if a microphone is involved, he could be responsible for the bangs, the whispers, the cries in the night."

"And the temperature fluctuations as well," Nate added, jaw tightening. "If the thermostat is connected to an app on his phone, he could drop a room's temperature with the touch of a button." He raked a hand through his hair. "Fair warning, lady... If I ever come face to face with this piece of shit, I can't be held responsible for what I do."

Isabella smiled. "I'm right there with ya, bud. If only..."

A wheezing sound from behind caused them both to turn.

Hand raking at her throat, Luna stood at the top of the landing, gasping for breath. Her eyes were wide, her lips swollen. The skin on her face was flushed and blotchy.

"Lune?" Isabella asked, rushing to her side. "Sweetheart, what is it?"

Grabbing Isabella's wrist in a death grip, Luna whispered, "Can't breathe. Anaphylaxis."

Nate sped by them and rushed down the stairs. "Where's her EpiPen?" he yelled.

"Top dresser drawer in her bedroom!" Isabella shouted back. She put an arm around Luna. "Come on, honey…we need to get you to the hospital!".

Terrified, Isabella half-carried, half-dragged, Luna down the steps. By the time they reached the foyer, Nate was standing by, EpiPen in hand.

"Do it!" Isabella shouted. "In her thigh!"

Nate bent forward and pushed the device against her leg.

Nothing happened.

"Shit! The fucking thing is broken!" Nate yelled.

Isabella, on the verge of hysteria, screamed, "Where's the other one?"

"There was only one in the drawer!" Nate said. "What about her purse?'

"She left it at her office! Oh, God!"

Nate tossed the useless EpiPen aside, swooped Luna into his arms, and ran to the front door. "Let's go!" he said over his shoulder, snatching Isabella's car keys from the foyer table. "I'm driving!"

In tears, terrified for her friend, Isabella dashed out after him, slamming the door behind her. Together they laid Luna in the back seat of the car. Isabella climbed in beside her and tucked her friend's head onto her lap.

"Nate, please!" Isabella begged. "Go quickly!"

He did, weaving and honking all the way to the hospital.

And, just as he pulled into the emergency room entrance, Luna Lake—Isabella's lifelong friend and the closest thing she had to a sister—stopped breathing.

# CHAPTER
# THIRTY-ONE

Nate walked into the waiting room of Savannah General Hospital, holding two steaming cups of coffee. "Any word?"

Isabella rubbed her temples. "No, nothing yet. At least they got her breathing again," she said, taking the cup Nate offered, grateful for its warmth. "Thanks."

"Another headache?" he asked, taking the seat beside her. "You might want to get that checked, sweetheart. You seem to have those a lot more than other people."

"I know," she agreed. "But it's only been since we moved to Rosemear. I've been wondering if there is black mold or something."

Nate remained quiet, lost in thought. Eventually, he said, "You know, the whole thing with Luna is very odd, isn't it?"

She frowned. "How do you mean?"

He set his coffee on a side table and rubbed his thighs. "I'm not sure. It just feels 'off' to me. Didn't you say Luna's only allergy was to penicillin?"

"Yes, as far as I know. It's so severe that she usually carries two EpiPens in her purse. I keep a pair of them here for her as well, just in case."

Nate cleared his throat. "I only saw one in the drawer."

"I know. But I swear there were two," Isabella said softly.

"Maybe it's the suspicious cop in me, but don't you find it strange that not only did she somehow come in contact with an allergen that could kill her, but that the one thing that could save her life malfunctioned?"

"And the other EpiPen I kept for her is missing," she said dully.

"Right. And, although I don't know her well, she's a nurse who knows the dangers of anaphylaxis. I'd expect her to be extra cautious."

Her mouth twisted. "Which is why we keep two here and two in her purse. Maybe she has another allergy we are unaware of. Food? Something on the pizza?" She looked down, eyes brimming with tears. "All I know is that I can't lose her, Nate. I will go insane for real if that happens."

He wrapped an arm around her shoulder. "She's scrappy and tougher than nails. No way she's going down without a fight."

Twenty minutes later, a doctor wearing a white coat over scrubs and carrying a clipboard entered the waiting room. "Isabella Boyd?" he asked, expression neutral.

Isabella's breath hitched, and she and Nate slowly stood.

The balding doctor, whose name tag read "Paul Alexander, MD," smiled. "Your friend will be fine. It was touch-and-go there for a minute, but we've managed to stabilize her."

Relieved, Isabella collapsed into Nate's arms, tears streaming down her face.

Dr. Alexander checked his clipboard. "You told the triage nurse the only allergy you know of is penicillin, correct?"

"Yes," Isabella said. "Luna has such a severe reaction to it she carries two, sometimes three, EpiPens with her. And at work—she's a nurse practitioner—she won't even handle penicillin."

"It sounds as though she's cautious enough, leading me to believe it was an accidental exposure. Tell me, do you currently have any antibiotics at home?"

Isabella shook her head. "No, nothing. We just moved here and haven't even found a primary doctor yet." She paused a moment. "Can we see her?"

The doctor nodded. "Briefly, but don't be surprised if she doesn't say much. Her body has gone through a multi-system trauma and needs rest." He cleared his throat. "I'd like to keep her overnight. A small percentage of these cases end up with biphasic anaphylaxis, a secondary reaction that causes a recurrence of symptoms. I'd also like to run more tests. Luna may have developed a second deadly allergy she isn't aware of, and if we can't identify it, next time…"

He didn't need to finish the sentence—Isabella understood his warning.

*Next time, we won't be so lucky.*
*Next time, Luna will die.*

*Rosemear*
*August 9ᵗʰ*
*10 p.m.*

The house was pitch black when Isabella and Nate returned from the hospital.

Nate unlocked the door and tossed the car keys on the foyer table. "Guess in our panic, we forgot to leave on a light or two."

Isabella latched the front door. "Well, we had other things on our mind, right?"

"Right," Nate said, stuffing his hands into his pockets. "So, um, I…I was thinking," he stuttered, "about maybe staying here.

Just for tonight."

Isabella's eyes narrowed. "Stay here? Overnight?"

He gulped, suddenly uncomfortable. "No, not like that," he said, "not in a sexual way. It's just with the kids gone and Luna in the hospital, I don't feel comfortable leaving you here alone."

"You don't feel..." Isabella said, tamping down a flicker of irritation. "Look, Nate, while I understand you're only trying to protect me, it's not necessary. I'm not made of glass. I'm a thirty-three-year-old woman who happens to have a mean streak and a helluva left hook."

Nate grinned. "Mean streak? I've seen newborn kittens meaner than you."

"Ahh, but sometimes, those meek pussycats turn out to be tigers."

"Sure, but..."

Isabella stopped him. "Let's table this for now, okay? It's late, and I'm cranky. Why don't you find a nice bottle of white in the wine cabinet? While you do that, I'll throw together a tray of cheese and crackers."

"Yes, ma'am," he said, smiling as she headed to the kitchen.

*Beautiful, witty, and tough as nails. You're in deep shit, Decker.*

When Nate entered the kitchen with a bottle of Riesling, Isabella was at the refrigerator, her back to him, gathering an assortment of cheese.

He snagged a red rose from a vase of flowers on the table and moved behind her. Wrapping an arm around her torso, he placed his chin on her shoulder and presented it to her. "A red rose, milady?"

Isabella chuckled, took the offering, and turned. "Thank you, it's lovely. I should know; I bought it."

"True, but I was desperate," he joked. "Look, I didn't mean

to imply you were a porcelain doll, Bella. I know you can defend yourself, but the hard truth is that I don't trust your husband. Something is happening here besides him spying or recording you without consent."

"Like?"

"I'm not sure. Call it a gut feeling."

The peal of Isabella's phone halted their discussion. "Speak of the devil. Sorry, but he has the kids. I have to take this."

Nate nodded, and she answered the phone.

"Everything okay?" she asked, skipping any false pleasantries.

"Why wouldn't it be?" Spencer snapped.

Sighing, she said, "It's late, Spence. What do you want?"

"Jesus, Iz, no need to be a bitch about it. I thought you'd like to know that Ellie wants to come home."

"Oh, no! Is she sick?"

"Just for home. Will you be around tonight if I bring the kids back?"

Isabella nearly laughed. Ellie wasn't homesick; her asshole father just couldn't handle the responsibility of caring for his children. "Tonight? I guess, as long as there isn't an emergency with Luna. She's in the hospital."

"That right?" Spencer said. "Did someone finally have enough of her mouth and pop her a shot?"

"Oh, for fuck's sake! Can you pretend to be decent for one stupid minute? Luna had an allergic reaction tonight and nearly died!"

"Wow, that's rough. Wonder what caused it."

"The doctors are trying to figure that out now. Somehow, she came in contact with an allergen, sending her into anaphylaxis."

"Tragic," Spencer said, unmoved. "Did she blow up like a balloon? Wish I'd seen it."

Anger building, Isabella tried to hold her tongue. She failed miserably.

"I'm sure if you checked your spy cameras," she said through gritted teeth, "you could see the whole episode unfold."

He hesitated. "Spy cameras? I've no idea what you're talking about. Be there in fifteen minutes."

Isabella hung up and turned to Nate. "He's bringing the kids back," she said, laughing bitterly. "He only picked them up last night. Father of the year, right?" Wrinkling her nose, she added, "I'm sorry, but you should probably go. It's better if you aren't here when he comes."

Nate shook his head. "Not a good idea. I'll hang out upstairs when he drops them off, but I'm not leaving."

She started to object, and he held up his hand. "Look, you can be pissed off at me all you want. This asshole is dangerous. I can feel it in my bones." He studied her smooth skin and the smattering of freckles across her nose and cheeks. She looked more like a college kid than a woman in her thirties. "Luna told me Spencer hates her and has threatened her more than once. He hinted at going after her nursing license."

"And cornered her in the kitchen of our old house," Isabella added, suddenly nauseous. "What are you saying, Nate?"

He rubbed the back of his neck. "What if he found a more permanent solution to get Luna out of your life? What if he tampered with her EpiPens?"

She paled. "No, no, he couldn't! How would he even know she'd need them? Besides, he'd need access to…" She stopped, a hand flying to her mouth.

"Access to what?" he asked.

"Remember when I told you I fainted after hearing Anna's voice?"

"I do."

"Well, that day, when I woke up," she said, wide-eyed, "I heard noises coming from Luna's room and went to investigate. Spencer was in there."

"In her room?" Nate growled. "Son of a bitch! There'd be no

reason for him to be in there, right?"

Isabella shook her head. "No. He said he was looking for smelling salts."

"Bullshit," Nate hissed. "Tell me—have you always kept extra pens for her?"

Isabella nodded. "Yes, and there was an extra bottle of her allergy pills. Since she's here so often, and her hay fever is notoriously bad this time of year, it made sense to keep extra allergy meds on hand. And the bedroom EpiPens were more for my peace of mind than hers."

"Fuck," Nate whispered. "You remember the last thing she did before she got sick? We were checking out the hidden camera, and she kept sneezing."

The realization hit Isabella like a freight train. "Yes, I remember! She went to take her pills!"

"And Spencer is a pharmaceutical rep with access to almost any drug imaginable," he said. "Including penicillin."

Isabella gasped. "No, no—impossible! Spencer is a lot of things, but Christ, Nate, to tamper with her meds? Her EpiPens? You're talking about murder!"

"Attempted murder, since Luna survived," Nate said. "I'm sorry, Isabella, but I think he's been gaslighting you for months. That alone is a sick kind of mental and emotional abuse." He placed his hands on her shoulders. "In the last four years, you were nearly destroyed after the loss of your parents and Anna Rae. Spencer knows how close you were to the edge."

"Meaning?"

"Meaning, what better way to send you over that cliff than to remove the one person who's always had your back?"

"Oh, my God!" Isabella said, turning to rush out of the kitchen. "I need to check those pills!"

Nate stopped her. "Wait! Did Spencer have gloves when you found him in Luna's room?"

She frowned. "Not that I remember."

"Then let's not touch anything. If he did this, his fingerprints should be all over that pill bottle."

"And the EpiPen," Isabella added. "Although I'm not sure where that went."

"I tossed it somewhere when it malfunctioned," Nate said. "We'll look for it later. In the meantime, play it cool when Spencer comes. I don't want him to know we're on to him. If I'm right, he's looking at a long prison sentence. We'll file a report tomorrow, and I'll bring this case to my supervisor. We need to dust that bottle and the epinephrine injector for prints."

"And analyze the camera," she murmured. "You really think Spencer did this?"

He took her hand. "I've dealt with men like him my entire career, Bella. He's a narcissist and, I suspect, a con man. The only thing he loves more than attention is money."

"That's very true," Isabella said, looking down at Nate's hand, entwined with hers. "I hate to say it, but you should hide now. He'll be here any minute." She smiled sadly. "So much for our ghost hunt, huh? I'd hoped to get answers about this place and the ghosts who remain here."

He squeezed her hand. "We will. Don't forget, Roma is coming tomorrow."

"Yeah, about that. Maybe I should cancel? Roma is Luna's friend, after all. And now the kids will be here."

Nate gently pulled her toward the staircase. "No, don't cancel. I can ask Marnie to watch them. That was the original plan, anyway. And with any luck, Luna will be released tomorrow." He brought her hand to his lips and kissed her knuckles. "I'm right upstairs if you need me. If anything strikes you as the least bit worrisome, call out. Understood?"

She threw back her shoulders and saluted. "Yes, sir, Officer, sir."

"Nobody likes a wise guy," he said with a laugh as he started up the stairs.

Five minutes after Nate headed to the second floor, the doorbell rang. Isabella crossed the foyer and opened the plantation doors to find Spencer, a backpack over each shoulder, standing on the small porch.

He was alone.

"Um," she said, brows dipped. "Where are the kids?"

Spencer walked through the front door, reeking of cheap perfume and alcohol. "They both fell asleep in the car. I thought we should talk alone for a few minutes before I carry them inside."

Suspicious, Isabella asked, "Talk about what?"

"About us." He laid the backpacks on the floor. "Come with me to the kitchen and let's pour a drink."

"It's late, Spence, and I'm exhausted. Can we not do this now?"

"Then when?" he snapped. "If it's not that bitch Luna sticking her nose in where it doesn't belong, it's that fucking cop that keeps sniffing around." He sneered. "You giving him the goods, Iz? You fuckin' him?"

Shocked, Isabella said, "What are you talking about? Nate is my friend."

"Your 'friend,'" Spencer mocked. "Sure he is."

"He is. What I'm wondering is how you know about him."

Spencer ignored her and stomped to the kitchen, Isabella right behind him. Grabbing a beer from the fridge, he opened it with his teeth and spat the cap on the floor. It was a stupid, juvenile trick he'd learned in college.

Isabella hoped he'd crack a tooth.

After chugging half the bottle, he wiped his mouth with the back of his hand. "I have a right to know if my wife is spreading her legs for another man."

"Wrong, Spencer!" she shouted, suddenly furious. "You forfeited that right when you started an affair with your assistant!

Now, go get my kids and then get the fuck out of here before I have you arrested!"

He giggled. "Arrested for what? Having a beer in my own house?"

"No, for driving my kids around when you're obviously drunk!" Silently chastising herself, wondering how she had ever loved this man, she hissed, "I'm warning you… I *will* call the police!"

Spencer's eyes flashed, and he grabbed her by the neck. "No need to use a phone, right?" he taunted, words slurred. "Just call out to your boyfriend upstairs."

Isabella pulled at the fingers wrapped around her throat. "You think you're so clever, asshole? Listening to a private conversation?" She repositioned her hands, trying to work a finger under the thumb that was crushing her trachea. "I-I know exactly what you've been up to," she rasped, trying to kick his shins. "You tried to kill Luna, didn't you? You switched her allergy pills with penicillin, and she nearly died!"

He grinned. "Nearly? That's too bad. So close, too." He started walking backward to the kitchen counter, Isabella's throat still in his hand. The more he dragged her, the tighter his grip became against her windpipe.

"Let. Go!" she wheezed, afraid she would die tonight, even with help right upstairs.

Simply because she couldn't produce a sound louder than a whisper.

Ignoring her pleas, Spencer jerked open a drawer and withdrew a massive carving knife. Holding it beneath her chin, he moved his mouth close to her ear. "It was a senseless tragedy," he said softly. "If only she'd sought help! Poor, broken Isabella, in the throes of psychosis, stabbed her cop lover to death before slitting her own throat." He sighed wistfully. "Yet, her husband, a forgiving soul, would ask friends and family to recall the woman she once was— rather than the killer she'd become."

Stomach roiling as the room spun, Isabella closed her eyes, moments away from losing consciousness.

"And the best part? I have a paper trail to prove your instability—psych ward admissions, years of therapy, countless prescription medications. And let's not forget your attempted overdose. You'd be long gone if it weren't for me." He licked her cheek. "Yes, even back then, I was covering my bases."

Enjoying the power it gave him, Spencer released some of the pressure on her throat.

Because seeing how much she could withstand before passing out had become a game.

"Are you still with me, Iz?" he asked, pushing the knife into the tender flesh of her neck and drawing blood. "Because, honestly, this is much harder than last time. Before, all I had to do was replace your anti-anxiety meds with a kickass anti-psychotic like Haldol and some powerful antidepressants. The combination alone should have killed you."

Isabella, growing weaker, still managed to find her voice. "You drugged me?"

Spencer started laughing, a maniacal-sounding chitter. "Of course! I've been drugging you for years, idiot!" He grew serious. "But that one time... Shit, how the fuck was I supposed to know when I gave you your 'Advil' that it would knock you out? Anna was sleeping and not supposed to be hurt!"

Bile rose to her throat, and anger shot through her veins. Isabella no longer cared about the knife under her chin or the fingers circling her neck.

Because she no longer cared about breathing. Or dying.

All that mattered was getting revenge against the man whose hate and selfishness had taken Anna Rae.

Using her last ounce of strength, Isabella jerked her knee up as hard as she could, connecting with Spencer's groin.

A whoosh of air, followed by a tiny yelp, escaped his lips. He dropped the knife onto the floor mat and released Isabella's throat, doubling over as waves of pain shot from his testicles to the pit of his stomach. Hands clutching his ballsack, he choked down the vomit that had risen in his throat.

Isabella watched, feeling a strength and confidence she hadn't felt since Anna's death. Seeing Spencer now, bent over in agony, she felt neither pity nor remorse for what she'd done.

Rather, she'd love to do it again.

She didn't get the chance.

Spencer coughed and started to rise, a string of expletives and threats spewing from his lips.

As he moved toward Isabella, they both felt a change in the air.

A wave of static electricity bathed their bodies, peppering their skin with goosebumps and lifting the hairs on their arms as a familiar smell filled the room.

Lavender.

Together, they watched as a ripple, an undulating flutter of space and time, shimmered before them. Within this pulsing wave, a minor breach began to form.

A minuscule opening offering a glimpse into another dimension.

Soon, the hole grew wider, spanning the width of the kitchen.

Transfixed, momentarily forgetting their current circumstances, they froze, gaping at the wispy void until a translucent, spectral woman stepped through.

"Abigail?" Isabella whispered.

"The fuck is that?" Spencer yelled, slamming his fist on the table and rattling the vase of flowers. "How the hell are you doing this, Isabella?"

"It's not me, jackass!" she hissed between clenched teeth. "It's the lady of the house. It's Abigail Charles."

Abigail smiled shyly, nodding her thanks to Isabella before glaring at Spencer.

Growling, fists flying, he lunged toward the ghostly vision.

Abigail recoiled and, with a screech of pent-up rage that was at once heartbreaking and deafening, raised a kitchen chair overhead and smashed it against Spencer's skull, raining wooden splinters and chair legs all over the floor.

Grunting, he spun and dropped to one knee.

But within seconds, he started to rise again.

Crouched low, one hand cradling his head, he stumbled toward Isabella. "Now, you're fucking dead!" he rasped.

Panicked, she scanned the area around her for a weapon. Spotting a broken chair leg to her right, she picked it up and began to swing blindly.

On the third swing, she connected.

The sharp crack as Spencer's jaw shattered echoed throughout the kitchen.

His arm shot out as, dazed, he flailed desperately for something to hold on to. His hand slapped the kitchen table and it rocked violently, sending the crystal vase crashing to the floor.

When Nathan Decker, the man hiding upstairs, the man rapidly falling in love with Isabella Boyd, heard the crack of wood splintering, followed by an explosive shattering of glass, he jumped to his feet.

And started to run.

# CHAPTER THIRTY-TWO

*Rosemear*
*August 10ᵗʰ*
*1:00 a.m.*

After personally placing a handcuffed Spencer Boyd into the back of a squad car, Nate returned to the kitchen and found Isabella sweeping up tiny pieces of shattered glass.

"Here," he said, taking the broom from her hands, "let me do that. Why don't you check on the kids?"

She smiled. "I can't believe they slept through all of this. Thanks for carrying them in for me." She shook her head. "Man, I suspect we're all looking at years of therapy. Especially them."

Nate leaned on the broom handle and shrugged. "Kids are more resilient than we give them credit for. They'll work it out."

Isabella nodded. "I guess. Um, is he—is he gone?"

Nate winked. "Drove into the sunset in the back of a Savannah PD squad car, handcuffed and Mirandized." His eyes landed on the bruises on her neck, the cut on her chin. A flash of anger marred his handsome face before he reined it in. "Tonight," he growled, "was the last time that son of a bitch will ever lay a hand on you."

"God, I hope so." She dragged the kitchen trash can over to the pile of glass on the floor. "You know what I don't get? Why did he save me?"

"Save you?"

"Yes. Right after Anna died, I tried to, you know, end it," she said, embarrassed to say it out loud. "As much as I love Sam and Ellie, the thought of Anna being all alone messed with my mind. I took a bunch of pills from Spencer's pharmaceutical bag. Normally, that bag would be under lock and key, but this day..." She let the thought hang in the air. "Anyway, he found me unconscious and rushed me to the hospital."

Nate's brow wrinkled. "An unlocked bag filled with prescription meds and within reach of an emotionally devastated woman. Kind of convenient, don't you think?"

Isabella went rigid. "You think it was deliberate? If so, why save me?"

Nate waved a hand. "Who the fuck knows with that guy. Maybe his original plan was not to kill you but to get you out of the way. And him saving you, becoming the 'hero,' would divert suspicion from him later."

"If that's true, he must have hated me for years. Like, long before Anna died." She gave Nate a beaming smile. "Is it weird to be happy right now? To feel relief and a simple peace at knowing the truth?"

He leaned the broom against the wall and took her in his arms. "No, not at all. You're free, Isabella. Free to live and laugh and love again." He brushed a soft kiss over her forehead. "Only this time, with the right person."

She hugged him tightly. "I don't know what would have happened if you weren't here to help me, Nate," she whispered. "Thank you."

Smiling, he released her. "I did very little, actually. By the time

I rushed in here, you and Abigail had everything under control." He winked. "You make a good team."

She rubbed his arm, feeling his bicep contract at her touch. "So you saw it, right? Abigail, the portal? I know I sound like a broken record, but think of it as my sanity check."

"I saw her, Bella," Nate said, grabbing the broom again and sweeping shards of glass closer to the dustpan. "I saw her and that alternate dimension or big-ass plane thing clear as day. You aren't crazy, and I owe you an apology for ever doubting you."

She stopped him from sweeping and kissed his cheek. "You owe me nothing. You've been a rock and a true friend. I'm grateful to have you in my life." She smiled shyly. "But just to be clear—do you always carry a set of handcuffs? Or were you hoping to get lucky tonight, Officer Decker?"

He roared with laughter. "If I were going to play games with you, Ms. Boyd, it would be with something much softer and less likely to bruise." His eyes darkened. "Because I'm not into pain when pleasuring a woman."

A sudden flush of warmth bathed her body. The atmosphere in the kitchen had gone from playful banter to something else. Something more intimate, steamier.

Something erotic.

Feeling it, too, he changed the subject. "Well, I don't know about you, but I'm beat. Is it okay if I crash on your couch tonight? If I come banging into Marnie's at this hour, I'll wake the whole house."

"Oh, of course," she said, flustered. "I'll-I'll get you some blankets. What time do we have to be at the police station in the morning?"

Nate yawned. "Nine or ten. I thought we could drop the kids off with my sister and then go. After we give our formal statements, we can stop by the hospital and see if we can break Luna out of there."

"Oh, I hope so. Doing an investigation without her doesn't

seem right." Exhausted and out of things to say, she headed upstairs to the linen closet. "Be right back with your bedding."

Nate watched her leave, cursing God and fate and the shitty timing of the universe.

Because he was seeing clearly for the first time since they'd met and knew he wasn't falling in love with her.

That ship had already sailed.

And right now, she was still a married woman and far too vulnerable to board that vessel with him and sail into the sunset.

Isabella, wearing a light summer scarf to hide the bruises on her neck, walked hand in hand with Nate out of the police station.

After nearly three hours of questioning, photographing Isabella's injuries, and taking written statements, the police charged Spencer Boyd with aggravated assault for his attack on Isabella. The lead detective on the case also told them that once they'd received the results of Luna's blood screen and processed the prints they'd found on the pill bottle, Spencer, if found guilty, would be looking at decades in prison for attempted murder.

When they reached the car, Nate opened the passenger-side door. "Know what else I heard from the guy working the case?"

"If you tell me, will you have to kill me?"

Nate chuckled. "Nothing so drastic. However, keep in mind he was doing me a favor, so the information he provided is strictly off the record."

"My lips are sealed."

"Okay, so, according to Detective Mullins, your husband has been singing like a canary since this morning. Despite his Miranda warning, he waived his right to counsel and started an interesting chat with investigators."

"That doesn't sound like Spencer."

"Maybe not, but once he was informed that his lover agreed to testify against him …"

"Wait! Julia is turning on him?"

Nate leaned on her open door. "Ms. Cox was notified early today that she was being looked at as an accessory. One of the detectives who spoke to her put a bug in her ear, telling her that if she cooperated fully, she might not get charged."

"And she caved? So much for loyalty!"

"Well," he said cryptically, "not exactly. They might have led Spencer to believe that before they closed the deal."

"Hah! Brilliant!"

He secured her door and jogged to the driver's side. Once behind the wheel, he asked, "Hey, are you hungry? It's after one, and I just realized we didn't eat breakfast."

She shook her head. "If it's okay with you, I'd like to go to the hospital and check on Luna."

"Done," he said, pulling out of the parking lot. "And, if she's ready to be sprung, we can return to Rosemear, and I'll make us all a fabulous lunch!"

Isabella made a face. "Hotdogs?"

"And beans! Don't forget about the beans!"

*Rosemear*
*August 10ᵗʰ*
*4:00 p.m.*

Isabella paced the den. "Are you sure you're up to this, Luna? We can try to reschedule Roma for another time."

Sitting on the couch with her feet propped up, Luna rolled her eyes. "Jaysus, I'm fine! I swear to God, Izzy-B, I've only been here for thirty minutes! If you don't stop fussing over me, I'll go insane and take you with me!"

Nate snorted. "Well, that's funnier than it would have been a week ago!"

"Yeah," Isabella said tartly. "It's hilarious. So, sue me if I don't want to watch you blow up like the Stay Puft Marshmallow Man again."

"I know, I know," she said, reaching for Isabella's hand. "But I swear on my last boyfriend's life, I'm fine!"

"You hated your last boyfriend!"

"Did I?" Luna said innocently. "Anyway, I'm okay and happy to be home. The only thing that would make me happier is knowing the fucker who put me in the hospital is suffering!"

"Allegedly," Nate said, using air quotes. "But he's locked up for now, and I can tell you that is *not* a pleasant experience."

Isabella frowned. "Allegedly? As far as I'm concerned, there's no question in my mind. That bastard knew all about Luna's allergy, how severe it was, and switched her meds anyway. He was willing to kill her to get to me, and that's seven shades of fucked up."

Luna snapped her fingers. "Maybe we bail him out, take him for a nice boat ride down in Hilton Head." She winked at Isabella. "At night. In a boat with chains and a cement block on board."

Nate slapped his hands over his ears. "La, la, la, I hear nothing! I'm a cop, remember?"

"That's why we keep you around," Luna teased. "You're a rock-solid alibi."

"Touché." He smiled and checked his watch. "Only a few hours until six. Is there anything we need to do to prepare for this lady's visit? Candles? Creepy music? Garlic cloves and holy water?"

Luna laughed. "She's not banishing vampires or performing an exorcism, Decker—just getting a feel for the energy. First, she'll try to communicate with the ghosts here."

"And then?" Isabella asked.

"Then she'll probably do a séance and house cleansing."

"A séance?" Isabella said, eyes wide. "As in raising the dead for a fireside chat? Yeah, not sure I like the sound of that."

"Hey, it's not like you see in the movies. Roma is respectful and knows what the boundaries are." Luna stood and walked to the portrait of the Hawthornes, still leaning against the desk, front side away from them. Nodding to it, she asked, "Have you told Nate about the ever-changing picture, Iz?"

"That they changed again? I did. I think that's the scariest part of this haunting. Truthfully, I haven't looked at it since we noticed the eyes shift from right to left."

Luna picked up the painting, turned it, and held it in front of her. "Uh-oh," she said, hesitating before turning the portrait to face the others. "It seems as though they still haven't found the 'look' they seek."

"Holy…," Nate whispered, dumbfounded.

Isabella stared, open-mouthed, at the portrait. "I don't understand!" she gasped. "How can this be?"

Because the portrait had, once again, changed.

The four Hawthorne children, dressed in their Sunday best, were no longer standing near the teal sofa.

They were sitting on it.

And William and Lillian were gone.

*Rosemear*
*August 10th*
*6:00 p.m.*

Roma Lee, a short, plump woman in her sixties, entered Rosemear carrying a multi-colored, quilted bag over one arm.

She wore her black hair short and wire-framed glasses over bright green eyes. Her garb—head scarf, hoop earrings, and a dozen bangle bracelets—seemed straight out of a psychic handbook.

Isabella tried to hide her grin. Roma's vibe reminded her of Zoltar, the animatronic gypsy fortune teller at fairs and arcades.

"Roma Lee!" Luna squealed, wrapping her arms around her friend. "It's been too long! How are things? Any gossip from the other side you'd care to share?" She raised a brow. "Any word from Elvis?"

Roma pulled her glasses down to the tip of her nose and peered over the frame. "You know my clients insist on discretion, Luna Lake. Even if Elvis was standing next to you at this very moment, I couldn't tell you."

Luna's eyes widened, and she whipped her head from side to side. "Is he?"

Roma rolled her eyes. "Honestly?"

"So, that's a no, then?"

"Uh, yeah. It's a no."

After a tour of the house, Isabella led her guests to the dining room. "Before we start, can I get you anything, Roma?"

"Nothing, except…perhaps you could close the blinds? I work better in low lighting."

After the shades were drawn, Isabella said, "Shall we tell you our experiences so far? What we've seen and heard?"

Roma shook her head. "No. Going in blind to an active haunt leads to more reliable results." She smiled. "I can't be biased if I know nothing of your experiences here."

Luna clicked her tongue. "Told ya she was good!"

Winking, Roma lit a few candles and began.

"This house," she said, eyes half-mast, "is like a funhouse mirror. Nothing is as it seems."

"I-I agree," Isabella said.

"Shhh!" Luna admonished with a whisper. "She has to get it all out before we interrupt her. Otherwise, she loses the connection."

"Sorry," Isabella mouthed. "It's my first…whatever this is."

"I sense several souls here," Roma continued, her face glowing in the flickering candlelight. "Many are confused and unable to move on."

"They're lost?" Nate asked, forgetting Luna's instructions.

Roma stared straight ahead. "Not lost, Nate. Trapped." She turned to Isabella. "Have you found any belongings, statues, anything unusual hidden in the walls here?"

"Yes! Luna and I found bones behind the plaster of my daughter's room while searching for an awful smell."

"And symbols," Luna added. "We found a daisy wheel and the initials 'A.M.' carved in the wood."

Roma nodded. "A hexafoil. It's known as a witches' mark and was thought to protect a home from evil. The 'A.M.' stands for 'Ave Maria.'"

Nate whistled. "Invoking both witches and the mother of God. Talk about covering your bases."

Roma nodded and closed her eyes. "Immurement, the act of placing items inside a wall, has a strange history. Centuries ago, people placed coins, shoes, or kitchen utensils within their walls for good luck and protection."

"And bones?" Nate asked. "Why did they use those?"

"Both to protect the home and to shield the occupants from harm. That smell you speak of is not from decay. Instead, the odor is a manifestation of a wrongful act."

"What act?" Isabella whispered.

"The act of disturbing the dead."

The room went still.

Roma continued. "After several tragedies, someone went to a lot of trouble to seal this home. Rosemear was blanketed with a protection spell—one that included disinterring bodies—to keep evil away. Unfortunately, I fear it worked too well."

"How do you mean?" Nate asked.

"Whoever did this was desperate and didn't think it through. A shield to keep ghosts from entering a home also means they cannot leave it."

"Trapping them," Isabella said sadly. "Good and bad spirits alike. Can you break the spell?"

Roma nodded. "Yes, and I will before I leave." She hesitated. "I must tell you that there are powerful magics at work here, both dark and light. They can cloud your memories and make you doubt what you see."

"That would explain a lot, Bella," Luna said. "The time gaps, not recalling the blue room…"

"Ah, yes," Roma said. "Painting a ceiling or walls haint blue goes back centuries as well. It was believed that the blue color could fool spirits into leaving."

Isabella looked at Nate. "Exactly as you said. The blue tricks them into thinking it's sky or sea." She smiled shyly. "How'd you get to be so smart?"

Nate chuckled.

"Tell me," Roma said to Isabella, "are you missing personal items?"

"Yes, an earring and charcoal pencils. My sunglasses that were missing have been, uh, returned."

"The little boy is taking them," Roma said. "He gives them to the woman who protects him from the others."

"Abigail," Luna whispered.

"Yes," Roma said. She closed her eyes, swayed a bit, and whimpered. When she opened them again, Luna gasped.

Roma's green eyes had turned honey brown.

"Lune?" Isabella said softly. "Um, is that supposed to happen?"

"I think she's channeling Abigail," Luna whispered back.

"Maybe she can change the channel," Nate cracked, "before I shit my pants."

Isabella giggled, and Luna silenced her with a kick to the shins.

"Can you not…" Isabella froze mid-sentence, mesmerized by a series of lights forming over Roma's head.

Nate and Luna saw it, too.

"Orbs," Luna whispered. "Dozens of them!"

Eyes still closed, Roma moaned softly.

"You okay, Rome?" Luna asked.

"So much death here," she murmured. "And so much anger."

Isabella nibbled her thumbnail. "Did Abigail speak? Did she tell you what happened to the Hawthornes and Clyde Baldwin?"

"Unfortunately," Roma said, "that's not how it works. The dead only reveal what they want to reveal. Abigail told me she looks after Martin and keeps him from the bad spirits, what the child calls the Meanies." She wiped her brow with a handkerchief that was tucked into her sleeve. "Channeling sometimes feels like a sprint. It's very taxing on the living."

"I understand. Thank you for helping us."

"Of course. You know, I did get, um, something upsetting from Abigail," Roma said. "Did you know she was murdered and buried alive?"

"Oh, God," Isabella said, horrified. "We didn't know for sure, but apparently, my daughter did. Ellie seems to have a connection with Martin."

"That makes sense. Child spirits often seek the comfort of another child."

"Did Abigail say who killed her?" Nate asked.

"No. All she said was that the house was 'alive' with magic. The tragic loss of life connected to Rosemear over the years was orchestrated, at least in part, by the bad spirits trapped here. Murders, suicides, sickness…all set in motion by ghosts with evil intent." She stood and slung her bag over her shoulder. "I will attempt to liberate the souls imprisoned here, but know this… A broken protection spell does not guarantee a spook-free home. Breaking that seal will give spirits, good or bad, an exit. But it will not force them to take it.

"Understood," Isabella said. "And thanks again."

Roma nodded and turned to leave. "Oh," she said, "there is one thing Abigail kept repeating. I've no idea what it means."

"What's that?" Isabella asked.

Roma shrugged. "That, regarding her death, a picture is worth a thousand words."

And just like that, Isabella knew where to find the missing journal pages.

# EPILOGUE

*Rosemear*
*November 28th*
*Thanksgiving Day*
*11:30 a.m.*

Isabella stood at the kitchen counter, singing Christmas carols while kneading a bowl of homemade stuffing.

Luna, peeling potatoes at the table, rolled her eyes. "Can we get through one holiday before going to the next? Ugh, I don't even want to think about it. Shiny, happy people, mobs of them, each willing to kill another just for the latest phone, toy, or gadget. Makes me cuckoo."

"Fine, Ebenezer, I won't sing." Isabella flipped the bowl of stuffing into a casserole dish, washed and dried her hands, and sat beside Luna. "Nate, Marnie, and Matt will be here about twelve."

Luna plopped a peeled potato into a bowl and looked at her friend. "And how are you, Izzy-B? Does the house feel lighter to you?"

"It does. I think the truth had to come out for us all to find closure."

"Which is why I'm glad you discovered those missing journal pages. How did you know to look behind the corners of the portrait?"

"Abigail's clue, mostly. 'A picture is worth a thousand words' is pretty specific." She rested her chin in her hands. "I still can't believe Edward blocked out the circumstances of Abigail's death for years."

"An alcoholic blackout," Luna explained. "Apparently, Edward's memory returned in snippets. In the grips of a blackout, someone can do things they have no recollection of doing."

"And, in his guilt, he hid the last few pages. He wanted it documented but not accessible. Very odd."

"For sure," Luna agreed. "So, Edward was the killer all along, huh?"

"Yep. He killed his parents in a drunken rage after learning of their sins. William Hawthorne ordered Clyde Baldwin to rape Abigail. He wanted to punish Edward for who he chose to love."

"Bastard."

"Exactly. It's sickening. When Edward discovered what his father did, he lost it and killed him."

"Then stabbed Lillian for poisoning his mother, Sarah," Luna said. "But what I don't get..." She hesitated. "Hell, I don't get much! Why did Maggie push Abigail down the stairs in the first place? How come Edward didn't report it to the authorities? And, most importantly, why did he let the two men who helped Abigail hang for the overseer's death?"

Isabella shrugged. "I don't pretend to have all the answers, but I suspect Edward's sister was blackmailing him. If he ratted Margaret out for killing Abigail, she'd see him hanged for the murders of his father and stepmother."

"And the gentlemen who were actually hanged?"

"Abraham and Virgil. According to a witness named Joseph, after Abigail accidentally stabbed Clyde with the pitchfork,

Abraham and Virgil pushed the pitchfork a bit deeper. I think they were trying to protect her. I also believe if Edward had been sober the day the workers at Rosemear hanged the men, he would have stopped it. Call it a gut feeling."

"But he wasn't sober," Luna said matter-of-factly.

"No, he wasn't. He passed out after binge drinking and had no idea until it was too late. The men were hanged right outside Ellie's room in that big oak tree." Tears filled her eyes. "I think the tapping noise we were hearing was the memory of their bodies swinging into the side of the house."

Luna blew out a breath. "Like a residual memory that Rosemear was holding on to."

"Yes," Isabella said softly.

Luna carried the pot of peeled potatoes to the sink. "So, are they gone? The ghosts here?"

"Nope," Isabella laughed. "But it's just Abigail and Martin, and although I enjoy having them here, I suspect it won't be for long. Eventually, they'll gather the courage to move on."

"Isn't it strange how Abigail got trapped here, though? I mean, if Roma and Ellie are right, she didn't die in the house, so how did she break through the protection barrier?"

"Great question. Roma spoke about powerful magic here, so maybe someone good decided Martin needed a champion and drew her in."

"And once in, she couldn't leave."

"Perhaps. Anyway, I think everyone else here, including young Harry Taylor, has moved on. Nate and I removed Ellie's other walls and gathered the human remains. We reburied them in a small coffin, and I've ordered a grave marker. I hope it brings them peace."

Luna wiped her hands on a towel. "It's so sad. I wish we knew who they were."

"I know, but at least they're back where they belong."

"And free." Luna took a chair next to Isabella. "So, do the kids know yet?" she asked, voice low. "About what happened to Spencer?"

"Well, they know what he did to land in prison, and they know he isn't coming home. I can't imagine what's going through their minds, though. I mean, he was a bastard, but he was their father."

A few weeks after his arrest, Spencer's lover, Julia Cox, had posted bail, and he was released. The pair had attempted to flee the country and were caught on their way to the Canadian border, and Spencer had been tossed back in jail.

Luna glanced toward the kitchen entrance. "Do the kids know about… you know," she whispered.

"Not yet," Isabella said. "I'm working with a therapist to figure out the best way to break the news."

Three weeks earlier, while incarcerated, Spencer had been attacked in the food line by a man who demanded his plate of mashed potatoes. By the time officers separated the men, the attacker, a four-hundred-pound inmate nicknamed "Tiny," had nearly severed Spencer's head with a metal cafeteria tray.

He had died on the scene and would never stand trial.

"You know the worst part?" Luna said. "We'll never know everything he's done."

"Well, we know some. Julia Cocksucker is spilling her guts. She told the cops Spencer was drugging me, had been for years."

"Hence the headaches, I bet," Luna snarled.

"Right. And he was gaslighting me with only a camera, a thermostat controlled by his phone, and a voice-changing app." Suddenly, her eyes filled with tears.

"What is it?" Luna asked, rubbing her shoulder.

"It's just that Nate…well, he said Julia mentioned my parents and the break-in. About how Spencer may have been involved. You know how much he coveted money."

"So he orchestrated the home invasion? Had a part in killing your parents?" The color drained from Luna's face. "Jesus, are you freaking kidding me?"

"It's still too early to know, but nothing Spencer did would surprise me. It just breaks my heart to think that if I'd never met him, my folks might still be alive."

"You can't play the 'what if' game, toots," Luna said, wrapping her friend in her arms. "You wouldn't have the kids if you'd never met him."

"True. I still can't get my head around his hatred for me." Isabella sniffed. "He killed Anna Rae, Lune. Or, at least, his actions did. Knocking me out…"

"I know, I know," Luna soothed. "But at least you can let go of the guilt you've been carrying for years. Anna's death is on *his* shoulders, not yours." She ground her teeth. "Good thing that fucker is dead, or I'd take him out back and cut off his microscopic…."

The sound of feet pounding down the stairs stopped her.

"Ma!" Sam yelled. "They're here! *She's* here!"

"Yes, come on, Momma!" Ellie yelled. "Hurry, so we can all see!"

Isabella and Luna followed the children out the front door into the cool November air.

Shielding her eyes from the glaring sun, Isabella called out to Nate. "Well? Did you bring the goods?"

He smiled a beautiful smile and bent low to the ground. Immediately, a fluffy ball of black and white came racing up the driveway.

Midget, as it turned out, had not been queasy from scavenging, nor had she been getting fat from too much food.

She'd gotten pregnant on one of the many occasions the dog-sitter had lost her.

"Look at her, Momma!" Ellie cried, kneeling, pressing her face against the pup's downy head. "Isn't she beautiful?"

"She sure is, Bug."

Once they'd discovered Midge was pregnant, Isabella had

asked for one of the puppies. "Okay," Nate had said, "but you may need to reach out to Maury Povich to find out who the father is."

Of the six puppies in the litter, Nate had found homes for five of them.

A sixth, a male Matty had named Jethro, would stay with the Bensons. Nate would be moving to an apartment after Christmas and wanted his sister and nephew to have an added layer of security.

"Where's Marnie?" Luna asked.

"Coming. There's about twenty minutes left on the pumpkin pie."

Isabella linked hands with Nate. They'd gotten closer over the last few months and even had some 'adult' dates.

And, although it was still too early for either of them to make a lifelong commitment, Nate had seen her at her 'ugly-crying' worst and her 'laugh until you pee your pants' best.

And he hadn't headed for the hills yet.

She took that as an excellent omen.

"I have to go check on the bird," she said. "Hang tight... I'll be back in a flash."

"Uncle Nate!" Matthew yelled. "Can we go out back and play ball with the dogs?"

Nate bent forward and kissed Isabella lightly on the lips. "Duty calls."

"Don't forget Luna," Isabella teased. "It's your turn to watch her."

"Hey!" Luna said, walking toward the kids, Midge at her side. "I heard that!"

Isabella squeezed Nate's hand. "You really are a wonderful uncle, Nathan Decker."

He kissed her again, longer this time. With a whisper, he said, "You think I'm a good uncle? Oh, lady... wait until you see me as a dad."

Heart fluttering and head spinning, she took a moment to

watch everyone—her family—as they laughed their way to the backyard.

Ten minutes later, Isabella stood in the den, wondering why she'd entered the room.

It was as if some unknown force had called to her, urging her to the rolltop desk and the portrait still hidden from sight.

The last few months had been a whirlwind, and she'd forgotten about it.

Until now.

Curious, perplexed by this compulsion to look at it, she picked it up and flipped it around.

And immediately started to laugh.

"Oh, my God, Abigail!" she shouted, spinning in place while holding up the picture. "Are you responsible for this?"

She heard a giggle and smelled lavender, but Abigail Charles did not appear.

"Abby, this is…this is amazing," Isabella whispered, tears in her eyes. "Thank you."

She centered the frame on top of the desk and smiled.

William, Lillian, and the oldest Hawthorne children were gone from the portrait.

In their place, seated on the teal couch and dressed in their Sunday best, were Martin Hawthorne and Anna Rae Boyd.

And behind them—backs straight and smiles beaming—stood Abigail Charles and her one true love.

Prophet Jones.

# ACKNOWLEDGMENTS

Any worthwhile endeavor requires a dash of patience, a cup of faith, and a whole lot of support from the people you love.

In my case, my family and friends are my army, marching me to victory.

Family is everything, and I have the best. To my husband, Mark, and children Jennifer, Brian, Jared, John, and Jordan… thanks a million for sticking with me as I left the security of a nursing career to try my hand at this author thing.

It hasn't been easy—I haven't been easy—but you've been by my side the entire journey. I am forever grateful, and love you all beyond measure.

Special shout-out to my incredible daughter and technical assistant, Jordan Noll. Without you, my books would be living a sad and lonely life, gathering dust as a file on my laptop. Thanks, Jobes!

The only thing better than watching your children grow and thrive is doing it all over again. To my beautiful grandbabies, Declan, Raylan, David, Connor, Mila, Dean, Piper, and Emma James…I love you all with a ferocity that is, at times, excessive and scary.

But I don't care. ☺

To my amazing mom and royal grammar queen, Mary Quinn. Once again, you've helped me slay dragons using a pen rather than a sword. Thank you for banishing those pesky grammatical errors and always being my first Beta reader! Love you, Momma!

And to my siblings Lori Martin and James Quinn—my first best friends, my loudest cheerleaders, and my ports in the storm. Together, we are the power of three and can accomplish anything.

I adore you, you filthy animals.

To my 'bonus' children—Lara Noll, Jessica Noll, Peter Barreira Noll, Vanessa Collins, and Chelsea Ryan. I could not love you more if I birthed you myself (but that would mean I gave birth ten times, which is yikes!). Love youse guys!

Friendships that survive as we journey through life are rare indeed. Cyndi Boyd, you've pushed me and encouraged me to succeed. You've not complained as I've dragged you state-to-state for book research; not balked as I asked you to partake in some pretty spooky ghost investigations. I cannot recall a time when you haven't had my back.

Thank you, my friend. Love you madly.

Sometimes in life, the universe intercedes, knowing what we need the most even before we do. I needed someone, a connection close to what I'd had years ago before death took my best friend.

So that bestie, that heavenly angel, Lisa Ferenc, sent me that connection.

Karen Colonnello, my 'best fuckin' friend'... You are the lantern that helped me find my way when I was in a lonely and dark place. We share the same dorky sense of humor, the same values, the same passion for life. When I count my blessings, I count that day in September when we first met.

Thank you for being my friend. I love you.

Special shout-out to Walter Ferenc and Jim Piotrowski...You

guys will always be part of my 'five.' Love you both.

Jennifer McIntyre, extraordinary editor, confidante, and friend…what can I say? We are basically the same person, split in two and living in different countries (which is probably a good thing. Oh, the trouble we would cause if we lived in the same zip code!). I've watched in awe as you've slain dangling participles and vanquished incomplete sentences with a smile on your face, maintaining your sense of humor with a cute meme or a quick 'bring out yer dead!' joke.

I adore you, JennyMac, and am beyond grateful for your expertise and your friendship.

To Laura Boyle, a talented cover designer with the patience of a saint. Thank you, Laura.

To my Beta readers, Kelly Coleman and Hilary Barber… The only thing I value more than your critique of my work is your friendship. Thanks a million.

Finally, as always, I tip my hat to my 'other' family, the men and women in blue. Law enforcement is a calling, and I stand in awe of every one of you who answered that call. Despite the anger and hatred you face from some in society, you still show up every day, not only doing your job but going that extra mile (I'm looking at you, BBO ♥).

Please know that most Americans see you for what you are…

Brave. Determined. Selfless.

And irreplaceable.

Peace out, my friends.

—Q

# BOOK CLUB
# DISCUSSION
# QUESTIONS

## The Characters

1. Creating authentic and diverse characters when writing a book is often challenging. In reading *Rosemear,* did you feel a particular connection to one of the characters? If so, what pulled you in?

2. Mental health can be a fragile thing. In *Rosemear,* Isabella experienced the greatest fear in a parent's life—to outlive their children. What is your greatest fear? How do you deal with it?

3. We learn early on that Spencer Boyd is a snake and a terrible husband to Isabella. Despite that, she stayed with him for far longer than most women would. How about you? Would you stay and try to work on a failing marriage or head for the hills? What is the one sin your spouse could commit that, in your eyes, would be unforgivable?

4. Luna Lake is Isabella's confidante and closest

friend. What word immediately jumps to your mind if you had to sum up her personality?

5. Despite how much we love where we live, an awful neighbor can shatter our peace. Nathan Decker was, luckily for Isabella, a great neighbor and caring friend. Have you had a terrific neighbor who could never be replaced? Or a terrible one that still gives you nightmares?

6. Abigail Charles faced numerous personal trials and tragedies. Despite that, she remained optimistic that better things were coming. Did you connect with her character's optimism? Knowing the challenges she'd face in an interracial relationship in that era, do you think she should have stepped away from any romance with Edward?

## THE CREEPS

1. This book has many scary moments involving the supernatural. What, if anything, scared you the most? Do any scenes stick in your mind as being especially nightmarish or creepy?

2. *Rosemear* is rife with ghosts, both good and evil. Do you believe in the paranormal? Why or why not?

3. In line with the above question, if you believe that life after death exists, have you personally experienced anything supernatural? If so, would you be willing to share it with me for a future non-fiction book I am planning?

## THE FINAL CHAPTERS

1. I always try to include little-known facts in my books for readers to enjoy. Did you learn anything

from *Rosemear* about investigating the paranormal?
Have you ever conducted an investigation or been
on a ghost hunt? Were you able to find any evidence of spirit activity? (Orbs, bangs, whispers,
doors closing, electronics going wonky, etc.)

2.   Isabella and Nate became closer as the pages pro-
gressed. How did you feel about their relationship,
given that Isabella was still technically married?
Were you satisfied with the pairing?

3.   Finally, how did you like the ending? Did you feel
the book answered all your questions and ended on
a positive note? Would you recommend *Rosemear*
to a friend? Why or why not?

Thanks for reading and I hope you enjoyed exploring the haunted
halls of *Rosemear!*

# WANT MORE QUINN?

For updates, bonus content, and special giveaways, visit me at Quinnnoll.com and sign up for my newsletter!

Aside from *Rosemear,* check out my Shadow Sisters Trilogy, a series about a serial killer who targets a woman who can see the dead. *The Apostle's Fury, The Disciple's Fury,* and *The Final Fury* are all available on Amazon or wherever fine books are sold.

Until next time!
Happy Reading!

*Quinn Noll*

www.Quinnnoll.com
facebook.com/Quinn.Noll
instagram.com/QuinnNollWrites